THE HOLY WAR

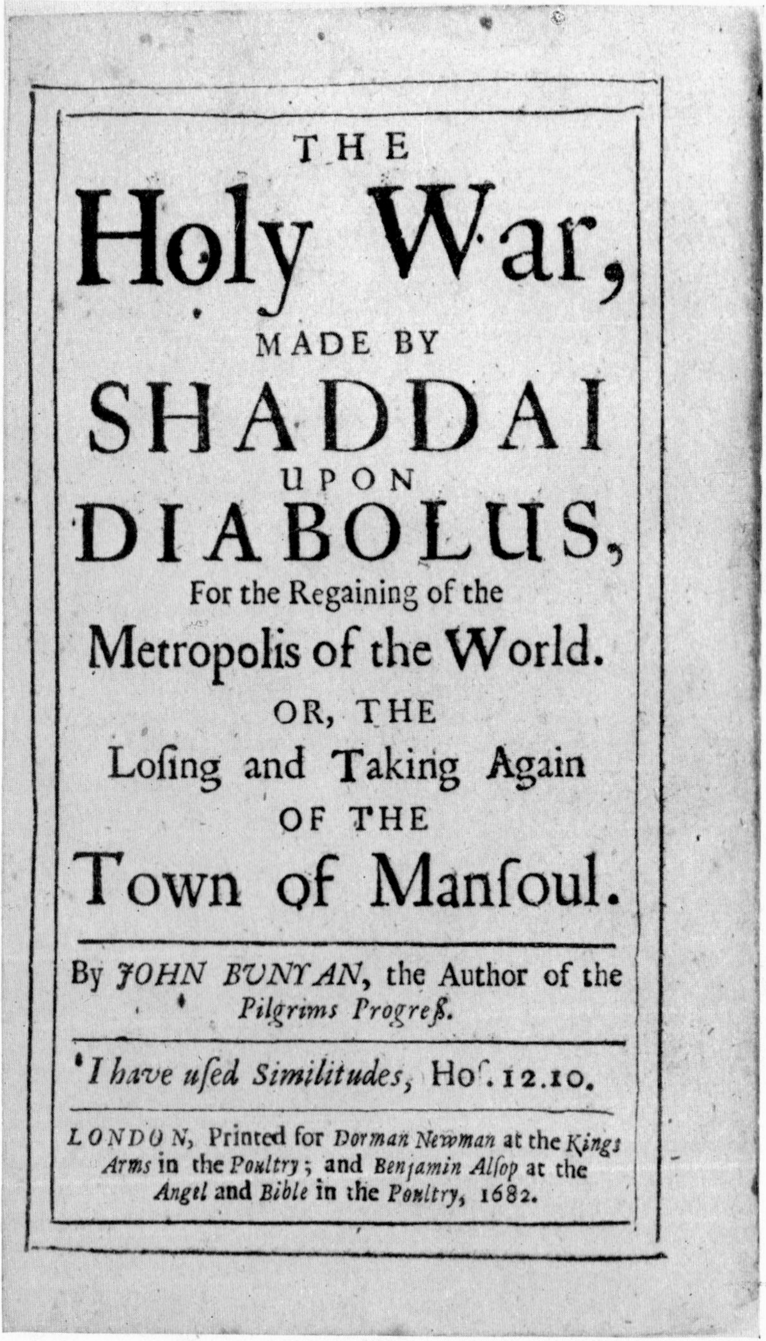

THE

Holy War,

MADE BY

SHADDAI

UPON

DIABOLUS,

For the Regaining of the

Metropolis of the World.

OR, THE

Loſing and Taking Again

OF THE

Town of Manſoul.

By *JOHN BUNYAN*, the Author of the *Pilgrims Progreſs*.

I have uſed Similitudes, Hoſ. 12.10.

LONDON, Printed for *Dorman Newman* at the *Kings Arms* in the *Poultry*; and *Benjamin Alſop* at the *Angel* and *Bible* in the *Poultry*, 1682.

Title-page of *The Holy War* from the first edition, 1682
(Bodleian Library, Oxford)

JOHN BUNYAN

THE HOLY WAR

made by Shaddai upon Diabolus. For the Regaining of the Metropolis of the World. Or, the Losing and Taking Again of the Town of Mansoul

EDITED BY

ROGER SHARROCK

AND

JAMES F. FORREST

OXFORD
AT THE CLARENDON PRESS
1980

Oxford University Press, Walton Street, Oxford OX2 6DP

OXFORD LONDON GLASGOW
NEW YORK TORONTO MELBOURNE WELLINGTON
KUALA LUMPUR SINGAPORE HONG KONG TOKYO
DELHI BOMBAY CALCUTTA MADRAS KARACHI
NAIROBI DAR ES SALAAM CAPE TOWN

Published in the United States by
Oxford University Press, New York

British Library Cataloguing in Publication Data

Bunyan, John
The Holy War – (Oxford English texts)
I. Title II. Sharrock, Roger III. Forrest
James F
823'.4 PR3329.H1 79.40264
ISBN 0-19-811887-2

Printed in Great Britain
at the University Press, Oxford
by Eric Buckley
Printer to the University

PREFACE

BUNYAN'S second great allegory, while constantly admired, has never enjoyed the popularity of *The Pilgrim's Progress*. Though there have been many editions since the first, they have not been on the scale of those of the former work, and in the last century they have been few. Since Mabel Peacock (Oxford, 1892, with *The Heavenly Footman*) and John Brown (Cambridge, 1905, with *The Life and Death of Mr. Badman*) one can only draw attention to the modern-spelling edition by James F. Forrest (New York and Toronto, 1967).

Much of the research involved in the preparation of this edition was made possible by the generous assistance of the Central Research Fund of the University of London and the Social Science and Humanities Research Council of Canada, and to these bodies the editors acknowledge their indebtedness and offer thanks. They also wish to record the help provided by the following libraries: University of Alberta (Special Collections), Bedford County Library, Bodleian Library, British Library, Bunyan Meeting, Congregational Library (London), Folger Shakespeare Library, Harvard University (Houghton Library), Huntington Library, J. P. Morgan Library, Leicester University Library, New York Public Library, and the University of Texas Library.

Like *Grace Abounding* and *The Pilgrim's Progress*, and the forthcoming *Mr. Badman*, Bunyan's other personal and fictional works, *The Holy War* appears alongside the theological and evangelical *Miscellaneous Works*, sharing their format but not their numbering in volume series.

R. S.
J. F. F.

CONTENTS

REFERENCES AND ABBREVIATIONS

[*The place of publication, unless otherwise stated, is London*]

BUNYAN'S WORKS

The Works of That Eminent Servant of Christ, Mr. John Bunyan, ed. Charles Doe	*1692 Folio*
The Works of John Bunyan, ed. George Offor (3 vols., Glasgow, Edinburgh, and London, 1860–2)	Offor
The Miscellaneous Works of John Bunyan, general editor Roger Sharrock (Oxford, 1976–)	Oxford Bunyan
Grace Abounding to the Chief of Sinners, ed. Roger Sharrock (Oxford, 1962)	*G.A.*
The Pilgrim's Progress from This World to That Which Is to Come, ed. J. B. Wharey, rev. Roger Sharrock (Oxford, 1960)	*P.P.*
The Holy War, ed. James F. Forrest (Toronto and New York, 1967)	Forrest
The Holy War (the present edition)	*H.W.*

OTHER WORKS

John Brown, *John Bunyan: His Life, Times, and Work*, rev. ed. Frank Mott Harrison (1928)	Brown
Calendar of State Papers Domestic, 1682, and *1683–5* (3 vols., 1934–8)	*C.S.P.D.*
The Church Book of Bunyan Meeting, 1650–1821, facsimile edition with introduction by G. B. Harrison (1928)	*Church Book*
Dictionary of National Biography	*D.N.B.*
Frank Mott Harrison, *A Bibliography of the Works of John Bunyan* (Oxford, 1932)	Harrison
David Ogg, *England in the Reign of Charles II* (2 vols., Oxford, 1963)	Ogg
Oxford English Dictionary	*O.E.D.*
H. R. Plomer, *A Dictionary of the Printers and Booksellers . . . from 1668 to 1725* (Oxford, 1922)	Plomer
Roger Sharrock, *John Bunyan* (1968)	Sharrock

INTRODUCTION

(i) *Bunyan's Life and Ministry from 1678 to 1688*

LIKE Defoe in the next generation, Bunyan came to fiction late and produced at least one popular masterpiece. He was 50 when the First Part of *The Pilgrim's Progress* was published in 1678. At two-yearly intervals in the next six years he published three more works of allegorical fiction: *The Life and Death of Mr. Badman* (1680), which is more a realistic tale than a true allegory in spite of the name of the chief character; *The Holy War* (1682); and the Second Part of *The Pilgrim's Progress* (1684), the story of Christiana and her children. But his incursions into imaginative writing did not alter the general character of his literary production. The same flow of books in the form of extended sermons, with their texts, divisions, reasons, and uses in the characteristic style of the period, continued to issue from his pen, rising to something of a climax in 1688, the year of his death, when seven books appeared.

The considerable bulk of his writings represents only part of his activity in the last ten years of his life. Though *The Pilgrim's Progress* made him known far beyond the Bedford neighbourhood, he continued to minister to the Nonconformist congregation there and to its affiliated churches in Bedfordshire, Huntingdonshire, Hertfordshire, and Cambridgeshire. These are the years in which he acquired the nickname of 'Bishop Bunyan' and in which he poured out his energies in strenuous preaching tours into the countryside; there were also visits to London where he apparently gave one of the Tuesday lectures at Pinners' Hall, Old Broad Street,[1] and also preached from George Cokayne's pulpit in Red Cross Street, Southwark.[2] There is also a persistent legend that Bunyan preached

[1] The title-page of *The Greatness of the Soul* (1683) has 'First preached in Pinners Hall'. The Hall was in Old Broad Street and the London merchants endowed a series of lectures there, the first being given by Bates, Manton, Owen, Baxter, Collins, and Jenkyn; they are probably the 'valiant Worthies' who in the Second Part of *P.P.* battle with Popery in the shape of 'a Monster out of the Woods' (*P.P.*, p. 350; Brown, p. 367).

[2] George Cokayne, celebrated among the Independent ministers, preached the

in Zoar Street Chapel, Gravel Lane, Southwark, at Bankside and close to the site of the former Globe Playhouse; however, the ground on which the chapel was built was not leased out for that purpose until 1687: it therefore seems unlikely that Bunyan ever preached there unless it was on one of his last visits to London in 1688.[1] Thomas Barlow, Bishop of Lincoln, exercised a manner of patronage over the Zoar Street meeting-house, and according to one version of the story he permitted Bunyan to preach there as a friend of his former pupil John Owen.[2] Yet another version has Bunyan preaching in an alley in Zoar Street. All that may be deduced is that Bunyan had a strong connection with Southwark Nonconformist meetings through his friendship with George Cokayne, that he certainly preached in Red Cross Street, and may have done at other meeting-houses.[3] The Red Cross Street church moved to Hare Court in 1692, four years after Bunyan's death, and it is worth noting that in the original list of deacons at Hare Court is the name of John Strudwick, in whose house Bunyan had died after his last visit to London in August 1688.[1] He was a grocer at the sign of the Star in Snow Hill. Bunyan's last sermon had been preached 'at Mr. Gamman's meeting' in Whitechapel. This seems to be John Gammon who is listed in the Lay Subsidies in the Public Record Office as paying

fast sermon before the House of Commons on 29 Nov. 1648; he was presented to the living of St. Pancras, Soper Lane, under the Cromwellian religious establishment, and, being ejected in 1662, continued to hold meetings in his own house in Red Cross Street (opposite where Dr. Williams's Library now stands) until a church for the use of the congregation was built in Hare Court between Aldersgate and Paul's Alley. Cokayne also ministered to a congregation at his home, Cotten End, Cardington, Bedfordshire, where he was associated with Bunyan's publisher Nathaniel Ponder and with Bunyan himself (A. G. Matthews, *Calamy Revised* (Oxford, 1934), p. 124; Walter Wilson, *The History and Antiquities of Dissenting Churches and Meeting Houses, in London, Westminster, and Southwark, including the Lives of their Ministers, from the rise of Nonconformity to the Present Time* (1808–14), iii. 277–81; G. Lyon Turner, *Original Records of Nonconformity under Persecution and Indulgence* (1911), ii. 855, 985).

[1] Wilson, op. cit. iv. 188–9.

[2] Owen was instrumental in obtaining Bunyan's release from his second imprisonment (John Asty, *Memoirs of the Life of Dr. Owen*, in *A Complete Collection of the Sermons of . . . John Owen, D.D.* (1721), p. xxx; William Orme, *Memoirs of the Life, Writings, and Religious Connections of John Owen, D.D.* (1820), pp. 398–9). Orme repeats Asty's account of how Owen intervened with Barlow to obtain Bunyan's release but convincingly relates it to the second imprisonment, not the first, since Barlow was not consecrated as Bishop of Lincoln till 1675. He adds that Owen was frequently in the practice of hearing Bunyan preach when he came to London.

[3] Oxford Bunyan, vol. ii, pp. xvii–xviii.

tax on four hearths in Stepney and who was the author of *Christ, a Christian's Life* (1691).[1] It is impossible to know how much earlier the connection with Gammon's church had been established. The church is said to have met in Boar's Head Yard. Bunyan's known acquaintance with Owen leads one to believe that he may at times have been offered the use of the latter's pulpit in Moorfields. Finally, we have the testimony of Charles Doe, the Southwark comb-maker and his first editor, that he had first heard Bunyan preaching at Stephen More's meeting which was usually held in Winchester Yard, Southwark:

It was at this time of persecution that I heard Mr. Bunyan came to London sometimes and preached; and because of his fame, and I having read some of his books, I had a mind to hear him. And accordingly I did, at Mr. More's meeting in a private house; and his text was, 'The fears of the wicked shall come upon him, but the desires of the righteous shall be granted'.[2]

The period of persecution referred to is that of the renewal of penal legislation against Nonconformists after the accession of James I (1685–6). The sermon provided the basis for *The Desires of the Righteous Granted* later published by Doe with other posthumous works in the Folio of 1692. Doe's description in *The Struggler* of Bunyan at the height of his fame preaching to a large congregation in London must refer to the last year of his life when, after the Second Declaration of Indulgence, public worship outside the Establishment was once more permitted:

When Mr. Bunyan preached in London, if there were but one day's notice given, there would be more people come together to hear him preach than the meeting-house could hold. I have seen to hear him preach, by my computation, about twelve hundred at a morning lecture by seven o'clock on a working day, in the dark winter-time. I also computed about three thousand that came to hear him one Lord's Day at London, at a town's-end meeting-house, so that half were fain to go back again for want of room, and then himself was fain at a back-door to be pulled almost over people to get upstairs to his pulpit.[3]

1 P.R.O., *Lay Subsidies*, 252/30; Brown, p. 372.
2 Charles Doe, *A Collection of the Experience of the Work of Grace* (1700), p. 52.
3 Charles Doe, *The Struggler*, in Offor, iii. 766–7.

Both Doe's reminiscences refer to the latter part of the last ten years of Bunyan's life. Yet there is nothing to prevent our dating his association with London city churches from an earlier period; the publication of *The Pilgrim's Progress* had of course spread his reputation to a far wider audience of readers than he had ever enjoyed before; but there are two further reasons for assigning his London contacts to a much earlier date. First, his controversy with the Strict Particular Baptists in 1672–3 had brought him into prominence among the ministers of those churches which, like Bedford, advocated an open-communion basis for membership rather than an insistence on adult baptism as a condition of entry. The works in question are *A Confession of my Faith and Reason of my Practice* (1672), *Differences in Judgment about Water-Baptism* (1673), *Peacable Principles and True* (1674). His arguments had been supported by Independents of distinction such as Henry Jessey and the Oxford scholar John Tombes. He knew Owen at any rate by 1677: Asty's *Life of Owen* (1721) gives an account of how on the instigation of Bishop Barlow he offered a bond as surety for Bunyan's release from an imprisonment which must have been the shorter second imprisonment in that year.[1] Secondly, Bunyan's increasing responsibility for the Independent churches in the Bedfordshire area and as far afield as Braintree in Essex led him into contacts which concerned the transfer of brethren who became resident in London to communion with metropolitan congregations. An example is found among the sparse entries in the Bedford *Church Book* for the period between 1676 and 1682 (sparse, no doubt, because Bunyan had little time to keep them in full); the entry is late in 1682 and is in Bunyan's handwriting:

The Church of Christ in and about Bedford to the Church of Christ walking with our beloved Brother Cockain in London, wisheth abundance of grace by Jesus Christ. Beloved Brethren, we commend unto you our beloved Brother William Breeden, who is one of us, but by reason that his place of habitation is with you in London, and so remote from us; and becaus he desireth that his distance from us might not be a bar as to his Christian communion; and also becaus he desireth to be helped forward in his Christian course by haveing

[1] *The Church Book of Bunyan Meeting*, fac. edn. by G. B. Harrison (1928), p. 72.

admittance by you into all Christ's ordinances; therefore we pray you in the bowels of Christ to receive him, and to be a nurs to him in the lord. John Bunyan, John Fenn, Anthony Harrington, &c.[1]

Other entries concern the choosing of additional elders and deacons and resolutions to provide 'That the several meetings that are upheld by the congregation to witt; Bedford, Kemston, Malden, Cotton End, Edworth, and Gamlingay be better supplied'. The advice of George Cokayne, together with that of Henry Jessey and John Simpson, had been asked by the Bedford church as long ago as 1659 when they were seeking an assistant for John Burton as pastor. Bunyan's personal acquaintance with Cokayne was of long standing since the latter was a Bedfordshire man and a near neighbour; in his house at Cotton End John Whiteman, a Bedford elder, preached in 1672.[2] The picture of increasing evangelizing activity is borne out by Archbishop Sheldon's religious census of 1676. In the five parishes of the town of Bedford there are listed 121 adult Protestant Nonconformists as against the 30 recorded in the return of 1669; in the whole of the Lincoln diocese the Nonconformists were 1 in 21 of the population, in the county of Bedford 1 in 12, and in the town of Bedford 1 in 10, which may indicate Bunyan's increasing personal influence and certainly reveals the importance of the community to which he ministered.[3]

During these years of activity hardly anything is known of his personal life except that he continued to live with his family in a cottage in St. Cuthbert Street, Bedford. There is only the evidence, chronologically vague, in the brief contemporary accounts of his journeys and his sermons. This can only be supplemented by reference to his other writings in the period.

(ii) *Bunyan's Writings from* The Pilgrim's Progress, *Part One, to* The Holy War

All Bunyan's sermon treatises throughout his life employ relentlessly the same contrast between free grace and bondage to worldly

1 Ibid.

2 *Church Book*, p. 53.

3 G. Lyon Turner, *Original Records of Nonconformity under Persecution and Indulgence* (1911), i. 63–8, ii. 851–61.

values, between the genuine awakening of the soul to Christ and adherence to the law. However, a difference may be detected between the writings of this period and those of the first imprisonment (1660–72). In the previous decade Bunyan had written closely to his own experience: 'I preached what I felt, what I smartingly did feel, even that under which my poor Soul did groan and tremble to astonishment. Indeed I have been as one sent to them from the dead; I went my self in chains to preach to them in chains, and carried that fire in my own conscience that I perswaded them to beware of.'[1] From *A Few Sighs from Hell* onwards he had attempted to open to others in threateningly objective terms the terrors that had haunted his conscience at the time of his conversion. The terrors of hell are not absent from the tracts of the 1670s, but there are signs of a new inclination to stress on the mercy and relief available to Christians.

Instruction for the Ignorant (1675) is a short and homely catechism, 'fitted for the capacity of the weakest', which may mean that if not intended for children it was designed for new members of the Bedford congregation. Since the evidence points to the greater part of the First Part of *The Pilgrim's Progress* having been written during the first imprisonment, it must be presumed that this work came later. The prefatory letter to the Bedford church speaks of the author 'being driven from you in presence, not affection', and is subscribed, 'Yours to serve by my ministry, when I can, to your edification and consolation'. The inference is that Bunyan was in hiding, or had at any rate temporarily abstained from preaching, following the issue of an ecclesiastical warrant against him on 4 March 1675 for preaching or teaching at a conventicle (a result of the royal proclamation of 3 February suppressing all conventicles and ordering the names of those not presenting themselves at their parish church to be listed by the bishops' officers).[2]

Saved by Grace, or a Discourse of the Grace of God was issued in 1676, as may be learned from its entry in the Term Catalogues for Trinity Term in that year. But no copy has survived and the first

[1] *G.A.*, pp. 85–6.

[2] *Tudor and Stuart Proclamations 1485–1714*, ed. R. Steele, (1910), i. 368 and 369; see David Ogg, *England in the Reign of Charles II* (2nd edn., Oxford, 1963), ii. 529–30.

available edition is that provided in Doe's Folio; the date of first publication is also confirmed by Doe's *Catalogue* of 1698. *The Strait Gate: or the Great Difficulty of going to Heaven* also appeared in 1676. It is based on the text Luke 13: 24, and its sharp, dry portraits of hypocrites and false professors provide an introduction to the world of minor characters in *The Pilgrim's Progress*; it is likely that the sermon treatise was written not long before or after Bunyan was working on the first part of the allegory. However, the book about 'the way and race of saints' spoken of in the prefatory verses to *The Pilgrim's Progress*, the work which Bunyan set aside as thoughts for the fiction crowded in upon him ('Breed so fast'), was not *The Strait Gate* but *The Heavenly Footman*, a figurative sermon in which St. Paul's metaphor of the Christian's race for a prize is turned into something more like a cross-country walk. Many of the admonitions in *The Heavenly Footman* to those who run or walk point directly to the episodes and the phraseology of *The Pilgrim's Progress*:

> Beware of by-paths, take heed that thou dost not turn into those lanes which lead out of the way.
>
> Take Heed that you have not an ear open to every one that calleth after you as you are on your journey.
>
> The Cross is the standing way-mark by which all they that go to glory must pass by.

Again, there is strong internal evidence that *The Heavenly Footman* was written, and presumably published, long before the first extant edition of 1698 by Doe (the one containing his *Catalogue* of Bunyan's sixty books). In the work he recommends to the reader an early and raw book, *A Few Sighs from Hell*; he also speaks of 'that little time that I have been a professor'; and declares, 'Do not have too much company with some Anabaptists, though I go under that name myself'. After the 1672–3 controversy with the London Strict Particular Baptist leaders, Kiffin, Danvers, and Paul, Bunyan expressly repudiated the sectarian label 'Baptist'. Thus, if we take into account also the close relationship between the spiritual autobiography of *Grace Abounding* and the allegory of the soul in *The Pilgrim's Progress*, the indications are that the latter, together with *The Heavenly Footman*, was written between 1666 and 1672, in the second half of Bunyan's first imprisonment, and during one of the rare periods of any length in which no other works by him appeared.

Instruction for the Ignorant, *Saved by Grace*, and *The Strait Gate* were all published by Francis Smith, as had been the slightly earlier *Light for Them that Sit in Darkness* (1675). As a publisher of Nonconformist books Smith had his difficulties with the authorities. As he stated before a Committee of the House of Lords in 1677, he had had seized an impression printed for him of Henry Danvers's *Infant Baptism* (a rejoinder to Bunyan's *Differences in Judgment about Water-Baptism No Bar to Communion*). After this date Smith published no more books by Bunyan with the exception of the third edition of *Grace Abounding* (1679) though he appears to have remained in business until 1683 with a possible spell in Holland to avoid further prosecution.[1]

Come and Welcome to Jesus Christ, published in 1678 within a few months of the First Part of *The Pilgrim's Progress*, continues to strike the fervent and evangelical note of these works of 1675–8. The printer was Benjamin Harris. The work is an enlargement of a sermon on John 6: 37: 'Him that cometh to me I will in nowise cast out.' Its increasing use of everyday imagery shows Bunyan storing material which is to enrich the imaginative life of his first allegory; both the metaphorical liveliness and the new tenderness in the treatment of the theme of free salvation through the mercy of Christ are carried on into *The Holy War* of four years later: a conspicuous feature of *The Holy War* is the manner in which after each backsliding the people of Mansoul are forgiven by their prince Emanuel again and again, right to the very end of the narrative which still leaves them imperfect and struggling to await his final coming:

> Remember therefore, O my *Mansoul*, that thou art beloved of me; as I have therefore taught thee to watch, to fight, to pray, and to make war against my foes, so now I command thee to believe that my love is constant to thee. O my *Mansoul*, how have I set my heart, my love

[1] He was called 'Elephant' Smith; a dedicated printer of 'fanatic' pamphlets, he was consistently persecuted by the licenser Roger L'Estrange who confiscated his stock in 1666 and on other occasions, including works by Bunyan (*The Injurious Proceedings against One Francis Smith*, 1680); Harrison, p. xvi.

upon thee, watch. Behold, I lay none other burden upon thee, than what thou hast already, hold fast till I come.[1]

There is a marked similarity in the tenderness of tone and the firm confidence in the relation of Saviour and creature exhibited in many passages of *Come and Welcome* if allowance be made for sermon style with its sharp reiterated blows of question and answer:

The promise is large, Christ will in nowise cast out. Let the best master of arts on earth show me if he can any condition in this text that depends upon any qualification in us. They shall come? Shall they come? Yes, they shall come. But how if they want those things, those graces, power and heart without which they cannot come? Why, *shall come* answereth all this and all things else. And him that cometh shall in nowise be cast out. Let him be as red as blood, let him be as red as crimson. Some men are blood-red sinners, crimson sinners, sinners of a double dye, dipped and dipped again before they come to Jesus Christ.[2]

As is Bunyan's habit there is continual lexical play on a single word. The sinner is, in Puritan jargon, a coming sinner who comes and is welcome to Christ; but Christ also is coming, to save the sinner on the Day of Judgement.

It is less easy to find parallels in *The Holy War* for the similes from country life in *Come and Welcome* which often appear in a cluster where a general dynamic impulse, as of moving forward but meeting hindrances, seems naturally to proliferate along different shoots of metaphor:

Discouraging thoughts are like unto cold weather, they benumb the senses and make us go ungainly about our business; but the sweet and warm gleads of promise are like the comfortable beams of the sun which liven and refresh. You see how little the bee and fly do play in the air in winter; why the cold hinders them from doing it; but when the wind and the sun is warm, who so busy as they? He that comes to Christ cannot, it is true, always get on as fast as he would. Poor coming soul, thou art like the man that would ride full gallop whose horse would hardly trot. Now the desire of his mind is not to be judged by the slow pace of the dull jade he rides on, but by the hitching and kicking and spurring as he sits on his back. Thy flesh

[1] *H.W.*, p. 250. [2] *Come and Welcome to Jesus Christ*, in Oxford Bunyan, viii.

is like this dull jade, it will not gallop after Christ, it will be backward though thy soul and heaven lie at stake.[1]

This looks backward to the crucially important visionary experience he had as a young man after hearing the poor women of Bedford 'talking about the things of God'. Then he thought he saw the sun shining on one side of a wall while he was left in cold and darkness on the other side. Also, in its ready passing from one image to another, it anticipates the homely comparisons scattered through the incidental conversations in *The Pilgrim's Progress*, Part One. If there is less of this incidental, illustrative imagery in *The Holy War* it is because we have forsaken the country for the city, Elstow for Bedford, and the city image of a great corporation in turmoil and under external threat is more simple and unified, less in need of external embroidery, than its predecessor the allegory of the journey. *The Pilgrim's Progress*, unexpectedly, is closer to the sermon structure, the continuous march of a reiterated text in need of exposition and amplification all along its course; while the meaning of *The Holy War* is implicit in the unified developments of its plot: there are no episodes and no expository digressions. The powerful unconscious attraction of the journey metaphor may have obscured this comparative aspect of the two works and prevented our doing justice to the later allegory. *The Pilgrim's Progress* is as it were united at a deeper level which dissolves any ill effects from its strange mixture of modes, of dreaming and preaching, of satire and the communication of the fruits of religious vision. *The Holy War* shows how far Bunyan had advanced, not in genius or total imaginative achievement, but in the construction of a bold, firm, and ambitious narrative. To borrow the language of the romantics, *The Pilgrim's Progress* is a Gothic, its successor a classical work.

Come and Welcome was extremely popular and it passed through twelve editions (their numberings are confused) before 1720. But six years elapsed between the first and second editions and for this reason it was suggested by Frank Mott Harrison that its attraction may have been partly due to the increasing popularity of *The Pilgrim's Progress*, published probably a few months before. The printer of *Come and Welcome*, Benjamin Harris, was pilloried during

[1] *Come and Welcome to Jesus Christ*, in Oxford Bunyan, viii.

the Tory reaction of 1681 and fled to New England in 1686; editions subsequent to the third bear the names of Elizabeth Harris and John Harris, members of his family.[1]

The last sermon tract of this prolific decade was *A Treatise of the Fear of God* (1679) printed by Nathaniel Ponder. The first edition contains the request that the reader should correct the errors 'occasioned by the Printer, by reason of the absence of the Author'. The entries in the *Church Book* for this year are brief and in a hand other than that of Bunyan. A tradition was long preserved near Braintree in Essex that Bunyan was at Bocking End there writing a book. As usual there is little evidence to support surmise.[2] We can only note that *The Life and Death of Mr. Badman*, the considerable work of fiction intervening between the two allegories, was published in 1680, again by Nathaniel Ponder.

The Fear of God distinguishes between true and superstitious fear, between humility and the subjection to unnecessary penances and formal observances. There are some topical references to the practices of Catholics, then suffering from the alarm and persecution following on the supposed Popish Plot. But again, in drawing his distinction Bunyan is inclined to let the sinner down gently in comparison with the uncompromising dialectic of the early works, and the stress is on the grace of God which can melt a hard heart.

The period of two years between 1680 and 1682 is a striking gap in Bunyan's continuous record of publication from 1655 onwards. Was he working on *The Holy War*, a long and carefully constructed work which could not have been carpentered together from sermon notes? And was some of this time spent at Bocking End, so that it was the allegory and not the novel which was composed there? Again, there is only reasonable surmise to go upon. One can only note the strong contrast between the two works. *Badman* is the straightforward story of a single life with a sententious commentary and a few cautionary short tales thrown in for good measure; it looks

[1] H. R. Plomer, *A Dictionary of the Printers and Booksellers . . . from 1668 to 1725* (Oxford, 1922), pp. 144–6; John Dunton, *Letters from New England* (edn. 1867), p. 144.

[2] F. M. Harrison mentioned 'a tradition rife at Bocking-End, Braintree, Essex' but gives no further authority (Harrison, p. 23). The *Church Book* under the date 'The 7th of the 12th month' (7 Mar. 1677) commits one of its brethren, Samuel Hensman, to fellowship with 'the Church of Christ in and about Braintree'; see also Brown, p. 302.

back to and grows out of the realistic episodes of *The Pilgrim's Progress* concerning rogues and hypocrites met along the way. *The Holy War* is an elaborate construction with several layers of allegory, unlike any other book that Bunyan wrote. Though, when judged by the standards of formal realism which Defoe and his successors were later to observe, *Badman* is a very imperfect novel, the interest of the formal distinction between the two works remains and suggests a swing of attitude in Bunyan's writing in this period; he moves away from a satirical and hortatory realism and returns to the more inward vision which constitutes the heart and core of *The Pilgrim's Progress*, Part One, but in a purer and more abstract form without concessions to realism in the shape of mimetic episodes and with a single, consistent system of allegorical nomenclature. If *Badman* does not look forward very keenly or very far to the new novel, it may properly be placed with the books of judgement and sensational anecdote, a purely seventeenth-century genre of which Reynolds's *God's Revenges against the Crying Sin of Murder* is a prime example. This is still to emphasize the separateness of *The Holy War* which in its devotion to a single allegorical system, complex references for that system, and a realism restricted merely to *tone* of presentation, looks back in chronological isolation to the high genre of allegory, to the folk and morality elements in *The Faerie Queene*, to Lydgate's Deguileville, and to *Piers Plowman.*[1]

(iii) *The Contemporary Background and Bedford Corporation*

In *The Holy War* it cannot be denied that the struggle for man's soul is seen as emphatically a political transaction (the charge once

[1] Cf. the presence of folk and romance elements in *P.P.* discussed by Harold Golder in 'Bunyan's Valley of the Shadow', *M.P.* xxvii (1929), 55–72, and 'Bunyan and Spenser', *P.M.L.A.* xlv (1930), 216 f., and my note on the fight with Apollyon in Part One in *P.P.* pp. 322–3. The relationship to the tradition represented by *The Pilgrimage of the Soul of Man* was fully discussed in *The Ancient Poem of Guillaume de Guileville entitled Le Pélérinage de l'Homme compared with the Pilgrim's Progress of John Bunyan edited from Notes collected by the late Mr. Nathaniel Hill* (1858), and more critically by J. B. Wharey, *A Study of the Sources of Bunyan's Allegories, with Special Reference to Deguileville's Pilgrimage of Man* (Baltimore, 1904) but I do not find that attention has been paid to the conclusions of *Piers Plowman* and *H.W.*, conclusions in which 'nothing is concluded' and the Christian struggle continues outside the text.

brought by Bagehot against Milton's handling of his theme in *Paradise Lost*). What may be less clear to the present-day reader is that the changes in the government of the town and its officials brought about by Diabolus's usurpation closely reflect a revolution in English local government occurring in the years when Bunyan wrote.

From 1678 onwards the agitation over the Popish Plot had enabled the country party, Shaftesbury, and the city of London to make headway against Charles II and the court interest. The interests of the Nonconformists were closely identified with those of the country party and Bunyan speaks as a typical Whig, Protestant, and anti-Papist when he writes during this period:

Our days indeed had been days of trouble, especially since the discovery of the Popish plot, for then we began to fear cutting of throats, of being burned in our beds, and of seeing our children dashed in pieces before our faces. But looking about us, we found we had a gracious king, brave parliaments, a stout city, good lord-mayors, honest sheriffs, substantial laws against them, and these we made the object of our hope, quite forgetting the direction in this exhortation—let Israel hope in the Lord.[1]

Bunyan must have had in mind the Whig sheriffs, Slingsby Bethell, Pilkington, and Shute, supporters of Shaftesbury and advocates of the Bill to exclude the Duke of York from the throne. The germinal idea of *The Holy War*, an honest municipality in danger of destruction if it does not trust in the Lord, is implicit in this passage.

In the general election of February 1679, the first for nineteen years, the country party was victorious in most constituencies including Bedfordshire. There Lord Bruce was defeated by Lord William Russell, the son of the Duke of Bedford, later to be executed for treason under the Tory reaction. Edmund Verney wrote: 'I hear the Bedfordshire election cost £6,000. They were three days a-polling. But Lord Bruce and his party lost it by five hundred votes, whereat the Earl of Ailesbury his father was extremely angry.'[2] But from the spring of 1681 a Tory reaction and revenge was set in

[1] *Israel's Hope Encouraged; or, What Hope Is, and how Distinguished from Faith: With Encouragement for a Hoping People* (Offor, i. 585).
[2] Verney MSS., 24 Feb. 1678–9.

motion. Earlier that year Charles had dissolved the Parliament held at Oxford after it had sat only one day; subsequently he issued a declaration explaining the reasons for his dissolving his last two parliaments and urging that the laws against Nonconformists must now be prosecuted more zealously. Addresses of thanks for this declaration poured in to the King from those in the royal interest in boroughs and counties; there was one from the Lord-Lieutenant, Deputy Lieutenant, justices, and gentlemen of the county of Bedford in June 1681.[1] The intense political divisiveness of the time and the treatment of religion as an instrument of state policy have a direct bearing on Bunyan's story in *The Holy War*.

The trial and condemnation of Stephen College and other Protestant agitators was succeeded by the impeachment of Shaftesbury. When the Middlesex grand jury threw this out with an Ignoramus in November 1681 Charles and his ministers sought other means to strengthen the royal interest against Whigs and Nonconformists in London and the corporate towns. With the support of the lords-lieutenant and local magnates the borough charters were scrutinized with a view to their surrender, the curbing of civic rights, and the imposition of new charters under which Whig and Nonconformist councillors would lose their offices. The case of Bedford illustrates what was happening all over the country. In April 1681 an Order in Council was issued to inquire whether all the officials of the corporation had complied with the regulations of the Corporation Act. On its being found that the town chamberlains had not duly taken the sacrament their places were declared void and the Deputy Recorder, Robert Audley, was accused before the Council at Whitehall of being 'an enemy to the Government and to the Church of England, and a great countenancer of conventicles and phanaticks in the town of Bedford'.[2]

[1] *The Humble Address of the Lieutenant, Deputy-Lieutenant, Justices of the Peace, Military Officers, Clergy, Gentlemen and Freeholders of the County of Bedford:* 'But your Majestie's late Gracious declaration, as it hath made us the most obliged, so should we be the most ungrateful people in the world if we did not profess (what we here in all humility do) our most hearty and thankful resentment of the Royal Assurance you are pleased to give us therein to remove all the reasonable fears and causeless jealousies which some ill men . . . have endeavoured to insinuate into the people' (*Bedfordshire Notes and Queries*, ed. F. A. Blaydes (1886), pp. 6–7; Brown, p. 315).

[2] Dr. Williams's MSS. i. 320, Sir William Morrice's Entering Book.

Audley was not himself a Dissenter but it seems clear that he had tolerated the separatist church of which Bunyan was pastor. He had been an officer on the King's side throughout the Civil War. He defended himself before the Council, at first with some success. But Lord Bruce and his father were soon to obtain their revenge. It was recorded in the Minute Book of Bedford Corporation: 'It is ordained that from henceforth Mr. Audley, ye Deputy Recorder, shall not have any vote in Common Councill or other Assemblies of the Corporacon.'[1] The mayor, Paul Cobb, an old enemy of Bunyan at the time of his first imprisonment in 1661, was a tool of Lord Bruce who wrote to him: 'Mr. Mayor, I received your letter, and am glad to find by it that you have made so good a choice in ye room of Mr. Audley. I have taken occasion to applaud your actions since you came in your office where it was well resented.' In October 1683 fifty-three new burgesses were created including some who had been concerned in Bunyan's prosecution after the Restoration, the magistrate Sir Francis Wingate, and the commissary William Foster; a month later twenty-three more names were added to the burgess roll including members of prominent Royalist families like the Dyves and the Chesters. A majority of safe men as burgesses made the rest of the proceedings a foregone conclusion. On 8 January 1684 the Council resolved that the old charter be surrendered and petition made to the King for a new one, 'with like privileges as the former was, or such other priviledges as hee shall be pleased to grant'.[1] The Privy Council had decided a week before that the new charter for Bedford should pass all seals and offices without charge.[2] With a packed corporation the progress towards a new charter was rapid. It was formally brought down from London on 19 July 1684 by the Earl of Ailesbury in person with a great concourse. They were met near Elstow by a deputation from the town and later the Earl gave an address before the guildhall in which he 'was pleased to tell them how great his Majesties grace and favour had been to them (although undeservedly) and how highly they were obliged from thence both to approve themselves eminently loyal, and continue so for ever'. The new Deputy

[1] *The Minute Book of Bedford Corporation*, xxv.
[2] *C.S.P.D. 1683–1685*, 195.

Recorder gave a charge to the grand jury in the same vein.[1] The new charter gave the King power to remove members of the corporation at his pleasure, and the only considerable extra privilege granted the town was the right to hold two new fairs yearly. The gist of what had been achieved is implied in a letter of Ailesbury to the Secretary of State in which he hopes that the corporation of Bedford will now be loyal, while at the same time offering to bring forward the name of 'an honest gentleman' willing to serve as High Sheriff.[2]

The remodelling of the corporation of Mansoul, with a new Lord Mayor and a new Recorder, Lustings in place of Understanding and Forget-good in place of Conscience, closely reflects the imposed reform of the Bedford municipality. The bravery of Mr. Conscience who will not serve Diabolus's design recalls the behaviour of the upright and independent-minded Robert Audley: 'For as for Mr. Recorder, he was a man of courage and faithfulness to speak truth at every occasion, and he had a tongue as bravely hung as he had a head filled with judgment. Now this man Diabolus could by no means abide, because he could not by all wiles, trials, stratagems, and devices that he could use, make him wholly his own.'[3] It comes as something of a surprise to find that the process of creating new burgesses, surrendering the old charter, and obtaining the new one, belongs to the years 1683–4, a full year after the publication of *The Holy War*. The campaign against Audley and against influential Nonconformists in the borough was begun much earlier, but it is still not necessary to see Bunyan's fable as a judicious prophecy of Bedford's immediate future, as John Brown did.[4] Bunyan's common sense about political affairs, so evident in his writings and in the caution which he displayed when the terror reached its height at the beginning of the reign of James II, together with his contacts with all manner of men among the separated brethren, may indeed have enabled him to make shrewd guesses as to what would happen to the corporation under the pressure of the local magnates and the Crown. But at a time when letters, petitions, talk, and pamphlet

[1] *Bedfordshire Notes and Queries*, ed. F. A. Blaydes (1886), p. 8; Brown, p. 320.

[2] *C.P.S.D. 1683–1685*, ii (1938), 35.

[3] *H.W.*, p. 18–19.

[4] Brown, pp. 315–21.

warfare were contributing to a national crisis of proportions not seen since the eve of the Civil War, that common sense would also be drawn to look beyond the frontiers of Bedfordshire and to draw conclusions. Although the climax was reached in 1683–4 the attack on the corporations had begun before 1682, and Bunyan had material to his hand without indulging in prophecy or guesswork. The town of Northampton, a not too distant neighbour of Bedford, had already received its new charter by 25 September 1681 after voluntarily surrendering the old. On that day the mayor and aldermen met the Earl of Peterborough, Lord-Lieutenant of the county, on the edge of the town, just as the Bedford gentry and municipality had met Lord Ailesbury. The mayor received the charter on his knees in the name of the corporation, 'with due reverence, joy and gratitude of mind'. The Deputy Recorder in his speech denounced the conduct of those recently wielding civic power: 'Is there any among you have been tainted with ill principles? . . . Now there is an eye upon you which will have respect to justice as well as to mercy.'[1] Quite apart from the example of Robert Audley, the Recorder's office was a key one in this epoch of municipal revolution because of the role he played in elections, and in the new regulations for many towns his powers were extended (for instance at Bewdley, Worcestershire, which surrendered its old charter on 28 July 1684 and received a new one in May 1685): 'The powers and status of the recorder were enlarged in a number of minor but significant ways. He now had the nomination of the deputy recorder who was a very important officer at election times.'[2] In that period of out-and-out party struggle, the atmosphere of which is captured in *The Holy War* and translated into the terms of Christian allegory, the Recorder's voice was indeed that of a troubled and tried conscience, whether in Mansoul, Bedford, or many another English town.

(iv) *A Complex Epic*

The Holy War has an elaborate plot which contains a number of climaxes and reversals and covers three distinct phases of the

[1] Bodleian MS. Ashmole 1674, no. 79.

[2] See Peter Styles, 'The Corporation of Bewdley under the Later Stuarts', *University of Birmingham Historical Journal*, i (1958–9), 111.

history of the city of Mansoul. Throughout the allegory of the city, the assaults upon it by Diabolus and his instruments, and its two liberations by Emanuel, the allegory operates on at least three levels, those of Christian or world history, of the life of the individual soul, and of recent and contemporary English history; there may also be detected a fourth level of millenarian history relating to the events described in Revelation. But as in Langland or Spenser, not all these levels of reference are kept in play at the same time, and there are large parts of the narrative where one level, especially the second, is predominant at the expense of the others. Before analysing this complex scheme a brief summary of the story which provides the vehicle may be useful.

Bunyan begins with an account of the fall from heaven of Diabolus (Satan) and the rebel angels and their resolve to revenge themselves by seizing the newly created town of Mansoul, 'one of the chief works and delights of King Shaddai' (God the Father). Diabolus sits down with his host to besiege Mansoul and persuades its citizens to open the gates to him by a trick which alludes to the temptation in Eden. He remodels the corporation, replacing the Recorder, Mr. Conscience, by Mr. Forget-good; there is also a new Lord Mayor, the Lord Lustings, in the place of Mr. Understanding, and the Lord Wilbewill, who represents human free will, takes service under the new government. However, Shaddai resolves to recapture the town; he first sends an army of forty thousand men representing the Old Testament and the Mosaic law: the captains are Boanerges, Conviction, Judgment, and Execution. Their attacks weaken the resolution of the townspeople and Understanding and Conscience gradually return to their allegiance. But it is only the arrival of Shaddai's son Emanuel with a fresh army which routs the Diabolonian hordes and delivers the town. After their unconditional surrender the people are pardoned and given a new charter. Emanuel appoints the Lord Chief Secretary (the Holy Spirit) to be their principal preacher; the Diabolonian usurpers are tried and condemned.

Diabolonians still lurk underground in the town: and they are assisted by Mr. Carnal Security to breed complacency and pride in Mansoul. Its enemies emerge from holes and corners while Emanuel silently withdraws. Diabolus attacks again with an army of Doubters. He succeeds in winning the town a second time, but Lord Wilbewill, his chief opponent, holds out in a citadel of which Mr. Godly-fear is the keeper. During a long and wretched time the besieged constantly petition the Prince to relieve them; at last a petition inspired by the Lord Chief Secretary is effectual and Emanuel is moved to return and to liberate the city for a second time. Yet a third time Diabolus raises an army, a combination of Doubters and Bloodmen (persecutors), twenty-five thousand strong, but he is again defeated and most of the Doubters slain; those who escape to plot further treasons are captured, tried, and sentenced to death. In his closing speech Emanuel makes clear that the enemy will never be entirely eliminated but will continue as an irritant and a constant temptation within the walls of Mansoul to remind them that they must hold fast.

Diabolus's first attempt on Mansoul represents the temptation in Eden and the Fall; in fact the form of the siege allegory is blatantly abandoned when, immediately after incidents of epic action, the shooting of Captain Resistance as he stands on guard at the gate, and the death of Lord Innocency, we are told that the people of the town are offered the forbidden fruit of the tree of the knowledge of good and evil:

> . . . they looked, they considered, they were taken with the forbidden fruit: *they took thereof and did eat*; and having eaten, they became immediately drunken therewith. So they opened the gates, both Eargate, and Eyegate, and let in Diabolus with all his bands . . .[1]

The mixture of modes, of political and military allegory with straightforward Biblical narrative, may seem clumsy, but it is no different from the method Bunyan sometimes adopts in *The Pilgrim's Progress*, for instance in episodes when the journey metaphor is abandoned and Christian and Hopeful discourse directly of matters of grace and salvation. The subsequent rule of Diabolus and the remodelled corporation of Mansoul thus represents at the historical level the period between the Fall of Man and the Redemption; within this period the first, less effectual attempts at relief by

[1] *H.W.*, p. 17.

the captains Boanerges, Conviction, Judgment, and Execution, span the period of Old Testament history and particularly recall the exhortations of the prophetic books.

After Emanuel's liberation of the town and granting of a new charter we enter the Christian era. The second lapse of the town is harder to fit within a scheme of cosmic chronology; it may, however, reflect the rise of the Papacy and the decline of Christian belief and practice from the ideals of the primitive church: then the second relief of the city by Emanuel would correspond to the Protestant Reformation. The third series of attacks by Diabolus with his armies of Doubters and Bloodmen are figurative of the successive threats to Protestant Christianity in the sixteenth and seventeenth centuries, the threat by the Spanish Armada, the extensions of Catholic power during the Thirty Years' War, and finally the encroachments of the civil power on the gathered churches in Bunyan's own lifetime and within his own experience: his imprisonments and those of other Nonconformists and the persecution of Dissenters under the Clarendon code and subsequent legislation.

It will be seen that the historical perspective thus apparent is a telescoped vision; we move from a broad sweep of Christian chronology to the details of Bunyan's own time. But this telescoping of cosmic history is found also in many of the apocalyptic commentators of the period. It is, for instance, encountered in Joseph Mede's highly celebrated *Clavis Apocalyptica* (1627). Mede assigns the pouring out of the first four vials in Revelation 16 to, respectively, the reforming movements of Wiclif and Huss, the Reformation of Luther and Calvin, the defeat of the Spanish Armada by a Protestant England, and the victories of Gustavus Adolphus against the Catholic Imperialists. The fifth vial signifies the destruction of Rome; the sixth the conversion of the Jews, a theme of serious and topical interest in the 1640s and 1650s to which a poet like Marvell, building slender and protective aesthetic fabrics from the terrible political realities of his time, could direct an oblique and ironic gaze.[1] The pouring out of the last vial of

[1] 'And you should, if you please, refuse Till the conversion of the Jews' ('To his Coy Mistress'). An account of the last days slightly differing from that of Mede and painstaking in its detail is that of Henry Archer, *The Personall Reign of Christ Upon Earth* (1642); Archer concludes that the conversion of the Jews would take place

God's wrath against the forces of Antichrist is yet to come, and it is noticeable how the intervals between each prophetic epoch are rapidly diminishing. It was possible, as William Haller has pointed out, for Englishmen who were contemporaries of Mede, inspired by Puritan preachers and lecturers, to look upon the great religious and political events of their time, signalled by the meeting of the Long Parliament and the fall of Laud and Strafford, as harbingers of the final epoch which would usher in the last age, the final defeat of Antichrist, the end of secular history, and the thousand-year rule of Christ and his saints.[1]

Mede's book went through three editions and its English translation by Richard More (*The Key of the Revelation*, 1650) was authorized to be published by the Long Parliament. It is not necessary to suppose that Bunyan had read it but it seems probable that he had encountered the same material and the same chiliastic views in other books and in countless sermons and godly conversations. The static dialogues already mentioned in *The Pilgrim's Progress* are, after all, faithful reproductions of the spiritual searchings of the Puritan and sectarian saints. The white vesture prepared for the inhabitants of Mansoul and the ecstatic final expression of his love for them by Emanuel again reveal this definite but by no means preponderant millenarian strain.

Once Diabolus has gained admission into the town and remodelled the corporation, it is then that the allegory begins to work on two parallel levels. Mansoul is still mankind, now fallen, but it is also the individual soul, hardened by sin and before the reception of grace. Unlike much in Spenser's allegory in *The Faerie Queene*, where the historical level sometimes seems somewhat coldly abstracted from the moral and theological (Duessa as False Religion and Mary Queen of Scots would be an instance), Bunyan always holds in front of us as a cohesive agent linking the theme of the

about 1650 or 1656, and that therefore 'it is likely that *Christ's* comming from Heaven, and raysing the dead, and beginning his kingdome, and the thousand years, will bee about the yeare of our Lord 1700 for it is to be about fortie-five yeares after 1650 or 1656'.

[1] See the English translation, *The Key of the Revelation*, by Richard More (1650), pp. 60 and 114–25, and the discussions in William Haller, *Liberty and Reformation in the Puritan Revolution* (New York, 1955), pp. 49–50, and Michael Fixler, *Milton and the Kingdoms of God* (1964), esp. pp. 24–5.

individual soul and the theme of Christian history, the stuff of lively fiction that is in the foreground of his metaphor, the presence throughout the work of a vivid, bustling civic community, like Bedford or any other seventeenth-century county town: thus the single soul in time is linked with the whole world and its time, and we are prepared to overlook the occasional artistic anomalies, as when the Genesis story of the Fall is forced into the narrative, or when the condemned Diabolonians are barbarously put to death 'at the cross'.

The fusion of psychological and historical allegory was no doubt made easier by the tendency which Bunyan shared with other Baptists, but also with the Quakers in whom it is more pronounced, to treat God's dealings with Israel and indeed the whole Old Testament narrative as an analogue of the soul's history.[1] The tendency is poignantly displayed in Bunyan's agonized searching of the Scriptures in *Grace Abounding*, where every single text encountered, damning or saving, is applied to his immediate personal condition. Most of the civic officials of Mansoul fit more suitably into the personal allegory: the Recorder is Mr. Conscience, whose thundering voice can still make Mansoul tremble when his place is taken by Mr. Forget-good; Diabolus builds a tower to shut out the sun from the Lord Mayor's house (the understanding is darkened) and puts a new Lord Mayor in his place, the Lord Lustings; and the Lord Wilbewill, perhaps the most interesting of the characters in the book, takes service under the new governor. The cardinal role given to human free will is an assurance of Bunyan's essential Christian orthodoxy, in which he differs from the antinomians of his time and social group though sharing many features of their style; his attitude is firmly laid down in *The Heavenly Footman*:

I tell you the will is all: that is one of the chief things that turns the wheel either backwards or forwards; and God knoweth that full well, and so likewise doth the devil; and therefore they both endeavour very much to strengthen the will of their servants. God, he is for making of his willing people to serve him; and the devil, he doth

[1] As in the personal narrative of a member of his congregation: 'And before I came to my Brothers, my Soul was made like the Chariotts of Aminnadab, and I was wounderfully bourne upp' (*The Narrative of the Persecution of Agnes Beaumont in 1674*, ed. G. B. Harrison (1929), p. 77).

what he can to possess the will and affection of those that are his, with love to sin . . .[1]

As the large and bold canvas of the work unfolds we see the same narrative sustaining the story of the Redemption as well as the saga of an individual conversion. Shaddai hears the news of the surrender of his beloved Mansoul, and he accepts the offer of his son Emanuel to recover the town in an episode which is parallel to the Son's offering of himself in *Paradise Lost*, iii; but the captains who are first sent against the town, Boanerges (powerful preaching), Conviction, Judgment, and Execution, represent the terrors of the Mosaic law as they are applied to the arousing of spiritual awareness in an individual: nearly every Puritan spiritual biography begins with an awakening sermon.

If the interpretation of later events and the second attack on the city is less clear at the world-historical level, except for the vague millenarian thread already mentioned, it is plain at the level of conversion-allegory, where as in *The Pilgrim's Progress* the order of the experiences recounted in *Grace Abounding* is exactly repeated. Once more a second period of spiritual doubt is recapitulated, with its 'very great storm' of temptations, just as in the autobiography there is the sequence despair–faith–despair, and as in *The Pilgrim's Progress* Doubting Castle follows the Valley of the Shadow of Death, with a long period of recovery intervening. The Doubters sent against the town do not represent intellectual questioning of belief; they stand for various forms of despair concerning their salvation on the part of convinced Christians. The nine companies of Doubters include the Election-doubters, the Grace-doubters, the Vocation-doubters, and so on. Their long and dangerous attack is delivered when the citizens have become careless, 'all taken with the words of this tattling Diabolonian gentleman', Carnal Security. An important marginal note at this point says, ''Tis not Grace received but Grace improved, that preserves the soul from temporal dangers':[2] again one is reminded of the orthodox view of the necessary co-operative activity of human nature with which Bunyan balances his Calvinist belief in salvation by free grace. The Mansoulians have neglected to improve their talent, and when they awake to the danger, Christ

[1] *The Heavenly Footman*, in Offor, iii. 383. [2] *H.W.*, p. 152.

has departed, they have forgotten the promises previously declared to them, and have in their remorse become an easy prey to the Doubters. It is the story of Doubting Castle over again. As in Bunyan's conversion experience, when the Doubters force their way into the town they strike terror by their blasphemies:

Oh the fearful state of *Mansoul* now! now every corner swarmed with outlandish *Doubters*; Red-coats and Black-coats, walked the town by clusters, and filled up all the houses with hideous noises, vain Songs, lying stories and blasphemous language against *Shaddai* and his Son.[1]

The statement that the occupation of the town and the siege of Heart Castle lasted 'about two years and a half' is again autobiographical and corresponds to Bunyan's second period of despair, the 'very great storm' of temptations. After a short interval the Bloodmen succeed the Doubters, just as in *Grace Abounding* Bunyan passes from the account of his spiritual doubts to the legal persecution of his imprisonment with a very brief passage on his ministry. Emanuel's second occupation of the town is, in terms of the allegory of the soul, a final assurance of grace. Prayers for assurance have at last been answered, but the life of the believer is not yet perfected; Carnal Sense and Unbelief still remain within the walls (a typically Calvinist comment on the survival of concupiscence even into the higher stages of sanctification).

As Bunyan becomes more and more engaged in recounting battles and sieges he appears to be stirred by a deep nostalgia for his own military past as a raw recruit in a county levy in the First Civil War. This nostalgia leads him to recollect the millenarian hopes of the early years of the Bedford church; at a time when, under the Protectorate, Fifth Monarchy agitation was going on, we find Gifford, the founder of the church, using millenarian language at the beginning of the *Church Book*, and the brethren in correspondence with the London Fifth Monarchy congregation of Peter Chamberlen.[2] Gifford too had served in the army like Thomas Harrison and so many other Baptists of that persuasion. The Fifth Monarchy agitators of the Commonwealth period thought that the

[1] *H.W.*, p. 205.

[2] See the Minute Book of this church in Lothbury, Bodleian, Rawlinson MS. D828; Sharrock, p. 51.

Stuart rule, and after that the Protectorate, was the continuation of the fourth or Roman monarchy, only to be ended by the advent of King Jesus. In Revelation the fourth monarchy is the reign of the Beast, and the corresponding period in *The Holy War* is the period of Mansoul's corruption under Carnal Security and the assaults of the Doubters and Bloodmen. The high-water mark of persecution when the Doubters break into the town is parallel to the slaying of the witnesses (Rev. 11). Emanuel's second liberation would then be the millennium (the renewal of the citizens' white garments is a strong hint of this), and the last attack of the Bloodmen would be the warfare associated with Gog and Magog:

> And when the thousand years are expired, Satan shall be loosed out of his prison.
>
> And shall go out to deceive the nations which are in the four quarters of the earth, Gog and Magog, to gather them together to battle: the number of whom is as the sand of the sea.
>
> And they went up on the breadth of the earth, and compassed the camp of the saints about, and the beloved city; and fire came down from God out of heaven, and devoured them. (Rev. 20: 7–9.)

However, the reader can only note the strain and the quality of apocalyptic fervour and guess approximately at the correspondences. For the extraordinary poetry of Revelation with its abrupt movement from one vision to the next makes it just as difficult for one to discern how Bunyan as allegorist interpreted its revolutions as it was for the political Fifth Monarchy men to apply its chronology to contemporary events.

The glances at current history hardly amount to a distinct level of the allegory. The episode of the Bloodmen refers to the persecution of the Nonconformists after the Restoration. The appointment by Diabolus of Mr. Filth who encourages the publication of wanton songs and ballads is a hit at Roger L'Estrange, who, as licenser of the press, had acted harshly towards Nonconformist writers and printers, including one of Bunyan's own printers, Francis Smith; L'Estrange was also noted for the scurrility of his own pamphlets.[1]

[1] In the last four years of the reign L'Estrange's principal organs for attacking the Dissenters were *Heraclitus Ridens* and *The Observator*; Ogg, ii. 709–10.

In the period of the Doubters the city is stricken by plague and some time afterwards a Diabolonian plot is detected by Mr. Prywell in circumstances which recall informers' reports of incidents in the Popish Plot: he hears a murmuring 'at a place called Vile-hill', and draws near to eavesdrop on the conspirators. When, at the second council of devils, Lucifer advocates that, as a prelude to a second campaign, Mansoul shall be allowed to grow rich, there seems to be an allusion to those spiritual and moral dangers for Nonconformists of prosperity in trade which Bunyan had lately described in *The Life and Death of Mr. Badman*. Mr. Penniwise-Pound-foolish and Mr. Get-ith'-hundred-and-lose-ith'-shire are to be sent among the burgesses who will thus become taken up with much business and surfeited with the good things of the world.[1]

These complex layers of significance show Bunyan as the latest representative of the tradition of multiple allegory as practised by Langland and Spenser. As with them, the tradition had been passed on to him from the source which inspired the middle ages: Biblical exegesis. In spite of the Reformers' stress on the supremacy of the literal sense, relics of the old fourfold interpretation continued to be applied, usually to Canticles and Revelation, but to other books of the Bible as well. In the posthumously published *Exposition on the First Ten Chapters of Genesis* Bunyan detects one literal and three allegorical meanings as being present in the text at the same time; the flood is a real historical event, but it is also a type of the enemies of the Church, of water baptism under the New Testament, and finally 'of the last and general overthrow of the world by fire and brimstone'.[2] This is the manner of proceeding which comes naturally to Bunyan in his epic of the Christian warfare.

The Holy War is an ambitious work with a power and sweep in its continuous narrative that certainly entitles it to be called an epic. *The Pilgrim's Progress*, in terms of literary construction, seems episodic in comparison, sustained only by the metaphor of the journey and the road, and yet Bunyan has so entered into that

[1] *H.W.*, p. 216; there is also some similarity to the episode of By-ends and his companions in *P.P.*, pp. 98–106.

[2] *Exposition on the First Ten Chapters of Genesis*, in Offor, ii. 466.

metaphor as to have become the creator of a myth universally communicable. This is why *The Holy War*, with all its fine qualities, remains inferior to the earlier allegory: it does not possess that mythic power, and we marvel rather at its narrative flow, sustained interest, and combination of heroic dignity with human variety. Now Bunyan is the self-conscious writer, attempting what might be called the typical second novel, a book aiming higher than the first, more literary, and drawing less on personal experience. He is seeking to provide at the popular level the equivalent of a heroic subject treated in the grand manner. As for the epic poet, a certain degree of detachment is necessary; he is no longer the dreamer, but an observer, and the new tone of grandeur and universality is introduced in the first paragraph, just as the opening words of *The Pilgrim's Progress* create an atmosphere of visionary immediacy:

In my Travels, as I walked through many Regions and Countries, it was my chance to happen into that famous *Continent* of *Universe*; a very large and spacious Countrey it is. It lieth between the two Poles, and just amidst the four points of the Heavens. It is a place well watered, and richly adorned with Hills and Valleys, bravely situate; and for the most part (at least where I was) very fruitful, also well peopled, and a very sweet Air . . .

I learned much of their mother-tongue, together with the Customs, and manners of them among whom I was . . . Yea I had (to be sure) even lived and died a Native among them (so was I taken with them and their doings) had not my Master sent me home to his House, there to do business for him and to over-see business done.[1]

From his heavenly viewpoint the author is carried above the spacious country of Universe and the corporation of Mansoul, so that he can regard them with a sublime detachment. After the first paragraph, the 'I saw', 'I beheld', of the visionary, so frequent in the earlier allegory, do not recur. No dreamer awakes at the end of the book, when with the first person narrator long forgotten Christ addresses Mansoul in a conclusion of epic splendour and amplitude.

It has been suggested that the image of Christian warfare gives a less full and satisfying account of the Christian life than the image of the pilgrimage of the soul, because by seeing life as a continual conflict between the powers of light and darkness the ordinary

[1] *H.W.*, p. 7.

general tenor of human life is neglected. There may be some truth in this view, but the criticism is hardly just to Bunyan since he is careful to relieve the military tensions of Mansoul with civic bustle and satiric humour. Another objection that has often been made, as for example by Froude, is to the double nature of the action in which Mansoul is captured and relieved twice and many incidents like the trials of the Diabolonian traitors are re-enacted in only slightly differing form. The same charge has been made against *Beowulf*. But both in *Beowulf* and in *The Holy War* something is gained from the absence of a neat dramatic construction: a sense of the range and breadth of human endeavour, heroic in the one case, waiting on God with mingled weakness and aspiration in the other. And, like *Piers Plowman*, *The Holy War* has an open conclusion: all is not at an end and the final coming of King Shaddai is yet to be.

Tribute must be paid to the skill with which every detail of a huge theological structure is translated into some allegorical incident or character. The most interesting parts of the allegory are those involving some degree of tension between symbol and idea. The citizens of Mansoul are free agents and their great man Wilbewill has a certain Restoration swagger and independence about him; when he takes service under Diabolus he demonstrates the *corruptio optimi*, only to redeem himself by exemplary courage during the second siege. But there is nothing strictly incompatible with Bunyan's Calvinist doctrine; it is simply that when dogma is transferred to fiction the stresses are bound to appear different. Milton's Satan steals the limelight (until the appearance of Adam and Eve) and the unregenerate Wilbewill has a similar tarnished splendour, because they are characters who make decisions and act. The sanctified will is able to curb the affections only through the assistance of grace; but when this principle is coaxed into the fable it has a different effect, and makes Wilbewill seem rather a fine fellow:

> The Lord *Wilbewill* also, he took the charge of the watching against the Rebels within . . . ever since he took penance for his fault, he has showed as much honesty and bravery of spirit as any he in *Mansoul*.[1]

[1] *H.W.*, p. 195; there may be some relation of Wilbewill with the first Lord Bruce who is described as a humane person and a scholar; the reception of Emanuel's

Elsewhere the predominant impression is of the ingenuity with which the doctrinal points are made. Ear-gate is the vital gate of the town. Tradition, Human Wisdom, and Man's Invention enlist in the army of Shaddai, but when taken prisoners are ready to change sides; here is the mechanic preacher's jaundiced comment on ministers who had accepted the Restoration church settlement, like Edward Fowler, Bunyan's opponent in controversy; the incident is a small excursus in the manner of some of Langland's incidents involving names, a gargoyle having nothing to do with the main structure of the work. The doctrine of free grace is effectively illustrated when Emanuel, after the rejection of numerous petitions, grants an entirely undeserved mercy to the rebel town. When Diabolus attempts to negotiate, Emanuel maintains that Mansoul is his by purchase, and refuses to consider any proposals for a truce; the Devil, now transformed in Pauline terms, which Bunyan must have had in mind, into 'an angel of light', offers to establish and maintain 'a sufficient ministry, besides lecturers, in Mansoul', but it will not do; here is another out-and-out condemnation of the establishment. Throughout there is the play of an ever alert intellectual skill in building analogies, as well as Bunyan's accustomed shrewdness of observation. Only rarely does there appear to be an unbridgeable emotional gap between the idea and the similitude, and then it is when Bunyan has been betrayed by his absolute trust in the language of the Bible. Thus, because the Epistle to the Galatians speaks of crucifying the affections and lusts,[1] the condemned Diabolonians are put to death by literal crucifixion. It is the naivety of Bunyan's Biblical realism, not his ferocity, that causes this slip.

Allegorical skill is combined with realism and humour in the episode of the trial of the Diabolonians. Necessity had given Bunyan a good working knowledge of court procedure and he uses it to advantage, though he had certainly profited from the study of a previous allegorical trial of vices in Richard Bernard's *The Isle of Man*

charter bears resemblance with the reception of the new charter in Bedford in 1684 when a troop of citizens met the party from London outside the town in splendid array (*D.N.B.*, Lord Bruce of Ampthill, later Earl of Ailesbury; Brown, pp. 319–20).

[1] Galatians 5: 24: 'And they that are Christ's have crucified the flesh with the affections and lusts.'

(1627).[1] False-peace brought to the bar denies the indictment, a common form of defence in criminal cases in the seventeenth century, claiming that he is incorrectly named and that his real name is Peace. The crier summons any in court who can give information to stand forth, and Search-truth testifies to having known the prisoner:

My Lord, I know, and have known, this man from a child, and can attest that his name is *False-peace*. I knew his father, his name was *Mr. Flatter*, and his mother before she was married was called by the name of *Mrs. Soothup* . . . I was his play-fellow only I was somewhat older than he; and when his mother did use to call him home from his play, she used to say, *False-peace*, *False-peace*, come home quick or I'll fetch you . . . I can remember that when his mother did use to sit at the door with him, or did play with him in her arms, she would call him twenty times together, My little False-peace, My pretty False-peace . . . O my little bird False-peace; and how do I love my child. The gossips also know it is thus though he has the face to deny it in open court.[2]

Moral argument is directed through the conceit of the denial of the indictment and aided by an unfailing ear for common speech to achieve an effortlessly true domestic genre picture. Later there is the episode of the hiring fair where Covetousness, Lasciviousness, and Anger change their names to Prudent Thrifty, Harmless-mirth, and Good-zeal, respectively. The Lord Wilbewill engages Harmless-mirth as his lackey, 'because Lent was almost out'. The disguised vices are described as: 'Three lusty fellows they were to look on and they were clothed in sheep's russet'.

In fact the colloquial English of *The Holy War* is as muscular and racy as in any other of Bunyan's fictions. There is actually more plain style and less sermon rhetoric than in *The Pilgrim's Progress* or *Badman* because there are no pious dialogues between believers employing a register of Puritan devotion. Everything is assimilated to the fable. When the scriptural promises of the new covenant of grace are touched on, it is by relating how the prince Emanuel, feasting his subjects in heroic style, sends the chief men of Mansoul many 'good bits' from his table. Bunyan does indeed make one or

[1] *The Isle of Man: Or, the Legall Proceedings in Manshire against Sin* (4th edn., 1627); see Roger Sharrock, 'The Trial of Vices in Puritan Fiction', *Baptist Quarterly*, xiv. 3–12.

[2] *H.W.*, p. 127.

two uneasy experiments with a kind of epic diction to dress out his grand theme and then prudently abandons them. The traces in the text are slight. Conscience has to preside over 'all terrene and domestic matters'; a hundred pages later Bunyan has forgotten the meaning of the exotic word 'terrene' and writes of Diabolonian soldiers encamping before Eye-gate, 'in what terrene and terrible manner they could'. We also find 'dolorous notes' and 'the profundity of your craft'. But a natural soundness of judgement prevents him from allowing the heroic theme to impose any major alteration on his style.[1] Elsewhere the popular flavour is as strong as ever. A rumour spreads through the town 'as a snowball loses nothing by rolling'. Incredulity, describing to Diabolus the execution of his companions, says he would have 'drunk of the same cup' if he had not escaped from the town. When Mr. Profane takes a secret message to Diabolus from his supporters in Mansoul, he pauses at Hell-gate to gossip with Cerberus, and 'they were presently as great as beggers'. Carnal Security, who brings Mansoul 'to dance after his pipe', chides the more cautious citizens for their fear of being 'sparrow-blasted'.

In most of these turns of phrase Bunyan has the benefit of the inventiveness of the folk; his own genius lies in judicious selection and loyalty to the resources of common speech. There are few similes which are not proverbs, or which do not possess clear characteristics of the proverb, even if their currency is not elsewhere recorded. It is as if the main drive of Bunyan's creativeness went into the larger imagery of the allegory of Mansoul, and in language he was content to make use of what lay ready to his hand. But there are also examples of his ability to invest his images from common life with original imaginative power. He sees the routed army of the Doubters 'spread upon the ground dead men, as one would spread dung upon the land', and here he is effectively reaching towards epic seriousness and epic grimness. There is formal splendour too in the parallels and contrasts of the graduated series of assaults on Mansoul, the different captains and their different scutcheons. But comedy will keep breaking in.

[1] E. M. W. Tillyard in *The English Epic and Its Background* (1954) lays more stress on the epic aspect of the work.

NOTE ON THE TEXT

COMPARED with that of *The Pilgrim's Progress*, the success of *The Holy War* was initially most modest. Despite the title-page's trading on the author's fame, only two editions were produced during Bunyan's lifetime, the first in 1682 and the second in 1684, while a third edition was not called for until 1696.

The first edition was published by Dorman Newman and Benjamin Alsop, the octavo volume being advertised in the Term Catalogue for Hilary Term, 1681–2. Why these men, who had not previously been responsible for any of Bunyan's books, should have been entrusted with the publication of such an important work is not known; but there is room for speculation in that the publisher to whom Bunyan had earlier assigned his most significant labours, the dependable Nathaniel Ponder, was currently experiencing some difficulties. Ponder was involved in a bitter dispute over the printing of unauthorized editions of *The Pilgrim's Progress*, and in 1681 he was named among the defendants in an action for assault brought by Bartholomew Sprint against some printers and booksellers in London and Oxford.[1] Perhaps Bunyan did not want to add to his friend's burden at this time or perhaps Ponder himself was simply too busy or preoccupied to undertake publication of another lengthy volume immediately. Whatever the reason, *The Holy War* was delivered into the hands of two remarkable entrepreneurs. One of the most prominent publishers of his day, Newman was ultimately driven into bankruptcy through unwise speculation, though not before he had produced Bunyan's *The Advocateship of Jesus Christ* (1688) and announced plans for a Folio edition of Bunyan, an enterprise later undertaken by Charles Doe and published by William Marshall in 1692.[2] Alsop was likewise celebrated. Named with Ponder as a co-defendant in the Sprint action, he was described

[1] See Frank Mott Harrison, 'Nathaniel Ponder: The Publisher of *The Pilgrim's Progress*', *The Library*, 4th ser., xv (Dec. 1934), 257–94; Plomer, pp. 240–1.

[2] Plomer, p. 217.

by his successor, John Dunton, as 'a first-rate book-seller' if 'a wild sort of a Spark', who with an eye to the main chance eventually gave up his business to take a commission in Monmouth's army.[1] Subsequent to his partnership with Newman in *The Holy War*, Alsop published no fewer than four of Bunyan's treatises, all printed under his well-known sign of 'the *Angel* and *Bible* in the *Poultry*'.

Satisfactory as the Newman–Alsop collaboration proved, it did not survive the first edition. The second edition of 1684 bears the imprint of Dorman Newman alone; nor is there sufficient evidence to explain the discontinuance of the relationship. While Harrison's suggestion that their separation was due to Alsop's departure seems plausible enough, it still remains conjecture, for at some point in 1684 Alsop brought out yet another Bunyan tract, *Seasonable Counsel*, the issue of which is not, unfortunately, recorded in the Term Catalogues.[2] Since the second *Holy War* was in print apparently as early as May of that year, Alsop's absence or imminent disengagement need not have precluded his association with the venture. Some other possibility may thus account for the change. The point is not without significance, because the very existence of the 1684 edition in the form in which we have it is, to say the least, extremely questionable.

No modern editor who aspires to establish a reliable text of *The Holy War* can fail to come to grips with the curious phenomenon of this 1684 version. What perplexes is not simply that it contains serious anomalies, but that it seems to have been treated in its own time as totally authentic. The book was noticed in the Term Catalogue for Easter, 1684, and Newman continued to advertise it until at least 1688, when he listed it in a catalogue of some twenty Bunyan works appended to *The Advocateship of Jesus Christ*, describing it there as 'An useful Book'. Not only so, but the physical structure of the volume has its own integrity, as the following abbreviated bibliographical description indicates:[3]

[1] Plomer, p. 5.

[2] Harrison, p. xxiii. In 1684 Alsop produced Bunyan's *A Holy Life* through his agent, B. W.: the publication, however, was inexplicably delayed, the work having been advertised in the Term Catalogue for Michaelmas, 1682. See Harrison, p. 48.

[3] What follows incorporates part of a brief article by James F. Forrest, 'The Authenticity of the 1684 Edition of Bunyan's *Holy War*', *The Papers of the Bibliographical Society of America*, 72 (First Quarter, 1978), 89–91. The author gratefully

THE SECOND EDITION, 1684

Title: [within double rule] THE / Holy War, / MADE BY / CHRIST / UPON THE / DEVIL, / For the Regaining of / MAN: / Or, the Losing and Taking Again / OF THE / Town of Mansoul. / [rule] / *The second Edition.* / [rule] / By *JOHN BUNYAN*, the Author of the *Pilgrims Progress.* / [rule] / *I have used Similitudes*, Hos. 12. 10 / [rule] / LONDON, Printed for Dorman Newman at the / *Kings Arms* in the *Poultry*, 1684.

Variant: THE / Holy WAR / Betwixt / CHRIST / And the / DEVILL
Collation: 12°: A^4 B–M^{12} N^8
Pagination: 144 leaves, pp. [8] 1–20 12 22–119 126 125 122–33 341 135–56 142 158–70 11 172–92 213–76 278 278–89 300–9 [310] [= 288]

Apart from the surprising change of title, the main discrepancy is in pagination. The oddities in enumeration are no doubt partly a consequence of the numerous abridgements made from the text of 1682 (comprising about 20 per cent of the whole), but they are also symptomatic of a standard of typography much inferior to that of the first edition. Set on paper of poorer quality, the print is closer, each page bearing thirty-six lines compared with the earlier edition's thirty-two, so that in its make-up the duodecimo volume of 1684 reflects the exercise of thrift.

Since there is no conclusive evidence that Bunyan oversaw the printing of any of his works, the onus is on those who would assert his involvement in this instance. But the testimony of aesthetics inhibits the argument. To recall the original title, *The Holy War, made by Shaddai upon Diabolus, for the Regaining of the Metropolis of the World. Or the Losing and Taking Again of the Town of Mansoul*, is at once to feel it wholly inconceivable that the author could have acceded to the change of title (especially to one so tentative and uncertain as the presence of a variant may suggest), subverting as that inevitably does his allegorical intent. Moreover, the kinds of substantive alterations made in the 1684 edition are not such as Bunyan would ever have contrived. Like allegorists before him, notably Spenser, Bunyan delights in catalogues and lists, as

acknowledges permission from the editor of that journal to make use of the material here.

demonstrated by the parallel rehearsings of opposing captains with their heraldic panoplies or the repeated naming of jurors at the trial of the Diabolonians in Mansoul: their presentation is a ritual that functions through reinforcement and delay to etch the import on the mind, and the artful process is therefore essential to the message. Yet the ill-considered dropping of a double listing of these jurors (sig. H5) or the incongruous decision not to enumerate the Doubters' captains while parading those of the Bloodmen (M8^{v}) is precisely the sort of insensitive abbreviation practised in this version. A similar heedlessness is evident in the curtailment of the second of Bunyan's beloved court scenes by dispensing with the indictment (N1^{v}), another bizarre omission which Bunyan (one can reasonably hold) with his intimate and personal knowledge of English court procedure would not have countenanced; in the deletion of some of his most characteristic and significant marginalia (D12^{v}, E11^{v}, G4^{r}, H8^{r}, H9^{r}); and above all, in the gross excision of a number of his finest passages, including those relating to the joy of the townsfolk over their unexpected pardon (G1^{v}, G2^{r}, G4^{r}), the triumphal entry of the Prince into the town (G6^{v}) and its jubilee to celebrate the occasion of Emanuel's residence (M6^{v}). Lamentable as indeed these are, the general shortening might be felt less keenly, were the cuts always discreetly managed; but some of them are really maladroit and inept. While an attempt is usually made to maintain the narrative flow, the editor sometimes nods, whereupon the sense becomes discontinuous. Thus we are informed that Diabolus is put 'into another fright', after all mention of his earlier one has been erased (E5^{r}, E4^{v}); we are told of 'more talk between Profane and Cerberus', when in fact the previous racy dialogue between them has been expunged (K6^{r}, K2^{v}). Perhaps the most serious break occurs in the description of Carnal Security's sly proceedings, where the narrative is abruptly terminated in mid-sentence by the account of Emanuel's crying over Mansoul (I4^{r}); in this instance, only a preserved marginal comment helps to keep us on course, even as we are made sharply aware of editorial manipulation.

Despite these occasional lapses, it may be claimed that the guiding principle of abridgement is to create as inexpensive an edition as possible without losing good sense. That so much of the original text is retained surely bespeaks this simple desire for economy rather than exposes a darker motive. While it is true that in its typographical arrangement (closeness of print, paragraphs run together, and so on) the book betrays certain features typical of a pirated edition, the question of piracy must be left open in the absence of information concerning the precise circumstances of publication. What remains incontestable, however, is that this edition of 1684 must be rejected on aesthetic grounds as spurious, and its lack of authority is only further attested to by the fact that those responsible for the third edition of 1696, when the work was 'reprinted by the Assigns of *B.A.* and sold by *Nat. Ponder* in *London-Yard*, the West-End of St. *Pauls* Church', ignored it to return to the text of the first edition.

Once the second edition has been dismissed, the copy-text becomes that of the first edition.

THE FIRST EDITION, 1682

[within double rule] THE / Holy War, / MADE BY / SHADDAI / UPON / DIABOLUS, / For the Regaining of the / Metropolis of the World. / OR, THE / Losing and Taking Again / OF THE / Town of Mansoul. / [rule] / By *JOHN BUNYAN*, the Author of the / *Pilgrims Progress.* / [rule] / *I have used Similitudes*, Hos. 12. 10. / [rule] / *LONDON*, Printed for *Dorman Newman* at the *Kings* / *Arms* in the *Poultry*; and *Benjamin Alsop* at the / *Angel* and *Bible* in the *Poultry*, 1682.

Collation: 8°: A⁴, B–Z⁸, Aa–Cc⁸ [$4–A3, A4] (with insert before A1 and insert before B1); 204 leaves, pp. [i–viii] 1–397 [398–400] (misprinting 97 as 67) in headline against outer margin of type-page.

Contents: Free end-paper. Inset: engraved portrait of Bunyan facing title-page. A1ʳ: title (verso blank). A2ʳ: [beneath double rule] 'TO THE READER' with text in verse (init. T⁴) ending on A4ʳ (verso blank); below, '*Jo. Bunyan.*' and rule. Inset: engraved folding plate of Bunyan (full length) superimposed on Mansoul between Shaddai's army and forces of Diabolus. B1ʳ: [beneath two unequal double rules] HT, with text (init. I⁴) ending on Cc7ʳ (verso blank) with rule; below, '*FINIS.*' and rule. Cc8ʳ: [beneath two rows of acorn type-ornaments: one row turned up, the other down] *An ADVERTISE-MENT* / *to the READER.* with text of 32 lines of verse (init. S²) ending on Cc8ᵛ with anagram '*Nu hony in a B.*'; below, '*JOHN BUNYAN.*' Free end-paper.

Head-title: A / RELATION / OF THE / Holy War, &c.

Running titles: A2v–A4r: [within double rule] To the Reader. B1v–Cc7r: [within double rule] *The Holy War*. [*VVar* HKL(i) M(o) O(i) PR(o) T(i) VYZ(o) Bb(i) Cc(o); *war* FGKNQTXBblr DEIMPSYAa2r B3r C4r]

Catchwords: B8v on C1r Giant's [Gyant's] C8v (i)mpreg- [impregnable] D8v of E8v should F8v First ('The' misplaced in text) [The] G8v to H8v his I8v *may* K8v before L8v Well, M8v Now N8v *loath* [*loth*] O8v ever P3v (*pro*)*mi*- [*promise*] Q8v But R8v *above* S8v it T8v them- [themselves] V8v *hold*, X8v after Y8v So Z8v the Aa8v the Bb8v (*me*)*ditation*,

Plates: Portrait of '*John Bunnyon*' measures 132 × 75 mm and is inscribed 'R White Sculp'. The folding plate of Bunyan as type of Mansoul measures 139 × 182 mm and is unsigned. Both portraits are undoubtedly by the same engraver, Robert White, whose pencilled sketch of the author on vellum (Cracherode Collection, British Museum) is their basis, as it is also of the famous 'sleeping-man' portrait included in the third edition of *The Pilgrim's Progress* (1679).[1]

Copies examined: Bedford County Library (two copies); Bodleian; British Library; Congregational Library, London; Folger Shakespeare Library; Harvard University; Henry E. Huntington Library; New York Public Library; University of Alberta (two copies); University of Texas.

The first edition exists in three different states. Of the copies examined, that in the Congregational Library, London, alone shows the original setting, in which 'bare' on l. 11 of V3v (inner forme) appears as 'bear'. This mis-spelling was evidently soon noticed and corrected to create the second state represented by most of the copies listed. The press was afterwards stopped a second time to substitute 'standard-bearer' for 'Ancient-bearer' on ll. 16, 26, and 31 of the same page, and 'Standards' for 'Ancients' on l. 4 of V4r on the same forme (all these type-lines display evidence of crowding, the result of inserting an additional letter within the line) to produce the third and final state found in one of the two copies located in Bedford County Library and in the copies of the Henry E. Huntington and University of Texas libraries.

Since the unaltered reading of the second state is not patently incorrect, the question naturally arises why it was felt necessary to make the change. It is hardly credible that the proof-reader was merely following his copy with unusual fidelity at this point, for the repetitive nature of the substitution surely argues deliberate

[1] On White's talents in portraiture see Horace Walpole, *Anecdotes of Painting*, with adds. by the Revd. James Dallaway (3 vols., London, 1849), iii. 947–53.

intent on the part of reader or author to rewrite the text. Apparently the motive was to achieve consistency. The lines in question form part of a terrifying tabulation of Diabolus's vicious officers that begins on V3^{r} with the depiction of 'Captain *Rage*' who is said to have a 'Standard-bearer', and the catalogue as a whole constitutes a satanic parody of an earlier roll-call of Emanuel's glorious captains, each of whom is mustered with his appropriate 'Standard-bearer' (H4^{r}). The same title is again used to denote the aides to the Bloodmen's captains (Aa5^{v}–Aa6^{r}). But given this late desire for uniformity in parallel situations of allegorical stock-taking, the case for preferring 'Standard-bearer' over 'Ancient-bearer' is by no means irresistible. No attempt is made to obtain consistency earlier in the text, for the term '*Ancient*-bearer' remains attributed (F7^{r}), however significantly, to Diabolus's own attendant. Moreover, though it has been claimed with reference to Shakespeare's Iago that there is a precise distinction between 'ancient' and 'standard-bearer' concerning the nature and function of appointment, nothing indicates that a nice discrimination of duty is implied here; indeed, the evidence points the other way, because details of the passage in question accord, not merely with the other inventories mentioned, but also with an initial listing of Shaddai's four captains, where the designation employed is actually 'Ensign' (E2^{r}).[1] One notes, however, that 'ancient' is a phonetic corruption of 'ensign'; that the post was 'often borne by men of honourable descent'; and that *O.E.D.* cites an Act of James I (1606) which specifically debars any 'recusant convict' from holding office as 'ancient-bearer'.[2] As the term in this case refers solely to the rascals of Diabolus's camp, it may not be too outlandish to suggest that Bunyan is applying it pejoratively within a sophisticated allegory where such ironic inversion is frequent. Whatever the truth, in the belief that some zealous printing-house reader may have inadvertently thwarted the author's design in an attempt to 'improve' the text, and that 'Ancient-bearer' can furnish a richer reading, the second-state rendering has been preferred.

[1] H. H. Furness (ed.), *A New Variorum Edition of Shakespeare. Othello* (Philadelphia, 1886; rep. New York, 1963), pp. 13–14.

[2] Furness, p. 13; *O.E.D.*, sb. 3.

The text that follows is printed from one of the two copies of the first edition in the possession of the University of Alberta, which acquired the item (Accession No. 382034) in 1962 as part of a remarkable Bunyan collection assembled by the late Ralph E. Ford of Bedford. The book retains only about half of the original folding-plate (in most other copies this is missing altogether), but is otherwise well preserved; its make-up tends to corroborate Harrison's view that Alsop and Newman were among the most careful printers of Bunyan's works.[1] What printing errors occur are generally inconsequential and have normally been tacitly corrected. Changes of any significance are duly recorded in footnotes. Capitalization, spelling, and punctuation have not been tampered with, though it has not been thought illegitimate to alter the pointing on those few occasions when the reader's need for clarity has seemed paramount: the original accidentals were in any event most probably perfected by the printer.[2] The aim throughout has been to present a text that most fully accords with Bunyan's artistic conception.

Although *The Holy War* has never gained the massive popular acclaim of *The Pilgrim's Progress*, it has proved to be among the most durable of Bunyan's longer works. The eighteenth century treated it with respect. Following the third edition of 1696, reprints were issued in 1700 and 1703, and a fourth edition came out in 1707; thereafter, at least six more editions were published before the version printed by Samuel Wilson in his revision of the second volume of Doe's edition of the *Works* (1736–7). From then until near the close of the nineteenth century there were at least twenty-five more editions, including the first annotated edition by W. Mason (1782) to which Samuel Adams (according to the B.M. Catalogue) contributed explanatory and hortatory notes. In America the book was first printed about 1736. During the past century a few scholarly editions have appeared: among them might be mentioned those by John Brown (1887), Mabel Peacock (1892), and James F. Forrest (1967).

Bunyan's international reputation ensured early recognition for

[1] Harrison, p. xxvii.

[2] Cf. Roger Sharrock (ed.), *Grace Abounding to the Chief of Sinners* (Oxford, 1962), p. xxxviii.

the book on the Continent. A Dutch translation (*Den Heyligen Oorlog*') was published at Amsterdam in 1685 and a German one (*Der heilige Krieg*) at Hamburg in 1694. The many later translations in a variety of tongues testify not only to the fame of the author but to his allegory's distinctive merit.

TO THE READER.

'TIS *strange to me, that they that love to tell*
Things done of old, yea, and that do excell
Their Equals in Historiology,
Speak not of Mansoul's *wars, but let them lye*
Dead, like old Fables, *or such worthless things,*
That to the Reader *no advantage brings:*
When men, let them make what they will their own,
Till they know this, are to themselves unknown.
Of Stories I well know there's divers sorts,
Some foreign, some domestick; and reports
Are thereof made as fancy leads the Writers;
(By Books a man may guess at the Inditers.)
Some will again of that which never was,
Nor will be, feign, (and that without a cause)
Such matter, raise such mountains, tell such things
Of Men, of Laws, of Countries, and of Kings:
And in their Story seem to be so sage,
And with such gravity cloath ev'ry Page,
That though their Frontice-piece says all is vain,
Yet to their way Disciples they obtain.
But, Readers, *I have somewhat else to do,*
Than with vain stories thus to trouble you;
What here I say, some men do know so well, True Christians.
They can with tears and joy the story tell.
The Town of Mansoul *is well known to many,*
Nor are her troubles doubted of by any
That are acquainted with those Histories The Scriptures.
That Mansoul, *and her Wars* Anatomize.
Then lend thine ear to what I do relate
Touching the Town of Mansoul *and her state,*
How she was lost, took captive, made a slave;

And how against him set, that should her save.
Yea, how by hostile ways, she did oppose
Her Lord, and with his enemy did close.
For they are true, he that will them deny,
Must needs the best of records vilifie.
For my part I (my self) was in the Town,
Both when 'twas set up, and when pulling down,
I saw Diabolus *in his possession,*
And Mansoul *also under his oppression.*
Yea, I was there when she own'd him for Lord,
And to him did submit with one accord.
When Mansoul *trampled upon things Divine,*
And wallowed in filth as doth a swine:
When she betook her self unto her arms,
His Counsels. *Fought her* Emanuel, *despis'd his charms,*
Then I was there, and did rejoice to see
Diabolus *and* Mansoul *so agree.*
Let no man then count me a Fable-maker,
Nor make my name or credit a partaker
Of their derision: what is here in view,
Of mine own knowledg, I dare say is true.
I saw the Princes *armed men come down*
By troops, by thousands, to besiege the Town.
I saw the Captains, *heard the* Trumpets *sound,*
And how his forces cover'd all the ground.
Yea, how they set themselves in battel-ray,
I shall remember to my dying day.
I saw the Colours *waving in the wind,*
And they within to mischief how combin'd,
To ruin Mansoul, *and to make away*
Her Soul. *Her* Primum mobile *without delay.*
I saw the Mounts cast up against the Town,
And how the slings were plac'd to beat it down.
I heard the stones fly whizzing by mine ears,
(What longer kept in mind than got in fears),
I heard them fall, and saw what work they made,
Death. *And how old* Mors *did cover with his shade*

The face of Mansoul*: and I heard her cry,*
Wo worth the day in dying I shall die.
I saw the Battering Rams, and how they play'd
To beat ope Ear-gate, *and I was afraid,*
Not only Ear-gate, *but the very Town*
Would by those Battering Rams be beaten down.
I saw the fights, and heard the captains shout,
And in each battel saw who fac'd about:
I saw who wounded were, and who were slain; Lusts.
And who when dead, would come to life again.
I heard the cries of those that wounded were,
(While others fought like men bereft of fear)
And while they cry, kill, kill, was in mine ears,
The Gutters ran, not so with blood as tears.
Indeed the Captains *did not always fight,*
But then they would molest us day and night;
Their cry, up, fall on, *let us take the Town,*
Kept us from sleeping, or from lying down.
I was there when the Gates *were broken ope,*
And saw how Mansoul *then was stript of hope.*
I saw the Captains *march into the Town,*
How there they fought, and did their foes cut down.
I heard the Prince bid Boanerges *go*
Up to the Castle, and there siese his foe,
And saw him and his fellows bring him down
In chains of great contempt quite through the Town.
I saw Emanuel *when he possest*
His Town of Mansoul, *and how greatly blest*
A Town, his gallant Town of Mansoul *was,*
When she receiv'd his pardon, liv'd his Laws.
When the Diabolonians *were caught,*
When try'd, and when to execution brought,
Then I was there; yea, I was standing by
When Mansoul *did the rebels crucifie.*
I also saw Mansoul *clad all in white,*
And heard her Prince call her his hearts delight.
I saw him put upon her Chains of Gold,

And Rings, and Bracelets, goodly to behold.
What shall I say, I heard the peoples *cries,*
And saw the Prince wipe tears from Mansouls *eyes.*
I heard the groans, and saw the joy of many:
Tell you of all, I neither will, nor can I.
But by what here I say, you well may see
That Mansouls *matchless Wars no Fables be.*
Mansoul! *the desire of both Princes was,*
One keep his gain would, t'other gain his loss;
Diabolus *would cry the Town is mine,*
Emanuel *would plead a right Divine*
Unto his Mansoul*; then to blows they go,*
And Mansoul *crys, these Wars will me undo.*
Mansoul! *her Wars seem'd endless in her eyes,*
She's lost by one, becomes another's prize.
And he again that lost her last would sware,
Have her I will, or her in pieces tare.
Mansoul, *it was the very seat of war,*
Wherefore her troubles greater were by far,
Than only where the noise of War is heard,
Or where the shaking of a sword is fear'd,
Or only where small skirmishes are fought,
Or where the fancy fighteth with a thought.
She saw the swords of fighting men made red,
And heard the cries of those with them wounded;
Must not her frights then be much more by far
Than theirs that to such doings strangers are?
Or theirs that hear the beating of a Drum,
But not made fly for fear from house and home?
Mansoul, *not only heard the Trumpets sound,*
But saw her Gallants gasping on the ground.
Wherefore we must not think that she could rest
With them, whose greatest earnest is but jest:
Or where the blustring threatning of great Wars.
Do end in Parleys, or in wording Jars.
Mansoul, *her mighty Wars, they did portend*
Her weal or wo, and that world without end.

Wherefore she must be more concern'd than they
Whose fears begin, and end the self-same day.
Or where none other harm doth come to him
That is engag'd, but loss of life or limb,
As all must needs confess that now do dwell
In Universe, *and can this story tell.*
Count me not then with them that to amaze
The people, set them on the stars to gaze,
Insinuating with much confidence,
That each of them is now the residence
Of some brave Creatures; yea, a world they will
Have in each Star, though it be past their skill
To make it manifest to any man,
That reason hath, or tell his fingers can.
But I have too long held thee in the Porch,
And kept thee from the Sun-shine with a Torch.
Well, now go forward, step within the dore,
And there behold five hundred times much more
Of all sorts of such inward Rarities
As please the mind will, and will feed the eyes
With those, which if a Christian, thou wilt see
Not small, but things of greatest moment be.
Nor do thou go to work without my Key,
(In mysteries men soon do lose their way)
And also turn it right if thou wouldst know
My riddle, and wouldst with my heifer plow.
It lies there in the window, *fare thee well,*
My next may be to ring thy Passing-Bell. The margent.

Jo. Bunyan.

A

RELATION

OF THE

Holy War, &c.

IN my Travels, as I walked through many Regions and Countries, it was my chance to happen into that famous *Continent* of *Universe*; a very large and spacious Countrey it is. It lieth between the two Poles, and just amidst the four points of the Heavens. It is a place *well* watered, and richly adorned with Hills and Valleys, bravely situate; and for the most part (at least where I was) very fruitful, also well peopled, and a very sweet Air.

The people are not all of one complexion, nor yet of one Language, mode, or way of Religion; but differ as much as ('tis said) do the Planets themselves. Some are right, and some are wrong, even as it happeneth to be in lesser Regions.

In this Countrey, as I said, it was my lot to travel, and there travel I did, and that so long, even till I learned much of their mother-tongue, together with the Customs, and manners of them among whom I was. And to speak truth, I was much delighted to *see*, and *hear* many things which I saw and heard among them: Yea I had (to be sure) even lived and died a Native among them, (so was I taken with them and their doings) had not my Master sent for me home to his House, there to do business for him and to over-see business done.

A natural state pleasing to the flesh.

Christ.

Now, there is in this gallant Country of *Universe*, a *fair* and *delicate Town*, a Corporation, called *Mansoul*: a Town for its Building so curious, for its Situation so commodious, for its Priviledges so advantagious; (I mean with reference to its Original) that I may say of it, as was said before, of the

Man.

Continent in which it is placed, *There is not its equal under the whole Heaven.*

As to the Situation of this Town, it lieth just between the two worlds, and the first founder, and builder of it, so far as [Scriptures.] by the best, and most Authentick records I can gather, was [The Almighty.] one *Shaddai*; and he built it for his own delight. He made it the [Gen. 1. 26.] mirrour, and glory of all that he made, even the Top-piece beyond any thing else that he did in that Countrey: yea, so [Created.] goodly a Town was *Mansoul*, when first built, that it is said [Angels.] by some, the Gods at the setting up thereof, came down to see it, and sang for joy. And as he made it goodly to behold, so also mighty to have Dominion over all the Country round about. Yea all was commanded to acknowledge *Mansoul* for their *Metropolitan*, all was injoyned to do homage to it. Ay, the Town it self had *positive* commission, and power from her King to demand service of all, and also to subdue any, that any ways denied to do it.

[The heart.] There was reared up in the midst of this Town, a most famous and stately Palace; for strength, it might be called a *Castle*; for pleasantness, a Paradise; for largeness, a place so [Eccl. 3. 11.] copious as to contain all the world. This place, the King Shaddai intended but for himself *alone*, and not another with him: partly because of his own delights, and partly because he would not that the terror of strangers should be upon the Town. This place *Shaddai* made also a Garrison of, [The powers of the Soul.] but committed the keeping of it, only, to the men of the Town.

The wall of the Town was well built, yea so fast and firm was it knit and compact together, that had it not been for the Townsmen themselves, they could not have been shaken, or broken for ever.

[The body.] For here lay the excellent wisdom of him that builded *Mansoul*, that the Walls could never be broken down, nor hurt, by the most mighty adverse Potentate, unless the Towns-men gave consent thereto.

This famous Town of *Mansoul* had five gates, in at which to come, out at which to go, and these were made likewise answerable to the Walls: to wit *Impregnable*, and such as could never be opened nor forced, but by the will and leave of those within. The names of the Gates were these, *Ear-gate*, *Eye-gate*, *Mouth-gate*, *Nose-gate* and *Feel-gate*.

The five Sences.

Other things there were that belonged to the Town of *Mansoul*, which if you adjoyn to these, will yet give farther demonstration to all, of the glory and strength of the place. It had always a sufficiency of provision within its Walls; it had the best, most wholesome, and excellent Law that then was extant in the world. There was not a Rascal, Rogue, or Traiterous person then within its Walls: They were all true men, and fast joyned together; and this you know is a great matter. And to all these, it was always (so long as it had the goodness to keep true to *Shaddai* the King) his countenance, his protection, and it was his delight, *&c.*

The state of Mansoul at first.

Well, upon a time there was one *Diabolus*, a mighty *Gyant*, made an assault upon this famous Town of *Mansoul*, to take it, and make it his own habitation. This *Gyant* was King of the *Blacks* or *Negroes*, and a most raving Prince he was. We will if you please first discourse of the Original of this *Diabolus*, and then of his taking of this famous Town of *Mansoul*.

The Devil.

Sinners the fallen Angels.

The Original of *Diabolus*.

This *Diabolus* is indeed, a great and mighty Prince, and yet both poor and beggerly. As to his Original, he was at first, one of the Servants of King *Shaddai*, made, and taken and put by him into most high and mighty place, yea was put into such Principalities as belonged to the best of his Territories and Dominions. This *Diabolus* was made *Son of the morning*, and a brave place he had of it: It bought him much glory, and gave him much brightness, an income that might have contented his *Luciferian* heart, had it not been insatiable, and inlarged as Hell it self.

Isa. 14. 12

Well, he seeing himself thus exalted to greatness and honour, and raging in his mind for higher state, and degree, what doth he but begins to think with himself, how he might be set up as Lord over all, and have the sole power under *Shaddai*. (Now *that* did the King reserve for his Son, yea, and had already bestowed it upon him) wherefore he first consults with

2 Pet. 2. 4.
Jude 6.

himself what had best to be done, and then breaks his mind to some other of his companions, to the which they also agreed. So in fine, they came to this issue, that they should make an attempt upon the Kings Son to destroy him, that the Inheritance might be theirs. Well, to be short, the Treason (as I said) was concluded, the time appointed, the word given, the Rebels rendezvouzed, and the assault attempted. Now the King, and his Son being *All*, and always *Eye*, could not but discern all passages in his Dominions; and he having always love for his Son, as for himself, could not, at what he saw, but be greatly provoked, and offended: wherefore what does he, but takes them in the very *nick* and first *Tripp* that they made towards their design, convicts them of the Treason, horrid Rebellion, and Conspiracy that they had devised, and now attempted to put into practice: and casts them altogether out of all place of trust, benefit, honour, and preferment; this done, he banishes them the Court, turns them down into the horrible Pits, as fast bound in Chains, never more to expect the least favour from his hands, but to abide the judgment that he had appointed: and that forever, and yet,

Now they being thus cast out of all place of trust, profit, and honour, and also knowing that they had lost their Princes favour for ever, (being banished his Court and cast down to the horrible Pits) you may be sure they would now add to their former pride, what malice and rage against *Shaddai*, and

1 Pet. 5. 8. against his Son they could. Wherefore roving, and ranging in much fury from place to place (if perhaps they might find something that was the Kings) to revenge, by spoiling of that, themselves on him, at last they happened into this spacious Countrey of *Universe*, and steer their course towards the Town of *Mansoul*; and considering that that Town was one of the chief works, and delights of King *Shaddai*: what do they, but after Counsel taken, make an assault upon that. I say they knew that *Mansoul* belonged unto *Shaddai*, for they were there when he built it, and Beautified it for himself. So when they had found the place they shouted horribly for joy, and roared

on it as a Lyon upon the prey: saying, now we have found the prize, and how to be revenged on King *Shaddai* for what he hath done to us. So they sate down and called a Council of War, and considered with themselves what ways and methods they had best to ingage in, for the winning to themselves this famous Town of *Mansoul*: and these four things were then propounded to be considered of.

A Council of War held by *Diabolus* and his fellows against the Town of *Mansoul.*

Proposals.

First, *Whether they had best, all of them to shew themselves, in this design to the Town of* Mansoul.

Secondly, *Whether they had best to go and sit down against* Mansoul, *in their now ragged, and beggarly guise.*

Thirdly, *Whether they had best to shew to* Mansoul *their intentions, and what design they came about, or whether to assault it with words and ways of deceit.*

Fourthly, *Whether thay had not best, to some of their Companions to give out private orders to take the advantage, if they see one, or more of the principal Townsmen, to shoot them: if thereby they shall judge their cause and design will the better be promoted.*

To the first proposal.

It was answered to the first of these Proposals, in the Negative, to wit, that it would not be best that all should shew themselves before the Town: because the appearance of many of them might alarm, and fright the Town. Whereas, a *few* or but *one* of them, was not so likely to do it. And to inforce this advice to take place, 'twas added further, that if *Mansoul* was frighted, or did take the alarm. 'Tis impossible, said *Diabolus* (for he spake now) that we should take the Town: for that none can enter into it without its own consent. Let therefore but few, or but one assault *Mansoul*, and in mine opinion said *Diabolus*, let me be he. *Wherefore to this they all agreed*, and then to the second Proposal they came, namely, *Whether they had best to go and sit down before* Mansoul, *in their now ragged and beggarly guise.* To which it was answered also in the Negative, by no means; and that because, though the Town of *Mansoul*, had been made to know, and to have to do before now, with things that are invisible; they did never as yet see any of their fellow Creatures in so sad, and Rascal condition as they. And this was the advice of that fierce

The second proposal.

Alecto. *Apollyon.* *Alecto.* Then said *Apollyon*, the advice is pertinent, for even one of us appearing to them as we are now, must needs, both beget, and multiply such thoughts in them, as will both put them into a consternation of spirit, and necessitate them to put themselves upon their guard: And if so, said he, Then, as my Lord *Alecto* said but now, 'tis in vain for us to think of *Beelzebub.* taking the Town. Then said that mighty Gyant *Beelzebub*, The advice that already is given is safe, for though the men of *Mansoul* have seen such things as we *once were*, yet hitherto they did never behold such things as we *now are*. And 'tis best in mine opinion to come upon them in such a guise, as is common to, and most familiar among them. To this when they had consented: The next thing to be considered was, in what shape, hue or guise, *Diabolus* had best to shew himself, when he went about to make *Mansoul* his own. Then one said *Lucifer.* one thing, and another the contrary, at last *Lucifer* answered, that in his opinion, 'twas best that his Lordship should assume the body of some of those Creatures that they of the Town had dominion over. For quoth he, these are not only familiar to them, but being under them they will never imagin that an attempt should by them be made upon the Town; and to blind all, let him assume the body of one of these beasts Gen. 3. 1. Rev. 20. 1, 2. that *Mansoul* deems to be wiser than any of the rest. This advice was applauded of all, so it was determined that the Giant *Diabolus* should assume the *Dragon*, for that he was in those days as familiar with the Town of *Mansoul* as now is the bird with the Boy. For nothing that was in its primitive state was at all amazing to them. Then they proceeded to the third thing which was,

The third proposal. 3. *Whether they had best to shew their intentions, or the design of his coming to* Mansoul, *or no*? This also was answered in the Negative; because of the weight that was in the former reasons, to wit, for that *Mansoul* were a strong people, a strong people in a strong *Town*, whose *Wall* and *Gates* were impregnable, (to say nothing of their Castle) nor can they by any means be won but by their own consent. Besides said *Legion.* *Legion*, (for he gave answer to this) a discovery of our intentions, may make them send to their King for aid, and if that be done, I know, quickly what time of day 'twill be with us. Therefore let us assault them in all pretended fairness, covering of our intentions with all manner of lies, flatteries, delusive words; feigning of things that never will be, and promising of that to them, that they shall never find: This is the way to win *Mansoul*, and to make them of themselves to open their Gates to us; yea, and to desire us too, to come in to them.

And the reason why I think that this project will do, is, because the people of *Mansoul* now, are every one simple and innocent; all honest and true: nor do they as yet know what it is to be assaulted with Fraud, Guile, and Hypocrisy. They are strangers to lying and desembling lips; wherefore, we cannot, if thus we be disguised, by them at all be discerned, our Lies shall go for true sayings, and our dissimulations for upright dealings. What we promise them, they will in that believe us: especially, if in all our Lies and feigned words, we pretend great love to them, and that our design is only their advantage, and honour. Now there was not one bit of a reply against this, this went as currant down, as doth the water down a steep descent: wherefore they go to consider of the last Proposal which was,

4. *Whether they had not best to give out orders to some of their Company, to shoot some one or more of the principal of the Townsmen: if they judge that their cause may be promoted thereby.* *The fourth Proposal.*

This was carried in the Affirmative, and the man that was designed by this Stratagem to be destroyed, was one Mr. *Resistance*, otherwise called *Captain Resistance*. And a great man in *Mansoul*, this Captain *Resistance* was; and a man that the Giant *Diabolus*, and his band, more feared than they feared the whole Town of *Mansoul* besides. Now who should be the Actor to do the murder; that was the next, and they appointed one *Tisiphane*, a fury of the Lake to do it. *Of Capt. Resistance.*

They thus having ended their Council of War, rose up, and assay'd to do as they had determined; they marched towards *Mansoul*, but all in a manner invisible, save one only *The result of their Counsel.*

one; nor did he approach the Town in his own likeness, but under the shade, and in the body of the *Dragon*.

So they drew up, and sate down before *Ear-gate*, for that was the place of hearing for all without the Town, as *Eye gate* was the place of *perspection*. So, as I said, he came up with his Train to the *Gate*, and laid his ambuscado for Captain *Resistance* within Bow-shot of the Town. This done, the Giant ascended up close to the *Gate*, and called to the Town of *Mansoul* for audience. Nor took he any with him, but one *Ill-pause*, who was his Orator in all difficult matters. Now, as I said, he being come up to the Gate, (as the manner of those times was) sounded his Trumpet for Audience. At which the chief of the Town of *Mansoul*, such as my Lord *Innocent*, my Lord *Willbewill*, my Lord *Mayor*, Mr. *Recorder*, and Captain *Resistance* came down to the Wall to see who was there, and what was the matter. And my Lord *Willbewill*, when he had looked over and saw who stood at the Gate, demanded, what he was, wherefore he was come, and why he roused the Town of *Mansoul* with so unusual a sound.

Diabolus marches up to the Town and calls for Audience.

The Lords of *Mansoul* appeared.

Diab. *Diabolus then, as if he had been a Lamb, began his Oration and said, Gentlemen of the famous Town of* Mansoul, *I am, as you may perceive no far dweller from you, but near, and one that is bound by the King to do you my homage, and what service I can; wherefore that I may be faithful to my self, and to you, I have somewhat of concern to impart unto you. Wherefore grant me your Audience and hear me patiently. And first, I will assure you, it is not my self but you; not mine, but your advantage that I seek by what I now do, as will full well be made manifest, by that I have opened my mind unto you. For Gentlemen, I am (to tell you the truth) come to shew you how you many obtain great, and ample deliverance from a bondage that unawares to your selves, you are captivated and inslaved under.* At this the Town of *Mansoul* began to prick up its ears, and what is it, pray what is it thought they: and he said, *I have somewhat to say to you concerning your King, concerning his Law, and also touching your selves. Touching your King, I know he is great and potent, but yet, all that he hath said to you, is neither true, nor yet*

Diabolus his Oration.

Mansoul ingaged.

9 *Ill-pause*] *All-pause*

for your advantage. 1. *'Tis not true, for that wherewith he hath hitherto awed you, shall not come to pass, nor be fulfilled, though you do the thing that he hath forbidden. But if there was danger, what a slavery is it to live always in fear of the greatest of punishments, for doing so small and trivial a thing, as eating of a little fruit is.* 2. *Touching his Laws, this I say further, they are both unreasonable, intricate and intolerable. Unreasonable as was hinted before, for that the punishment is not proportioned to the offence. There is great difference, and disproportion betwixt the life, and an Apple: yet the one must go for the other by the Law of your* Shaddai. *But it is also intricate, in that he saith, first, you may eat of all; and yet after, forbids the eating of* one. *And then in the last place, it must needs be intolerable, for as much as that fruit which you are forbidden to eat of (if you are forbidden any) is that, and that alone, which is able by your eating, to minister to you, a good, as yet unknown by you. This is manifest by the very name of the tree, it is called the* Tree of knowledge of good and evil, *and have you that knowledge as yet? No, no, nor can you conceive how good, how pleasant, and how much to be desired to make one wise it is, so long as you stand by your Kings commandment. Why should you be holden in ignorance and blindness? Why should you not be enlarged in knowledge and understanding? And now! Ah ye inhabitants of the famous Town of* Mansoul, *to speak more particularly to your selves, you are not a free people! You are kept both in bondage and slavery, and that by a grievous threat; no reason being anexed, but so I will have it, so it shall be. And is it not grievons to think on, that that very thing that you are forbidden to do, might you but do it, would yield you both wisdom and honour; For then your eyes will be opened, and you shall be as Gods. Now since this is thus, quoth he, can you be kept by any Prince in more slavery, and in greater bondage than you are under, this day? You are made underlings, and are wrapt up in inconveniences, as I have well made appear? For what bondage greater than to be kept in blindness, will not reason tell you, that it is better to have eyes than to be without them; and so to be at liberty, to be better than to be shut up in a dark and stinking cave.*

Diabolus his subtilty made up of lies.

And just now while *Diabolus* was speaking those words to *Mansoul*, *Tisiphane* shot at Captain *Resistance*, where he stood

Captain *Resistance* slain.

on the Gate, and mortally wounded him in the head; so that he to the amazement of the Townsmen, and the incouragement of *Diabolus*, fell down dead quite over the Wall. Now when Captain *Resistance* was dead (and he was the only man of War in the Town) poor *Mansoul* was wholly left naked of Courage, nor had she now any heart to resist. But this was as the Devil would have it. Then stood forth that He, Mr. *Ill-pause*, that *Diabolus* brought with him, who was his Orator, and he addressed himself to speak to the Town of *Mansoul*: The tenure of whose Speech here follows.

Mr. *Ill-pause* his speech to the Town of *Mansoul*.

Ill-pause. Gentlemen, quoth he, it is my Masters happiness, that he has this day a quiet and teachable Auditory; and it is hoped *by us*, that we shall prevail with you not to cast off good advice: my Master has a very great love for you, and although, as he very well knows, that he runs the hazzard of the anger of King *Shaddai*, yet love to you will make him do *more than that*. Nor doth there need that a word more should be spoken to confirm for truth what he hath said; there is not a word but carries with it self-evidence in its Bowels; the very name of the Tree may put an end to all Controversie in this matter. I therefore at this time shall only add this advice to you under, and by the leave of my Lord, (and with that he made *Diabolus* a very low Congee.) Consider his words, look on the Tree, and the promising Fruit thereof; remember also that yet you know but little, and that this is the way to know more: And if your Reasons be not conquered to accept of such good Council, you are not the men that I took you to be. But when the Townsfolk saw that the Tree was good for food, and that it was pleasant to the eye, and a Tree to be desired to make one wise, they did as old *Ill-pause* advised, they took and did eat thereof. Now, this I should have told you before that even then, when this *Ill-pause* was making of his speech to the Towns-men, my Lord *Innocency*, (whether by a shot from the Camp of the Giant, or from some sinking qualm that suddenly took him, or whether by the stinking breath of that Treacherous Villain old *Ill-pause*, for so I am most apt to think) sunk down in the place where he stood, nor could he be

My Lord *Innocency's* death.

brought to life again. Thus these two brave men died; brave men I call them, for they were the beauty and glory of *Mansoul*, so long as they lived therein: nor did there now remain any more, a noble spirit in *Mansoul*, they all fell down, and yielded obedience to *Diabolus*, and became his Slaves and Vassals as you shall hear.

The Town taken, and how.

Now these being dead what do the rest of the Towns-folk, but as men that had found a fools Paradise, they presently, as afore was hinted, fall to prove the truth of the Gyant's words, and first they did as *Ill-pause* had taught them, they looked, they considered, they were taken with the forbidden fruit, *they took thereof, and did eat*: and having eaten, they became immediately drunken therewith; so they opened the Gates, both *Ear-gate*, and *Eye-gate*, and let in *Diabolus* with all his bands, quite forgetting their good *Shaddai*, his Law, and the judgement that he had annexed with solemn threatning to the breach thereof.

Diabolus, having now obtained entrance in at the Gates of the Town, marches up to the middle thereof, to make his conquest as sure as he could, and finding by this time the affections of the people warmly inclining to him, he as thinking 'twas best striking while the Iron is hot, made this further deceivable speech unto them saying, *Alas my poor* Mansoul! *I have done thee indeed this service, as to promote thee to honour, and to greaten thy liberty, but Alas! Alas! Poor* Mansoul, *thou wantest now one to defend thee, for assure thy self that when* Shaddai *shall hear what is done, he will come: for sorry will he be that thou hast broken his bonds, and cast his cords away from thee. What wilt thou do, wilt thou after enlargement suffer thy priviledges to be invaded and taken away? or what wilt resolve with thyself.* Then they all with one consent said to this Bramble, do thou Reign over us. So he accepted the motion and became the King of the Town of *Mansoul*. This being done, the next thing was, to give him possession of the Castle, and so, of the whole strength of the Town. Wherefore, into the Castle he goes (it was, that which *Shaddai* built in *Mansoul* for his own delight, and pleasure). This now was become a Den, and hold for the Giant *Diabolus*.

He is entertained for their King.

He is possessed of the Castle and fortified it for himself.

Now having got possession of this stately Palace, or Castle what doth he, but make it a Garrison for himself, and strengthens and fortifies it with all sorts of provision against the King *Shaddai*, or those that should endeavour the regaining of it, to him, and his obedience again.

He new modelleth the Town.

This done, but not thinking himself yet secure enough, in the next place, he bethinks himself of new modelling the Town; and so he does, setting up one, and putting down another at pleasure. Wherefore my Lord Mayor, whose name was my Lord *Understanding*, and Mr. Recorder whose name was Mr. *Conscience*, those he puts out of place, and power.

My Lord Mayor put out of place.

2 Cor. 10. 4, 5.

Ephes. 4. 18, 19.

As for my Lord Mayor though he was an understanding man, and one too that had complied with the rest of the Town, of *Mansoul*, in admitting of the *Giant* into the Town; yet *Diabolus* thought not fit to let him abide in his former lustre and glory, because he was a seeing man. Wherefore he darkned it not only by taking from him his Office and power, but by building of an high and strong Tower, just between the Suns reflections, and the Windows of my Lords Palace: By which means his house and all, and the whole of his habitation, was made as dark as darkness itself. And thus being alienated from the light, he became as one that was born blind. To this his house, my Lord was confined, as to a Prison; nor might he upon his *parole* go further than within his own bounds. And now had he had an heart to do for *Mansoul*: What could he do for it, or wherein could he be profitable to her? So then, so long as *Mansoul* was under the power and government of *Diabolus*: (And so long it was under him, as it was obedient to him; which was, even until by a War it was rescued out of his hand.) So long my Lord Mayor was rather an impediment in, than an advantage to, the famous Town of *Mansoul*.

The Recorder put out of place.

As for Mr. *Recorder*, before the Town was taken, he was a man well read in the Laws of his King, and also a man of courage and faithfulness to speak truth at every occasion: And he had a tongue as bravely hung, as he had an head filled with judgement. Now this man, *Diabolus* could by no means abide, because, though he gave his consent to his coming into the Town, yet he could not, by all wiles, trials, Stratagems, and devices that he could use, make him wholly his own. True, he was much degenerated from his former King, and also much pleased with many of the Giants Laws, and service: but all this would not do for as much as he was not wholly his. He would now and then think upon *Shaddai*, and have dread of his Law upon him, and then he would speak with a voice, as great against *Diabolus*, as when a Lyon roareth. Yea, and would also at certain times when his fits were upon him (for you must know that some times he had terrible fits) make the whole Town of *Mansoul* shake with his voice: and therefore the now King of *Mansoul* could not abide him.

He sometimes speaks for his first King.

Diabolus therefore feared the *Recorder* more than any that was left alive in the Town of *Mansoul*, because, as I said his words did shake the whole Town; they were like the ratling-thunder, and also like Thunder-claps. Since therefore the *Giant* could not make him wholly his own, what doth he do but studies all that he could, to debauch the old Gentleman, and by debauchery, to stupifie his mind, and more harden his heart in ways of vanity. And as he attempted, so he accomplished his design: He debauched the man, and by little and little, so drew him into sin and wickedness, that at last he was not only debauched as at first: and so by consequence defiled, but was almost (at last, I say) past all Conscience of sin. And this was the farthest *Diabolus* could go. Wherefore he be-thinks him of an other project, and that was to perswade the men of the Town that Mr. Recorder was mad, and so not to be regarded. And for this he urged his fits, and said, if he be himself, why doth he not do thus always? but, quoth he, as all mad folk have their fits, and in them their raving language; so hath this old and doating Gentleman. Thus by one means or another, he quickly got *Mansoul* to slight, neglect, and despise what ever Mr. *Recorder* could say. For besides what already you have heard, *Diabolus* had a way to make the old Gentleman, when he was merry, unsay and deny what he in his fits had affirmed. And indeed, this was the next way to make himself ridiculous, and to cause that no man

He is more debauched than before.

The Town taken off from heeding of him.

How conscience becomes so ridiculous, as with Carnal men it is.

should regard him. Also now he never spake freely for King *Shaddai*, but always by force and constraint. Besides, he would at one time be hot against that, at which at another he would hold his peace. So uneven was he now in his doings. Sometimes he would be, as if fast a sleep, and again sometimes, as dead even then when the whole Town of *Mansoul* was in her career after vanity, and in her dance after the Giants pipe.

Wherefore, sometimes when *Mansoul* did use to be frighted with the thundring voice of the *Recorder* that was, and when they did tell *Diabolus* of it, he would answer, that what the old Gentleman said, was neither of love to him, nor pity to them, but of a foolish fondness that he had to be prating: and so would hush, still, and put all to quiet again. And that he might leave no argument unurged that might tend to make them secure, he said, and said it often; O *Mansoul*! Consider that notwithstanding the old Gentlemans rage, and the rattle of his high and thundring words, you hear nothing of *Shaddai* himself (when lyar, and deceiver, that he was, every out cry of Mr. *Recorder* against the sin of *Mansoul*, was the voice of God in him to them.) But he goes on and sayes, You see that he values not the loss, nor rebellion of the Town of *Mansoul*, nor will he trouble himself with calling of his Town to a reckoning for their giving of themselves to me. He knows that though ye were his, now you are lawfully mine; so leaving us one to another, he now hath shaken his hands of us.

Satanical Rhetorick.

Moreover O *Mansoul*! quoth he, Consider how I have served you, even to the uttermost of my power; and that with the best that I have, could get, or procure for you in all the world: Besides, I dare say, that the Laws and customes that you now are under, and by which you do homage to me, do yield you more solace and content, than did the Paradise that at first you possessed. Your liberty also, as your selves do very well know, has been greatly widened, and enlarged by me; whereas I found you a pen'd up people. I have not laid any restraint upon you; you have no Law, Statute, or Judgment of mine to fright you; I call none of you to account for your doings, except the Madman, you know who I mean: I have granted you to

His flatteries.

Conscience.

live, each man like a Prince in his own, even with as little controul from me, as I my self have from you.

Men sometimes angry with their Consciences.

And thus would *Diabolus* hush up, and quiet the Town of *Mansoul*, when the Recorder that was, did at times molest them: Yea, and with such cursed Orations as these, would set the whole Town in a rage, and fury against the old Gentleman: Yea, the Rascal crue, at sometimes would be for destroying of him. They have often wished (in my hearing) That he had lived a thousand miles off from them: his company, his words, yea, the sight of him, and especially when they remembered how in old times he did use to threaten and condemn them; (for all he was now so debauched) did terrifie and afflict them sore.

Ill thoughts.

Of fears.

But all wishes were vain, for I do not know how, unless by the power of *Shaddai*, and his wisdom, he was preserved in being amongst them. Besides, his house was as strong as a Castle, and stood hard to a strong Hold of the Town: moreover, if at any time any of the crue or rabble attempted to make him away, he could pull up the sluces, and let in such floods, as would drown all round about him.

The will.

But to leave Mr. *Recorder*, and to come to my Lord *Willbewill*, another of the Gentry of the famous Town of *Mansoul*. This *Willbewill* was as high born, as any man in *Mansoul*, and was as much if not more a Freeholder than many of them were: besides, if I remember my tale aright, he had some priviledge peculiar to himself in the famous Town of *Mansoul*: Now together with these, he was a man of great strength, resolution, and courage, nor in his occasion could any turn him away. But I say, whether he was proud of his estate, priviledges, strength or what, (but sure it was through pride of something) he scorns now to be a slave in *Mansoul*; and therefore resolves to bear Office under *Diabolus*, that he might (such an one as he was) be a petty Ruler and Governour in *Mansoul*. And (head-strong man that he was) thus he began betimes; for this man, when *Diabolus* did make his Oration at *Eargate*, was one of the first that was for consenting to his words, and so accepting of his counsel as wholesome, and that was for the opening of the Gate, and for letting him into the Town: wherefore *Diabolus* had a kindness for him; and therefore he designed for him a place: And perceiving the valour and stoutness of the man, he coveted to have him for one of his great ones, to act and do in matters of the highest concern.

The *Will* takes place under *Diabolus*.

So he sent for him, and talked with him of that secret matter that lay in his breast but there needed not much perswasion in the case. For as at first he was willing that *Diabolus* should be let into the Town; so *now* he was as willing to serve him there. When the Tyrant therefore perceived the willingness of my Lord to serve him, and that his mind stood bending that way, he forthwith made him the *Captain* of the *Castle*, Governour of the *Wall*, and keeper of the Gates of *Mansoul*: Yea there was a Clause in his Commission, *That nothing without him should be done in all the Town of* Mansoul. So that now next to *Diabolus* himself, who but my Lord *Willbewill* in all the Town of *Mansoul*; nor could any thing now be done, but at his *Will* and *Pleasure* throughout the Town of *Mansoul*. He had also one Mr. *Mind* for his Clerk, a man to speak on, every way like his Master: For he and his Lord were in *principle* one, and in practice not far asunder. And now was *Mansoul* brought under to purpose, and made to fulfil the lusts of the will and of the mind.

Heart. Flesh. Senses.

Rom. 8. 7.

Mr. *Mind* my Lords Clerk.

Ephes. 2. 2, 3, 4.

But it will not out of my thoughts, what a desperate one this *Willbewill* was, when power was put into his hand. First, he flatly denyed that he owed any suit or service to his former Prince, and Liege-Lord. This done, in the next place he took an Oath, and swore fidelity to his great Master *Diabolus*, and then being stated and setled in his places, offices, advancements and preferments; oh! you cannot think unless you had seen it, the strange work, that this workman made in the Town of *Mansoul*.

The carnal will opposeth conscience.

First, he maligned Mr. *Recorder* to death, he would neither indure to see him, nor to hear the words of his mouth; he would shut his eyes when he saw him, and stop his ears when he heard him speak: Also he could not indure that so much as a fragment of the Law of *Shaddai* should be any where seen in the Town. For example, his Clerk Mr. *Mind* had some old, rent, and torn parchments of the Law of good *Shaddai* in his house, but when *Willbewill* saw them, he cast them behind his back. True Mr. *Recorder* had some of the Laws in his study, but my Lord could by no means come at them: He also thought and said, That the windows of my old Lord *Mayor's* house, were alwayes too light for the profit of the Town of *Mansoul*. The light of a candle he could not indure. Now nothing at all pleased *Willbewill*, but what pleased *Diabolus* his Lord.

Neh. 9. 26.

Corrupt will loves a dark understanding.

There was none like him to trumpet about the Streets, the brave nature, the wise conduct, and great glory of the King *Diabolus*: He would range and rove throughout all the Streets of *Mansoul*, to cry up his illustrious Lord, and would make himself even as an abject, among the base and *Rascal crue*, to cry up his valiant Prince. And I say, when, and wheresoever he found these Vassals, he would even make himself as one of them. In all ill courses he would act without bidding, and do mischief without commandment.

Vain thoughts.

The Lord *Willbewill* also had a Deputy under him, and his name was Mr. *Affection*; one that was also greatly debauched in his principles, and answerable thereto in his life: He was wholly given to the flesh, and therefore they called him *Vile Affection*: Now there was he, and one *Carnal Lust*, the daughter of Mr. *Mind* (like to like quoth the Devil to the Collier) that fell in love, and made a match, and were married; and as I take it, they had several children, as *Impudent*, *Black-mouth* and *Hate-reproof*: these three were black boyes: and besides these they had three daughters, as *Scorn-Truth*, and *Slight-God*, and the name of the youngest was *Revenge*; these were all married in the Town, and also begot and yielded many bad brats, too many to be here inserted. But to pass by this.

Rom. 1. 25.

A match betwixt vile affection and carnal lust.

When the Gyant had thus ingarrisoned himself in the Town of *Mansoul*, and had put down and set up whom he thought good: he betakes himself to *defacing*. Now there was in the market place in *Mansoul*, and also upon the Gates of the Castle, an image of the blessed King *Shaddai*, this image was so exactly ingraven (and it was ingraven in gold) that it did the most resemble *Shaddai* himself of any thing that then was extant in the world. This he basely commanded to be defaced, and it was as basely done by the hand of Mr. *No-Truth*. Now you must know, that as *Diabolus* had commanded, and that by the hand of Mr. *No-Truth* the Image of *Shaddai* was defaced, He likewise gave order that the same Mr. *No-Truth* should set up in its stead the horrid and formidable Image of *Diabolus*: to the great contempt of the former King, and debasing of his Town of *Mansoul*.

What *No-Truth* did.

All Law books destroyed that could be so.

Moreover, *Diabolus* made havock of all remains of the Laws and Statutes of *Shaddai*, that could be found in the Town of *Mansoul*: to wit, such as contained either the Doctrines of *Morals*, with all *Civil* and *Natural* Documents. Also relative severities he sought to extinguish. To be short, there was nothing of the remains of good in *Mansoul* which he, and *Willbewill* sought not to destroy: for their design was to turn *Mansoul* into a bruit, and to make it like to the sensual sow: by the hand of Mr. *No-truth*.

1 Joh. 2.

When he had destroyed what Law, and good orders he could, then further to effect his design, namely, to alienate *Mansoul* from *Shaddai* her King, he commands and they set up his own vain Edicts, Statutes and Commandments, in all places of resort, or concourse in *Mansoul*, to wit such as gave liberty to the *lusts of the flesh, the lusts of the eyes, and the pride of life* which are not of *Shaddai, but of the world.* He incouraged, countenanced and promoted lasciviousness, and all ungodliness there. Yea much more did *Diabolus* to incourage wickedness in the Town of *Mansoul*, he promised them peace, content, joy, and bliss in doing his commands, and that they should never be called to an account for their not doing the contrary. And let this serve to give a taste to them that love to hear tell of what is done beyond their knowledge, a far off in other Countries.

Now *Mansoul* being wholly at his beck, and brought wholly

to his bow: nothing was heard or seen therein but that which tended to set up him.

They have a new Lord Mayor and a new Recorder.

But now, he having disabled the Lord *Mayor*, and Mr. *Recorder* from bearing of Office in *Mansoul*: and seeing that the Town, before he came to it, was the most ancient of Corporations in the world; and fearing, if he did not maintain greatness, they at any time should object that he had done them an injury: Therefore, I say, (that they might see that he did not intend to lessen their Grandeur, or to take from them any of their advantagious things) he did chuse for them a Lord Mayor, and a Recorder, himself: and such as contented *them* at the heart, and such also as pleased *him* wondrous well.

The new Lord Mayor.

The name of the Mayor that was of *Diabolus*'s making, was, the Lord *Lustings*. A man that had neither *Eyes* nor *Ears*, all that he did whether as a man, or as an Officer, he did it naturally as doth the beast. And that which made him yet the more ignoble, though not to *Mansoul*, yet to *them* that beheld, and were grieved for its ruins, was, that he never could favour good, but evil.

The new Recorder.

The Recorder, was one whose name was *Forget-good*. And a very sory fellow he was. He could remember nothing but mischief, and to do it with delight. He was naturally prone to do things that were hurtful; even hurtful to the Town of *Mansoul*, and to all the dwellers there. These two therefore, by their power, and practice, example and smiles upon evil; did much more Grammer, and settle the common people in hurtful ways. For who doth not perceive but when those that sit aloft, are vile, and corrupt themselves; they corrupt the whole Region and Country where they are.

Thoughts.

He doth make them new Aldermen, and who.

Besides these, *Diabolus* made several Burgesses, and Aldermen in *Mansoul*: such as out of whom the Town, when it needed, might chuse them Officers, Governours, and Magistrates. And these are the names of the chief of them Mr. *Incredulity*, Mr. *Haughty*, Mr. *Swearing*, Mr. *Whoreing*, Mr. *Hard heart*, Mr. *Pitiless*, Mr. *Fury*, Mr. *No-truth*, Mr. *Stand-to-lies*, Mr. *False Peace*, Mr. *Drunkenness*, Mr. *Cheating*, Mr.

Atheism, Thirteen in all. Mr. *Incredulity*, is the eldest, and Mr. *Atheism* the youngest of the Company.

There was also an election of Common Council men, and others; as Bailiffs, Serjeants, Constables, and others, but all of them like to those a forenamed, being either Fathers, Brothers, Cousins, or Nephews to them. Whose names, for brevities-sake I omitt to mention.

He buildeth three strong holds, their names, and Governours.

When the Giant had thus far proceeded in his work, in the next place he betook him to build some strong holds in the Town. And he built three that seemed to be impregnable. The first he called the Hold of *Defiance*, because it was made to command the whole Town, and to keep it from the knowledge of its ancient King. The second he called *Midnight hold*, because it was builded on purpose to keep *Mansoul* from the true knowledge of it self. The third was called *Sweet sin-hold*, because by that he fortified *Mansoul* against all desires of good. The first of these Holds stood close by *Eyegate*, that as much as might be, light might be darkned there. The second was builded hard to the *Old Castle*, to the end that that might be made more blind (if possible.) And the third stood in the Market Place.

He that *Diabolus* made Governour over the first of these, was one *Spite-God*, a most blasphemous wretch. He came with the whole rabble of them that came against *Mansoul* at first, and was himself one of themselves. He that was made the Governour of *Midnight-hold* was one *Love-no-light*. He was also of them that came first against the Town. And he that was made the Governour of the Hold called *Sweet-sin* Hold, was one whose name was *Love-flesh*, he was also a very leud fellow, but not of that Country where the other are bound. This fellow could find more sweetness when he stood sucking of a lust, than he did in all the Paradise of God.

Diabolus has made his Nest.

And now *Diabolus* thought himself safe; He had taken *Mansoul*; He had ingarrisoned himself therein; He had put down the old Officers, and had set up new ones; He had defaced the Image of *Shaddai*, and had set up his own; He had spoiled the old Law Books, and had promoted his own vain lies; He had made him new Magistrates, and set up new Aldermen; He had builded him new Holds, and had man'd them for himself. And all this he did to make himself secure in case the good *Shaddai*, or his Son, should come to make an incursion upon him.

Tidings carried to the Court of what had happened to *Mansoul.*

Now you may well think, that long before this time word, by some or other could not but be carried to the good King *Shaddai*, how his *Mansoul* in the Continent of *Universe* was lost; and that the Runagate Giant *Diabolus*, once one of his Majesties Servants, had in Rebellion against the King made sure thereof for himself: Yea tidings were carried and brought to the King thereof, and that to a very circumstance.

As first, How *Diabolus* came upon *Mansoul* (they being a simple people and innocent) with craft, subtlety, lies and guile; *Item*, That he had treacherously slain the right noble and valiant Captain, their Captain *Resistance*, as he stood upon the Gate with the rest of the Townsmen; *Item*, How my brave Lord *Innocent* fell down dead (with grief some say, or with being poisoned with the stinking breath of one *Ill-pause*, as say others) at the hearing of his just Lord, and rightful Prince *Shaddai* so abused by the mouth of so filthy a *Diabolian*, as that Varlet *Ill-pause* was. The Messenger further told, That after this *Ill-pause* had made a short Oration to the Townsmen, in behalf of *Diabolus* his Master, the simple Town believing that what was said was true, with one consent did open *Ear-gate*, the chief Gate of the *Corporation*, and did let him with his Crue into a Possession of the famous Town of *Mansoul*. He further shewed how *Diabolus* had served the Lord *Mayor*, and Mr. *Recorder*, to wit, That he had put them from all place of power and trust; *Item*, He shewed also that my Lord *Willbewill*, was turned a very Rebel and Runagate, and that so was one Mr. *Mind* his Clerk, and that they two did range and revel it all the Town over, and teach the wicked ones their wayes. He said moreover, That this *Willbewill* was put into great trust. And particularly that *Diabolus* had put into *Willbewill*s hand , all the strong places in *Mansoul*: And that Mr. *Affection* was made my Lord *Willbewill*'s Deputy in his most rebellious affairs. Yea, said the Messenger, this monster, Lord *Willbewill*, has openly disavowed his King *Shaddai*, and hath horribly given his faith and plighted his Troth to *Diabolus*.

Also said the Messenger, besides all this, the new King or rather rebellious Tyrant over the once famous, but now perishing Town of *Mansoul*, has set up a Lord *Mayor*, and a *Recorder* of his own. For Mayor he has set up one Mr. *Lustings*, and for *Recorder*, Mr. *Forget-good*: two of the vilest of all the Town of *Mansoul*. This faithful Messenger also proceeded and told what a sort of new *Burgesses*, *Diabolus* had made, also that he had builded several strong Forts, Towers, and strong Holds in *Mansoul*. He told too, the which I had almost forgot, how *Diabolus* had put the Town of *Mansoul* into Arms, the better to capacitate them on his behalf to make resistance against *Shaddai* their King, should he come to reduce them to their former obedience.

Grief at Court to hear the Tidings.

Now this Tidings-teller did not deliver his Relation of things in private but in open Court, the King and his Son, high Lords, chief Captains, and Nobles, being all there present to hear. But by that they had heard the whole of the story, it would have amazed one, to have seen, had he been there to behold it, what sorrow and grief, and compunction of spirit there was among all sorts, to think that famous *Mansoul* was now taken: only the King, and his Son foresaw all this long before, yea, and sufficiently provided for the relief of *Mansoul*, though they told not every body thereof: Yet because they also would have a share in condoling of the misery of *Mansoul*, therefore they also did, and that at a rate of the highest degree, bewail the losing of *Mansoul*. The King said plainly, *That it grieved him at the heart*, and you may be sure that his Son was not a whit behind him. Thus gave they conviction to all about them, that they had love and compassion for the famous Town of *Mansoul*. Well, when the King and his Son were retired into the Privy-Chamber, there they again consulted about what they had designed before, to wit, *That as* Mansoul *should in time be suffered to be lost; so as certainly it should be recovered again;* recovered I say, in such a way as that

Gen. 6. 5, 6.

The secret of his purpose.

both the King and his Son would get themselves eternal fame and glory thereby. Wherefore after this consult, the son of *Shaddai* (a Sweet and comly person, and one that had alwayes great affection for those that were in affliction, but one that had mortal enmity in his heart against *Diabolus*, because he was designed for it, and because he sought his Crown and Dignity.) This Son of *Shaddai*, I say, having stricken hands with his Father, and promised that he would be his servant to recover his *Mansoul* again, stood by his resolution, nor would he repent of the same. The purport of which agreement was this; To wit, *That at a certain time prefixed by both, the Kings Son should take a journey into the Countrey of* Universe, *and there in a way of Justice and equity, by making of amends for the follies of* Mansoul, *he should lay a foundation of her perfect deliverance from* Diabolus, *and from his Tyranny.*

The Son of God.

Isa. 49. 5.
1 Tim. 1. 15.
Hos. 13. 14.

A brave design on foot for the Town of *Mansoul*.

Moreover *Emanuel* resolved to make, at a time convenient, a war upon the Giant *Diabolus*, even while he was possessed of the Town of *Mansoul*. And that he would fairly by strength of hand drive him out of his *hold*, his *nest*, and take it to himself, to be his habitation.

By the Holy *Ghost*.

This now being resolved upon, order was given to the Lord chief *Secretary*, to draw up a fair Record of what was determined, and to cause that it should be published in all the Corners of the Kingdom of *Universe*. A short Breviat of the Contents thereof, you may if you please take here as follows.

The Holy Scriptures

Let all men know who are concerned, That the Son of Shaddai *the great King, is ingaged by Covenant to his Father, to bring his* Mansoul *to him again; Yea and to put* Mansoul *too, through the power of his matchless love, into a far better, and more happy condition than 'twas in before it was taken by* Diabolus.

The Contents.

These papers therefore were published in several places, to the no little molestation of the Tyrant *Diabolus*, for now thought he, I shall be molested, and my habitation will be taken from me.

But when this matter, I mean this purpose of the King and his Son, did at first take air at Court: who can tell how the

Among the Angels.

high Lords, chief Captains, and noble Princes that were there, were taken with the business. First, they whispered it one to another, and after that it began to ring out throughout the Kings Palace, all wondring at the glorious design that between the King and his Son was on foot for the miserable Town of *Mansoul*. Yea the Courtiers could scarce do any thing, either for the King or Kingdom, but they would mix with the doing thereof, a noise of the love of the King and his Son, that they had for the Town of *Mansoul*.

Diabolus perplexed at the News.

Nor could these Lords, high Captains, and Princes, be content to keep this News at Court, yea before the Records thereof were perfected, themselves came down and told it in *Universe*. At last it came to the ears, as I said, of *Diabolus*, to his no little discontent. For you must think it would perplex him to hear of such a design against him: well, but after a few casts in his mind, he concluded upon these four things.

He concluded on several things.

First that this News, this good tidings (if possible) should be kept from the ears of the Town of *Mansoul*: For said he, if they shall once come to the knowledge that *Shaddai* their former King, and *Emanuel* his Son, are contriving of good for the Town of *Mansoul*: what can be expected by me, but that *Mansoul* will make a revolt from under my hand and government, and return again to him.

First how to keep the News from *Mansoul*.

The *Will* ingaged against the Gospel.

Good thoughts must be kept out of the Town of *Mansoul*.

Now to accomplish this his design, he renews his flattery with my Lord *Willbewill*, and also gives him strict charge and command, that he should keep watch by day, and by night at all the gates of the Town, especially *Eargate* and *Eyegate*: For I hear of a design, quoth he, a design to make us all Traytors, and that *Mansoul* must be reduced to its first bondage again. I hope they are but flying stories quoth he, however let no such news by any means be let into *Mansoul*, lest the people be dejected thereat: I think my Lord it can be no welcome news to you, I am sure it is none to me. And I think that at this time it should be all our wisdoms and care, to nip the head of all such rumors as shall tend to trouble our people: Wherefore I desire my Lord, that you will in this matter do as I say, let there be strong guards daily kept at every Gate of the Town, Stop also and examine, from whence such come that you perceive do from far come hither to trade; nor let them by any means be admitted into *Mansoul*, unless you shall plainly perceive that they are favourers of our excellent Government. I command moreover, said *Diabolus*, that there be spies continually walking up and down the Town of *Mansoul*, and let them have power to suppress, and destroy, any that they shall perceive to be plotting against us, or that shall prate of what by *Shaddai* and *Emanuel* is intended.

All good thoughts and words in the Town are to be suppressed.

This therefore was accordingly done, my Lord *Willbewill* hearkned to his Lord and Master, went willingly after the commandment, and with all the diligence he could, kept any that would, from going out abroad, or that sought to bring this tidings to *Mansoul*, from coming into the Town.

Secondly, This done, in the next place, *Diabolus* that he might make *Mansoul* as sure as he could, frames and imposes a new Oath, and horrible covenant upon the Townsfolk:

A new Oath imposed upon *Mansoul*.

To wit, *That they should never desert him, nor his Government, nor yet betray him, nor seek to alter his Laws: but that they should own, confess, stand by, and acknowledge him for their rightful King in defiance to any that do or hereafter shall, by any pretence, Law, or title what ever lay claim to the Town of Mansoul*. Thinking belike that *Shaddai* had not power to absolve them from this Covenant with death, and agreement with Hell. Nor did the silly *Mansoul* stick or boggle at all at this most monstrous ingagement, but as if it had been a Sprat in the mouth of a Whale, they swallowed it without any chewing. Were they troubled at it? Nay, they rather bragged and boasted of their so brave fidelity to the Tyrant their pretended King, swearing that they would never be Changlings, nor forsake their Old Lord for a New.

Isa. 28. 15.

Thus did *Diabolus* tye poor *Mansoul* fast, but jealousie that never thinks it self strong enough, put him in the next place upon another exploit, which was yet more, if possible, to debauch this Town of *Mansoul*: wherefore he caused by the hand of one Mr. *Filth*, an odious, nasty, lascivious piece of beastliness to be drawn up in writing, and to be set upon the Castle Gates: whereby he granted, and gave licence to all his

Odious Atheistical Pamphlets and filthy Ballads & Romances full of baldry.

true and trusty sons in *Mansoul*, to do whatsoever their lustful appetites prompted them to do, and that no man was to lett, hinder, or controul them, upon pain of incurring the displeasure of their Prince.

Reasons of his thus doing.

Now this he did for these Reasons:

1. That the Town of *Mansoul* might be yet made weaker and weaker, and so more unable, should tidings come, that their redemption was designed: to believe, hope, or consent to the truth therof. For reason sayes, The bigger the Sinner, the less grounds of hopes of mercy.

2. The second reason was, If, perhaps *Emanuel* the Son of *Shaddai* their King, by seeing the horrible, and prophane doings of the Town of *Mansoul*, might repent, tho' entred into a Covenant of redeeming them, of pursuing that Covenant of their redemption; for he knew that *Shaddai* was holy, and that his Son *Emanuel* was holy, yea, he knew it by woful experience: for, for the iniquity and sin of *Diabolus*, was he cast from the highest Orbs. Wherefore what more rational than for him to conclude that thus, for sin, it might fare with *Mansoul*. But fearing also lest this knot should break, he bethinks himself of another, to wit:

3. Thirdly, To endeavour to possess all hearts in the Town of *Mansoul*, that *Shaddai* was raising of an Army, to come to overthrow, and utterly to destroy this Town of *Mansoul*, (and this he did to forestal any tidings that might come to their ears, of their deliverance) for thought he, if I first brute this, the tidings that shall come after, will all be swallowed up of this; for what else will *Mansoul* say, when they shall hear that they must be delivered, but that the true meaning is, *Shaddai intends to destroy them*: Wherefore, he summons the whole Town into the *Market place*, and there with deceitful Tongue thus he addresses himself unto them.

The place of hearing and of considering.

Gentlemen, and my very good Friends, You are all as you know my legal Subiects, and men of the famous Town of Mansoul; *you know how from the first day that I have been with you until now, I have behaved my self among you, and what liberty, and great priviledges you have injoyed under my Government, I hope to your honour, and mine, and also to your content and delight; Now my famous* Mansoul, *a noise of trouble there is abroad, of trouble to the Town of* Mansoul, *sorry I am thereof for your sakes. For I received but now by the Post from my Lord* Lucifer, (*and he useth to have good intelligence*) *That your old King* Shaddai, *is raising of an Army to come against you, to destroy you root and branch: and this O* Mansoul! *is now the cause, that at this time I have called you together; namely to advise what in this juncture is best to be done; for my part, I am but one, and can with ease shift for my self, did I list to seek my own ease, and to leave my* Mansoul *in all the danger: But my heart is so firmly united to you, and so unwilling am I to leave you; that I am willing to stand and fall with you, to the utmost hazzard that shall befal me. What say you? O my* Mansoul! *will you now desert your old friend; or do you think of standing by me. Then as one man*, with one mouth, they cried out together, *Let him die the death that will not.*

Then said *Diabolus* again, '*Tis in vain for us to hope for quarter, for this King knows not how to shew it: True perhaps, he at his first sitting down before us, will talk of and pretend to mercy, that thereby with the more ease, and less trouble, he may again make himself the master of* Mansoul; *what ever therefore he shall say, believe not one syllable or tittle of it, for all such language is but to overcome us, and to make us while we wallow in our blood, the Trophies of his merciless victory. My mind is therefore, that we resolve to the last man, to resist him, and not to believe him upon any terms*, For in at that door will come our danger. *But shall we be flattered out of our lives? I hope you know more of the rudiments of Politicks than to suffer your selves so pitifully to be served.*

Very deceivable language.

But suppose he should, if he gets us to yield, save some of our lives or the lives of some of them that are underlings in Mansoul, *what help will that be to you that are the chief of the Town, especially of you whom I have set up, and whose greatness has been procured by you through your faithful sticking to me? And suppose again, that he should give quarter to every one of you, be sure he will bring you into that bondage under which you were captivated before, or a worse, and then what good will your lives do you? Shall you with him live in pleasure as you do now? No, no, you must be bound by Laws that will pinch you, and be made to do that which at present is hateful to you;*

Lying language.

He is afraid of losing of *Mansoul.*

He puts them upon Arming of themselves.

I am for you if you are for me, and it is better to dye valiantly, than to live like pitiful Slaves, But I say, the life of a Slave, will be counted a life too good for Mansoul *now. Blood, blood, nothing but blood is in every blast of* Shaddai's *Trumpet against poor* Mansoul *now; Pray be concerned, I hear he is coming, up, and stand to your Armes, that now while you have any leisure, I may learn you some feats of War. Armour for you I have, and by me it is; Yea, and it is sufficient for* Mansoul *from top to toe; nor can you be hurt by what his force can do, if you shall keep it well girt and fastned about you: Come therefore to my Castle and welcome, and harness yourselves for the war. There is Helmet, Breast-plate, Sword and Shield, and what not, that will make you fight like men.*

His Helmet. Deut. 29. 19.

1. *My* Helmet, *otherwise called an headpiece,* is hope of doing well at last what lives soever you live: *This is that which they had, who said,* that they should have peace tho' they walked in the wickedness of their heart, to add drunkenness to thirst; *A piece of approved Armour this is, and who ever has it and can hold it, so long no Arrow, Dart, Sword, or Shield can hurt him; this therefore keep on, and thou wilt keep off many a blow my* Mansoul.

His Breast-plate. Rev. 9. 9.

2. *My* Breast-Plate *is a* Breast-Plate of Iron; *I had it forged in* mine own Countrey, *and all my Souldiers are armed therewith, in plain language it is an* hard heart, *an heart as hard as Iron, and as much past feeling as a stone, the which if you get, and keep, neither mercy shall win you, nor judgment fright you. This therefore is a piece of Armour, most necessary for all to put on that hate* Shaddai, *and that would fight against him under my Banner.*

His Sword. Psal. 57. 4. Psal. 64. 3. Jam. 3.

3. *My* Sword *is a* Tongue that is set on fire of Hell, *and that can bend it self to speak evil of* Shaddai, *his Son, his wayes, and people; Use this, it has been tryed a thousand times twice told; whoever hath it, keeps it, and makes that use of it as I would have him, can never be conquered by mine enemy.*

His Shield. Job. 15. 26. Psal. 76. 3. Mar. 6. 5, 6.

4. *My* Shield is unbelief, *or calling into question the truth of the word, or all the sayings that speak of the judgment that* Shaddai *has appointed for wicked men, use this Shield; many attempts he has made upon it, and sometimes, 'tis true, it has been bruised; but they that have writ of the wars of* Emanuel *against my servants, have testified that he could do no mighty work there because of their unbelief:*

Now to handle this weapon of mine aright, it is, not to believe things, because they are true, of what sort or by whom soever asserted; if he speaks of Judgment, care not for it; if he speaks of mercy care not for it; if he promises, if he swears that he would do to Mansoul, *if it turns, no hurt but good; regard not what is said, question the truth of all; for it is to wield the Shield of unbelief aright, and as my servants ought and do: and he that doth otherwise loves me not, nor do I count him, but an Enemy to me.*

5. *Another part or piece, said* Diabolus *of mine excellent Armour is*, a dumb and prayerless Spirit, *a spirit that scorns to cry for mercy; wherefore be you my* Mansoul, *sure that you make use of this:* What! *cry for quarter, never do that, if you would be mine; I know you are stout men, and am sure that I have clad you with that which is Armour of proof; wherefore to cry to* Shaddai *for mercy, let that be far from you: Besides all this, I have a Maul, Fire-brands, Arrows and Death, all good hand-weapons, and such as will do execution.*

He backs all with a speech to them.

After he had thus furnished his men with Armour and Armes, he addressed himself to them in such like words as these, *Remember quoth he, that I am your rightful King, and that you have taken an Oath, and entred into Covenant to be true to me and my cause; I say remember this, and shew your selves stout, and valiant men of* Mansoul. *Remember also the kindness that I have alwayes shewed to you, and that without your petition; I have granted to you external things, wherefore the Priviledges, Grants, Immunities, Profits, and honours wherewith I have indowed you, do call for at your hands, returns of loyalty, my Lyon-like men of* Mansoul; *And when so fit a time to shew it, as when another shall seek to take my dominion over you, into their own hands; One word more and I have done: Can we but stand, and overcome this one shock or brunt, I doubt not but in little time, all the world will be ours; And when that day comes, my true hearts, I will make you Kings, Princes and Captains, and what brave dayes shall we have then?*

Diabolus having thus armed, and fore-armed his Servants and Vassals in *Mansoul*, against their good and Lawful King *Shaddai*; in the next place he doubleth his Guards, at the Gates of the Town, and he takes himself to the Castle, which was his strong Hold: His Vassals also to shew their wills, and

They of *Mansoul* shew their loyalty to the Gyant.

supposed (but ignoble) gallantry, exercise themselves in their Arms every day, and teach one another feats of War; they also defied their Enemies, and sang up the praises of their Tyrant; they threatned also what men they would be, if ever things should rise so high, as a War between *Shaddai* and their King.

Shaddai prepareth an Army for the recovery of *Mansoul*

The words of God.

Now all this time, the good King, the King *Shaddai* was preparing to send an Army to recover the Town of *Mansoul* again from the Tyranny of their pretended King *Diabolus*: But he thought good at the first, not to send them by the hand and conduct of brave *Emanuel* his son, but under the hand of some of his Servants, to see first by them the temper of *Mansoul*; and whether by them they would be won to the obedience of their King. The Army consisted of above forty thousand, all true men: For they came from the Kings own Court, and were those of his own chusing.

The Captains names.

They came up to *Mansoul* under the conduct of four stout Generals, each man being a Captain of ten thousand men, and these are their names, and their signs. The name of the first was *Boanerges*. The name of the second was Captain *Conviction*. The name of the third was Captain *Judgment*; And the name of the fourth was Captain *Execution*: These were the Captains that *Shaddai* sent to regain *Mansoul*.

Psal. 60. 4.

These four Captains (as we said) the King thought fit in the first place to send to *Mansoul*, to make an attempt upon it; for indeed generally in all his Wars he did use to send these four Captains in the Van, for they were very stout and rough-hewen men, men that were fit to break the ice, and to make their way by dint of Sword, and their men were like themselves.

To each of these Captains the King gave a Banner that it might be displayed because of the goodness of his cause and because of the right that he had to *Mansoul*.

Mark. 3. 17.

First to Captain *Boanerges*, for he was the chief, to him, I say, was given ten thousand men; His Ensign was Mr. *Thunder*, he bare the black Colours, and his Scutcheon was the three burning Thunder-Bolts.

The second Captain was Captain *Conviction*, to him also was given ten thousand men; his Ensign's name was Mr. *Sorrow*, he did bear the pale Colours, and his Scutcheon was the Book of the Law wide open, from whence issued a flame of fire. Deut. 33. 2.

The third Captain was Captain *Judgment*, to him was given ten thousand men; his Ensigns name was Mr. *Terror*, he bare the red Colours, and his Scutcheon was a burning fiery furnace. Matt. 13. 40, 41.

The fourth Captain was Captain *Execution*; to him was given ten thousand men: his Ensign was one Mr. *Justice*, he also bare the red Colours, and his Scutcheon was a fruitless tree with an Ax laying at the root thereof. Matt. 3. 10.

These four Captains, as I said, had every one of them under his command ten thousand men, all of good fidelity to the King, and stout at their Military actions.

Well, the Captains and their forces, their men and Under Officers, being had upon a day by *Shaddai* into the Field, and there called all over by their names, were then and there put into such harness, as became their degree and that service that now they were going about for their King.

Now when the King had mustered his Forces, (*for it is he that mustereth the Host to the Battel*) he gave unto the Captains their several Commissions: with charge and commandment in the audience of all the Souldiers that they should take heed faithfully and couragiously to do and execute the same. Their Commissions were for the substance of them the same in form, though as to name, title, place and degree of the Captains there might be some, but very small variation: And here let me give you an account of the matter and summ contained in their Commission.

A Commission from the great Shaddai *King of* Mansoul, *to his trusty and noble Captain, the Captain* Boanerges, *for his making War upon the Town of* Mansoul.

‘O! Thou *Boanerges*, one of my stout and thundring Captains, over one ten thousand of my valiant and faithful Servants: Go thou in my name with this thy Force to the miserable Town of *Mansoul*, and when thou comest thither, offer them first conditions of peace; and command them, that

Their Commission. Mat. 10. 11. Luk. 10. 5.

casting off the yoke and tyranny of the wicked *Diabolus*, they return to me their rightful Prince and Lord; command them also that they cleanse themselves from all that is his in the Town of *Mansoul*, (and look to thy self that thou hast good satisfaction touching the truth of their obedience.) Thus when thou hast commanded them (if they in truth submit thereto) then do thou to the uttermost of thy power, what in thee lies, to set up for me a Garrison in the famous Town of *Mansoul*; Nor do thou hurt the least Native that moveth or breatheth therein, if they will submit themselves to me, but treat thou such as if they were thy Friend or Brother; for all such I love, and they shall be dear unto me: And tell them that I will take a time to come unto them, and to let them know that I am merciful.

1 Thes. 2. 7, 8, 9, 10, 11.

'But if they shall notwithstanding thy Summons and the producing of thy Authority, resist, stand out against thee, and rebel: then do I command thee to make use of all thy cunning, power, might, and force to bring them under by strength of hand. Farewel.'

Thus you see the summ of their Commissions, for as I said before, for the substance of them, they were the same that the rest of the noble Captains had.

They prepare for a March.

Wherefore they having received each Commander his authority, at the hand of their King. The day being appointed, and the place of their Rendezvouz prefixed; each Commander appeared in such gallantry, as became his cause and calling. So after a new entertainment from *Shaddai*: With flying Colours, they set forward to march towards the Famous Town of *Mansoul*. Captain *Boanerges* led the Van: Captain *Conviction* and Captain *Judgment* made up the main Body: And Captain *Execution* brought up the *Rere*. They then having a great way to go, (for the Town of *Mansoul* was far off from the Court of *Shaddai*) they marched through the Regions and Countries of many people, not hurting, or abusing any, but blessing where ever they came. They also lived upon the Kings cost in all the way they went.

Eph. 2. 13, 17.

Having travelled thus for many dayes, at last they came within sight of *Mansoul*: the which when they saw, the Captains could for their hearts do no less than for a while bewail the condition of the Town; for they quickly saw how that it was prostrate to the will of *Diabolus*, and to his wayes and designs.

Well, to be short, the Captains came up before the Town, march up to *Eargate*, sit down there (for that was the place of hearing). So when they had pitched their Tents, and intrenched themselves, they addressed themselves to make their Assault.

The world are convinced by the well ordered life of the godly.

Now the Townsfolk at first, beholding so gallant a Company, so bravely accoutred, and so excellently disciplined, having on their glittering Armour, and displaying of their flying Colours: could not but come out of their Houses and gaze. But the cunning Fox *Diabolus*, fearing that the people, after this sight should on a suddain Summons, open the Gates to the Captains, came down with all haste from the Castle, and made them retire into the body of the Town, who when he had them there, made this lying and deceivable speech unto them.

Diabolus alienates their minds from them.

'Gentlemen, quoth he, although you are my trusty and well beloved Friends, yet I cannot but (a little) chide you for your late uncircumspect action: in going out to gaze on that great and mighty force, that but yesterday sat down before (and have now intrenched themselves in order to the maintaining of a Siege against the famous) Town of *Mansoul*, Do you know who they are? whence they come? and what is their purpose in sitting down before the Town of *Mansoul*? They are they of whom I have told you long ago, that they would come to destroy, destroy this Town, and against whom I have been at the cost to arm you with cap-a-pe for your body, besides great fortifications for your mind; Wherefore then did you not rather, even at the first appearance of them, cry out, fire the *Beacons*, and give the whole Town an Alarm concerning them, that we might all have been in a posture of defence, and a been ready to have received them with the highest acts of defiance, then had you shewed your selves

That's false Satan.

Satan greatly afraid of Gods Ministers, that they will set

Mansoul against him.

He stirs them up to bid defiance to the Ministers of the Word.

men to my liking, whereas by what you have done, you have made me half afraid; I say half afraid, that when they and we shall come to push a *Pike*, I shall find you want courage to stand it out any longer. Wherefore have I commanded a watch, and that you should double your Guards at the Gates? Wherefore have I indeavoured to make you as hard as Iron, and your hearts as a piece of the nether Milstone? was it think you, that you might shew your selves Women, and that you might go out like a company of Innocents to gaze on your mortal foes! Fy, fy, put your selves into a posture of defence, beat up the Drum, gather together in warlike manner, that our Foes may know that, before they shall conquer this Corporation, there are valiant men in the Town of *Mansoul*.

'I will leave off now to chide, and will not further rebuke you: but I charge you, that hence forwards, you let me see no more such actions. Let not hence forward a man of you, without order first obtained from me, so much as shew his head over the Wall of the Town of *Mansoul*: You have now heard me, do as I have commanded, and you shall cause me that I dwell securely with you, and that I take care as for my self, so for your safety and honour also. Farewel.'

When Sinners hearken to Satan they are set in a rage against godliness.

Now were the Townsmen strangely altered: they were as men stricken with a panick fear: they ran to and fro through the Streets of the Town of *Mansoul* crying out, help, help, The men that turn the World upside down are come hither also; nor could any of them be quiet after, but still as men bereft of wit, they cryed out, The destroyers of our peace and people are come: this went down with *Diabolus*. 'Ay!' quoth he to himself, 'this I like well, now it is as I would have it, now you shew your obedience to your Prince; hold you but here, and then let them take the Town if they can.'

The Kings Trumpet sounded at *Eargate*.

Well, before the Kings Forces had sat before *Mansoul* three dayes, Captain *Boanerges* commanded his Trumpeter to go down to *Eargate*, and there in the name of the great *Shaddai* to summons *Mansoul* to give audience to the message that he in his Masters name was to them commanded to deliver. So the Trumpeter, whose name was, *Take heed what you hear*,

They will not hear.

went up as he was commanded to *Eargate*, and there sounded his Trumpet for a hearing: but there was none that appeared, that gave answer or regard; For so had *Diabolus* commanded. So the Trumpeter returned to his Captain, and told him what he had done, and also how he had sped. Whereat the Captain was grieved, but bid the Trumpeter go to his Tent.

A second Summons repulsed.

Again Captain *Boanerges* sendeth his Trumpeter to *Eargate*, to sound as before for an hearing; But they again kept close, came not out, nor would they give him an answer, so observant were they of the command of *Diabolus* their King.

A Council of War.

Then the Captains, and other Field-Officers, called a Council of War to consider what further was to be done for the gaining of the Town of *Mansoul*, and after some close and thorough debate upon the contents of their Commissions, they concluded yet to give to the Town by the hand of the forenamed Trumpeter, another Summons to hear; but if that shall be refused said they, and that the Town shall stand it out still: Then they determined, and bid the Trumpeter tell them so, that they would indeavour, by what means they could, to *compel* them by force to the obedience of their King.

Luk. 14. 23.

A third Summons.

So Captain *Boanerges* commanded his Trumpeter to go up to *Eargate* again, and in the name of the great King *Shaddai* to give it a very loud Summons to come down without delay to *Eargate*, there to give audience to the Kings most noble Captains. So the Trumpeter went, and did as he was commanded: he went up to *Eargate*, and sounded his Trumpet, and gave a third Summons to *Mansoul*: He said moreover, That if this they should still refuse to do, the Captains of his Prince would with might come down upon them, and indeavour to reduce them to their obedience by force.

Isa. 58. 1.

The Lord *Willbewill* his Speech to the Trumpeter.

Then stood up my Lord *Willbewill*, who was the Governor of the Town, (this *Willbewill* was that Apostate of whom mention was made before) and the keeper of the Gates of *Mansoul*. He therefore with big and ruffling words demanded of the Trumpeter who he was? whence he came? and what was the cause of his making so hideous a noise at the gate, and speaking such insufferable words against the Town of *Mansoul*.

The Trumpeter. The Trumpeter answered, 'I am servant to the most noble Captain, Captain *Boanerges*, General of the Forces of the great King *Shaddai*, against whom both thy self with the whole Town of *Mansoul* have rebelled, and lift up the heel; and my Master the Captain hath a special message to this Town, and to thee as a member thereof: The which if you of *Mansoul* shall peaceably hear, so: and if not, you must take what follows.'

Willbewill Then said the Lord *Willbewill*, 'I will carry thy words to my Lord, and will know what he will say.'

The Trumpeter. But the Trumpeter soon replyed, saying, 'Our message is, not to the Gyant *Diabolus*, but to the miserable Town of *Mansoul*: nor shall we at all regard what answer by him is made; nor yet by any for him. We are sent to this Town to recover it from under his cruel Tyranny, and to perswade it to submit, as in former times it did, to the most excellent King *Shaddai*.'

Willbewill. Then said the Lord *Willbewill*, 'I will do your errand to the Town.'

The Trumpeter. The Trumpeter then replyed, 'Sir, do not deceive us, lest in so doing, you deceive your selves much more.' He added moreover, 'For we are resolved, if in peaceable manner you do not submit your selves: then to make a War upon you, and to bring you under by force. And of the truth of what I now say, this shall be a sign unto you, you shall see the black Flag with its hot burning-thunderbolts set upon the mount to morrow, as a token of defiance against your Prince, and of our resolutions to reduce you to your Lord, and rightful King.'

The Trumpeter returns to the Camp. So the said Lord *Willbewill* returned from off the Wall, and the Trumpeter came into the Camp. When the Trumpeter was come into the Camp, the Captains and Officers of the mighty King *Shaddai*, came together to know, if he had obtained a hearing, and what was the effect of his errand: So the Trumpeter told, saying, 'When I had sounded my Trumpet, and had called aloud to the Town for a hearing: My Lord *Willbewill* the Governour of the Town, and he that hath charge of the Gates came up, when he heard me sound, and looking over the wall, he asked me what I was? whence I came? and what was the cause of my making this noyse? so I told him my errand, and by whose Authority I brought it. Then, said he, I will tell it to the Governour and to *Mansoul*: and then I returned to my Lords.'

Then said the brave *Boanerges*, 'Let us yet for a while, lie still in our Trenches, and see what these Rebels will do.' Now when the time drew nigh that audience by *Mansoul* must be given to the brave *Boanerges* and his companions: It was commanded that all the men of war throughout the whole Camp of *Shaddai*, should as one man stand to their Arms, and make themselves ready, if the Town of *Mansoul* shall hear, to receive it forthwith to mercy; but if not, to force a subjection. So the day being come, the Trumpeters sounded, and that throughout the whole Camp, that the men of War might be in a readiness for that which then should be the work of the day. But when they that were in the Town of *Mansoul*, heard the sound of the Trumpets throughout the Camp of *Shaddai*, and thinking no other, but that it must be in order to storming the Corporation: they at first were put to great consternation of Spirit, but after they a little were setled again, they also made what preparation they could for a War, if they did storm; else to secure themselves.

Carnal Souls make a wrong interpretation of the design of a Gospel Ministry.

Well, when the utmost time was come, *Boanerges* was resolved to hear their answer; wherefore he sent out his Trumpeter again to summons *Mansoul* to a hearing of the message that they had brought from *Shaddai*. So he went and sounded, and the Townsmen came up, but made *Eargate* as sure as they could. Now when they were come up to the top of the Wall, Captain *Boanerges* desired to see the *Lord Mayor*, but my Lord *Incredulity* was then *Lord Mayor*, for he came in the room of my Lord *Lustings*. So *Incredulity*, he came up and shewed himself over the Wall; but when the Captain *Boanerges* had set his eyes upon him, he cryed out aloud, *This is not he, where is my Lord* Understanding, *the ancient* Lord Mayor *of the Town of* Mansoul, *for to him I would deliver my message?*

Zach. 7. 11.

Boanerges refuses to make *Incredulity* a Judge of what he had to deliver to the famous Town of *Mansoul*.

Then said the Gyant, (for *Diabolus* was also come down) to the Captain; Mr. Captain, *You have by your boldness given to*

Mansoul *at least four Summons to subject herself to your King: by whose Authority I know not; nor will I dispute that now, I ask therefore what is the reason of all this ado, or what would you be at if you knew your selves?*

Boanerges obtains a hearing.

His Speech.

Then Captain *Boanerges*, *whose was the black Colours, and whose Scutcheon was the three burning-thunder-bolts*, (taking no notice of the Gyant or of his speech), thus addressed himself to the Town of *Mansoul*; 'Be it known unto you, O unhappy and rebellious *Mansoul*! That the most Gracious King, the great King *Shaddai* my Master, hath sent me unto you with Commission (and so he shewed to the Town his broad Seal) to reduce you to his obedience. And he hath commanded me, in case you yield, upon my Summons, to carry it to you as if you were my Friends, or Brother; but he also hath bid, that if after Summons to submit, you still stand out and rebel, we should indeavour to take you by force.'

The Speech of Captain *Conviction*.

Rom. 3. 10, 11, 12, 13, 14, 15, 16, 17, 18, 19, 23. Chap. 16. 17, 18.

Psal. 50. 21, 22.

Then stood forth Captain *Conviction* and said, (*his was the pale Colours, and for his Scutcheon he had the Book of the Law wide open* &c.) 'Hear O *Mansoul*! Thou, O *Mansoul*, wast once famous for innocency, but now thou art degenerated into lies and deceit: Thou hast heard what my Brother, the Captain *Boanerges* hath said, and it is your wisdom, and will be your happiness to stoop to, and accept of conditions of peace and mercy when offered; specially when offered by one, against whom thou hast rebelled, and one who is of power to tear thee in pieces, for so is *Shaddai* our King, nor when he is angry, can any thing stand before him. If you say you have not sinned, or acted rebellion against our King, the whole of your doings since the day that you cast off his service (and there was the beginning of your sin) will sufficiently testify against you: what else means your harkening to the Tyrant, and your receiving him for your King? what means else your rejecting of the Laws of *Shaddai*, and your obeying of *Diabolus*? yea, what means this your taking up of Arms against, and the shutting of your gates upon us, the faithful servants of your King? Be ruled then, and accept of my Brothers invitation, and overstand not the time of mercy, but agree with thine

Luk. 12. 58, 59.

adversary quickly. Ah *Mansoul*, suffer not thy self to be kept from mercy, and to be run into a thousand miseries, by the flattering wiles of *Diabolus*: Perhaps that piece of deceit may attempt to make you believe that we seek our own profit in this our service; but know 'tis obedience to our King, and love to your happiness, that is the cause of this undertaking of ours.

'Again, I say to thee O *Mansoul*, consider if it be not amazing grace that *Shaddai* should so humble himself as he doth, now he by us reasons with you, in a way of intreaty and sweet perswasions, that you would subject your selves to him. Has he that need of you, that we are sure you have of him? No, no, but he is merciful, and will not that *Mansoul* should dye, but turn to him and live.'

2 Cor. 5. 18, 19, 20, 21.

Then stood forth Captain *Judgment*, *whose was the red Colours, and for a Scutcheon he had the burning fiery Furnace*, and he said: 'O ye the Inhabitants of the Town of *Mansoul*! that have lived so long in rebellion and acts of Treason against the King *Shaddai*: Know that we come not to day to this place, in this manner, with our message of our own minds, or to revenge our own quarrel; it is the King my Master that hath sent us to reduce you to your obedience to him, the which if you refuse, in a peaceable way ro yield, we have Commission to compel you thereto. And never think of your selves, nor yet suffer the Tyrant *Diabolus* to perswade you to think, that our King by his power is not able to bring you down, and to lay you under his feet, for he is the Former of all things, and if he touches the Mountains they smoak. Nor will the Gate of the Kings clemency stand alwayes open, for the day that shall burn like an Oven is before him, yea it hasteth greatly, it slumbreth not.

Captain *Judgment* his speech to *Mansoul*.

'O *Mansoul*! is it little in thine eyes that our King doth offer thee mercy, and that after so many provocations? yea he still holdeth out his golden Scepter to thee, and will not yet suffer his Gate to be shut against thee, wilt thou provoke him to do it? If so, consider of what I say; *To thee it is opened no more for ever. If thou sayest thou shalt not see him, yet judgment*

Mal. 4. 1.
2 Pet. 2. 3.
Job. 36. 14.
Ch. 36. 18.
Psal. 9. 7.
Is. 66. 15.

is before him; therefore trust thou in him: Yea, because there is wrath, beware, lest he take thee away with his stroak; then a great ransome cannot deliver thee. Will he esteem thy riches? no, not gold, nor all the forces of strength. He hath prepared his Throne for Judgment; for he will come with fire, and with his Chariots like a whirl-wind, to render his anger with fury, and his rebukes with flames of fire. Therefore O *Mansoul* take heed, lest after thou hast fulfilled the judgment of the wicked, Justice and Judgment should take hold of thee.' Now while the Captain *Judgment* was making of this Oration to the Town of *Mansoul*, it was observed by some that *Diabolus* trembled: But he proceeded in his parable and said, 'O thou woful Town of *Mansoul*! wilt thou not yet set open thy Gate to receive us, the Deputies of thy King, and those that would rejoyce to see thee live? *Can thine heart endure, or can thy hands be strong in the day that he shall deal in Judgment with thee?* I say canst thou indure to be forced to drink as one would drink sweet Wine, the Sea of wrath that our King has prepared for *Diabolus* and his Angels? Consider, betimes consider.'

Ezek. 22. 14.

The Speech of Captain *Execution.*

Then stood forth the fourth Captain, the noble Captain *Execution*, and said: 'O Town of *Mansoul*! once famous, but now like the fruitless bough; *once* the delight of the high ones, but now a Den for *Diabolus*: Hearken also to me, and to the words that I shall speak to thee in the name of the great *Shaddai. Behold the Ax is laid to the root of the Trees, every Tree therefore that bringeth not forth good fruit, is hewen down and cast into the fire.*

Mat. 3. 7, 8, 9, 10.

'Thou, O Town of *Mansoul*! hast hitherto been this fruitless Tree, thou barest nought but Thorns and Bryers. Thy evil fruit sore-bespeaks thee not to be a good Tree: Thy Grapes are Grapes of Gall, thy clusters are bitter. Thou hast rebelled against thy King, and lo we, the Power and Force of *Shaddai*, are the Ax that is laid to thy roots; What saist thou, wilt thou turn? I say again, tell me before the first blow is given, wilt thou turn? Our Ax must first be laid *to* thy root, before it be laid *at* thy root; it must first be laid *to* thy root *in a way of threatning*, before it is laid *at* thy root *by way of Execution*; and

Deut. 32. 32.

between these two is required thy repentance, and this is all the time that thou hast. What wilt thou do? wilt thou turn? or shall I smite? If I fetch my blow *Mansoul*, down you go: For I have Commission to lay my Ax *at*, as well as *to* thy roots, nor will any thing, but yielding to our King, prevent doing of *Execution*. What art thou fit for O *Mansoul*, if mercy preventeth not, but to be hewn down, and cast into the fire and burned?

'O *Mansoul*! patience and forbearance do not act for ever: a year or two, or three they may; but if thou provoke by a three years rebellion, and thou hast already done more than this, Then what follows, but cut it down, nay after *that thou shalt cut it down*. And dost thou think that these are but threatnings, or that our King has not power to execute his words? O *Mansoul*! thou wilt find that in the words of our King, when they are by sinners made little or light of, there is not only threatning, but burning Coals of fire.

Luk. 13. [7, 9]

'Thou hast been a cumber ground long already, and wilt thou continue so still? thy sin has brought this Army to thy Walls, and shall it bring it in Judgment to do *Execution* into thy Town? Thou hast heard what the Captains have said, but as yet thou shuttest thy Gates, speak out *Mansoul*, wilt thou do so still? or wilt thou accept conditions of peace?'

These brave speeches of these four noble Captains, the Town of *Mansoul* refused to hear, yet a sound thereof did beat against *Eargate*, though the force thereof could not break it open. In fine the Town desired a time to prepare their answer to these demands. The Captains then told them, 'That if they would throw out to them one *Ill-pause*, that was in the Town, that they might reward him according to his works; then they would give them time to consider: but if they would not cast him to them over the Wall of *Mansoul*, then they would give them none: for said they, "we know that so long as *Illpause* draws breath in *Mansoul*, all good consideration will be confounded, and nothing but mischief will come thereon." '

Mansoul desires time to make answer.

Upon what conditions the Captains would give them time.

Then *Diabolus*, who was there present, being loth to lose his *Ill-pause*, because he was his Orator (and yet be sure he

Diabolus interrupts them and sets *Incredulity* to answer them.

had, could the Captains have laid their fingers on him) was resolved at this instant to give them answer by himself, but then changing his mind, he commanded the then Lord Mayor, the Lord *Incredulity* to do it: saying, 'My Lord do you give these Runagates an answer, and speak out that *Mansoul* may hear and understand you.'

His Speech.

So *Incredulity* at *Diabolus*'s command began and said: 'Gentlemen, you have here, as we do behold, to the disturbance of our Prince, and the molestation of the Town of *Mansoul*, camped against it: but from whence you come, we will not know; and what you are, we will not believe. Indeed you tell us in your terrible Speech, that you have this Authority from *Shaddai*, but by what right he commands you to do it, of that we shall yet be ignorant.

'You have also by the Authority aforesaid, Summoned this Town to desert her Lord, and for protection, to yield up her self to the great *Shaddai* your King: flatteringly telling her, that if she will do it, he will pass by and not charge her with her past offences.

'Further, You have also to the terror of the Town of *Mansoul*, threatned with great and sore destructions to punish this Corporation if she consents not to do as your wills would have her.

The true picture of unbelief.

'Now Captains, from whence soever you come, and though your designs be never so right; yet know ye, that neither my Lord *Diabolus*, nor I his servant *Incredulity*, nor yet our brave *Mansoul*, doth regard either your persons, message, or the King that you say hath sent you: His power, his greatness, his vengeance we fear not; nor will we yield at all to your Summons.

'As for the War that you threaten to make upon us, we must therein defend ourselves as well as we can: and know ye, that we are not without wherewithal to bid defiance to you. And in short, for I will not be tedious: I tell you that we take you to be some Vagabond Runagate Crew, that having shaken off all obedience to your King, have gotten together in tumultuous manner, and are ranging from place to place to see, if, through the flatteries you are skilled to make, on the one side, and threats wherewith you think to fright, on the other; to make some silly Town, City, or Country, to desert their place and leave it to you: But *Mansoul* is none of them.

'To conclude, we dread you not, we fear you not, nor will we obey your summons: Our gates we keep shut upon you, our place we will keep you out of: Nor will we long thus suffer you to sit down before us. Our people must live in quiet: your appearance doth disturb them: wherefore arise with Bag and Baggage, and be gone, or we will let fly from the *Walls against you.'

Luk. 11. 21.
* Flesh.

This Oration made by Old *Incredulity*, was seconded by desperate *Willbewill*, in words to this effect. 'Gentlemen, we have heard your demands, and the noise of your threats, and have heard the sound of your summons, but we fear not your force, we regard not your threats, but will still abide as you found us. And we command you, that in three days time you cease to appear in these parts, or you shall know, what it is, once to dare offer to rouze the Lion *Diabolus*, when asleep in his Town of *Mansoul*.'

The speech of the Lord *Willbewill*.

The Recorder whose name was *Forget-good*, he also added as followeth. 'Gentlemen, My Lords, as you see, have with milde and gentle words, answered your rough and angry speeches; they have moreover, in my hearing, given you leave quietly to depart as you came. Wherefore take their kindness and be gone, we might have come out with force upon you, and have caused you to feel the dint of our Swords: but as we love ease and quiet our selves; so we love not to hurt or molest others.'

The speech of *Forget-good* the Recorder.

Then did the Town of *Mansoul* shout for joy, as if by *Diabolus* and his Crew, some great advantage had been gotten of the Captains. They also rang the Bells, and made merry, and danced upon the Walls.

The Town resolved to withstand the Captains.

Diabolus also returned to the Castle, and the *Lord Mayor* and *Recorder* to their place: But the Lord *Willbewill* took special care that the Gates should be secured with double guards, double bolts, and double locks and bars. And that *Eargate* (especially) might the better be looked to, for that was the Gate in at which the Kings forces sought most to enter; The Lord *Willbewill* made one old Mr. *Prejudice* (an angry and ill-conditioned fellow) Captain of the Ward at that Gate, and put under his power sixty men, called *Deaf-men*: men advantagious for that service, for as much as they mattered no words of the Captains, nor of their Souldiers.

The band of *Deaf-men* set to keep *Eargate*.

The Captains resolved to give them Battel.

Now when the Captains saw the answer of the great ones, and that they could not get an hearing from the old Natives of the Town, and that *Mansoul* was resolved to give the Kings Army battel: they prepared themselves to receive them, and to try it out by the power of the arm. And first they made their force more formidable against *Eargate*. For they knew that unless they could penetrate that, no good could be done upon the Town. This done, they put the rest of their men in their places. After which they gave out the word, which was, *ye must be born again*. Then they sounded the Trumpet, then they in the Town made them answer, with shout against shout, charge against charge, and so the Battel began. Now they in the Town had planted upon the Tower over *Eargate*, two great *Guns*, the one called *High-mind*, and the other *Heady*. Unto these two Guns they trusted much, they were cast in the Castle by *Diabolus*'s founder, whose name was Mr. *Puff-up*, and mischievous pieces they were. But so vigilant and watchful, when the Captains saw them, were they, that though sometimes their shot would go by their ears with a *Whizz*, yet they did them no harm. By these two Guns the Townsfolk made no question but greatly to annoy the Camp of *Shaddai*, and well enough to secure the Gate, but they had not much cause to boast of what execution they did, as by what follows will be gathered.

The Battel begun.

Two guns planted upon *Eargate*.

The famous *Mansoul* had also some other small pieces in it, of the which they made use against the Camp of *Shaddai*.

They from the Camp also, did as stoutly, and with as much of that as may (in truth) be called Valour, let fly as fast at the Town, and at *Eargate*: For they saw that unless they could break open *Eargate*, 'twould be but in vain to batter the Wall.

The sentenc and power of the word.

Now the Kings Captains had brought with them several slings and two or three *Battering-Rams*; with their slings therefore they battered the houses and people of the Town, and with their Rams they sought to break *Eargate* open.

The Town stoutly stands out and the Captains return to their Winter Quarters.

The Camp and the Town had several skirmishes, and brisk encounters, while the Captains with their Engins made many brave attempts to break open or beat down the Tower that was over *Eargate*, and at the said Gate to make their entrance: But *Mansoul* stood it out so lustily, through the rage of *Diabolus*, the valour of the Lord *Willbewill*, and the conduct of old *Incredulity* the Mayor, and Mr. *Forgetgood*, the Recorder, That the charge and expence of that Summers Wars, (on the Kings side) seemed to be almost quite lost, and the advantage to return to *Mansoul*: But when the Captains saw how it was, they made a fair retreat, and intrenched themselves in their Winter Quarters. Now in this War, you must needs think there was much loss on both sides, of which be pleased to accept of this brief account following.

An account of this War with reference to the loss on both sides.

The Kings Captains when they marched from the Court to come up against *Mansoul* to War; as they came crossing over the Country, they happened to light upon three young fellows that had a mind to go for Souldiers; proper men they were, and men of courage, (and skill) to appearance. Their names were Mr. *Tradition*, Mr. *Human-wisdom*, and Mr. *Mans Invention*. So they came up to the Captains, and proffered their service to *Shaddai*. The Captains then told them of their design, and bid them not to be rash in their offers: But the young men told them, they had considered the thing before, and that hearing they were upon their march for such a design, came hither on purpose to meet them, that they might be listed under their Excellencies. Then Captain *Boanerges*, for that they were men of *Courage*, listed them into his company, and so away they went to the War.

Three new Souldiers.

Now when the War was begun, in one of the briskest skirmishes, so it was, that a Company of the Lord *Willbewills* men sallyed out at the Sallyport, or Postern of the Town, and fell in upon the Rear of Captain *Boanerges* men, where these

They are taken prisoners.

three fellows happened to be, so they took them Prisoners, and away they carried them into the Town; where they had not lain long in durance, but it began to be noised about the Streets of the Town, what three notable Prisoners the Lord *Willbewills* men had taken, and brought in Prisoners out of the Camp of *Shaddai*. At length tidings thereof was carried to *Diabolus* to the Castle, to wit, what My Lord *Willbewills* men had done, and whom they had taken prisoners.

They are brought before *Diabolus*, and are content to fight under his banner.

Then *Diabolus* called for *Willbewill*, to know the certainty of this matter. So he asked him and he told him; then did the *Gyant* send for the prisoners, who when they were come, demanded of them who they were, whence they came, and what they did in the Camp of *Shaddai*; and they told him. Then he sent them to ward again. Not many days after he sent for them to him again, and then asked them if they would be willing to serve him against their former Captains: They then told him, that they did not so much live by *Religion*, as by the fates of *Fortune*. And that since his Lordship was willing to entertain them, they should be willing to serve him. Now while things were thus in hand, there was one Captain *Anything*, a great doer in the Town of *Mansoul*, and to this Captain *Anything* did *Diabolus* send these men, with a note under his hand to receive them into his Company; the Contents of which Letter were thus.

Anything.

He therefore sends them to Captain *Anything* with a Letter.

Anything, *my Darling, the three men that are the bearers of this Letter, have a desire to serve me in the War; nor know I better to whose conduct to commit them, than to thine: Receive them therefore in my name, and as need shall require make use of them against* Shaddai *and his men. Farewell.* So they came and he received them, and he made of two of them Serjeants, but he made Mr. *Mans invention*, his *Ancient*-Bearer. But thus much for this, and now to return to the Camp.

Anything receives them into his service.

They of the Camp did also some execution upon the Town, for they did beat down the roof of the old Lord Mayors house, and so laid him more open than he was before. They had almost (with a sling) slain My Lord *Willbewill* outright: But he made a shift to recover again. But they made a notable

The Roof of old *Incredulities* house beat down.

slaughter among the *Aldermen*, for with one only shot they cut off six of them: To wit, Mr. *Swearing*, Mr. *Whoring*, Mr. *Fury*, Mr. *Stand-to lies*, Mr. *Drunkenness*, and Mr. *Cheating*.

Six Aldermen slain.

They also dismounted the two Guns that stood upon the Tower over *Eargate*, and laid them flat in the dirt. I told you before that the Kings noble Captains had drawn off to their Winter Quarters, and had there intrenched themselves and their carriages, so as with the best advantage to their King, and the greatest annoyance to the enemy, they might give seasonable and warm alarms to the Town of *Mansoul*. And this design of them did so hit, that I may say they did almost what they would to the molestation of the Corporation.

The two great Guns dismounted.

For now could not *Mansoul* sleep securely as before, nor could they now go to their debaucheries with that quietness as in times past. For they had from the Camp of *Shaddai* such frequent, warm, and terrifying alarms; yea, alarms upon alarms, first at one Gate and then at another, and again, at all the Gates at once, that they were broken as to former peace. Yea, they had their alarms so frequently, and that when the nights were at longest, the weather coldest, and so consequently the *season* most *unseasonable*; that that Winter was to the Town of *Mansoul* a Winter by it self. Sometimes the Trumpets would sound, and sometimes the slings would *whorle* the stones into the Town. Sometimes ten thousand of the Kings Souldiers would be running round the Walls of *Mansoul* at midnight, shouting and lifting up the voice for the battel. Sometimes again, some of them in the Town would be wounded, and their cry and lamentable voice would be heard, to the great molestation of the now languishing Town of *Mansoul*. Yea so distressed, with those that laid siege against them, were they, that I dare say, *Diabolus* their King had in these days his rest much broken.

Continual alarms given to *Mansoul*.

The effects of convictions though common if abiding.

The Town much molested.

In these days, as I was informed, new thoughts, and thoughts that began to run counter one to another, began to possess the minds of the men of the Town of *Mansoul*. Some would say, *there is no living thus*: others would then reply, *this will be over shortly*: then would a third stand up and answer, *let us turn to*

Change of thoughts in *Mansoul*.

the King Shaddai, and so put an end to these troubles: And a fourth would come in with a fear saying, *I doubt he will not receive us.* The old Gentleman too, the Recorder, that was so before *Diabolus* took *Mansoul*; he also began to talk aloud, and his words were now to the Town of *Mansoul*, as if they were *great claps of thunder*. No noise now, so terrible to *Mansoul*, as was his, with the noise of the Souldiers and shoutings of the Captains.

Conscience speaks.

A famin in *Mansoul*. Luk. 15. 14, 15.

Also things began to grow scarce in *Mansoul*; now the things that her soul lusted after, were departing from her. Upon all her pleasant things there was a blast, and burning in stead of beauty. Wrinkles now, and some shews of the shadow of death, were upon the inhabitants of *Mansoul*. And now, O how glad would *Mansoul* have been to have injoyed quietness, and satisfaction of mind, though joyned with the meanest condition in the world!

They are summoned again to yield.

The Captains also, in the deep of this Winter, did send by the mouth of *Boanerges* Trumpeter, a summons to *Mansoul* to yield up her self to the King, the great King *Shaddai*. They sent it once, and twice, and thrice: Not knowing but that at some times there might be in *Mansoul* some willingness to surrender up themselves unto them, might they but have the colour of an invitation to do it under. Yea, so far as I could gather, the Town had been surrendred up to them before now, had it not been for the opposition of old *Incredulity*, and the *Fickleness* of the thoughts of My Lord *Willbewills*. *Diabolus* also began to rave, wherefore *Mansoul* as to yielding was not yet all of one mind, therefore they still lay distressed under these perplexing fears.

Mansoul in distress.

I told you but now that they of the Kings Army had this Winter sent three times to *Mansoul*, to submit her self.

The contents of the first summons.

The First time the Trumpeter went, he went with words of peace, telling of them, *that the Captains, the Noble Captains of* Shaddai, *did pity and bewail the misery of the now perishing Town of* Mansoul*; and was troubled to see them so much to stand in the way of their own deliverance. He said moreover, that the Captains bid him tell them, that if now poor* Mansoul *would humble her self, and turn,* *her former Rebellions, and most notorious treasons shonld by their merciful King be forgiven them, yea and forgotten too. And having bid them beware that they stood not in their own way, that they opposed not themselves, nor made themselves their own losers; He returned again into the Camp.*

Secondly, the second time the Trumpeter went, he did treat them a little more roughly. For after sound of Trumpet he told them, *That their continuing in their Rebellion did but chafe, and heat the spirit of the Captains, and that they were resolved to make a Conquest of* Mansoul, *or to lay their bones before the Town Walls.*

The contents of the second summons.

Thirdly, He went again the third time, and dealt with them yet more roughly; telling of them, *That now, since they had been so horribly prophane, he did not know, not certainly know, whether the Captains were inclining to mercy or judgment; only, said he, they commanded me to give you a summons to open the Gates unto them: So he returned, and went into the Camp.*

The contents of the third summons.

These three summons, and especialy the two last, did so distress the Town, that they presently call a consultation, the result of which was this, That My Lord *Willbewill* should go up to *Eargate*, and there with sound of Trumpet, call to the Captains of the Camp for a parly. Well, the Lord *Willbewill* sounded upon the Wall, so the Captains came up in their Harness with their ten thousands at their feet. The Townsmen then told the Captains, that they had heard and considered their summons, and would come to an agreement with them, and with their King *Shaddai*, upon such certain Terms, Articles, and Propositions as, *with* and *by* the order of their Prince, they to them, were appointed to propound. To wit, they would agree upon these grounds to be one people with them.

The Town sounds for a parly.

They propound conditions of agreement.

1. *If that those of their own company, as the now Lord Mayor, and their Mr.* Forgetgood, *with their brave Lord* Willbewill, *might under* Shaddai *be still the Governours of the Town, Castle, and Gates of* Mansoul.

Proposition the first.

2. *Provided that no man that now serveth under their great Gyant* Diabolus, *be by* Shaddai *cast out of house, harbor, or the freedom that he hath hitherto enjoyed in the famous Town of* Mansoul.

Proposition the second.

Proposition the third.

3. *That it shall be granted them, that they of the Town of* Mansoul *shall enjoy certain of their Rights, and priviledges: To wit, such as have formerly been granted them; and that they have long lived in the enjoyment of, under the Reign of their King* Diabolus, *that now is and long has been their only Lord, and great defender.*

Proposition the fourth.

4. *That no new Law, Officer, or Executioner of Law or Office, shall have any power over them, without their own choice and consent.*

These be our Propositions, or conditions of peace: And upon these terms, said they, we will submit to your King.

But when the Captains had heard this weak and feeble offer of the Town of *Mansoul*, and their high and bold demands: they made to them again by their noble Captain, the Captain *Boanerges*, this speech following.

Boanerges his answer.

'O ye inhabitants of the Town of *Mansoul*, when I heard your Trumpet sound for a Parley with us, I can truly say, I was glad; but when you said you were willing to submit your selves to our King and Lord, then I was yet more glad: But when by your silly provisoes, and foolish cavils, you lay the stumbling block of your inquity before your own faces; then was my gladness turned into sorrows, and my hopeful beginnings of your return, into languishing, fainting fears.

'I count, that old *Illpause*, the ancient enemy of *Mansoul*, did draw up those proposals that now you present us with, as terms of an agreement, but they deserve not to be admitted to sound in the ear of any man that pretends to have service for *Shaddai*. We do therefore joyntly, and that with the highest disdain, refuse, and reject such things as the greatest of iniquities.

2 Tim. 2. 19.

'But O *Mansoul*, if you will give your selves into our hands, or rather into the hands of our King; and will trust him to make such terms with, and for you, as shall seem good in his eyes, (and I dare say they shall be such as you shall find to be most profitable to you) then we will receive you, and be at peace with you: But if you like not to trust your selves in the arms of *Shaddai* our King, then things are but where they were before, and we know also what we have to do.'

Old *Incredulity's* reply.

Then cryed out old *Incredulity* the Lord Mayor, and said, And who, being out of the hands of their Enemies, as ye see we are now, will be so foolish as to put the staff out of their own hands, into the hand of they know not who? I for my part will never yield to so unlimited a proposition. Do we know the manner and temper of their King? 'Tis said by some, that he will be angry with his Subjects, if but the breadth of an hair they chance to step out of the way: And of others, that he requireth of them much more than they can perform. Wherefore it seems O *Mansoul*, to be thy wisdom, to take good heed what thou dost in this matter. For if you once yield, you give up your selves to another, and so you are no more your own. Wherefore to give up your selves to an unlimited power, is the greatest folly in the world. For now you indeed may repent; but can never justly complain. But do you indeed know, when you are his, which of you he will kill, and which of you he will save alive? Or whether he will not cut off every one of us, and send out of his own country another new people, and cause them to inhabit this Town.

Unbelief never is profitable in talk, but always speaks *mischievously*.

This speech of the Lord Mayor, *undid all*, and threw flat to the ground their hopes of an accord: Wherefore the Captains returned to their Trenches, to their Tents, and to their Men, as they were: and the *Mayor* to the *Castle*, and to his *King*.

This speech undid all but it did please the Devil.

Now *Diabolus* had waited for his return, for he had heard that they had been at their points. So when he was come into the Chamber of State, *Diabolus* saluted him, with, *Welcome My Lord: How went matters betwixt you to day?* So the Lord *Incredulity* (with a low congy) told him the whole of the matter, saying, Thus and thus, said the Captains of *Shaddai*, and thus and thus said I. The which when 'twas told to *Diabolus*, he was very glad to hear it, and said, *My Lord Mayor, my faithful* Incredulity, *I have proved thy fidelity above ten times already, but never yet found thee false. I do promise thee, if we rub over this brunt, to prefer thee to a place of honour, a place far better than to be Lord Mayor of* Mansoul. *I will make thee my Universal Deputy, and thou shalt, next to me, have all Nations under thy hand; yea, and thou shalt lay bands upon them that they may not resist thee, not shall any of our Vassals walk more at liberty, but those that shall be content to walk in thy Fetters.*

Now came the Lord *Mayor* out from *Diabolus*, as if he had obtained a favour indeed; wherefore to his habitation he goes in great state, and thinks to feed himself well enough with hopes, until the time came that his greatness should be enlarged.

The Understanding and Conscience begin to receive conviction, and they set the soul in a hubbub.

But now, though the Lord Mayor and *Diabolus* did thus well agree, yet this repulse to the brave Captains put *Mansoul* into a *Mutiny*. For while Old *Incredulity* went into the Castle to congratulate his Lord with what had passed, the Old Lord Mayor that was so before *Diabolus* came to the Town, to wit, My Lord *Understanding*, and the old Recorder Mr. *Conscience*, getting intelligence of what had passed at *Eargate* (for you must know that they might not be suffered to be at that debate, lest they should then have *mutinied* for the Captains; but, I say, they got intelligence what had passed there, and were much concerned therewith) wherefore they, getting some of the Town together, *began to possess them with the reasonableness of the noble Captains demands, and with the bad consequences that would follow upon the speech of old* Incredulity, *the Lord Mayor*: To wit, how little reverence he shewed therein, either to the Captains, or to their King; also how he implicitly charged them with unfaithfulness; and treachery: For what less, quoth they, could be made of his words, when he said he would not yield to their proposition; and added moreover a supposition, that he would destroy us, when before, he had sent us word that he would shew us mercy. The multitude being now possessed with the conviction of the evil that old *Incredulity* had done, began to run together by companies in all places, and in every corner of the Streets of *Mansoul*, and first they began to mutter, then to talk openly, and after that they run to and fro, and cried as they run, *O the brave Captains of* Shaddai! *Would we were under the Government of the Captains, and of* Shaddai *their King*. When the Lord Mayor had intelligence that *Mansoul* was in an uproar, down he comes to appease the people, and thought to have

A mutiny in *Mansoul*.

15 *mutinied* for the Captains; but,] *mutinied*, for the Captains) But,

quashed their heat with the bigness and the shew of his countenance. But when they saw him, they came running upon him, and had doubtless done him a mischief, had he not betaken himself to house. However they strongly assaulted the house where he was, to have pulled it down about his ears; but the place was too strong, so they failed of that. So he taking some courage addressed himself, out at a Window, to the people in this manner.

Incredulity seeks to quiet the people. My Lord *Understanding* answers him.

Gentlemen, what is the reason, that there is here such an uproar to day?

Und. Then answered My Lord *Understanding*: It is even because that thou and thy Master have carried it not rightly, and as you should, to the Captains of *Shaddai*; for in three things you are faulty, First, in that you would not let Mr. *Conscience* and my self be at the hearing of your discourse. Secondly, In that you propounded such terms of peace, to the Captains, that by no means could be granted, unless they had intended that their *Shaddai*, should have been only a *Titular* Prince, and that *Mansoul* should still have had power by Law, to have lived in all lewdness and vanity before him, and so by consequence *Diabolus* should still here be King in power, and the other, only King in name. Thirdly, for that thou didst thy self, after the Captains had shewed us upon what conditions they would have received us to mercy, even undo all again with thy unsavory, and unseasonable, and ungodly speech.

Sin, and the Soul at odds.

Incred. When old *Incredulity* had heard this *Speech*, *He cried out*, *Treason*, *Treason. To your Arms*, *to your Arms*, *O ye*, *the trusty friends of* Diabolus *in* Mansoul.

Und. 'Sir, you may put upon my words, what meaning you please, but I am sure that the Captains of such an high Lord as theirs is, deserved a better treatment at your hands.'

They chide on both sides.

Incred. Then said old *Incredulity*, *This is but little better. But* Sir, *quoth he*, *what I spake*, *I spake for my Prince*, *for his Government*, *and the quieting of the people*, *whom by your unlawfull actions*, *you have this day set to mutiny against us.*

Cons. 'Then replyed the old Recorder, whose name was Mr. *Conscience*, and said, Sir, you ought not thus to retort upon what

My Lord *Understanding* hath said. 'Tis evident enough that he hath spoken the truth, and that you are an enemy to *Mansoul*, be convinced then of the evil of your saucy and malapert language, and of the grief that you have put the Captains to; yea, and of the damages that you have done to *Mansoul* thereby. Had you accepted of the conditions, the sound of the Trumpet, and the alarm of War had now ceased about the Town of *Mansoul*; but that dreadful sound abides, and your want of wisdom in your speech has been the cause of it.'

'*Incred.* Then said old *Incredulity*: Sir, if I live I will do your errand to *Diabolus*, and there you shall have an answer to your words. Mean while we will seek the good of the Town, and not ask Counsel of you.'

Understand. 'Sir, your Prince and you are both Foreigners to *Mansoul*, and not the Natives thereof. And who can tell but that when you have brought us into greater straits (when you also shall see that your selves can be safe by no other means than by flight) you may leave us and shift for your selves, or set us on fire, and go away in the smoak, or by the light of our burning, and so leave us in our ruins.

Incred. 'Sir, you forget that you are under a Governor, and that you ought to demean your self like a Subject, and know ye, when my Lord the King shall hear of this days work, he will give you but little thanks for your labour.'

Men of Arms come down.

Now while these Gentlemen were thus in their chiding words, down comes from the Walls and Gates of the Town, the Lord *Willbewill*, Mr. *Prejudice*, Old *Illpause*, and several of the new made *Aldermen* and *Burgesses*, and they asked the reason of the hubbub, and tumult. And with that every man began to tell his own tale, so that nothing could be heard distinctly: Then was a silence commanded, and the old Fox *Incredulity* began to speak; My Lord, quoth he, *here are a couple of peevish Gentlemen, that have, as a fruit of their bad dispositions, & as I fear, through the advice of one Mr.* Discontent, *tumultuously gathered this Company against me this day; and also atempted to run the Town into acts of Rebellion against our Prince.*

Then stood up all the *Diabolonians* that were present, and affirmed these things to be true.

A great confusion.

Now when they that took part with my Lord *Understanding*, and with Mr. *Conscience*, perceived that they were like to come to the worst, for that force and power was on the other side; they came in for their help and relief: so a great company was on both sides. Then they on *Incredulities* side, would have had the two old Gentlemen, presently away to prison; but they on the other side said they should not. Then they began to cry up parties again: The *Diabolonians* cried up old *Incredulity*, *Forgetgood*, the *new Aldermen*, and their great one *Diabolus*; and the other party, they as fast cried up *Shaddai*, the Captains, his Laws, their mercifulness, and applauded their conditions and ways. Thus the bickerment went a while, at last they passed from words to blows, and now there were knocks on both sides. The good old Gentleman, Mr. *Conscience* was knockt down twice by one of the *Diabolonians*, whose name was Mr. *Benumming*. And my Lord *Understanding* had like to have been slain with an *Harquebus*, but that he that shot wanted to take his aim aright. Nor did the other side wholly escape, for there was one Mr. *Rashhead*, a *Diabolonian*, that had his brains beaten out by Mr. *Mind*, the Lord *Willbewills* servant; and it made me laugh to see how old Mr. *Prejudice* was kickt and tumbled about in the dirt. For though a while since he was made Captain of a Company of the *Diabolonians*, to the hurt and damage of the Town; yet now they had got him under their feet; and I'll assure you he had by some of the Lord *Understandings* party, his crown soundly crackt to boot. Mr. *Anything* also, he became a brisk man in the broyle, but both sides were against him, because he was true to none. Yet he had for his malapertness, one of his legs broken, and he that did it, wisht it had been his neck. Much harm more was done on both sides, but this must not be forgotten; it was now a wonder to see My Lord *Willbewill* so indifferent as he was, he did not seem to take one side more than another, only it was perceived that he smiled to see how old *Prejudice* was tumbled up and down in the dirt. Also when Captain *Anything*

They fall from words to blows.

A hot Skirmish.

Harm done on both sides.

came halting up before him, he seemed to take but little notice of him.

The two old Gentlemen put in prison as the authors of this revel-rout.

Now when the uproar was over, *Diabolus* sends for My Lord *Understanding*, and Mr. *Conscience*, and claps them both up in prison as the ringleaders and managers of this most heavy riotous Rout in *Mansoul*. So now the Town began to be quiet again, and the prisoners were used hardly, yea, he thought to have made them away, but that the present juncture did not serve for that purpose: For that War was in all their Gates. But let us return again to our story: The Captains, when they were gone back from the Gate, and were come into the Camp again, called a Council of War, to consult what was further for them to do. Now some said, let us go up presently and fall upon the Town, but the greatest part thought, rather better 'twould be, to give them another summons to yield; and the reason why they thought this to be best, was, because, that so far as could be perceived, the Town of *Mansoul* now, was more inclinable than heretofore. And if, said they, while some of them are in a way of inclination, we should by ruggedness give them distast, we may set them further from closing with our summons, than we would be willing they should.

The Captains call a Council and consult what to do.

The result is, they send another Trumpeter, to summon the Town to yield.

Wherefore to this advice they agreed, and called a Trumpeter, put words into his mouth, set him his time, and bid him God speed. Well, many hours were not expired before the Trumpeter addressed himself to his journey. Wherefore coming up to the Wall of the Town, he steareth his course to *Eargate*; and there sounded, as he was commanded; They then that were within, came out to see what was the matter, and the Trumpeter made them this speech following.

The summons itself.

'O hard-harted, and deplorable Town of *Mansoul*, how long wilt thou love thy sinful, sinful simplicity, and ye fools delight in your scorning? As yet despise you the offers of peace, and deliverance? As yet will ye refuse the golden offers of *Shaddai*, and trust to the lies and falshoods of *Diabolus*? Think you when *Shaddai* shall have conquered you, that the remembrance of

33 your] their

these your carriages towards him, will yield you peace, and comfort: or that by ruffling language, you can make him afraid as a Grass-hopper? Doth he intreat you, for fear of you? Do you think that you are stronger than he? Look to the Heavens, and behold, and consider the Stars, how high are they? Can you stop the Sun from running his course, and hinder the Moon from giving her light? Can you count the numbers of the Stars, or stay the bottles of heaven? Can you call for the Waters of the Sea, and cause them to cover the face of the ground? Can you behold every one that is proud, and abase him? And bind their faces in secret? Yet these are some of the works of our King, in whose name, this day, we come up unto you: That you may be brought under his authority. In his name therefore I summon you again, to yield up your selves to his Captains.'

At this summons the *Mansoulians* seemed to be, at a stand, and knew not what answer to make: Wherefore *Diabolus* forthwith appeared, and took upon him to do it, himself, and thus he begins, but turns his speech to them of *Mansoul*.

The Town at a stand.

'Gentlemen, quoth he, and my faithful Subjects, if it is true that this Summoner hath said, concerning the greatness of their King, by his terror you will always be kept in bondage, and so be made to sneak. Yea, how can you now, though he is at a distance, indure to think of such a mighty one? And if not to think of him, while at a distance, how can you indure to be in his presence? I, your Prince, am familiar with you, and you may play with me, as you would with a Grass-hopper. Consider therefore, what is for your profit, and remember the immunities that I have granted you.

Diabolus makes a speech to the Town, and indeavours to terrifie it with the greatness of God.

'Farther, if all be true that this man hath said, how comes it to pass that the Subjects of *Shaddai*, are so inslaved in all places where they come? None in the *Universe* so unhappy as they, none so trampled upon as they.

'Consider, my *Mansoul*: would thou wert as loth to leave me, as I am loth to leave thee. But consider I say, the ball is yet at thy foot, liberty you have, if you know how to use it: Yea, a King you have too, if you can tell how to love and obey him.'

He drives *Mansoul* into despair.

Upon this speech, the Town of *Mansoul* did again harden their hearts, yet more, against the Captains of *Shaddai*. The thoughts of his greatness, did quite quash them, and the thoughts of his holiness, sunk them in despair. Wherefore after a short consult they (of the *Diabolonian* party they were) sent back this word by the Trumpeter, *That for their parts, they were resolved to stick to their King, but never to yield to* Shaddai: So it was but in vain to give them any further summons, for they had rather die upon the place than yield. And now things seemed to be gone quite back, and *Mansoul* to be out of *reach* or *call*; yet the Captains who knew what their Lord could do, would not yet be beat out of heart: they therefore send them another summons, more sharp and severe than the last, but the oftener they were sent to, to reconcile to *Shaddai*, the further off they were. *As they called them, so they went from them*, yea though they called them to the most high.

Mansoul grows worse and worse.

Hos. 11. 2.

The Captains leave off to summons and betake themselves to prayer.

So they ceased that way to deal with them any more, and inclined to think of another way. The Captains therefore did gather themselves together, to have free conference among themselves, to know what was yet to be done to gain the Town, and to deliver it from the Tyranny of *Diabolus*: And one said after this manner, and another after that. Then stood up the right noble, the Captain *Conviction*, and said my Brethren, mine opinion is this:

'*First*, That we continually play our slings into the Town, and keep it in a continual alarm, molesting of them day and night; by thus doing we shall stop the growth of their rampant spirit. For a Lion may be tamed, by continual molestation.

Secondly, 'This done, I advise that in the next place we with one consent draw up a Petition to our Lord *Shaddai*, by which, after we have shewed our King the condition of *Mansoul*, and of affairs here, and have begged his pardon for our no better success; we will earnestly implore his Majesties help, and that he will please to send us more force and power, and some gallant and well spoken Commander to head them, that so his Majesty may not lose the benefit of these his good beginnings, but may compleat his conquest upon the Town of *Mansoul*.'

To this Speech of the Noble Captain *Conviction*, they, as one man, consented, and agreed that a Petition should forthwith be drawn up, and sent by a fit man, away to *Shaddai* with speed. The contents of the Petition were thus.

'Most gracious, and glorious King, the Lord of the best world, and the builder of the Town of *Mansoul*. We have, dread Soveraign, at thy commandment, put our lives in Jeopardy, and at thy bidding made a War, upon the famous Town of *Mansoul*. When we went up against it, we did according to our Commission, first offer conditions of peace unto it. But they, Great King, set light by our Counsel, and would none of our reproof: They were for shutting of their Gates, and for keeping us out of the Town. They also mounted their Guns, they sallied out upon us, and have done us what damage they could, but we pursued them, with alarm, upon alarm, requiting of them with such retribution as was meet, and have done some execution upon the Town.

Mat. 22. 5. Prov. 1. Zech. 7. 10, 11, 12, 13.

'*Diabolus*, *Incredulity*, and *Willbewill*, are the great doers against us; now we are in our Winter quarters, but so as that we do yet with an high hand molest, and distress the Town.

'Once, as we think, had we had but one substantial friend in the Town, such as would but have seconded the sound of our summons, as they ought, the people might have yielded themselves: But there were none but Enemies there, nor any to speak in behalf of our Lord, to the Town: Wherefore though we have done as we could, yet *Mansoul* abides in a state of rebellion against thee.

'Now King of Kings, let it please thee to pardon the unsuccessfulness of thy servants, who have been no more advantageous in so desirable a work, as the conquering of *Mansoul* is: And send, Lord, as we now desire more forces to *Mansoul*, that it may be subdued; and a man to head them, that the Town may both love and fear.

'We do not thus speak, because we are willing to relinquish the Wars (for we are for laying of our bones against the place) but that the Town of *Mansoul* may be won for thy Majesty. We also pray thy Majesty, for expedition in this matter, that, after their conquest, we may be at liberty, to be sent about other thy gracious designs. *Amen.*'

Who carried this Petition.

The petition thus drawn up, was sent away with hast to the King, by the hand of that good man, Mr. *Love* to *Mansoul.*

To whom it was delivered.

When this Petition was come to the Palace of the King, who should it be delivered to, but to the Kings Son. So he took it and read it, and because the Contents of it pleased him well, he mended, and also in some things, added to the Petition himself. So after he had made such amendments, and additions as he thought convenient, with his own hand, he carried it in to the King: To whom when he had with obeysance delivered it, he put on authority, and spake to it himself.

The King receives it with gladness.

Now the King, at the sight of the Petition, was glad; but how much more think you, when it was seconded by his Son. It pleased him also to hear that his servants that camped against *Mansoul*, were so hearty in the work, and so stedfast in their resolves, and that they had already got some ground upon the famous Town of *Mansoul.*

The King calls his Son, and tells him that he shall go to conquer the Town of *Mansoul*, and he is pleased at it.

Wherefore the King called to him *Emanuel* his Son, who said here am I, my Father. Then said the King, thou knowest, as I do my self, the condition of the Town of *Mansoul*, and what we have purposed, and what thou hast done to redeem it. Come now therefore my Son, and prepare thy self for the War, for thou shalt go to my Camp at *Mansoul.* Thou shalt also there prosper, and prevail, and conquer the Town of *Mansoul.*

Heb. 10. He sollaceth himself in the thoughts of this work.

Then said the Kings Son: Thy Law is within my heart. I delight to do thy will. This is the day that I have longed for, and the work that I have waited for all this while. Grant me therefore what force thou shalt in thy wisdom think meet, and I will go, and will deliver from *Diabolus*, and from his power thy perishing Town of *Mansoul.* My heart has been often pained within me, for the miserable Town of *Mansoul.* But now 'tis rejoyced, but now 'tis glad; and with that he leaped over the Mountains for joy, saying:

I have not, in my heart, thought any thing too dear for *Mansoul*, the day of vengance is in mine heart, for thee my

Mansoul, and glad am I, that thou my Father, hast made me the Captain of their Salvation: And I will now begin to plague all those that have been a plague to my Town of *Mansoul*, and will deliver it from their hand.

Heb. 2. 10.

When the Kings Son had said thus to his Father, it presently flew like lightning round about at Court: Yea, it there became the only talk, what *Emanuel* was to go to do for the famous Town of *Mansoul*. But you cannot think how the Courtiers too, were taken with this design of the Prince. Yea, so affected were they with this work, and with the justness of the War, that the highest Lord, and greatest Peer of the Kingdom did covet to have Commissions under *Emanuel*, to go to help to recover again to *Shaddai*, the miserable Town of *Mansoul*.

The highest Peer in the Kingdom covets to go on this design.

Then was it concluded that some should go and carry tidings to the Camp, that *Emanuel* was to come to recover *Mansoul*, and that he would bring along with him so mighty, so impregnable a force that he could not be resisted. But oh, how ready were the high ones at Court, to run like Lacquies to carry these tidings to the Camp, that was at *Mansoul*. Now when the Captains perceived that the King would send *Emanuel* his Son, and that it also delighted the Son to be sent on this errand by the great *Shaddai* his Father: They also to shew, how they were pleased at the thoughts of his coming, gave a shout that made the Earth rent, at the sound thereof. Yea, the Mountains did answer again by Echo, and *Diabolus* himself did totter and shake.

The Camp shouts for joy when they hear the tidings.

For you must know, that though the Town of *Mansoul* it self, was not much, if at all, concerned with the project (for, alas for them, they were wofully besotted, for they chiefly regarded their pleasure and their lusts:) Yet *Diabolus* their Governour was, For he had his spies continually abroad, who brought him intelligence of all things, and they told him what was doing at Court against him, and that *Emanuel* would shortly certainly come with a power to invade him. Nor was there any man at Court, nor Peer of the Kingdom, that *Diabolus* so feared, as he feared this Prince. For if you

Diabolus afraid at the News of his coming.

remember, I shewed you before that *Diabolus* had felt the weight of his hand already. So that, since it was he that was to come, this made him the more afraid. Well, you see how I have told you that the Kings Son was ingaged to come from the Court to save *Mansoul*, and that his father had made him the Captain of the forces: The time therefore of his setting forth, being now expired, he addressed himself for his march, and taketh with him for his power, five Noble Captains and their forces.

The Prince addresses himself for his Journey.

Joh. 1. 29. Eph. 6. 16.

1. The first was that famous Captain, the Noble Captain *Credence*, his were the Red colours; and Mr. *Promise* bare them: and for a Scutcheon, he had the *Holy Lamb*, and *Golden Shield*. And he had ten thousand men at his feet.

Heb. 6. 19.

2. The second was that famous Captain, the Captain *Good-hope*, his were the Blue Colours: His Standard Bearer was Mr. *Expectation*; and for a Scutcheon he had the *Three Golden Anchors*. And he had ten thousand men at his feet.

1 Cor. 13.

3. The third Captain was that Valiant Captain, the Captain *Charity*: His Standard Bearer was Mr. *Pitiful*, his were the Green Colours; and for his Scutcheon, he had three *naked Orphans imbraced in the bosom*. And he had ten thousand men at his feet.

Mat. 10. 16.

4. The fourth was that Gallant Commander, the Captain *Innocent*: His Standard Bearer was Mr. *Harmless*; his were the White Colours, and for his Scutcheon, he had *the three Golden Doves*.

5. The fifth was the truly Loyal, and well beloved Captain, the Captain *Patience*: His Standard Bearer was Mr. *Suffer long*, his were the Black Colours; and for a Scutcheon, he had *three Arrows through the Golden Heart*.

Faith and Patience do the work. Heb. 6. 12.

These were *Emanuels* Captains, these their Standard Bearers, their Colours, and their Scutcheons, and these the men under their command. So as was said, the brave Prince took his march, to go to the Town of *Mansoul*. Captain *Credence* led the Van, and Captain *Patience* brought up the Rere. So the other three with their men made up the main

16 *Expectation*] *Exectation*

body. The Prince himself riding in his Chariot at the head of them.

But when they set out for their march, Oh how the Trumpets sounded; their Armor glittered, and how the Colours waved in the wind. The Princes Armor was all of Gold, and it shone like the Sun in the Firmament. The Captains Armor was of proof and was in appearance like the glittering Stars.

Their march.

There were also some from the Court that rode Reformades, for the love that they had to the King *Shaddai*, and for the happy deliverance of the Town of *Mansoul*.

Emanuel also when he had thus set forwards to go to recover the Town of *Mansoul*; took with him at the Commandment of his Father, forty four Battering Rams, and twelve slings, to whirle stones withal. Every one of these was made of pure Gold, and these they carried with them in the heart and body of their Army, all along as they went to *Mansoul*.

The holy Bible containing 66 Books.

So they marched till they came within less than a League of the Town: And there they lay till the first four Captains came thither, to acquaint him with matters. Then they took their Journey, to go to the Town of *Mansoul*, and unto *Mansoul* they came, but when the old Souldiers that were in the Camp saw that they had new forces to joyn with, they again gave such a shout before the Walls of the Town of *Mansoul* that it put *Diabolus* into another fright. So they sat down before the Town, not now as the other four Captains did, to wit, against the *Gates* of *Mansoul only*: but they invironed it round on every side; and beset it behind and before, so that now let *Mansoul* look which way it will, it saw force and power lie in Siege against it. Besides, there were mounts cast up against it.

The forces joyned with rejoycing.

***Mansoul* beleaguered round.**

The mount *Gracious* was on the one side, and Mount *Justice* was on the other. Farther, there were several small banks and advance ground, as *Plain truth-hill*, and *No sin-banks*, where many of the *Slings* were placed against the Town. Upon Mount *Gracious* were planted four, and upon Mount *Justice* were placed as many: and the rest were conveniently placed in several parts round about the Town. Five of the best *Battering*

Mounts cast up against it.

Rams, that is of the biggest of them, were placed upon Mount *Harken*, a Mount cast up hard by *Eargate* with intent to break that open.

Now when the men of the Town saw the multitude of the *Souldiers* that were come up against the place, and the *Rams* and *Slings*, and the *Mounts* on which they were planted; together with the *glittering* of the Armour and the waving of their Colours: they were forced to shift, and shift, and again to shift their thoughts; but they hardly changed for thoughts more stout, but rather for thoughts more faint. For though before, they thought themselves sufficiently guarded; yet now they began to think that no man knew what would be their *hap* or *lot*.

The heart of *Mansoul* begins to fail.

The *White Flag* hung out.

When the good Prince *Emanuel* had thus beleaguered *Mansoul*: In the first place he hangs out the *White Flag*, which he caused to be set up among the Golden slings that were planted upon *Mount Gracious*. And this he did for two reasons: 1. To give notice to *Mansoul* that he could and would yet be gracious if they turned to him. 2. And that he might leave them the more without excuse, should he destroy them, they continuing in their rebellion.

So the *White Flag*, with the three Golden *Doves* in it, was hanged out for two days together, to give them time, and space to consider. But they, as was hinted before, as if they were unconcerned, made no reply to the favourable Signal of the Prince.

The Red Flag hung out.

Then he commanded, and they set the *Red Flag*, upon that Mount called *Mount Justice*. 'Twas the *Red Flag* of Captain *Judgment*, whose Scutcheon was the *Burning Fiery Furnace*. And this also stood waving before them in the wind, for several days together. But look, how they carried it under the White Flag, when that was hanged out, so did they also when the Red one was: And yet he took no advantage of them.

The Black Flag hung out.

Then he commanded again that his servants would hang out the *Black Flag* of defiance against them, whose Scutcheon was the *three burning Thunder-bolts*. But as unconcerned was *Mansoul* at this, as at those that went before. But when the

Prince saw that neither mercy nor Judgment, nor execution of Judgment, would, or could come near the heart of *Mansoul*: He was touched with much compunction, and said surely this strange carriage of the Town of *Mansoul*, doth rather arise from ignorance of the manner, and feats of War; than from a secret defiance of us, and abhorrence of their own lives. Or if they know the manner of the War of their own; yet not the Rites and Ceremonies of the Wars in which we are concerned, when I make Wars upon mine enemy *Diabolus*.

Christ makes not War as the World does.

Therefore he sent to the Town of *Mansoul*, to let them know what he meant by those signs, and Ceremonies of the Flag, and also to know of them which of the things they will chuse, whether *Grace* and *Mercy*, or *Judgment*, and the *Execution* of judgment. All this while they kept their Gates shut with Locks, Bolts and Bars, as fast as they could. Their Guards also were doubled, and their Watch made as strong as they could. *Diabolus* also did pluck up what heart he could, to incourage the Town to make resistance.

He sends to know if they would have mercy or Justice.

The Towns-men also made answer to the Prince's messenger, in substance, according to that which follows.

Great Sir, *As to what, by your messenger you have signified to us, Whether we will accept of your mercy, or fall by your Justice, we are bound by the Law and Customs of this place, and can give you no positive answer. For it is against the Law, Government, and the Prerogative Royal of our King, to make either Peace or War without him. But this we will do, we will petition that our Prince will come down to the Wall, and there give you such treatment as he shall think fit, and profitable for us.*

The Towns-folks answer.

When the good Prince *Emanuel* heard this answer, and saw the Slavery and Bondage of the people, and how much content they were to abide in the Chains of the Tyrant *Diabolus*: It grieved him at the heart. And indeed, when at any time he perceived that any were contented under the Slavery of the Gyant, he would be affected with it.

Emanue grieved at the folly of *Mansoul*.

But to return again to our purpose. After the Town had carried this News to *Diabolus*, and had told him moreover,

14 their] there

that the Prince that lay in the Leaguer, without the Wall, waited upon them for an answer: He refused, and huffed as well as he could, but in heart he was afraid.

Diabolus afraid.

Then said he, I will go down to the Gates my self, and give him such an answer as I think fit. So he went down to *Mouth-gate*, and there addressed himself to speak to *Emanuel* (but in such language as the Town understood not) the Contents whereof were as follow.

His speech to the Prince.

O thou great Emanuel, *Lord of all the world, I know thee, that thou art the Son of the great* Shaddai! *Wherefore art thou come to torment me, and to cast me out of my possession? This Town of* Mansoul, *as thou very well knowest, is mine, and that by a twofold Right.* 1. *It is mine by right of Conquest, I won it in the open field. And shall the prey be taken from the mighty, or the lawful Captive, be delivered?* 2. *This Town of* Mansoul *is mine also by their subjection. They have opened the Gates of their Town unto me. They have sworn fidelity to me, and have openly chosen me to be their King. They have also given their Castle into my hands; yea, they have put the whole strength of* Mansoul *under me.*

Heart.

Moreover, this Town of Mansoul *hath disavowed thee: Yea, they have cast thy Law, thy name, thy image and all that is thine, behind their back: And have accepted, and set up in their room my Law, my name, mine image and all that ever is mine. Ask else thy Captains, and they will tell thee, that* Mansoul *hath, in answer to all their summons, shown Love, and Loyalty to me; but always disdain, despite, contempt, and scorn to thee, and thine: now thou art the just one, and the holy (and shouldest do no iniquity) depart then, I pray thee therefore from me, and leave me to my just inheritance, peacably.*

This Oration was made in the Language of *Diabolus* himself. For although he can, to every man, speak in their own language (else he could not tempt them all as he does) yet he has a language, proper to himself, and it is the language of the infernal cave, or black pit.

Wherefore the Town of *Mansoul* (poor hearts) understood him not, nor did they see how he crouched, and cringed, while he stood before *Emanuel* their Prince.

Yea, they all this while took him to be one of that power

and force that by no means could be resisted. Wherefore while he was thus intreating that he might have yet his residence there, and that *Emanuel* would not take it from him by force: The inhabitants boasted even of his valour, saying, *Who is able to make War with him.*

Well, when this pretended King, had made an end of what he would say: *Emanuel*, the Golden Prince stood up and spake: the Contents of whose words follow.

'Thou deceiving one, *said he*, I have in my Fathers name, in mine own name, and on the behalf, and for the good of this wretched Town of *Mansoul*, somwhat to say unto thee. Thou pretendest a right, a lawful right to the deplorable Town of *Mansoul*, when it is most apparent to all my Fathers Court, that the entrance which thou hast obtained in at the gates of *Mansoul*, was through thy lie & false-hood, Thou beliedst my Father, thou beliedst his Law, and so deceivedst the people of *Mansoul*. Thou pretendest that the people have accepted thee for their King, their Captain, and right Liege-Lord, but that also was by the exercise of deceit, and guile. Now if lying, wiliness, sinful craft and all manner of horrible hypocrisie, will go, in my Fathers Court (in which Court thou must be tryed) for equity and right, then will I confess unto thee that thou hast made a lawful conquest. But alas! What Thief what Tyrant, what Devil is there that may not conquer after this sort: But I can make it appear O *Diabolus*, that thou in all thy pretences to a conquest of *Mansoul*, hast nothing of truth to say. Thinkest thou this to be right, that thou didst put the ly upon my Father and madest him (to *Mansoul*) the greatest deluder in the world. And what saiest thou to thy perverting, knowingly, the right purport and intent of the Law? Was it good also that thou madest a prey of the innocency, and simplicity of the now miserable Town of *Mansoul*? Yea, thou didst overcome *Mansoul* by promising to them happiness in their transgressions, against my Fathers Law, when thou knewest, and couldest not but know, hadst thou consulted nothing but thine own experience, that that was the way to undo them. Thou hast also thy self (O! Thou Master of enmity) of spite, defaced my Fathers image in *Mansoul*, and set up thy own in its place; to the great contempt of my Father, the heightening of thy sin, and to the intolerable damage of the perishing Town of *Mansoul*.

'Thou hast moreover, (as if all these were but little things with thee) not only deluded & undone this place; but by thy lies, and fraudulent carriage hast set them against their own deliverance. How hast thou stired them up against my Fathers Captains, and made them to fight against those that were sent of him to deliver them from their bondage? All these things and very many more thou hast done against thy light, and in contempt of my Father, and of his Law: Yea, and with design to bring under his displeasure for ever, the miserable Town of *Mansoul*. I am therefore come to avenge the wrong that thou hast done to my Father, and to deal with thee for the Blasphemies, wherewith thou hast made poor *Mansoul* Blaspheme his name. Yea upon thy head, thou Prince of the infernal Cave, will I requite it.

'As for my self, O *Diabolus*, I am come against thee by lawful power, and to take by strength of hand, this Town of *Mansoul* out of thy burning fingers. For this Town of *Mansoul* is mine, O *Diabolus*, and that by undoubted right, as all shall see that will diligently search the most ancient, and most authentick Records, and I will plead my title to it, to the confusion of thy face.

'First, for the Town of *Mansoul*, my Father built and did fashion it with his hand. The Palace also that is in the midst of that Town, he built it for his own delight. This Town of *Mansoul* therefore is my Fathers, and that by the best of titles: And he that gainsays the truth of this, must lie against his soul.

'Secondly, O thou Master of the lie, this Town of *Mansoul* is mine.

Heb. 1. 2. Joh. 16. 15.

'1. For that I am my Fathers heir, his first born, and the only delight of his heart. I am therefore come up against thee in mine own right, even to recover mine own inheritance out of thine hand.

2. 'But further, as I have a right and title to *Mansoul*, by being my Fathers heir, so I have also by my Fathers donation. His it was, and he gave it me; nor have I at any time offended my Father that he should take it from me and give it to thee. Nor have I been forced by playing the Bankrupt to sell, or set to sale to thee, my beloved Town of *Mansoul*. *Mansoul* is my desire, my delight, and the joy of my heart. But,

Joh. 17.

Isa. 50. 1

3. '*Mansoul* is mine by right of purchase. I have bought it (O *Diabolus*) I have bought it to my self. Now since it was my Fathers and mine, as I was his heir, and since also I have made it mine by vertue of a great purchase, it followeth, that by all lawful right the Town of *Mansoul* is mine, and that thou art an Usurper, a Tyrant & Traytor in thy holding possession thereof. Now the cause of my purchasing of it was this: *Mansoul* had trespassed against my Father, now my Father had said, That in the day that they broke his Law, they should die. Now it is more possible for Heaven and earth to pass away, than for my Father to break his word. Wherefore when *Mansoul* had sinned indeed by harkening to thy lye, I put in and became a surety to my Father, body for body, and soul for soul, that I would make amends for *Mansoul*'s transgressions; and my Father did accept thereof. So when the time appointed was come, I gave body for body, soul for soul, life for life, blood for blood, and so redeemed my beloved *Mansoul*.

Mat. 5. 18.

O sweet Prince Emanuel!

4. 'Nor did I do this to the halves, my Fathers Law and Justice that were both concerned in the threatning upon transgression, are both now satisfied, and very well content that *Mansoul* should be delivered.

5. 'Nor am I come out this day against thee, but by commandment of my Father, 'twas he that said unto me, Go down and deliver *Mansoul*.

'Wherefore be it known unto thee (O thou fountain of deceit) and be it also known to the foolish Town of *Mansoul*, that I am not come against thee this day without my Father.

'And now (said the Golden-headed Prince) 'I have a word to the Town of *Mansoul* (but so soon as mention was made that he had a word to speak to the besotted Town of *Mansoul*, the Gates were double guarded, and all men *commanded* not to give him audience) so he proceeded, and said, 'O unhappy Town of *Mansoul*, I cannot but be touched with pity and compassion for thee. Thou hast accepted of *Diabolus* for thy King, and art become a nurse and minister of *Diabolonians* against thy Soveraign Lord. Thy Gates thou hast opened to him, but hast shut them fast against me; thou hast given him a hearing, but hast stopt thine ears at my cry; he brought to thee thy destruction, and thou didst receive both him and it: I am come to thee bringing Salvation, but thou regardest me not. Besides, thou hast as with Sacrilegious hands taken thy self with all that was mine in thee, and hast given all to my foe, and to the greatest enemy my Father has. You have bowed and subjected your selves to him, you have vowed and sworn your selves to be his. Poor *Mansoul*! what shall I do unto thee? shall I save thee, shall I destroy thee? What shall I do unto thee? shall I fall upon thee and grind thee to powder, or make thee a monument of the richest grace? What shall I do unto thee? Hearken therefore thou Town of *Mansoul*, hearken to my word, and thou shalt live. I am merciful, *Mansoul*, and thou shalt find me so: shut me not out at thy Gates.

Cant. 5. 2.

'O *Mansoul*, neither is my Commission nor inclination at all to do thee hurt; why flyest thou so fast from thy friend, and stickest so close to thine enemy? Indeed I would have thee, because it becomes thee, to be sorry for thy sin; but do not despair of life, this great force is not to hurt thee, but to deliver thee from thy bondage, and to reduce thee to thy obedience.

Joh. 12. 47.
Luk. 9. 56.

'My Commission indeed is to make a war upon *Diabolus* thy King, and upon all *Diabolonians* with him; for he is the strong man armed that keeps the house, and I will have him out; his spoils I must divide, his armour I must take from him, his hold I must cast him out of, and must make it an habitation for my self. And this, O *Mansoul*, shall *Diabolus* know, when he shall be made to follow me in chains, and when *Mansoul* shall rejoice to see it so.

'I could, would I now put forth my might, cause, that forthwith he should leave you and depart; but I have it in my heart so to deal with him, as that the justice of the war that I shall make upon him, may be seen and acknowledged by all. He hath taken *Mansoul* by fraud, & keeps it by violence and deceit, and I will make him bare and naked in the eyes of all observers.

'All my words are true, I am mighty to save, and will deliver my *Mansoul* out of his hand.' This speech was intended chiefly for *Mansoul*, but *Mansoul* would not have the hearing of it. They shut up *Ear-gate*, they barricado'd it up, they kept it lockt and boulted, they set a guard thereat, and commanded that no *Mansolonian* should go out to him, nor that any from the Camp should be admitted into the Town; all this they did, so horribly had *Diabolus* inchanted them to do, and seek to do for him, against their rightful Lord and Prince; wherefore no man, nor voice, nor sound of man that belonged to the glorious Host, was to come into the Town.

Emanuel prepares to make war upon *Mansoul*.

So when *Emanuel* saw that *Mansoul* was thus involved in sin, he calls his Army together (since now also his words were despised) and gave out a commandment throughout all his host to be ready against the time appointed. Now forasmuch as there was no way lawfully to take the Town of *Mansoul*, but to get in by the Gates, and at *Ear-gate* as the chief, therefore he commanded his Captains and Commanders to bring their *Rams*, their Slings, and their men, and place them at *Eye-gate* and *Ear-gate*, in order to his taking the Town.

Diabolus sends by the hand of his servant Mr. *Loth-to-stoop*, and by him he propounds conditions of peace.

When *Emanuel* had put all things in a readiness to bid *Diabolus* Battel, he sent again to know of the Town of *Mansoul*, if in peaceable manner they would yield themselves? or whether they were yet resolved to put him to try the utmost extremity? They then together with *Diabolus* their King called a Council of War, and resolved upon certain Propositions that should be offered to *Emanuel*, if he will accept thereof, so they agreed; and then the next was, who should be sent on this Errand. Now there was in the Town of *Mansoul* an old man a *Diabolonian*, and his name was Mr. *Loth-to-stoop*, a stiff man in his way, and a great doer for *Diabolus*; him therefore they sent, and put into his mouth what he should say. So he went and came to the Camp to *Emanuel*, and when he was come, a time was appointed to give him audience. So at the time he came, and after a *Diabolonian* Ceremony or two, he Tit. 1. 16. thus began and said, *Great Sir, that it may be known unto all men how good natured a Prince my master is, he hath sent me to tell your Lordship that he is very willing rather than to go to war, to deliver up* Mark this. *into your hands one half of the Town of* Mansoul. *I am therefore to know if your mightiness will accept of this Proposition.*

Then said *Emanuel*, the whole is mine by gift and purchase, wherefore I will never lose one half.

Mark this. Luk. 13. 25. Then said Mr. *Loth-to-stoop*, Sir, *my master hath said, that he will be content that you shall be the nominal and titular Lord of all, if he may possess but a part.*

Then *Emanuel* answered, The whole is mine really; not in name and word only: wherefore I will be the sole Lord and possessor of all, or of none at all of *Mansoul.*

Then Mr. *Loth-to-stoop* said again, *Sir, behold the condescension* Mark this. Act 5. 1, 2, 3, 4, 5. *of my master! He says that he will be content, if he may but have assigned to him some place in* Mansoul *as a place to live privately in, and you shall be Lord of all the rest.*

Then said the *Golden Prince*, All that the Father giveth me shall come to me; and of all that he hath given me I will lose nothing, no not a hoof, nor a hair. I will not therefore grant him, no not the least corner in *Mansoul* to dwell in, I will have all to my self.

Then *Loth-to-stoop* said again, *But, Sir, suppose that my Lord should resign the whole Town to you, only with this proviso, that he* Mark this. *sometimes when he comes into this Country, may for old acquaintance sake be entertained as a way-faring man for two days, or ten days, or a month, or so; may not this small matter be granted?*

2 Sam. 12. 1, 2, 3, 4, 5. Then said *Emanuel*, No. He came as a way-faring man to *David*, nor did he stay long with him, and yet it had like to have cost *David* his soul. I will not consent that he ever should have any harbour more there.

Then said Mr. *Loth-to-stoop*, Sir, *you seem to be very hard.*

Suppose my master should yield to all that your Lordship hath said, provided that his friends and kindred in Mansoul *may have liberty to trade in the Town, and to enjoy their present dwellings; may not that be granted, Sir?*

Sins and carna lusts.

Then said *Emanuel*, No; that is contrary to my Fathers will; for all, and all manner of *Diabolonians* that now are, or that at any time shall be found in *Mansoul*, shall not only lose their lands and liberties, but also their lives.

Rom. 6. 13. Col. 3. 5. Gal. 5. 24.

Then said Mr. *Loth-to-stoop* again, *But, Sir, may not my master, and great Lord, by Letters, by passengers, by accidental opportunities, and the like, maintain, if he shall deliver up all unto thee, some kind of old friendship with* Mansoul.

Mark this. Joh. 10. 8.

Emanuel answered, No, by no means; for as much as any such fellowship, friendship, intimacy or acquaintance in what way, sort or mode soever maintained, will tend to the corrupting of *Mansoul*, the alienating of their affections from me, and the endangering of their peace with my Father.

Mr. *Loth-to-stoop* yet added further, saying, *But great Sir, since my master hath many friends, and those that are dear to him in* Mansoul, *may he not, if he shall depart from them, even of his bounty and good nature, bestow upon them, as he sees fit, some tokens of his love and kindness, that he had for them, to the end that* Mansoul, *when he is gone, may look upon such tokens of kindness once received from their old friend, and remember him who was once their King, and the merry times that they sometimes enjoyed one with another, while he and they lived in peace together.*

Mark this. Rom. 6. 12, 13.

Then said *Emanuel*, No; for if *Mansoul* come to be mine, I shall not admit of, nor consent that there should be the least scrap, shred, or dust of *Diabolus* left behind, as tokens or gifts bestowed upon any in *Mansoul*, thereby to call to remembrance the horrible communion that was betwixt them and him.

Well Sir, said Mr. *Loth-to-stoop*, *I have one thing more to propound, and then I am got to the end of my commission: suppose that when my master is gone from* Mansoul, *any that yet shall live in the Town, should have such business of high concerns to do, that if they be neglected the party shall be undone; and suppose Sir, that no body can help in that case so well as my master and Lord; may not now my*

Mark this. 2 King. 1. 3, 6, 7.

master be sent for upon so urgent an occasion as this? or if he may not be admitted into the Town, may not he and the person concerned, meet in some of the Villages near Mansoul, *and there lay their heads together, and there consult of matters?*

This was the last of those ensnaring Propositions that Mr. *Loth-to-stoop* had to propound to *Emanuel* on behalf of his master *Diabolus*; but *Eman.* would not grant it, for he said, 1 Sam. 28. 15. There can be no case, or thing, or matter fall out in *Mansoul*, when thy master shall be gone, that may not be salved by my Father; besides, 'twill be a great disparagement to my Fathers 2 King. 1. 2, 3. wisdom and skill to admit any from *Mansoul* to go out to *Diabolus* for advice, when they are bid before, In every thing by prayer and supplication to let their requests be made known to my Father. Further this, should it be granted, would be to grant that a door should be set open for *Diabolus*, and the *Diabolonians* in *Mansoul* to hatch and plot and bring to pass treasonable designs to the grief of my Father and me, and to the utter destruction of *Mansoul*.

Lothtostoop departs.

When Mr. *Loth-to-stoop* had heard this answer, he took his leave of *Emanuel* and departed, saying, that he would do word to his master concerning this whole affair. So he departed and came to *Diabolus* to *Mansoul*, and told him the whole of the matter, and how *Emanuel* would not admit, no not by any means, that he when he was once gone out, should for ever have any thing more to do, either in, or with any that are of the Town of *Mansoul*. When *Mansoul*, and *Diabolus* had heard this relation of things, they with one consent concluded to use their best endeavour to keep *Emanuel* out of *Mansoul*, and sent old *Illpause*, of whom you have heard before, to tell the Prince and his Captains so. So the old Gentleman came up to the top of *Eargate*, and called to the Camp for a hearing: who when they gave audience he said, I have in commandment A speech of old *Illpause* to the Camp. from my high Lord to bid to tell it to your Prince *Emanuel*, *That* Mansoul *and their King are resolved to stand and fall together, and that it is in vain for your Prince to think of ever having of* Mansoul *in his hand, unless he can take it by force.* So some went and told to *Emanuel* what old *Illpause*, a *Diabolonian* in *Mansoul*, had said. Then said the Prince, I must try the power of my sword, for I will not (for all the rebellions and repulses that *Mansoul* has made against me) raise my siege and depart, but will assuredly take my *Mansoul* and deliver it from the hand of her enemy. And with that he gave out a commandment that Captain *Boanerges*, Captian *Conviction*, Captain *Judgment*, and Captain *Execution* should forthwith march up to *Eargate* with Trumpets sounding, Colours flying, and with shouting for the battel. Also he would that Captain *Credence* should join himself with them. *Emanuel* moreover gave order that Captain *Goodhope*, and Captain *Charity* should draw themselves up before *Eye-gate*. He bid also that the rest of his Captains and their men should place themselves for the best of their advantage against the enemy round about the Town, and all was done as he had commanded. Then he bid that the word should be given forth, and the word was at that time, *Emanuel*. Then was an alarm sounded, and the battering Rams were plaid, and the slings did whirl stones into the Town amain, and thus the battel began. Now *Diabolus* himself did manage the Townsmen in the war, and that at every gate; wherefore their resistance was the more forcible, hellish, and offensive to *Emanuel*. Thus was the good Prince engaged and entertained by *Diabolus* and *Mansoul* for several days together. And a sight worth seeing it was to behold how the Captains of *Shaddai* behaved themselves in this war.

Eph. 6. 17.

They must fight.

Preparations to the Battel.

And first for Captain *Boanerges* (not to undervalue the rest) he made three most fierce assaults, one after another, upon *Eargate*, to the shaking of the Posts thereof. Captain *Conviction* he also made up as fast with *Boanerges* as possibly he could, and both discerning that the Gate began to yield, they commanded that the Rams should still be played against it. Now Captain *Conviction* going up very near to the Gate, was with great force driven back, and received three wounds in the mouth. And those that rode *Reformades*, they went about to encourage the Captains.

Boanerges plays the man.

Conviction wounded.

Angels.

For the valour of the two Captains made mention of before, the Prince sent for them to his Pavilion, and commanded that a while they should rest themselves, and that with somewhat they should be refreshed. Care also was taken for Captain *Conviction*, that he should be healed of his wounds, the Prince also gave to each of them a chain of gold, and bid them yet be of good courage.

Goodhope and *Charity* play the men at *Eyegate*.

Nor did Captain *Goodhope*, nor Captain *Charity* come behind in this most desperate fight, for they so well did behave themselves at *Eyegate*, that they had almost broken it quite open. These also had a reward from their Prince, as also had the rest of the Captains, because they did valiantly round about the Town.

Captain *Boasting* slain.

In this Engagement several of the Officers of *Diabolus* were slain, and some of the Townsmen wounded. For the Officers there was one Captain *Boasting* slain. This *Boasting* thought that no body could have shaken the Posts of *Eargate*, nor have shaken the heart of *Diabolus*. Next to him there was one Captain *Secure* slain; this *Secure* used to say that the *blind* and *lame* in *Mansoul* were able to keep the Gates of the Town against *Emanuel*'s army. This Captain *Secure* did Captain *Conviction* cleave down the head with a two-handed-sword, when he received himself three wounds in his mouth.

2 Sam. 5. 6. Captain *Secure* slain.

Captain *Bragman* slain.

Besides these there was one Captain *Bragman*, a very desperate fellow, and he was Captain over a band of those that threw firebrands, arrows and death, he also received by the hand of Captain *Goodhope* at *Eyegate* a mortal wound in the breast.

Mr. *Feeling* hurt.

There was moreover one Mr. *Feeling*, but he was no Captain but a great stickler to encourage *Mansoul* to rebellion, he received a wound in the eye by the hand of one of *Boanerges* souldiers, and had by the Captain himself been slain, but that he made a sudden retreat.

Wilbewill hurt.

But I never saw *Wilbewill* so danted in all my life, he was not able to do as he was wont, and some say that he also received a wound in the leg, and that some of the men in the Princes army have certainly seen him limp as he afterwards walked on the wall.

9 open] upon

Many of the souldiers in *Mansoul* slain.

I shall not give you a particular account of the names of the souldiers that were slain in the Town, for many were maimed and wounded, and slain; for when they saw that the Posts of *Eargate* did shake, and *Eye-gate* was well nigh broken quite open; and also that their Captains were slain; this took away the hearts of many of the *Diabolonians*, they fell also by the force of the shot that were sent by the golden slings into the midst of the Town of *Mansoul*.

Lovenogood wounded.

Of the Townsmen there was one *Love no-good*, he was a Townsman, but a *Diabolonian*, he also received his mortal wound in *Mansoul*, but he died not very soon.

Illpause wounded.

Mr. *Illpause* also, who was the man that came along with *Diabolus* when at first he attempted the taking of *Mansoul*, he also received a grievous wound in the head, some say that his brain-pan was crackt; this I have taken notice of that he was never after this able to do that mischief to *Mansoul* as he had done in times past. Also old *Prejudice*, and Mr. *Anything* fled.

The White flag hung out again.

Now when the battel was over, the Prince commanded that yet once more the White-flag should be set upon mount *Gracious* in sight of the Town of *Mansoul*; to shew that yet *Emanuel* had grace for the wretched Town of *Mansoul*.

Diabolus's new prank.

When *Diabolus* saw the White flag hanged out again, and knowing that it was not for him but *Mansoul*; he cast in his mind to play another prank, to wit to see if *Emanuel* would raise his siege and be gone upon promise of a *reformation*. So comes down to the Gate one evening, a good while after the Sun was gone down, and calls to speak with *Emanuel*, who presently came down to the Gate, and *Diabolus* saith unto him.

His speech to *Emanuel*.

For as much as thou makest it appear by thy White flag that thou art wholly given to peace and quiet; I thought meet to acquaint thee that we are ready to accept thereof upon terms which thou maist admit.

I know that thou art given to devotion, and that holiness pleases thee; yea that thy great end in making a war upon Mansoul, *is, that it may be an holy habitation. Well, draw off thy forces from the Town, and I will bend* Mansoul *to thy bow.*

First, *I will lay down all acts of hostility against thee, and will be willing to become thy deputy, and will as I have formerly been*

Diabolus would be *Emanuel's* Deputy, and he would turn reformer.

against thee, now serve thee in the Town of Mansoul. *And more particularly,*

1. *I will perswade* Mansoul *to receive thee for their Lord, and I know that they will do it the sooner when they shall understand that I am thy deputy.*

2. *I will shew them wherein they have erred, and that transgression stands in the way to life.*

3. *I will shew them the holy Law unto which they must conform, even that which they have broken.*

4. *I will press upon them the necessity of a reformation according to thy Law.*

5. *And moreover that none of these things may fail, I my self at my own proper cost and charge will set up and maintain a sufficient Ministry, besides Lecturers, in* Mansoul.

6. *Thou shalt receive as a token of our subjection to thee continually year by year what thou shalt think fit to lay and levy upon us, in token of our subjection to thee.*

The Answer.

Then said *Emanuel* to him, O full of deceit, how movable are thy ways! how often hast thou changed and rechanged, if so be thou mightest still keep possession of my *Mansoul*, though as has been plainly declared before, I am the right heir thereof? Often hast thou made thy Proposals already, nor is this last a whit better than they. *And failing to deceive when thou shewedst thy self in thy black; thou hast now transformed thy self into an Angel of light, and wouldest to deceive, be now as a minister of righteousness.*

2 Cor. 11. 14.

Diabolus has no conscience to God, nor love to *Mansoul*.

'But know thou, O *Diabolus*, that nothing must be regarded that thou canst propound, for nothing is done by thee but to deceive; thou neither hast conscience to God, nor love to the Town of *Mansoul*; whence then should these thy sayings arise but from sinful craft and deceit? He that can of *list* and *will* propound what he pleases, and that wherewith he may destroy them that believe him, is to be abandoned with all that he shall say. But if righteousness be such a beauty-spot in thine eyes now, how is it that wickedness was so closely stuck to by thee before. But this is by the by.

'Thou talkest now of a reformation in *Mansoul*, and that thou thy self if I will please, will be at the head of that reformation, all the while knowing that the greatest proficiency that man can make in the Law, and the righteousness thereof, will amount to no more for the taking away of the curse from *Mansoul*, *than just nothing at all*, for a Law being broken by *Mansoul*, that had before upon a supposition of the breach thereof, a curse pronounced against him for it of God, can never by his obeying of the Law deliver himself therefrom. (To say nothing of what a reformation is like to be set up in *Mansoul*, when the Devil is become the *corrector of vice*.) Thou know'st that all that thou hast now said in this matter is nothing but guile and deceit; and is as it was the *first*, so is it the *last* card that thou hast to play. Many there be that do soon discern thee when thou shewest them thy *cloven foot*; but in thy *white*, thy *light*, and in thy *transformation* thou art seen but of a few. But thou shalt not do thus with my *Mansoul*, O *Diabolus*, for I do still love my *Mansoul*.

He knows that that will do no good which yet he propounds for the health of *Mansoul*.

'Besides, I am not come to put *Mansoul* upon works to live thereby, (should I do so, I should be like unto thee) but I am come that by me, and by what I have [done] and shall do for *Mansoul*, they may to my Father be reconciled, though by their sin they have provoked him to anger, and though by the Law they cannot obtain mercy.

'Thou talkest of subjecting of this Town to good, when none desireth it at thy hands. I am sent by my Father to possess it my self, and to guide it by the skilfulness of my hands into such a conformity to him as shall be pleasing in his sight. I will therefore possess it my self, I will dispossess and cast thee out: I will set up mine own standard in the midst of them: I will also govern them by new Laws, new Officers, new motives, and new ways: Yea, I will pull down this Town, and build it again, and it shall be as though it had not been, and it shall then be the glory of the whole Universe.'

All things must be new in *Mansoul*.

When *Diabolus* heard this, and perceived that he was discovered in all his deceits, he was confounded and utterly put to a *nonplus*; but having in himself the fountain of iniquity, rage, and malice against both *Shaddai* and his Son, and the

Diabolus confounded.

19 what I have [done] and shall do] what I have and shall do

beloved Town of *Mansoul*, what doth he but strengthen himself what he could to give fresh Battel to the noble Prince *Emanuel*? So then, now we must have another fight before the Town of *Mansoul* is taken. Come up then to the Mountains you that love to see military actions, and behold by both sides how the fatal blow is given; while one seeks to hold, and the other seeks to make himself master of the famous Town of *Mansoul*.

New preparations for to fight.

Diabolus therefore having withdrawn himself from the wall to his force that was in the heart of the Town of *Mansoul*, *Emanuel* also returned to the Camp; and both of them after their divers ways, put themselves into a posture fit to bid Battel one to another.

Diabolus despairs of holding of *Mansoul*, and therefore contrives to do it what mischief he can. Mar. 9. 26, 27.

Diabolus as filled with despair of retaining in his hands the famous Town of *Mansoul*, resolved to do what mischief he could (if indeed he could do any) to the army of the Prince, and to the famous Town of *Mansoul*, (For alas it was not the happiness of the silly Town of *Mansoul* that was designed by *Diabolus*, but the utter ruin and overthrow thereof); as now is enough in view. Wherefore he commands his Officers that they should then when they see that they could hold the Town no longer, do it what harm and mischief they could, renting and tearing of men, women and children. For, said he, we had better quite demolish the place, and leave it like a ruinous heap, than so leave it that it may be an habitation for *Emanuel*.

Emanuel again knowing that the next Battel would issue in his being made master of the place, gave out a Royal Commandment to all his Officers, high Captains, and men of War, to be sure to shew themselves men of War against *Diabolus*, and all *Diabolonians*; but favourable, merciful, and meek to all the old inhabitants of *Mansoul*. Bend therefore, said the Noble Prince, the hottest front of the Battel against *Diabolus* and his men.

So the day being come, the command was given, and the Princes men did bravely stand to their arms; and did as before, bend their main force against *Eargate*, and *Eyegate*. The word was then, *Mansoul* is *Won*; so they made their assault upon the Town. *Diabolus* also as fast as he could with the main of his power, made resistance from within, and his high Lords, and chief Captains for a time fought very cruelly against the Princes Army.

The Battel joined, and they fight on both sides fiercely.

But after three or four notable Charges by the Prince, and his Noble Captains, *Eargate* was broken open, and the bars and bolts wherewith it was used to be fast shut up against the Prince, was broken into a thousand pieces. Then did the Princes Trumpets *sound*, the Captains *shout*, the Town *shake*, and *Diabolus* retreat to his hold. Well, when the Princes forces had broken open the Gate, himself came up and did set his Throne in it; also he set his *standard* thereby, upon a mount that before by his men was cast up to place the mighty slings thereon. The mount was called mount *Hear-well*, there therefore the Prince abode, to wit, hard by the going in at the Gate. He commanded also that the Golden slings should yet be played upon the Town, especially against the *Castle*, because for shelter thither was *Diabolus* retreated. Now from *Eargate* the street was streight even to the house of Mr. *Recorder* that so was before *Diabolus* took the Town, and hard by his house stood the *Castle*, which *Diabolus* for a long time had made his irksome den. The Captains therefore did quickly clear that street by the use of their slings, so that way was made up to the heart of the Town. Then did the Prince command that Captain *Boanerges*, Captain *Conviction*, and Capt. *Judgment*, should forthwith march up the Town to the old *Gentlemans Gate. Then did the Captains in most warlike manner enter into the Town of *Mansoul*, and marching in with flying Colours, they came up to the *Recorders* house, (and that was almost as strong as was the Castle.) Battering Rams they took also with them to plant against the Castle-gates. When they were come to the house of Mr. *Conscience*, they knocked and demanded entrance. Now the old Gentleman not knowing as yet fully their design, kept his Gates shut all the time of this fight. Wherefore *Boanerges* demanded entrance at his Gates, and no man making answer, he gave it one stroke with

Eargate broken open.

The Princes Standard set up, and the Slings are plaid still at the Castle.

*Conscience.

They go up to the *Recorders* house.

They demand entrance.

the head of a Ram, and this made the old Gentleman *shake*, and his house to tremble and totter. Then came Mr. *Recorder* down to the Gate, and as he could with quivering lips, he asked who was there? *Boanerges* answered, We are the Captains and Commanders of the great *Shaddai*, and of the blessed *Emanuel* his Son, and we demand possession of your house for the use of our noble Prince. And with that the Battering Ram gave the Gate another shake: this made the old Gentleman tremble the more, yet durst he not but open the Gate: then the Kings forces marched in, namely the three brave Captains mentioned before. Now the *Recorders* house was a place of much convenience for *Emanuel*, not only because it was near to the Castle, and strong, but also because it was large, and fronted the Castle, the den where now *Diabolus* was; for he was *now* afraid to come out of his hold. As for Mr. *Recorder*, the Captains carried it very reservedly to him, as yet he knew nothing of the great designs of *Emanuel*; so that he did not know what judgment to make, nor what would be the end of such thundring beginnings. It was also presently noised in the Town, how the *Recorders* house was possessed, his rooms taken up, and his Palace made the seat of the War; and no sooner was it noised abroad but they took the alarm as warmly, and gave it out to others of his friends, (and you know as a snow-ball loses nothing by rolling) so in little time the whole Town was possessed, that they must expect nothing from the Prince but destruction; and the ground of the business was this, the *Recorder* was afraid, the *Recorder* trembled, and the Captains carried it strangely to the *Recorder*; so many came to see, but when they with their own eyes did behold the Captains in the Palace, and their battering Rams ever playing at the Castle-gates to beat them down; they were riveted in their fears, and it made them as in amaze. And, as I said, the man of the house would encrease all this, for whoever came to him, or discoursed with him, nothing would he talk of, tell them, or hear, but that death and destruction now attended *Mansoul*.

They go in.

They do keep themselves reserved from the *Recorder*.

His house the seat of War.

The office of Conscience when he is awakened.

For (quoth the old Gentleman) *you are all of you sensible that we all have been Traytors to that once despised, but now famously victorious and glorious Prince* Emanuel. *For he now, as you see, doth not only lye in close siege about us, but hath forced his entrance in at our Gates; moreover* Diabolus *flees before him, and he hath as you behold, made of my house a garrison against the Castle, where he is. I for my part have transgressed greatly (and he that is clean 'tis well for him.) But, I say, I have transgressed greatly in keeping of silence when I should have spoken, and in perverting of Justice when I should have executed the same. True, I have suffered something at the hand of* Diabolus *for taking part with the Laws of King* Shaddai; *but that alas! what will that do! Will that make compensation for the Rebellions and Treasons that I have done, and have suffered without gain-saying, to be committed in the Town of* Mansoul? *O I tremble to think what will be the end of this so dreadful and so ireful a beginning!*

Now while these brave Captains were thus busie in the house of the old *Recorder*, Captain *Execution* was as busie in other parts of the Town, in securing the back-streets, and the walls. He also hunted the Lord *Wilbewill* sorely, he suffered him not to rest in any corner. He pursued him so hard, that he drove his men from him, and made him glad to thrust his head into a hole. Also this mighty Warrier did cut three of the Lord *Wilbewils* Officers down to the ground; one was old Mr. *Prejudice*, he that had his Crown crackt in the mutiny; this man was made by Lord *Wilbewill* Keeper of *Eargate*, and fell by the hand of Captain *Execution*. There was also one Mr. *Backward to all but naught*, and he also was one of Lord *Wilbewils* Officers, and was the Captain of the two Guns that once were mounted on the top of *Eargate*, he also was cut down to the ground by the hands of Captain *Execution*. Besides those two there was another, a third, and his name was Captain *Treacherous*, a vile man this was, but one that *Wilbewill* did put a great deal of confidence in, but him also did this Captain *Execution* cut down to the ground with the rest.

The brave Exploits of the Captain *Execution*.

Old *Prejudice* slain.

Backward to all but naught slain.

Treacherous slain.

He also made a very great slaughter among my Lord *Wilbewils* souldiers, killing many that were stout and sturdy, and wounding of many that for *Diabolus* were nimble and active. But all these were *Diabolonians*, there was not a man, a native of *Mansoul* hurt.

Captain *Goodhope* doth slay Captain *Blindfold*.

Other feats of War were also likewise performed by other of the Captains, as at *Eyegate*, where Captain *Goodhope*, and Captain *Charity* had a charge, was great execution done; for the Captain *Goodhope* with his own hands slew one Captain *Blindfold*, the Keeper of that *Gate*; this *Blindfold* was Captain of a thousand men, and they were they that fought with *Mauls*; he also pursued his men, slew many, and wounded more, and made the rest hide their heads in corners.

And old *Illpause*.

There was also at that Gate Mr. *Illpause*, of whom you have heard before, he was an old man, and had a beard that reached down to his girdle, the same was he that was Orator to *Diabolus*, he did much mischief in the Town of *Mansoul*, and fell by the hand of Captain *Goodhope*.

What shall I say, the *Diabolonians* in these days lay dead in every corner, though too many yet were alive in *Mansoul*.

The old Townsmen meet and consult.

Now the old *Recorder*, and my Lord *Understanding* with some others of the chief of the Town, to wit such as knew they must stand and fall with the famous Town of *Mansoul*, came together upon a day, and after consultation had, did jointly agree to draw up a Petition, and to send it to *Emanuel*, now while he sat in the Gate of *Mansoul*. So they drew up their *Petition* to *Emanuel*, the contents whereof were this, *That they the old inhabitants of the now deplorable Town of* Mansoul, *confessed their sin, and were sorry that they had offended his Princely Majesty, and prayed that he would spare their lives.*

The Town does petition, and are answered with silence.

Unto this Petition he gave no answer at all, and that did trouble them yet so much the more. Now all this while the Captains that were in the *Recorders* house were playing with the battering Rams at the Gates of the Castle to beat them down. So after some time, labour and travel, the Gate of the Castle that was called *Impregnable*, was beaten open, and broken into several splinters; and so a way made to go up to the hold in which *Diabolus* had hid himself. Then was tidings sent down to *Eargate*, for *Emanuel* still abode there, to let him know that a way was made in at the Gates of the Castle of

The Castle Gates broke open.

Mansoul. But Oh! how the Trumpets at the tidings sounded throughout the Princes Camp, for that now the War was so near an end, and *Mansoul* it self of being set free.

Then the Prince arose from the place where he was, and took with him such of his men of War as were fittest for *that* Expedition, and marched up the street of *Mansoul* to the old *Recorders* house.

Emanuel marches into *Mansoul.*

Now the Prince himself was clad all in Armour of Gold, and so he marched up the Town with his Standard born before him; but he kept his countenance much reserved all the way as he went, so that the people could not tell how to gather to themselves love or hatred by his looks. Now as he marched up the street, the Townsfolk came out at every door to see, and could not but be taken with his person, and the glory thereof, but wondred at the reservedness of his countenance; for as yet he spake more to them by his actions and works, than he did by words or smiles. But also poor *Mansoul*, (as in such cases all are apt to do) they interpreted the carriages of *Emanuel* to them, as did *Josephs* Brethren his to them, even all the quite contrary way: For thought they, if *Emanuel* loved us, he would shew it to us by word or carriage, but none of these he doth, therefore *Emanuel* hates us. Now if *Emanuel* hates us, then *Mansoul* shall be slain, then *Mansoul* shall become a dunghill. They knew that they had transgressed his Fathers Law, and that against him they had been in with *Diabolus* his enemy. They also knew that the Prince *Emanuel* knew all this; for they were convinced that he was as an Angel of God, to know all things that are done in the earth. And this made them think that their condition was miserable, and that the good Prince would make them desolate.

How they interpret *Emanuels* carriages.

And thought they, what time so fit to do this in as now, when he has the bridle of *Mansoul* in his hand. And this I took special notice of, that the inhabitants (notwithstanding all this) could not; no, they could not, when they see him march through the Town, but cringe, bow, bend, and were ready to lick the dust of his feet. They also wished a thousand times over, that he would become their Prince and Captain, and would become their protection. They would also one to another talk of the comeliness of his Person, and how much for glory and valour he outstript the great ones of the world. But poor hearts, as to themselves their thoughts would change and go upon all manner of Extreams. Yea through the working of them backward and forward, *Mansoul* became as a ball tossed, and as a rolling thing before the whirlwind.

He comes up to the Castle, and commands *Diabolus* to surrender himself.

Now when he was come to the Castle-Gates, he commanded *Diabolus* to appear and to surrender himself into his hands. But Oh how loth was the beast to appear! how he stuck at it! how he shrunk! Ay, how he cringed! yet out he came to the Prince. Then *Emanuel* commanded, and they took *Diabolus* and bound him fast in chains, the better to reserve him to the Judgment that he had appointed for him. But *Diabolus* stood up to intreat for himself that *Emanuel* would not send him into the deep, but suffer him to depart out of *Mansoul* in peace.

He is taken and bound in chains.

When *Emanuel* had taken him and bound him in chains, he led him into the *Market-place*, and there before *Mansoul*, stript him of his armour in which he boasted so much before. This now was one of the acts of Triumph of *Emanuel* over his enemy, and all the while that the Giant was stripping, the Trumpets of the Golden Prince did sound amain; the Captains also shouted, and the soldiers did sing for joy.

Mansoul must behold it.

Then was *Mansoul* called upon to behold the beginning of *Emanuels* Triumph over him in whom they so much had trusted, and of whom they so much had boasted in the days when he flattered them.

Ephes. 4. He is bound to his Chariot-wheels.

Thus having made *Diabolus* naked in the eyes of *Mansoul*, and before the Commanders of the Prince; in the next place he commands that *Diabolus* should be bound with chains to his chariot wheels. Then leaving of some of his forces, to wit, Captain *Boanerges*, and Captain *Conviction*, as a guard for the Castle-gates, that resistance might be made on his behalf, (if any that heretofore followed *Diabolus* should make an attempt to possess it) he did ride in triumph over him quite through the Town of *Mansoul*, and so out at,

The Prince rides in Triumph over him, in the

11 Ay,] I

and before the Gate called *Eyegate*, to the Plain where his Camp did lye.

sight of *Mansoul.*

But you cannot think unless you had been there (as I was) what a shout there was in *Emanuels* Camp when they saw the *Tyrant* bound by the hand of their noble Prince, and tyed to his Chariot-wheels!

They sing.

And they said, He hath led captivity captive, he hath spoiled Principalities and Powers, *Diabolus* is subjected to the power of his sword, and made the object of all derision.

The *Reformades* joy.

Luk. 15. 7, 10.

Those also that rode *Reformades*, and that came down to see the Battel, they shouted with that greatness of voice, and sung with such melodious notes, that they caused them that dwell in the highest Orbs to open their windows, put out their heads, and look down to see the cause of that Glory.

The men of *Mansoul* taken with *Emanuel.*

The Townsmen also, so many of them as saw this sight, were as it were, while they looked, betwixt the earth and the Heavens. True, they could not tell what would be the issue of things as to them, but all things were done in such excellent methods, and I cannot tell how, but things in the management of them seemed to cast a smile towards the Town, so that their eyes, their heads, their hearts, and their minds, and all that they had were taken and held while they observed *Emanuels* order.

So when the brave Prince had finished this part of his Triumph over *Diabolus* his foe, he turned him up in the midst of his contempt and shame, having given him a charge no more to be a possessor of *Mansoul*. Then went he from *Emanuel*, and out of the midst of his Camp to inherit the parched places in a salt land, seeking rest but finding none.

Mat. 12. 43.

Now Captain *Boanerges* and Captain *Conviction* were both of them men of very great majesty, their faces were like the faces of Lions, and their words like the roaring of the Sea; and they still quartered in Mr. *Consciences* house, of whom mention was made before. When therefore the high and mighty Prince had thus far finished his Triumph over *Diabolus*, the Townsmen had more leisure to view and to behold the actions of these noble Captains. But the Captains carried it with that terrour and

The carriage of *Boanerges*, and of Captain

Conviction do crush the spirit of *Mansoul.*

dread in all that they did (and you may be sure that they had private instructions so to do) that they kept the Town under continual heart-aking, and caused (in their apprehension) the well-being of *Mansoul* for the future, to hang in doubt before them, so that (for some considerable time) they neither knew what rest or ease, or peace, or hope meant.

The Prince commands, & the Captains put the three chief of *Mansoul* in Ward.

Nor did the Prince himself, as yet, *abide* in the Town of *Mansoul*, but in his Royal Pavilion in the Camp, and in the midst of his Fathers forces. So at a time convenient, he sent special Orders to Captain *Boanerges* to summons *Mansoul*, the whole of the Townsmen, into the Castle yard, and then and there before their faces, to take my Lord *Understanding*, Mr. *Conscience*, and that notable one the Lord *Wilbewill*, and put *them* all three in Ward, and that they should set a strong Guard upon them there, until his pleasure concerning them were further known. The which orders when the Captains had put *them* in execution, made no small addition to the fears of the Town of *Mansoul*: for now to their thinking, were their former fears of the ruin of *Mansoul* confirmed. Now, what death they should die, and how long they should be in dying, was that which most perplexed their heads and hearts: yea, they were afraid that *Emanuel* would command them all into the deep, the place that the Prince *Diabolus* was afraid of; for they knew that they had deserved it. Also to die by the sword in the face of the Town, and in the open way of disgrace, from the hand of so good and so holy a Prince, that (too) troubled them sore. The Town was also greatly troubled for the men that were committed to Ward, for that they were their stay, and their guide, and for that they believed that if those men were cut off, their execution would be but the beginning of the ruin of the Town of *Mansoul*. Wherefore what do they, but together with the men in prison, draw up a Petition to the Prince, and sent it to *Emanuel* by the hand of Mr. *Wouldlive*. So he went and came to the Princes quarters, and presented the Petition: the sum of which was this.

Mansoul greatly distressed.

They send a Petition to *Emanuel* by the hand of Mr. *Wouldlive.*

Great and wonderful Potentate, Victor over Diabolus, *and Conqueror of the Town of* Mansoul*: We the miserable inhabitants of* *that most woful Corporation, do humbly beg that we may find favour in thy sight, and remember not against us former transgressions, nor yet the sins of the chief of our Town, but spare us according to the greatness of thy mercy, and let us not die, but live in thy sight: so shall we be willing to be thy servants, and if thou shalt think fit, to gather our meat under thy Table.* Amen.

So the Petitioner went as was said with his Petition to the Prince, and the Prince took it at his hand, but sent him away with silence. This still afflicted the Town of *Mansoul*, but yet considering that now they must either Petition, or die; for now they could not do any thing else; therefore they consulted again, and sent another Petition, and this Petition was much after the form and method of the former.

They are answered with silence.

But when the Petition was drawn up, by whom should they send it, was the next question; for they would not send this by him by whom they sent the first, (for they thought that the Prince had taken some offence at the manner of his deportment before him), so they attempted to make Captain *Conviction* their messenger with it, but he said, *That he neither durst nor would petition Emanuel for Traytors; nor be to the Prince an Advocate for Rebels.* Yet withal, said he, our Prince is good, and you may adventure to send it by the hand of one of your Town; provided he went with a rope about his head, and pleaded nothing but mercy.

They Petition again.

They cannot tell by whom to send it.

Well, they made through fear their delays as long as they could, and longer than delays were good, but fearing at last the dangerousness of them, they thought, but with many a fainting in their minds, to send their Petition by Mr. *Desires-awake*; so they sent for Mr. *Desires-awake*; now he dwelt in a very mean cottage in *Mansoul*, and he came at his neighbours request. So they told him what they had done, and what they would do concerning Petitioning, and that they did desire of him that he would go therewith to the Prince.

Then said Mr. *Desires-awake*, Why should not I do the best I can to save so famous a Town as *Mansoul* from deserved destruction? They therefore delivered the Petition to him, and told him how he must address himself to the Prince, and

Mr. *Desires-awake* goes with the Petition to the Prince

wisht him ten thousand good speeds. So he comes to the Princes Pavilion, as the first, and asked to speak with his Majesty: so word was carried to *Emanuel*, and the Prince came out to the man. When Mr. *Desires-awake* saw the Prince, he fell flat with his face to the ground, and cried out, *O that Mansoul might live before thee*! and with that he presented the Petition. The which when the Prince had read, he turned away for a while and wept, but refraining himself he turned again to the man (who all this while lay crying at his feet as at the first) and said to him, *Go thy way to thy place, and I will consider of thy requests.*

His Entertainment.

Now you may think that they of *Mansoul* that had sent him, what with guilt, and what with fear, lest their Petition should be rejected, could not but look with many a long look, and that too with strange workings of heart, to see what would become of their Petition: At last they saw their messenger coming back; so when he was come, they asked him how he fared, what *Emanuel* said? and what was become of the Petition. But he told them that he would be silent till he came to the *Prison* to my Lord *Mayor*, my Lord *Wilbewill* and Mr. *Recorder*. So he went forwards towards the Prison-house, where the men of *Mansoul* lay bound. But Oh! what a multitude flocked after to hear what the messenger said. So when he was come and had shewn himself at the Grate of the Prison, my Lord *Mayor* himself lookt as white as a clout, the *Recorder* also did quake: but they asked and said, *Come, good Sir, what did the great Prince say to you*? Then said Mr. *Desires-awake* when I came to my Lords Pavilion, I called, and he came forth; so I fell prostrate at his feet, and delivered to him my Petition, (for the greatness of his person, and the glory of his countenance would not suffer me to stand upon my legs.) Now as he received the Petition, I cried, *O that* Mansoul *might live before thee*! So when for a while he had looked thereon, he turned him about and said to his servant, *Go thy way to thy place again, and I will consider of thy requests.* The messenger added moreover, and said, *The Prince to whom you sent me, is such a one for beauty and glory, that whoso sees him must both love and fear him: I for my part can do no less, but I know not what will be the end of*

His return and answer to them that sent him.

these things. At this answer they were all at a stand, both they in prison, and they that followed the messenger thither to hear the news, nor knew they what, or what manner of interpretation to put upon what the Prince had said. Now when the prison was cleared of the throng, the prisoners among themselves began to Comment upon *Emanuels* words. My Lord Mayor said, *That the answer did not look with a rugged face; but* Wilbewill *said, it betokened evil; and the* Recorder, *that it was a messenger of death*. Now they that were left, and that stood behind, and so could not so well hear what the Prisoners said, some of them catcht hold of one piece of a sentence, and some on a bit of another, some took hold of what the messenger said, and some of the prisoners judgment thereon, so none had the right understanding of things; but you cannot imagin what work these people made, and what a confusion there was in *Mansoul* now.

Mansoul confounded at the answer.

The Prisoners judgment upon the Princes answer.

Misgiving thoughts breed confusion in *Mansoul*.

For presently they that had heard what was said, flew about the Town, one crying one thing, and another the quite contrary, and both were sure enough they told true, for they did hear they said with their ears what was said, and therefore could not be deceived. One would say, *We must all be killed*; another would say, *We must all be saved;* and a third would say, *that the Prince would not be concerned with* Mansoul; and a fourth, *that the prisoners must be suddenly put to death*. And as I said, every one stood to it, that he told his tale the rightest; and that all others but he were out. Wherefore *Mansoul* had now molestation upon molestation, nor could any man know on what to rest the sole of his foot; for one would go by now, and as he went, if he heard his neighbour tell his tale, to be sure he would tell the quite contrary, and both would stand in it that he told the truth. Nay some of them had got this story by the end, *That the Prince did intend to put* Mansoul *to the sword*. And now it begun to be dark, wherefore poor *Mansoul* was in sad perplexity all that night until the morning.

Mansoul in perplexity.

But so far as I could gather by the best information that I could get, all this hubbub came through the words that the *Recorder* said, when he told them, That in his Judgment the Princes answer was *a messenger of death*. 'Twas this that fired

What will guilt do.

the Town, and that began the fright in *Mansoul*; for *Mansoul* in former times did use to count that Mr. *Recorder* was a Seer, and that his sentence was equal *to the best of Oracles*; and thus was *Mansoul* a terrour to it self.

And now did they begin to feel what was the effects of stubborn rebellion, and unlawful resistance against their Prince. I say they now began to feel the effects thereof by guilt and fear that now had swallowed them up; and who more involved in the one but they that were most in the other, to wit the chief of the Town of *Mansoul*?

They resolve to Petition again.

To be brief, when the fame of the fright was out of the Town, and the prisoners had a little recovered themselves, they take to themselvs some heart, & think to Petition the Prince for life again. So they did draw up a 3*d* Petition, the Contents whereof was this.

Their Petition.

Prince Emanuel *the Great, Lord of all Worlds, and master of Mercy, we thy poor wretched, miserable, dying Town of* Mansoul, *do confess unto thy great and glorious Majesty, that we have sinned against thy Father and thee, and are no more worthy to be called thy* Mansoul, *but rather to be cast into the pit. If thou wilt slay us, we have deserved it. If thou wilt condemn us to the deep, we cannot but say thou art righteous. We cannot complain whatever thou dost, or however thou carriest it towards us. But Oh! let mercy reign! and let it be extended to us! O let mercy take hold upon us, and free us from our transgressions, and we will sing of thy mercy, and of thy judgment.* Amen.

Prayer attended with difficulty.

This Petition when drawn up was designed to be sent to the Prince as the first, but who should carry it, that was the question. Some said, let him do it that went with the first, but others thought not good to do that, and that because he sped no better. Now there was an old man in the Town, and his name was Mr. *Good-deed.* A man that bare only the name, but had nothing of the nature of the thing; now some were for sending of him, but the *Recorder* was by no means for that: For, said he, *we now stand in need of, and are pleading for mercy, wherefore to send our Petition by a man of this name will seem to cross the Petition it self; should we make Mr.* Good-deed *our messenger, when our Petition cries for mercy?*

Old *Good-deed* propounded as a fit person to carry the Petition, the old *Recorder* opposes it, and he is rejected.

Besides, quoth the old Gentleman, *should the Prince now, as he receives the Petition, ask him, and say, What is thy name? as no body knows but he will; and he should say, Old* Good-deed*; what, think you, would* Emanuel *say but this, Ay, is old* Good-deed *yet alive in* Mansoul, *then let old* Good-deed *save you from your distresses. And if he says so, I am sure we are lost, nor can a thousand of old* Good-deeds *save* Mansoul.

After the *Recorder* had given in his reasons why old *Good-deed* should not go with this Petition to *Emanuel*; the rest of the prisoners and chief of *Mansoul* opposed it also, and so old *Good-deed* was laid aside, and they agreed to send Mr. *Desires-awake* again; so they sent for him, and desired him that he would a second time go with their Petition to the Prince, and he readily told them he would. But they bid him that in any wise he should take heed that in no word or carriage he gave offence to the Prince, for by doing so, for ought we can tell, you may bring *Mansoul* into utter destruction, said they.

Now Mr. *Desires-awake*, when he saw that he must go of this Errand, besought that they would grant that Mr. *Wet-eyes* might go with him. Now this *Wet-eyes* was a near neighbour of Mr. *Desires*, a poor man, a man of a broken spirit; yet one that could speak well to a Petition. So they granted that he should go with him. Wherefore they address themselves to their business; Mr. *Desires* put a rope upon his head, and Mr. *Wet-eyes* went with hands wringing together. Thus they went to the Princes Pavilion.

Mr. *Desires-awake* goes again and takes one *Wet-eyes* with him.

Now when they went to Petition this third time, they were not without thoughts that by often coming they might be a burden to the Prince. Wherefore when they were come to the door of his Pavilion, they first made their apology for themselves, and for their coming to trouble *Emanuel* so often; and they said, That they came not hither to day, *for that they delighted in being troublesome, or for that they delighted to hear themselves talk; but for that necessity caused them to come to his Majesty; they could, they said, have no rest day nor night, because of their transgressions against* Shaddai, *and against* Emanuel *his Son. They also thought that some misbehaviour of Mr.* Desires-awake

Their Apology for their coming again.

the last time might give distaste to his Highness; and so cause that he returned from so merciful a Prince empty, and without countenance. So when they had made this apology, Mr. *Desires-awake* cast himself prostrate upon the ground as at the first, at the feet of the mighty Prince, saying, *Oh! that Mansoul might live before thee*! and so he delivered his Petition. The Prince then having read the Petition, turned aside a while as before, and coming again to the place where the Petitioner lay on the ground, he demanded what his name was, and of what esteem in the account of *Mansoul*? for that he above all the multitude in *Mansoul* should be sent to him upon *such* an *Errand*. Then said the man to the Prince, *O let not my Lord be angry; and why enquirest thou after the name of such a dead dog as I am? Pass by I pray thee, and take not notice of who I am, because there is, as thou very well knowest, so great a disproportion between me and thee. Why the Townsmen chose to send me on this Errand to my Lord, is best known to themselves, but it could not be, for that they thought that I had favour with my Lord. For my part I am out of charity with my self, who then should be in love with me? yet live I would, and so would I, that my Townsmen should; and because both they and my self are guilty of great transgressions, therefore they have sent me, and I am come in their names to beg of my Lord for mercy. Let it please thee therefore to incline to mercy, but ask not what thy servants are.*

The Prince talketh with them.

Mr. *Desires* free speech to his Prince.

Then said the Prince, And what is he that is become thy companion in this so weighty a matter? So Mr. *Desires* told *Emanuel*, that he was a poor neighbour of his, and one of his most intimate Associates, and his name said he, may it please your most excellent Majesty, is *Wet-eyes* of the Town of *Mansoul*. I know that there are many of that name that are naught, but I hope 'twill be no offence to my Lord, that I have brought my poor neighbour with me.

Then Mr. *Wet-eyes* fell on his face to the ground, and made this Apology for his coming with his neighbour to his Lord.

Mr. *Wet-eyes* Apology for his coming with his neighbor.

'O my Lord, quoth he, what I am, I know not my self, nor whether my name be feigned or true, especially when I begin to think what some have said, namely that this name was given me, because Mr. *Repentance* was my Father. Good men have bad children, and the sincere do often times beget hypocrites. My mother also called me by this name from my Cradle, but whether because of the moistness of my brain, or because of the softness of my heart, I cannot tell. I see dirt in mine own tears, and filthiness in the bottom of my prayers. But I pray thee (and all this while the Gentleman wept) that thou wouldest not remember against us our transgressions, nor take offence at the unqualifiedness of thy servants, but mercifully pass by the sin of *Mansoul*, and refrain from the glorifying of thy grace no longer.'

So at his bidding they arose, and both stood trembling before him, and he spake to them to this purpose.

The Princes answer.

'The Town of *Mansoul* hath grievously rebelled against my Father, in that they have rejected him from being their King, and did chuse to themselves for their Captain, a lyer, a murderer, and a runnagate-slave. For this *Diabolus*, and your pretended Prince, though once so highly accounted of by you, made rebellion against my Father and me, even in our palace and highest Court there, thinking to become a Prince and King. But being there timely discovered and apprehended, and for his wickedness bound in chains, and separated to the pit with those that were his companions, he offered himself to you, and you have received him.

The Original of *Diabolus*.

'Now this is, and for a long time hath been an high affront to my Father; wherefore my Father sent to you a powerful army to reduce you to your obedience. But you know how those men, their Captains, and their Counsels were esteemed of you, and what they received at your hand. You rebelled against them, you shut your Gates upon them, you bid them battel, you fought them, and fought for *Diabolus* against them. So they sent to my Father for more power, and I with my men are come to subdue you. But as you treated the servants, so you treated their Lord. You stood up in hostile manner against me, you shut up your Gates against me, you turned the deaf ear to me, and resisted as long as you could; but now I have made a conquest of you. Did you cry me mercy so long as you had hopes that you might prevail against me?

But now I have taken the Town, you cry; but why did you not cry before, when the white flag of my Mercy, the red flag of Justice, and the black flag that threatened Execution, were set up to cite you to it? Now I have conquered your *Diabolus*, you come to me for favour; but why did you not help me against the mighty? Yet I will consider your petition, and will answer it so as will be for my glory.

'Go bid Captain *Boanerges*, and Captain *Conviction*, bring the prisoners out to me into the Camp to morrow, and say you to Captain *Judgment*, and Captain *Execution*; Stay you in the Castle, and take good heed to your selves that you keep all quiet in *Mansoul* until you shall hear further from me': and with that he turned himself from them, and went into his Royal pavilion again.

So the petitioners having received this answer from the Prince, returned as at the first, to go to their companions again. But they had not gone far, but thoughts began to work in their minds, that no mercy as yet was intended by the prince to *Mansoul*: so they went to the place where the prisoners lay bound; but these workings of mind about what would become of *Mansoul*, had such strong power over them, that by that they were come unto them that sent them, they were scarce able to deliver their message.

But they came at length to the Gates of the Town (now the Townsmen with earnestness were waiting for their return) where many met them to know what answer was made to the Petition. Then they cried out to those that were sent, What news from the Prince, and what hath *Emanuel* said? But they said, that they must (as afore) go up to the prison, and there deliver their message. So away they went to the prison with a **multitude* at their heels. Now when they were come to the Grates of the prison, they told the first part of *Emanuels* speech to the prisoners, to wit, how he reflected upon their disloyalty to his Father and himself, and how they had chose, and closed with *Diabolus*, had fought for him, hearkened to him, and been ruled by him, but had despised him and his men. This made the prisoners look pale, but the messengers proceeded, and

*Of Inquisitive thoughts.

The messengers in telling their tale, fright the prisoners.

said, *He*, the Prince, said moreover, *that yet he would consider your Petition, and give such answer thereto as would stand with his glory*. And as these words were spoken, Mr. *Wet-eyes* gave a great sigh. At this they were all of them struck into their dumps, and could not tell what to say; fear also possest them in marvellous manner, and death seem'd to sit upon some of their *Eyebrows*. Now there was in the company a notable sharp-witted fellow, a mean man of estate, and his name was old *Inquisitive*, this man asked the *Petitioners* if they had told out every whit of what *Emanuel* said. And they answered, *Verily no*. Then said *Inquisitive*, I thought so indeed. Pray what was it more that he said unto you? Then they paused awhile, but at last they brought out all, saying, the Prince did bid us, bid Captain *Boanerges*, and Captain *Conviction* bring the prisoners down to him to morrow, and that Captain *Judgment*, and Captain *Execution* should take charge of the Castle and Town till they should hear further from him. They said also, *That when the Prince had commanded them thus to do, he immediately turned his back upon them, and went into his Royal Pavilion*.

Old Inquisitive.

But, O how this return, and specially this last clause of it, *that the prisoners must go out to the Prince into the Camp*, brake all their loins in pieces! Wherefore with one voice they set up a cry that reached up to the Heavens. This done, each of the three prepared himself to die, (and the **Recorder* said unto them, *This was the thing that I feared*), for they concluded that to morrow by that the Sun went down, they should be tumbled out of the world. The whole Town also counted of no other, but that in their time and order they must all drink of the same cup. Wherefore the Town of *Mansoul* spent that night in mourning and sackcloth, and ashes. The prisoners also when the time was come for them to go down before the Prince, dressed themselves in mourning *attire*, with *ropes* upon their head. The whole Town of *Mansoul* also, shewed themselves upon the wall, all clad in *mourning* weeds, if perhaps the Prince with the sight thereof might be moved with compassion. But Oh how the **Busie bodies* that were in the Town

*Conscience

*Vain thoughts.

of *Mansoul*, did now concern themselves! they did run here and there through the streets of the Town by companies, crying out as they ran in tumultuous wise, one after one manner, and another the quite contrary, to the almost utter distraction of *Mansoul*.

Well, the time is come that the prisoners must go down to the Camp, and appear before the Prince. And thus was the manner of their going down: Captain *Boanerges* went with a guard before them, and Captain *Conviction* came behind, and the prisoners went down bound in chains in the midst; so I say (the prisoners went in the midst, and) the Guard went with flying Colours behind and before, but the prisoners went with drooping spirits.

The prisoners had to trial.

Or more particularly thus:

How they went.

The prisoners went down all in Mourning, they put ropes upon themselves; they went on smiting of themselves on the breasts, but durst not lift up their eyes to Heaven. Thus they went out at the Gate of *Mansoul*, till they came into the midst of the Princes army, the sight and glory of which did greatly heighten their affliction. Nor could they now longer forbear, but cry out aloud, *O unhappy men! O wretched men of Mansoul!* Their Chains still mixing *their dolorous notes*, with the cries of the prisoners, made the noise more lamentable.

They fall down prostrate before him.

So when they were come to the door of the Princes Pavilion, they cast themselves prostrate upon the place; then one went in and told his Lord that the prisoners were come down. The Prince then ascended a Throne of State, and sent for the prisoners in; who when they came, did tremble before him, also they covered their faces with shame. Now as they drew near to the place where he sat, they threw themselves down before him; then said the Prince to the Captain *Boanerges*, Bid the prisoners stand upon their feet: then they stood trembling before him, and he said, *Are you the men that heretofore were the servants of Shaddai*? And they said, *Yes Lord, yes*. Then said the Prince again, *Are you the men that did suffer your selves to be corrupted, and defiled by that abominable one Diabolus?* And they said, We did more than suffer it, Lord; for we chose it of our

They are upon their trial.

own mind. The Prince asked further, saying, *Could you have been content that your slavery should have continued under his tyranny as long as you had lived*? Then said the prisoners, *Yes, Lord, yes*; for his ways were *pleasing* to our flesh, and we were grown aliens to a better state. *And did you*, said he, *when I came up against this Town of Mansoul, heartily wish that I might not have the victory over you*? *Yes*, Lord, *yes*, said they. Then said the Prince, *And what punishment is it, think you, that you deserve at my hand for these and other your high and mighty sins*? And they said, *Both death and the deep, Lord; for we have deserved no less.* He asked again, *If they had ought to say for themselves, why the sentence that they confessed that they had deserved, should not be passed upon them*? And they said, We can say nothing, Lord; thou art *just*, for we have sinned. Then said the Prince, *And for what are those ropes on your heads*? The prisoners answered, These *ropes are to bind us withal to the place of Execution, if mercy be not pleasing in thy sight. So he further asked, *If all the men in the Town of Mansoul were in this confession, as they*? And they answered, *All the *natives, Lord*; but for the **Diabolonians* that came into our Town when the Tyrant got possession of us, we can say nothing for them.

They condemn themselves.

*Sins. Prov. 5. 22.

*Powers of the Soul.

*Corruptions and lusts.

Then the Prince commanded that an **Herald* should be called, and that he should in the midst, and throughout the Camp of *Emanuel* proclaim, and that with sound of Trumpet, that the Prince, the son of *Shaddai*, had in his Fathers name, and for his Fathers glory, gotten a perfect conquest and victory over *Mansoul*, and *that the prisoners should follow him and say, Amen.* So this was done as he had commanded. And presently the *Musick that was in the upper region sounded *melodiously*. The *Captains* that were in the Camp shouted, and the *Souldiers* did sing songs of Triumph to the Prince, the *Colours* waved in the wind, and great joy was every where, only it was wanting as yet in the hearts of the men of *Mansoul*.

*A victory proclaimed.

*Joy for the victory.

Then the Prince called for the prisoners to come and to stand again before him, and they came and stood trembling. And he said unto them, *The sins, trespasses, iniquities, that you with the whole Town of Mansoul, have from time to time committed*

They are pardoned, and are commanded to proclaim it to morrow in *Mansoul*.

against my Father and me, I have power and commandment from my Father to forgive to the Town of Mansoul; and do forgive you accordingly. And having so said, he gave them written in Parchment, and sealed with seven Seals, a large and general pardon, commanding both my Lord *Mayor*, my Lord *Wilbewill* and Mr. *Recorder*, to proclaim, and cause it to be proclaimed to morrow by that the Sun is up, throughout the whole Town of *Mansoul*.

Their rags are taken from them. Isa. 61. 3.

Moreover the Prince stript the Prisoners of their mourning weeds, and gave them beauty for ashes, the oyl of joy for mourning, and the garment of praise for the spirit of heaviness.

A strange alteration.

Then he gave to each of the three, *Jewels* of Gold, and *precious* stones, and took away their *ropes*, and put chains of Gold about their necks, and *Ear rings* in their ears. Now the prisoners when they did hear the gracious words of Prince *Emanuel*, and had beheld all that was done unto them, fainted almost quite away; for the grace, the benefit, the pardon, was sudden, glorious, and so big, that they were not able without staggering to stand up under it. Yea, my Lord *Wilbewill* swounded out-right, but the Prince stept to him, put his everlasting arms under him, imbraced him, kissed him, and bid him be of good cheer, for all should be performed according to his word. He also did kiss and imbrace, and smile upon the other two that were *Wilbewills* companions, saying, take these as further tokens of my love, favour and compassions to you: and I charge you that you Mr. *Recorder* tell in the Town of *Mansoul* what you have heard and seen.

Their guilt.

Then were their *Fetters* broken to pieces before their faces, and cast into the air, and their *steps* were enlarged under them. Then they fell down at the feet of the *Prince*, and kissed his feet, and wetted them with tears; also they cried out with a mighty strong voice, saying, *Blessed be the glory of the Lord from this place*. So they were bid rise up, and go to the Town, and tell to *Mansoul* what the Prince had done. He commanded also that one with a *Pipe* and *Tabor* should go and play before them all the way into the Town of *Mansoul*. Then was fulfilled what they never looked for, and they were made to possess that

They are sent home with Pipe and Tabor.

which they never dreamt of. The Prince also called for the noble Captain *Credence*, and commanded that he and some of his Officers should march before the Noble men of *Mansoul* with flying Colours into the Town. He gave also unto Captain *Credence* a charge that about that time that the *Recorder* did read the general pardon in the Town of *Mansoul*, that at that very time he should with flying Colours march in at *Eyegate* with his ten thousands at his feet, and that he should so go until he came by the high street of the Town, up to the *Castle gates*, and that himself should take possession thereof against his Lord came thither. He commanded moreover that he should bid Captain *Judgment*, and Captain *Execution* to leave the strong-hold *to him*, and to withdraw from *Mansoul*, and to return into the Camp with speed unto the Prince.

Captain *Credence* guards them home. When Faith and Pardon meet together, *Judgment* and *Execution* depart from the heart.

And now was the Town of *Mansoul* also delivered from the terrour of the first four Captains and their men.

Well, I told you before how the prisoners were entertained by the noble Prince *Emanuel*, and how they behaved themselves before him, and how he sent them away to their home with *Pipe* and *Tabor* going before them. And now you must think that those of the Town that had all this while waited to hear of their death, could not but be exercised with sadness of mind, and with thoughts that pricked like thorns. Nor could their thoughts be kept to any one point; the wind blew with them all this while at great uncertainties, yea their hearts were like a balance that had been disquieted with shaking hand. But at last as they with many a long look looked over the wall of *Mansoul*, they thought that they saw some returning to the Town; and thought again, who should they be too, who should they be! at last they discerned that they were the prisoners; but can you imagin how their hearts were surprized with wonder! specially when they perceived also in what equipage, and with what honour they were sent home! they went down to the Camp in Black, but they came back to the Town in *White*; they went down to the Camp in *ropes*, they came back in chains of *Gold*; they went down to the Camp with their feet in *fetters*, but came back with their *steps*

A strange alteration.

inlarged under them; they went also to the Camp, *looking* for death, but they came back from thence with *assurance* of life; they went down to the Camp with *heavy* hearts, but came back again with *Pipe and Tabor* playing before them. So, so soon as they were come to *Eyegate*, the poor and tottering Town of *Mansoul*, adventured to give a shout; *and they gave such a shout as made the Captains in the Princes army leap at the sound thereof*. Alas! for them poor hearts, who could blame them, since their dead friends were come to life again? for 'twas to them as life from the dead, to see the ancients of the Town of *Mansoul* to shine in such splendour. They looked for nothing but the *Ax* and the *Block*; but behold! joy and gladness, comfort and consolation, and such melodious notes attending of them, that was sufficient to make a sick-man well. So when they came up, they saluted each other with welcome, welcome, and blessed be he that has spared you. They added also, We see, it is well with you, but how must it go with the Town of *Mansoul*, and will it go well with the Town of *Mansoul*, said they? Then answered them the *Recorder*, and my Lord *Mayor*, Oh! Tidings! glad tidings! good tidings of good! and of great joy to poor *Mansoul*! Then they gave another shout that made the earth to ring again. After this they enquired yet more particularly how things went in the Camp, and what message they had from *Emanuel* to the Town. So they told them all passages that had happened to them at the Camp, and every thing that the Prince did to them. This made *Mansoul* wonder at the wisdom and grace of the Prince *Emanuel*; then they told them what they had received at his hands for the whole Town of *Mansoul*; and the *Recorder* delivered it in these words, *PARDON, PARDON, PARDON* for *Mansoul*; and this shall *Mansoul* know to morrow. Then he commanded, and they went and summoned *Mansoul* to meet together in the Market-place to morrow, there to hear their general *Pardon* read.

Isa. 33. 24.

Conscience.

The Understanding.

O the joy of pardon of sin.

But who can think what a turn, what a change, what an alteration this hint of things did make in the countenance of the Town of *Mansoul*! no man of *Mansoul* could sleep that night for joy; in every house there was joy and musick, singing, and making merry, telling and hearing of *Mansouls* happiness, was then all that *Mansoul* had to do: and this was the burden of all their Song: *Oh! more of this at the rising of the Sun! more of this to morrow! Who thought yesterday, would one say, that this day would have been* such *a day to us? And who thought, that saw our prisoners go down in irons, that they would have returned in chains of gold! yea, they that judged themselves as they went to be judged of their Judg, were by his mouth acquitted, not for that they were innocent, but of the Princes mercy, and sent home with Pipe and Tabor.*

Town-talk of the Kings mercy.

But is this the common custom of Princes, do they use to shew such kind of favours to Traytors? No! this is only peculiar to *Shaddai*, and unto *Emanuel* his Son.

Now morning drew on apace, wherefore the Lord *Mayor*, the Lord *Wilbewill*, and Mr. *Recorder* came down to the Market-place at the time that the Prince had appointed, where the Townsfolk were waiting for them; and when they came, they came in that attire, and in that glory that the Prince had put them into the day before, and the street was lightened with their glory: so the *Mayor*, *Recorder*, and my Lord *Wilbewill*, drew down to *Mouthgate*, which was at the lower end of the Market-place, because that of old time was the place where they used to read publick matters. Thither therefore they came in their Robes, and their *Tabret* went before them. Now the eagerness of the people, to know the full of the matter, was great.

Then the *Recorder* stood up upon his feet, and first beckoning with his hand for a silence, he read out with loud voice the pardon. But when he came to these words, *The Lord, the Lord God merciful and gracious, pardoning iniquity, transgressions and sins;* and to them, *all manner of sin and blasphemy shall be forgiven, &c.* they could not forbear but leap for joy. For this you must know, that there was conjoined herewith every mans name in *Mansoul*; also the seals of the pardon made a brave shew.

The manner of reading the pardon.

Exod. 34
Mar. 3.

6 *thought*] *though*

Now they tread upon the flesh.

Lively and warm thoughts.

When the *Recorder* had made an end of reading the pardon, the Townsmen ran up upon the walls of the Town, and leaped and skipped thereon for joy, and bowed themselves seven times with their faces towards *Emanuels* Pavilion, and shouted out aloud for joy, and said, *Let Emanuel live for ever*. Then order was given to the young men in *Mansoul*, that they should ring the Bells for joy. (So the Bells did ring, and the people sing, and the musick go in every house in *Mansoul*.)

The carriage of the Camp.

Faith will not be silent when *Mansoul* is saved.

When the Prince had sent home the three prisoners of *Mansoul* with joy, and *Pipe* and *Tabor*; he commanded his Captains with all the Field-officers and Souldiers throughout his army to be ready in *that* morning, that the *Recorder* should read the pardon in *Mansoul*, to do his further pleasure. So the morning as I have shewed, being come, just as the *Recorder* had made an end of reading the pardon, *Emanuel* commanded that all the Trumpets in the Camp should sound, that the Colours should be displayed, half of them upon mount *Gracious*, and half of them upon mount *Justice*. He commanded also that all the Captains should shew themselves in all their Harness, and that the Souldiers should shout for joy. Nor was Captain *Credence*, though in the Castle, silent in such a day, but he from the top of the hold shewed himself with sound of Trumpet to *Mansoul*, and to the Princes Camp.

Thus have I shewed you the manner, and way that *Emanuel* took to recover the Town of *Mansoul* from under the hand and power of the Tyrant *Diabolus*.

The Prince displays his Graces before *Mansoul*.

Now when the Prince had compleated *these*, *the outward ceremonies of his joy*, He again commanded that his Captains and Souldiers should shew unto *Mansoul* some feats of War. So they presently addressed themselves to this work. But Oh! with what agility, nimbleness, dexterity and bravery did these military-men discover their skill in feats of War to the now gazing Town of *Mansoul*!

They marched, *they counter-marched*, *they opened to the right and left*, *they divided*, *and subdivided*, *they closed*, *they wheeled*, *made good their front and reer with their right and left wings*, *and twenty things*

8 house in *Mansoul*.)] house) in *Mansoul*.

more, with that aptness, and then were all as they were again, that they took, yea ravished the hearts that were in Mansoul to behold it. But add to this, *the handling of their arms, the managing of their weapons of war, were marvellous taking to Mansoul and me.*

They are ravished at the sight of them.

When this action was over, the whole Town of *Mansoul* came out as one man to the Prince in the Camp to thank him, and praise him for his abundant favour, and to beg that it would please his Grace to come unto *Mansoul* with his men, and there to take up their quarters for ever. And this they did in most humble manner, bowing themselves seven times to the ground before him. Then said he, *All peace be to you*: so the Town came nigh and touched with the hand the top of his Golden Scepter, and they said, *Oh! that the Prince* Emanuel *with his Captains and men of war would dwell in* Mansoul *for ever; and that his battering Rams and Slings might be lodged in her for the use and service of the Prince, and for the help and strength of Mansoul.* For said they, we have room for thee, we have room for thy men, we have also room for thy weapons of war, and a place to make a Magazine for thy Carriages. Do it, *Emanuel*, and thou shalt be King and Captain in *Mansoul* for ever. Yea, govern thou also according to all the desire of thy soul, and make thou Governours and Princes under thee of thy Captains and men of War, and we will become thy servants, and thy Laws shall be our direction.

They beg that the Prince and his men will dwell with them for ever.

Say and hold to it *Mansoul.*

They added moreover, and prayed his Majesty to consider thereof, for said they, if now after all this grace bestowed upon us thy miserable Town of *Mansoul*, thou shouldest withdraw, thou and thy Captains from us, the Town of *Mansoul* will die. Yea, said they, our blessed *Emanuel*, if thou shouldest depart from us now, now thou hast done so much good for us, and shewed so much mercy unto us; What will follow but that our joy will be as if it had not been, and our enemies will a second time come upon us with more rage than at the first? Wherefore we beseech thee, O thou the desire of our eyes, and the strength and life of our poor Town, accept of this motion that now we have made unto our Lord, and come and dwell in the midst of us, and let us be thy people. Besides, Lord, we do not

Their Fears.

know but that to this day many *Diabolonians* may be yet lurking in the Town of *Mansoul*, and they will betray us when thou shalt leave us, into the hand of *Diabolus* again; and who knows what designs, plots, or contrivances have passed, betwixt them about these things already; loth we are to fall again into his horrible hands. Wherefore let it please thee to accept of our Palace for thy place of residence, and of the houses of the best men in our Town for the reception of thy Souldiers, and their furniture.

The Princes question to *Mansoul*.

Then said the Prince, *If I come to your Town, will you suffer me further to prosecute that which is in mine heart against mine enemies and yours: yea will you help me in such undertakings?*

Their Answer.

They answered, We know not what we shall do, we did not think once that we should have been such Traytors to *Shaddai*, as we have proved to be: What then shall we say to our Lord? Let him put no trust in his Saints, let the Prince dwell in our Castle, and make of our Town a Garrison, let him set his noble Captains, and his Warlike Souldiers over us. Yea, let him conquer us with his love, and overcome us with his Grace, and then surely shall he be but with us, and help us, as he was, and did that morning that our pardon was read unto us, we shall comply with this our Lord, and with his ways, and fall in with his word against the mighty.

One word more, and thy servants have done, and in this will trouble our Lord no more. *We know not the depth of the wisdom of thee our Prince. Who could have thought that had been ruled by his reason, that so much sweet as we do now enjoy, should have come out of those bitter trials wherewith we were tried at the first? But, Lord, let light go before, and let love come after: yea, take us by the hand, and lead us by thy counsels, and let this always abide upon us, that all things shall be for the best for thy servants, and come to our* Mansoul, *and do as it pleaseth thee. Or, Lord, come to our* Mansoul, *do what thou wilt, so thou keepest us from sinning, and makest us serviceable to thy Majesty.*

He consenteth to dwell in *Mansoul*, and

Then said the Prince to the Town of *Mansoul* again, *Go return to your houses in peace, I will willingly in this comply with your desires. I will remove my Royal Pavilion, I will draw up my forces before* Eyegate *to morrow, and so will march forwards into the town of* Mansoul. *I will possess my self of your Castle of* Mansoul, *and will set my Souldiers over you; yea, I will yet do things in* Mansoul *that cannot be parallel'd in any Nation, Country or Kingdom under Heaven.*

promiseth to come in to morrow.

Then did the men of *Mansoul* give a shout, and returned unto their houses in peace; they also told to their kindred and friends the good that *Emanuel* had promised to *Mansoul*. And to morrow, said they, he will march into our Town, and take up his dwelling, he and his men in *Mansoul*.

Then went out the inhabitants of the Town of *Mansoul* with haste to the green trees, and to the meadows to gather boughs and flowers, therwith to strew the streets against their Prince, the son of *Shaddai*, should come; they also made Garlands, and other fine works to betoken how joyful they were, and should be to receive their *Emanuel* into *Mansoul*; yea, they strewed the street quite from *Eyegate* to the *Castle-gate*, the place where the Prince should be. They also prepared for his coming what musick the Town of *Mansoul* would afford, that they might play before him to the Palace his habitation.

Mansouls preparation for his reception.

So at the time appointed he makes his approach to *Mansoul*, and the Gates were set open for him, there also the Ancients and Elders of *Mansoul* met to salute him with a thousand welcomes. Then he arose and entred *Mansoul*, he and all his servants. The Elders of *Mansoul* did also go dancing before him till he came to the Castle-gates. And *this* was the manner of his going up thither. He was clad in his Golden Armour, he rode in his Royal Chariot, the Trumpets sounded about him, the Colours were displayed, his ten thousands went up at his feet, and the Elders of *Mansoul* danced before him. And now were the walls of the famous Town of *Mansoul* filled with the tramplings of the inhabitants thereof, who went up thither to view the approach of the blessed Prince, and his Royal Army. Also the Casements, Windows, Balconies and tops of the houses were all now filled with persons of all sorts to behold how their Town was to be filled with good.

He enters the Town of *Mansoul* and how.

Now when he was come so far into the Town as to the *Recorders* house, he commanded that one should go to C. *Credence*, to know whether the Castle of *Mansoul* was prepared to entertain his Royal presence (for the preparation of that was Act. 15. 9. left to *that Captain*) and word was brought that it was. Then was Captain *Credence* commanded also to come forth with his power to meet the Prince, the which was as he had commanded, done, and he conducted him into the Castle. Eph. 3. 17. This done, the Prince that night did lodg in the Castle with his mighty *Captains* and men of War, to the joy of the Town of *Mansoul*.

The Towns-men covet who shall have most of the Soldiers that belong to the Prince.

Now the next care of the Townsfolk was how the *Captains* and *Souldiers* of the Princes army should be quartered among them, and the care was not how they should shut their hands of them, but how they should fill their houses with them; for every man in *Mansoul* now had that esteem of *Emanuel* and his men, that nothing grieved them more, than because they were not enlarged enough, every one of them to receive the whole army of the Prince, yea they counted it their glory to be waiting upon them, and would in those days run at their bidding like *Lacquies*. At last they came to this result:

1. That Captain *Innocency* should quarter at Mr. *Reasons*.

2. That Captain *Patience* should quarter at Mr. *Minds*. This Mr *Mind* was formerly the Lord *Wilbewills* Clerk in time of the late rebellion.

How they were quartered in the Town of *Mansoul*.

3. It was ordered that Captain *Charity* should quarter at Mr. *Affections* house.

4. That Captain *Good-hope* should quarter at my Lord *Mayors*. Now for the house of the *Recorder*, himself desired, because his house was next to the *Castle*, and because from him it was ordered by the Prince, that if need be, the alarm should be given to *Mansoul*; It was, I say, desired by him that Captain *Boanerges*, and Captain *Conviction* should take up their quarters with him, even they and all their men.

5. As for Captain *Judgment*, and Captain *Execution*, my Lord *Wilbewill* took them, and their men to him, because he was to rule under the Prince for the good of the Town of

Rom. 6. 19. Eph. 3. 17.

Mansoul now, as he had *before* under the Tyrant *Diabolus* for the hurt and damage thereof.

6. And throughout the rest of the Town were quartered *Emanuels* forces, but Captain *Credence* with his men abode still in the Castle. So the Prince, his Captains, and his Soldiers were lodged in the Town of *Mansoul*.

Now the *Ancients* and *Elders* of the Town of *Mansoul* thought that they never should have enough of the Prince *Emanuel*; his person, his actions, his words and behaviour, were so pleasing, so taking, so desirable to them. Wherefore they prayed him, that though the Castle of *Mansoul* was his place of residence (and they desired that he might dwell there for ever) yet that he would often visit the streets, houses, and people of *Mansoul*. For, said they, Dread Soveraign, thy presence, thy looks, thy smiles, thy words, are the life, and strength, and sinews of the Town of *Mansoul*.

Mansoul inflamed with their Prince *Emanuel*.

Besides this, they craved that they might have without difficulty or interruption, continual access unto him, (so for that very purpose he commanded that the Gates should stand open) that they might there see the manner of his doings, the fortifications of the place, and the Royal mansion-house of the Prince.

They have access unto him.

When he spake, they all stopped their mouths, and gave audience; and when he walked, it was their delight to imitate him in his goings.

They learn of him.

Now upon a time *Emanuel* made a feast for the Town of *Mansoul*, and upon the Feasting-day the Townsfolk were come to the Castle to partake of his Banket. And he feasted them with all manner of outlandish food, food that grew not in the fields of *Mansoul*, nor in all the whole Kingdom of *Universe*. It was food that came from his Fathers Court, and so there was dish after dish set before them, and they were commanded freely to eat. But still when a fresh dish was set before them, they would whisperingly say to each other, *What is it*? for they wist not what to call it. They drank also of the water that was made wine; and were very merry with him. There was musick also all the while at the Table, and

Promise after promise.

Exod. 16. 15.

Brave entertainment.

Psa. 78. 24, 25.

man did eat Angels food, and had honey given him out of the rock; so *Mansoul* did eat the food that was peculiar to the Court, yea they had now thereof to the full.

I must not forget to tell you, that as at this Table there were *Musicians*; so they were not those of the Country, nor yet of the Town of *Mansoul*; but they were the Masters of the Songs that were sung at the Court of *Shaddai*.

Riddles.

Now after the feast was over, *Emanuel* was for entertaining the Town of *Mansoul* with some curious riddles of secrets drawn up by his Fathers Secretary, by the skill and wisdom of *Shaddai*; the like to these there is not in any Kingdom. These *Riddles* were made upon the King *Shaddai* himself, and upon *Emanuel* his Son, and upon his wars and doings with *Mansoul*.

The holy Scriptures.

Emanuel also expounded unto them some of those Riddles himself, but Oh how they were lightned! they saw what they never saw, they could not have thought that such rarities could have been couched in so few and such ordinary words. I told you before whom these *Riddles* did concern; and as they were opened, the people did evidently *see* 'twas so. Yea, they did gather that the things themselves were a kind of a *Pourtraicture*, and that of *Emanuel* himself; for when they read in the *Scheme* where the Riddles were writ, and looked in the face of the Prince, things looked so like the *one* to the *other*, that *Mansoul* could not forbear but say, This is the *Lamb*, this is the *Sacrifice*, this is the *Rock*, this is the *Red-Cow*, this is the *Door*, and this is the *Way*; with a great many other things more.

The end of that Banquet.

And thus he dismissed the Town of *Mansoul*. But can you imagin how the people of the Corporation were taken with this Entertainment? Oh they were transported with joy, they were drowned with wonderment, while they saw and understood, and considered what their *Emanuel* entertained them withal, and what mysteries he opened to them; and when they were at home in their houses, and in their most retired places they could not but sing of him, and of his actions. Yea, so taken were the Townsmen now with their Prince, that they would sing of him in their sleep.

Now it was in the heart of the Prince *Emanuel* to new *model* the Town of *Mansoul*, and to put it into such a condition as might be most pleasing to him, and that might best stand with the profit and security of the now flourishing Town of *Mansoul*. He provided also against insurrections at home, and invasions from abroad; such love had he for the famous Town of *Mansoul*.

Mansoul must be new modelled.

Wherefore he first of all commanded that the great slings that were brought from his Fathers Court when he came to the War of *Mansoul*, should be mounted, some upon the *Battlements* of the *Castle*, some upon the *Towers*, for there were Towers in the Town of *Mansoul*, Towers new built by *Emanuel* since he came thither. There was also an instrument invented by *Emanuel*, that was to throw stones from the Castle of *Mansoul*, out at *Mouth-gate*; an instrument that could not be resisted, nor that would miss of execution; wherefore for the wonderful exploits that it did when used, it went without a name, and it was committed to the care of, and to be managed by the brave Captain, the Captain *Credence*, in case of war.

The instruments of war mounted.

A nameless terrible instrument in *Mansoul*.

This done, *Emanuel* called the Lord *Wilbewill* to him, and gave him in commandment to take care of the Gates, the Wall and Towers in *Mansoul*; Also the Prince gave him the Militia into his hand, and a special charge to withstand all insurrections and tumults that might be made in *Mansoul* against the peace of our Lord the King, and the peace and tranquillity of the Town of *Mansoul*. He also gave him in commission, that if he found any of the *Diabolonians* lurking in any corner in the famous Town of *Mansoul*, he should forthwith apprehend them, and stay them, or commit them to safe custody, that they may be proceeded against according to Law.

Wilbewill promoted.

Then he called unto him the Lord *Understanding*, who was the old Lord *Mayor*, he that was put out of place when *Diabolus* took the Town, and put him into his former office again, and it became his place for his life time. He bid him also that he should build him a Palace near *Eye-gate*, and that he should build it in fashion like a Tower for defence. He bid

My Lord *Mayor* put into place.

him also that he should read in the *Revelation* of Mysteries all the days of his life, that he might know how to perform his Office aright.

Mr. *Knowledg* made *Recorder*.

He also made Mr. *Knowledg* the *Recorder*, not of contempt to old Mr. *Conscience*, who had been *Recorder* before; but for that it was in his Princely mind to confer upon Mr. *Conscience* another imploy; of which he told the old Gentleman he should know more hereafter.

The image of the Prince and his Father set up again in *Mansoul*. Rev. 22. 4.

Then he commanded that the Image of *Diabolus* should be taken down from the place where it was set up; and that they should destroy it utterly, beating of it into powder, and casting it into the wind, without the Town-wall. And that the image of *Shaddai* his Father should be set up again, with his *own*, upon the Castle gates. And that it should be more fairly drawn than ever; for as much as both his Father and himself were come to *Mansoul* in more grace and mercy than heretofore. He would also that his name should be fairly ingraven upon the front of the Town, and that it should be done in the best of Gold for the honour of the Town of *Mansoul*.

Some *Diabolonians* committed ro prison under the hand of Mr. *True-man* the Keeper.

After this was done, *Emanuel* gave out a Commandment that those three great *Diabolonians* should be apprehended, namely the two late Lord *Mayors*, to wit, Mr. *Incredulity*, Mr. *Lustings*, and Mr. *Forget good* the *Recorder*. Besides these, there were some of them that *Diabolus* made Burgesses and Aldermen in *Mansoul*, that were committed to Ward by the hand of the *now* valiant, and *now* right noble, the brave Lord *Wilbewill*.

And these were their names, Alderman *Atheism*, Alderman *Hard-heart*, and Alderman *False-peace*. The Burgesses were Mr. *No-truth*, Mr. *Pitiless*, Mr. *Haughty*, with the like. These were committed to close custody; and the *Gaolers* name was Mr. *True-man*; this *True man* was one of those that *Emanuel* brought with him from his Fathers Court, when at the first he made a war upon *Diabolus* in the Town of *Mansoul*.

Diabolus's strong-holds pull'd down.

After this the Prince gave a charge that the three strong holds that at the command of *Diabolus* the *Diabolonians* built in *Mansoul*, should be demolished, and utterly pulled down; of which Holds and their names, with their Captains and Governours, you read a little before. But this was long in doing, because of the largeness of the places, and because the stones, the timber, the iron, and all rubbish was to be carried without the Town.

When this was done, the Prince gave order that the Lord Mayor and Aldermen of *Mansoul*, should call a Court of *Judicature* for the *Trial* and *Execution* of the *Diabolonians* in the Corporation now under the charge of Mr. *True-man* the Gaoler.

A Court to be called to try the Diabolonians.

Now when the time was come, and the Court set, Commandment was sent to Mr. *True-man* the Gaoler to bring the Prisoners down to the Barr. Then were the prisoners brought down, pinioned, and chained together as the custom of the Town of *Mansoul* was. So when they were presented before the Lord Mayor, the *Recorder*, and the rest of the Honourable Bench, First, the *Jury* was impanelled, and then the *Witnesses* sworn. The names of the *Jury* were these, Mr. *Belief*, Mr. *True-heart*, Mr. *Upright*, Mr. *Hate-bad*, Mr. *Love-God*, Mr. *See-truth*, Mr. *Heavenly-mind*, Mr. *Moderate*, Mr. *Thankeful*, Mr. *Good-work*, Mr. *Zeal for God*, and Mr. *Humble*.

The Prisoners brought to the Bar.

The Jury *impanelled, and* witnesses *sworn.*

The names of the *Witnesses* were Mr. *Know-all*, Mr. *Tell true*, Mr. *Hate lies*, with my Lord *Wilbewill* and his man if need were.

So the prisoners were set to the Bar, then said Mr. *Do-right* (for he was the Town Clerk), set *Atheism* to the Bar, Gaoler. So he was set to the Bar. Then said the Clerk, *Atheism*, *hold up thy hand: Thou art here indicted by the name of* Atheism, (*an intruder upon the Town of* Mansoul) *for that thou hast perniciously and doultishly taught and maintained that there is no God, and so no heed to be taken to Religion. This thou hast done against the being, honour, and glory of the King, and against the peace and safety of the Town of* Mansoul. *What saist thou, art thou guilty of this Indictment, or not?*

Do-right the Clerk.

Atheism set to the Bar, his Indictment.

Atheism. Not Guilty.

His Plea.

Cry. *Call Mr.* Know-all, Mr. Tell true, *and* Mr. Hate-lies *into the Court.*

So they were called, and they appeared.

Clerk. Then said the Clerk, *You the Witnesses for the King, look upon the Prisoner at the Bar, do you know him?*

Know. Then said Mr. *Know-all*, Yes, my Lord, we know him, his name is *Atheism*, he has been a very pestilent fellow for many years in the miserable Town of *Mansoul*.

Cler. *You are sure you know him?*

Know. Know him! Yes, my Lord: I have heretofore too often been in his company, to be at this time ignorant of him. He is a *Diabolonian*, the son of a *Diabolonian*, I knew his Grandfather, and his Father.

Cler. *Well said: He standeth here indicted by the name of* Atheism, *&c. and is charged that he hath maintained and taught that there is no God, and so no heed need be taken to any Religion. What say you the Kings Witnesses, to this? is he guilty or not?*

Know. My Lord, I and he were once in *Vilains* Lane together, and he at that time did briskly talk of divers opinions, and then and there I heard him say, That for his part he did believe that there was no God. But, said he, I can profess one, and be as Religious too, if the company I am in, and the circumstances of other things, said he, shall put me upon it.

Cler. *You are sure you heard him say thus.*

Know. Upon mine Oath I heard him say thus.

Then said the Clerk, Mr. *Tell-true*, *What say you to the Kings Judges, touching the prisoner at the Bar?*

Tell. My Lord, I formerly was a great companion of his, (for the which I now repent me) and I have often heard him say, and that with very great stomachfulness, that he believed there was neither God, Angel, nor Spirit.

Cler. *Where did you hear him say so?*

Tell. In *Blackmouth*-lane, and in *Blasphemers* row, and in many other places besides.

Cler. *Have you much knowledge of him?*

Tell. I know him to be a *Diabolonian*, the son of a *Diabolonian*, and an horrible man to deny a Deity; his Fathers name was *Never-be-good*, and he had more children than this *Atheism*. I have no more to say.

Cler. Mr. Hate lyes *look upon the prisoner at the Bar, do you know him?*

Hate. My Lord, this *Atheism* is one of the vilest wretches that ever I came near, or had to do with in my life. I have heard him say that there is no God; I have heard him say that there is no world to come, no sin, nor punishment hereafter; and moreover, I have heard him say that 'twas as good to go to a Whore-house as to go to hear a Sermon.

Cler. *Where did you hear him say these things?*

Hate. In *Drunkards*-row, just at *Raskal*-lanes-end, at a house in which Mr. *Impiety* lived.

Lustings set to the Bar.

Cler. *Set him by*, Gaoler, *and set Mr.* Lustings *to the Bar.*

Mr. Lustings, *thou art here indicted by the name of* Lustings, (*an intruder upon the Town of* Mansoul) *for that thou hast Devilishly and Traiterously taught by practice and filthy words that it is lawful and profitable to man to give way to his carnal desires, and that thou for thy part hast not, nor never wilt deny thyself of any sinful delight as long as thy name is* Lustings. *How saist thou, art thou guilty of this Indictment or not?*

His Indictment.

His plea.

Lust. Then said Mr. *Lustings*, My Lord, I am a man of high birth, and have been used to pleasures and pastimes of greatness, I have not been wont to be snub'd for my doings, but have been left to follow my will as if it were Law. And it seems strange to me that I should this day be called into question for that, that not only I, but almost all men do either secretly or openly countenance, love, and approve of.

Cler. *Sir, we concern not our selves with your greatness (though the higher the better you should have been) but we are concerned, and so are you now, about an Indictment preferred against you. How say you, are you guilty of it, or not?*

Lust. Not guilty.

Cler. *Cryer*, call upon the Witnesses to stand forth, and give their Evidence.

Cry. Gentlemen, you the Witnesses for the King, come in and give in your Evidence for our Lord the King against the prisoner at the Bar.

Cler. Come, Mr. *Know-all*, look upon the prisoner at the Bar do you know him?

Know. Yes, my Lord, I know him.

Clerk. What's his name?

Know. His name is *Lustings*, he was the son of one *Beastly*, and his mother bare him in *Flesh-street*; she was one *Evil-concupiscence*'s daughter. I knew all the generation of them.

Cler. *Well said, You have here heard his* Indictment, *what say you to it, is he guilty of the things charged against him, or not?*

Know. My Lord, he has, as he saith, been a great man indeed; and greater in wickedness than by Pedigree, more than a thousand fold.

Cler. *But what do you know of his particular actions, and especially with reference to his* Indictment?

Know. I know him to be a swearer, a lyer, a Sabbath-breaker; I know him to be a fornicator, and an unclean person; I know him to be guilty of abundance of evils. He has been to my knowledg a very filthy man.

Cler. *But where did he use to commit his wickedness, in some private corners, or more open and shamelesly?*

Know. All the Town over, my Lord.

Cler. Come, Mr. *Tell-true*, what have you to say for our Lord the King against the prisoner at the Bar?

Tell. My Lord, all that the first Witness has said I know to be true, and a great deal more besides.

Cler. Mr. *Lustings*, do you hear what these Gentlemen say?

His second Plea.

Lust. I was ever of opinion that the happiest life that a man could live on earth, was to keep himself back from nothing that he desired in the world; nor have I been false at any time to this opinion of mine, but have lived in the love of my notions all my days. Nor was I ever so churlish, having found such sweetness in them my self, as to keep the commendations of them from others.

Court. Then said the Court. *There hath proceeded enough from his own mouth to lay him open to condemnation, wherefore set him by,* Gaoler, *and set* Mr. Incredulity *to the Bar.*

Incredulity set to the Bar.

Incredulity set to the Bar.

Cler. Mr. Incredulity, *thou art here Indicted by the name of* Incredulity, (*an intruder upon the Town of* Mansoul) *for that thou hast feloniously and wickedly, and that when thou wert an Officer in the Town of* Mansoul, *made head against the Captains of the great King* Shaddai, *when they came and demanded possession of* Mansoul; *yea thou didst bid defiance to the name, forces and cause of the King, and didst also, as did* Diabolus *thy Captain, stir up and encourage the Town of* Mansoul *to make head against, and resist the said force of the King. What saist thou to this Indictment? art thou guilty of it, or not?* His Indictment.

Then said *Incredulity*, I know not *Shaddai*, I love my old Prince, I thought it my duty to be true to my trust, and to do what I could to possess the minds of the men of *Mansoul* to do their utmost to resist strangers and foreigners, and with might to fight against them. Nor have I, nor shall I change mine opinion for fear of trouble, though you at present are possessed of place and power. His Plea.

Court. Then said the Court, the man as you see is incorrigible, he is for maintaining his Villanies by stoutness of words, and his rebellion with impudent confidence. And therefore set him by *Gaoler*, and set Mr. *Forget-good* to the Bar.

Forget-good set to the Bar. *Forgetgood* set to the Bar.

Cler. Mr. Forget-good, *thou art here Indicted by the name of* Forget-good (*an intruder upon the Town of* Mansoul) *for that thou when the whole affairs of the Town of* Mansoul *were in thy hand, didst utterly forget to serve them in what was good, and didst fall in with the Tyrant* Diabolus *against* Shaddai *the King, against his Captains, and all his host, to the dishonour of* Shaddai, *the breach of his Law, and the endangering of the destruction of the famous Town of* Mansoul. *What saist thou to this Indictment? art thou guilty or not guilty?* His Indictment.

Then said *Forget-good*, Gentlemen, and at this time my Judges, as to the Indictment by which I stand of several crimes accused before you, pray attribute my forgetfulness to mine *age*, and not to my *wilfulness*; to the *craziness* of my brain, and not to the *carelesness* of my mind, and then I hope I may by His Plea.

your charity be excused from great punishment, though I be guilty.

Then said the Court, *Forget-good, Forget-good, Thy forgetfulness of good was not simply of frailty, but of purpose, and for that thou didst loth to keep vertuous things in thy mind. What was bad thou couldest retain, but what was good thou couldest not abide to think of, thy age therefore, and thy pretended* craziness, *thou makest use of to blind the Court withal, and as a cloak to cover thy Knavery. But let us hear what the Witnesses have to say for the King against the prisoner at the Bar, is he guilty of this Indictment, or not?*

Hate. My Lord, I have heard this *Forget-good* say, That he could never abide to think of goodness, no not for a quarter of an hour.

Cler. *Where did you hear him say so?*

Hate. In *All-base*-lane, at a house next door to the Sign of *Conscience seared with an hot iron.*

Cler. Mr. *Know-all*, what can you say for our Lord the King against the prisoner at the Bar?

Know. My Lord, I know this man well, he is a *Diabolonian*, the son of a *Diabolonian*, his Fathers name was *Love-naught*, and for him I have often heard him say that he counted the very thoughts of goodness the most burdensome thing in the world.

Clerk. *Where have you heard him say these words?*

Know. In *Flesh*-lane right opposite to the Church.

Then said the Clerk, *Come*, Mr. Tell-true, *give in your Evidence concerning the prisoner at the Bar about that for which he stands here, as you see, indicted before this honourable Court.*

Tell. My Lord, I have heard him often say, he had rather think of the vilest thing than of what is contained in the Holy Scriptures.

Clerk. Where did you hear him say such grievous words?

Tell. Where? in a great many places, particularly in *Nauseous*-street, in the house of one *Shameless*, and in *Filth*-lane,* at the sign of the *Reprobate*, next door to the *Descent into the pit*.

Court. *Gentlemen, you have heard the Indictment, his Plea, and the testimony of the Witnesses.* Gaoler, *set* Mr. Hard-heart *to the Bar.*

Hard-heart set to the Bar.

He is set to the Bar.

Clerk. Mr. Hard-heart, *thou art here Indicted by the name of* Hard-heart, (*an intruder upon the Town of* Mansoul) *for that thou didst most desperately and wickedly possess the Town of* Mansoul *with impenitency and obdurateness, and didst keep them from remorse and sorrow for their evils, all the time of their apostasie from, and rebellion against the blessed King* Shaddai. *What saist thou to this Indictment, art thou guilty, or not guilty?*

Hard. My Lord, I never knew what remorse or sorrow meant in all my life: I am impenetrable. I care for no man; nor can I be pierced with mens griefs, their groans will not enter into my heart; whomever I mischief, whomever I wrong, to me it is musick, when to others mourning.

Court. *You see the man is a right* Diabolonian, *and has convicted himself. Set him by*, Gaoler, *and set* Mr. False-peace *to the Bar.*

***False-peace* set to the Bar.**

False-peace set to the Bar.

Mr. False-peace, *Thou art here Indicted by the name of* False-peace, (*an intruder upon the Town of* Mansoul) *for that thou didst most wickedly and satanically bring, hold, and keep the Town of* Mansoul, *both in her apostasie, and in her hellish rebellion, in a false, groundless and dangerous peace, and damnable security, to the dishonour of the King, the transgression of his Law, and the great damage of the Town of* Mansoul. *What saist thou, art thou guilty of this Indictment, or not?*

His plea.

Then said Mr. *False-peace*, Gentlemen, and you now appointed to be my Judges, I acknowledg that my name is Mr. *Peace*, but that my name is *False-peace*, I utterly deny. If your Honours shall please to send for any that do intimately know me, or for the midwife that laid my mother of me, or for the Gossips that was at my Christening, they will any, or all of them prove that my name is not *False-peace*, but *Peace*. Wherefore I cannot plead to this Indictment, for as much as my name is not inserted therein, and as is my *true* name, so also are my conditions. I was always a man that loved to live at quiet, and what I loved my self, that I thought others might love also.

He denies his name.

Wherefore when I saw any of my neighbours to labour under a disquieted mind, I endeavoured to help them what I could, and instances of this good temper of mine, many I could give: As,

Pleads his Goodness.

First, when at the beginning our Town of *Mansoul* did decline the ways of *Shaddai*, they, some of them afterwards began to have disquieting reflections upon themselves for what they had done; but I, as one troubled to see them disquieted sought out means to get them quiet again.

2. When the ways of the old world, and of *Sodom*, were in fashion; if any thing happened to molest those that were for the customes of the present times, I laboured to make them quiet again, and to cause them to act without molestation.

3. To come nearer home, when the wars fell out between *Shaddai* and *Diabolus*, if at any time I saw any of the Town of *Mansoul* afraid of destruction, I often used by some way, device, invention or other, to labour to bring them to peace again.

Wherefore since I have been always a man of so vertuous a temper, as some say a peace-maker is, and if a peace-maker be so deserving a man as some have been bold to attest he is. Then let me, Gentlemen, be accounted by you, who have a great name for justice and equity in *Mansoul*, for a man that deserveth not this inhumane way of treatment, but liberty, and also a licence to seek damage of those that have been my accusers.

Then said the *Clerk*, *Cryer*, make a Proclamation.

Cryer, *O Yes, for as much as the prisoner at the Bar hath denied his name to be that which is mentioned in the Indictment, the* Court *requireth that if there be any in this place that can give information to the* Court *of the original and right name of the prisoner, they would come forth and give in their Evidence, for the prisoner stands upon his own innocency.*

New Witnesses come in against him.

Then came two into the Court and desired that they might have leave to speak what they knew concerning the prisoner at the Bar; the name of the one was *Search-truth*, and the name of the other *Vouch-truth*: so the Court demanded of these men,

If they knew the prisoner, and what they could say concerning him, for he stands, said they, upon his own Vindication?

Then said Mr. *Search-truth*, My Lord, I—

Court. Hold, give him his Oath, then they sware him. So he proceeded.

Search. My Lord, I know, and have known this man from a child, and can attest that his name is *False peace*. I knew his Father, his name was Mr. *Flatter*, and his Mother before she was married was called by the name of Mrs. *Sooth up*; and these two when they came together, lived not long without this son, and when he was born, they called his name *False-peace*. I was his play-fellow, only I was somewhat older than he; and when his mother did use to call him home from his play, she used to say, *Falsepeace*, *Falsepeace*, come home quick, or I'le fetch you. Yea, I knew him when he sucked; and though I was then but little, yet I can remember that when his mother did use to sit at the door with him, or did play with him in her arms, she would call him twenty times together, My little *Falsepeace*, my pretty *Falsepeace*, and O my sweet Rogue, *Falsepeace*; and again, O my little bird, *Falsepeace*; and how do I love my child! The Gossips also know it is thus, though he has had the face to deny it in open Court.

Then Mr. *Vouch-truth* was called upon to speak what he knew of him. So they sware him.

Then said Mr. *Vouch-truth*, My Lord, all that the former Witness said is true; his name is *Falsepeace*, the son of Mr. *Flatter*, and of Mrs. *Soothup* his mother. And I have in former times seen him angry with those that have called him any thing else but *Falsepeace*, for he would say that all such did mock and nick-name him, but this was in the time when Mr. *Falsepeace* was a great man, and when the *Diabolonians* were the brave men in *Mansoul*.

Court. 'Gentlemen, you have heard what these two men have sworn against the prisoner at the Bar: and now Mr. *False-peace* to you, you have denied your name to be *False-peace*, yet you see that these honest men have sworn that t[his]

36 t[his]] *this* 1696

is your name. As to your Plea, in that you are quite besides the matter of your Indictment, you are not by it charged for evil doing, because you are a man of peace, or a peace-maker among your neighbours; but for that you did wickedly, and satanically bring, keep, and hold the Town of *Mansoul* both under its apostacy from, and in its rebellion against its King, in a false, lying, and damnable peace, contrary to the Law of *Shaddai*, and to the hazard of the destruction of the then miserable Town of *Mansoul*. All that you have pleaded for your self is, that you have denied your name, *&c.* but here you see we have Witnesses to prove that you are the man.

'For the peace that you so much boast of making among your neighbours, know that peace that is not a companion of truth and holiness, but that which is without this foundation, is grounded upon a lye, and is both deceitful and damnable; as also the great *Shaddai* hath said: thy Plea therefore has not delivered thee from what by the Indictment thou art charged with, but rather it doth fasten all upon thee.

'But thou shalt have very fair play, let us call the Witnesses that are to testifie, as to matter of fact, and see what they have to say for our Lord the King against the prisoner at the Bar.'

Clerk. Mr. Know-all, *what say you for our Lord the King against the Prisoner at the Bar?*

Know. My Lord, this man hath of a long time made it, to my knowledg, his business to keep the Town of *Mansoul* in a sinful quietness in the midst of all her leudness, filthiness and turmoils, and hath said, and that in my hearing, Come, come, let us fly from all trouble, on what ground soever it comes, and let us be for a quiet and peaceable life, though it wanteth a good foundation.

Clerk. *Come*, Mr. Hate-lies, *what have you to say?*

Hate. My Lord, I have heard him say, that peace, though in a way of unrighteousness is better than trouble with truth.

Clerk. *Where did you hear him say this?*

Hate. I heard him say it in *Folly-yard*, at the house of one Mr. *Simple*, next-door to the sign of the *Self-deceiver*. Yea, he hath said this to my knowledg twenty times in that place.

No-truth set to the Bar. His Indictment.

Clerk. 'We may spare further Witness, this Evidence is plain and full. Set him by, *Gaoler*, and set Mr. *No-truth* to the Bar. Mr. *No-truth*, thou art here Indicted by the name of *No-truth*, (an intruder upon the Town of *Mansoul*) for that thou hast always to the dishonour of *Shaddai*, and the endangering of the utter ruin of the famous Town of *Mansoul*, set thy self to deface, and utterly to spoil all the remainders of the law and image of *Shaddai* that have been found in *Mansoul* after her deep apostasie from her King to *Diabolus* the envious *Tyrant*. What saist thou, art thou guilty of this Indictment, or not?'

His Plea.

No. Not guilty, my Lord.

Then the Witnesses were called, and Mr. *Knowall* did first give in his Evidence against him.

Witnesses.

Know. My Lord, this man was at the pulling down of the Image of *Shaddai*; yea, this is he that did it with his own hands. I my self stood by and saw him do it, and he did it at the commandment of *Diabolus*. Yea, this Mr. *Notruth* did more than this, he did also set up the horned image of the beast *Diabolus* in the same place. This also is he that at the bidding of *Diabolus* did rent and tear, and cause to be consumed all that he could of the remainders of the Law of the King, even whatever he could lay his hands on in *Mansoul*.

Clerk. *Who saw him do this besides your self?*

Hate. I did, my Lord, and so did many more besides; for this was not done by stealth, or in a corner, but in the open view of all, yea he chose himself to do it publickly, for he delighted in the doing of it.

Clerk. Mr. *Notruth*, how could you have the face to plead not guilty, when you were so manifestly the doer of all this wickedness?

Notr. Sir, I thought I must say something, and as my name is, so I speak: I have been advantaged thereby before now, and did not know but by speaking *No truth*, I might have reaped the same benefit now.

Pityless set to the Bar.

Clerk. 'Set him by, *Gaoler*, and set Mr. *Pityless* to the Bar: Mr. *Pityless*, thou art here indicted by the name of *Pityless*, (an intruder upon the Town of *Mansoul*) for that thou didst most

His Indictment.

trayterously and wickedly shut up all bowels of compassion, and wouldest not suffer poor *Mansoul* to condole her own misery when she had apostatized from her rightful King, but didst evade, and at all times turn her mind awry from those thoughts that had in them a tendency to lead her to repentance. What saist thou to this Indictment? Guilty, or not guilty?'

His Plea.

Not guilty of *Pitylesness*: all I did was to *chear-up*, according to my name, for my name is not *Pityless*, but *Chear-up*; and I could not abide to see *Mansoul* incline to *Melancholy*.

Clerk. How! do you deny your name, and say it is not *Pityless* but *Chear-up*? Call for the Witnesses: What say you the Witnesses to this *Plea*?

Know. My Lord, his name is *Pityless*; so he hath writ himself in all papers of concern wherein he has had to do. But these *Diabolonians* love to counterfeit their names: Mr. *Covetousness* covers himself with the name of *good Husbandry*, or the like; Mr. *Pride* can when need is, call himself Mr. *Neat*, Mr. *Handsome*, or the like, and so of all the rest of them.

Clerk. Mr. Telltrue *what say you*?

Tel. His name is *Pityless*, my Lord; I have known him from a child, and he hath done all that wickedness whereof he stands charged in the Indictment; but there is a company of them that are not acquainted with the danger of damning, therefore they call all those melancholy that have serious thoughts how that state should be shunned by them.

Haughty set to the Bar.

Clerk. *Set* Mr. Haughty *to the Bar*. Gaoler. Mr. Haughty, *Thou art here indicted by the name of* Haughty, (*an intruder upon the Town of* Mansoul) *for that thou didst most Trayterously and Devillishly teach the Town of* Mansoul *to carry it loftily and stoutly against the summons that was given them by the Captains of the King* Shaddai. *Thou didst also teach the Town of* Mansoul *to speak contemptuously, and vilifyingly of their great King* Shaddai; *and didst moreover encourage, both by words and examples*, Mansoul, *to take up arms against the King and his Son* Emanuel. *How saist thou, art thou guilty of this Indictment, or not?*

His Indictment.

His Plea.

Haugh. Gentlemen, I have always been a man of courage and

valour, and have not used when under the greatest clouds, to sneak or hang down the head like a bulrush; nor did it at all at any time please me to see men veil their Bonnets to those that have opposed them. Yea, though their adversaries seemed to have ten times the advantage of them.

I did not use to consider who was my foe, nor what the cause was in which I was engaged. 'Twas enough to me if I carried it bravely, fought like a man, and came off a Victor.

The Court.

Court. Mr. Haughty, *you are not here Indicted for that you have been a valiant man, nor for your courage and stoutness in times of distress, but for that you have made use of this your pretended valour to draw the Town of* Mansoul *into acts of rebellion both against the great King and* Emanuel *his Son. This is the crime and the thing wherewith thou art charged in and by the Indictment. But he made no answer to that.*

Now when the Court had thus far proceeded against the prisoners at the Bar, then they put them over to the verdict of their Jury, to whom they did apply themselves after this manner:

The Court to the Jury.

The Juries charge.

Gentlemen of the Jury, you have been here, and have seen these men, you have heard their Indictments, their Pleas, and what the Witnesses have testified against them: Now what remains, is, that you do forthwith withdraw your selves to some place, where without confusion you may consider of what verdict in a way of truth and righteousness you ought to bring in for the King against them, and so bring it in accordingly.

They withdraw themselvs.

Then the Jury, to wit, Mr. *Belief*, Mr. *Trueheart*, Mr. *Upright*, Mr. *Hatebad*, Mr. *Lovegod*, Mr. *Seetruth*, Mr. *Heavenlimind*, Mr. *Moderate*, Mr. *Thankful*, Mr. *Humble*, Mr. *Goodwork*, and Mr. *Zealforgod*, withdrew themselves in order to their work: Now when they were shut up by themselves, they fell to discourse among themselves in order to the drawing up of their Verdict.

Their Conference among themselves.

And thus Mr. *Belief*, for he was the Foreman, began: Gentlemen, quoth he, for the men, the prisoners at the Bar, *for my part I believe that they all deserve death*. Very right, said Mr. *Trueheart*, I am wholly of your opinion: O what a mercy is it, said Mr. *Hate-bad*, that such Villains as these are apprehended! *Ai, Ai*, said Mr. *Lovegod, this is one of the joyfullest days that ever I saw in my life*. Then said Mr. *Seetruth, I know that if we judg them to death, our verdict shall stand before* Shaddai *himself*. Nor do I at all question it, said Mr. *Heavenlimind*; he said moreover, *When all such beasts as these are cast out of* Mansoul, *what a goodly Town will it be then*! Then said Mr. *Moderate*, it is not my manner to pass my judgment with rashness, but for these their crimes are so notorious, and the Witness so palpable, *that that man must be wilfully blind who saith the prisoners ought not to die. Blessed be God*, said Mr. *Thankful, that the Traytors are in safe custody*. And I join with you in this *upon my bare knees*, said Mr. *Humble*. I am glad also said Mr. *Goodwork*. Then said the warm man, and true hearted Mr. *Zeal-for God, Cut them off, they have been the plague, and have sought the destruction of* Mansoul.

Thus therefore being all agreed in their Verdict, they come instantly into the Court.

They are agreed of their Verdict, and bring them in guilty.

Clerk. Gentlemen of the Jury answer all to your Names: Mr. *Belief*, one: Mr. *Trueheart*, two: Mr. *Upright*, three: Mr. *Hatebad*, four: Mr. *Lovegod*, five: Mr. *Seetruth*, six: Mr. *Heavenlymind*, seven: Mr. *Moderate*, eight: Mr. *Thankful*, nine: Mr. *Humble*, ten: Mr. *Goodwork*, eleven: and Mr. *Zealforgod* twelve: Good men and true, stand together in your Verdict: are you all agreed?

Jury. Yes, my Lord.

Clerk. Who shall speak for you?

Jury. *Our Foreman*.

Clerk. *You the Gentlemen of the Jury being impannelled for our Lord the King to serve here in a matter of life and death, have heard the trials of each of these men the prisoners at the Bar: What say you, are they guilty of that, and those crimes for which they stand here Indicted, or are they not guilty?*

The Verdict.

Foreman. Guilty, my Lord.

Clerk. *Look to your Prisoners*, Gaoler.

This was done in the morning, and in the afternoon they received the sentence of death according to the Law.

The *Gaoler* therefore having received such a charge, put

them all in the inward prison, to preserve them there till the day of Execution, which was to be the next day in the morning.

Incredulity breaks prison.

But now to see how it happened, one of the prisoners, *Incredulity* by name, in the interim betwixt the Sentence and time of Execution, brake prison, and made his escape, and gets him away quite out of the Town of *Mansoul*, and lay lurking in such places and holes as he might, until he should again have opportunity to do the Town of *Mansoul* a mischief for their thus handling of him as they did.

No *Incredulity* found in *Mansoul.*

Now when Mr. *Truman* the *Gaoler* perceived that he had lost his Prisoner, he was in a heavy taking, because *he* that Prisoner was, to speak on, the very worst of all the gang: wherefore first he goes and acquaints my Lord *Mayor*, Mr. *Recorder*, and my Lord *Wilbewill* with the matter, and to get of them an Order to make search for him throughout the Town of *Mansoul*. So an Order he got and search was made, but no such man could now be found in all the Town of *Mansoul*.

He is gone to *Diabolus.*

All that could be gathered was, that he had lurked a while about the out-side of the Town, and that here and there one or other had a glimpse of him as he did make his escape out of *Mansoul*, one or two also did affirm that they saw him without the Town, going apace quite over the Plain. Now when he was quite gone, it was affirmed by one Mr. *Didsee*, that he ranged all over dry places, till he met with *Diabolus* his friend; and where should they meet one another but just upon *Hellgate-hill*.

But Oh! what a lamentable story did the old Gentleman tell to *Diabolus* concerning what sad alteration *Emanuel* had made in *Mansoul*?

He tells *Diabolus* what *Emanuel* now is doing in *Mansoul.*

As first, how *Mansoul* had, after some delays received a general pardon at the hands of *Emanuel*, and that they had invited him into the Town, and that they had given him the Castle for his possession. He said moreover, that they had called his Souldiers into the Town, coveted who should quarter the most of them; they also entertained him with the Timbrel, Song and Dance. But that, said *Incredulity*, that is the sorest vexation to me is, that he hath pulled down, O father, thy image, and set up his own, pulled down thy officers, and set up his own. Yea, and *Wilbewill*, that Rebel, who, one would have thought, should never have turned from us, he is now in as great favour with *Emanuel*, as ever he was with *thee*. But besides all this, this *Wilbewill* has received a special Commission from his Master to search for, to apprehend, and to put to death all, and all manner of *Diabolonians* that he shall find in *Mansoul*: Yea, and this *Wilbewill* has taken and committed to prison already eight of my Lords most trusty friends in *Mansoul*. Nay further, my Lord, with grief I speak it, they have been all arraigned, condemned, and I doubt before this executed in *Mansoul*. I told my Lord of eight, and my self was the ninth, who should assuredly have drunk of the same cup, but that through craft, I, as thou seest, have made mine escape from them.

Diabolus yells at this news.

When *Diabolus* had heard this lamentable story he yelled, and snuffed up the wind like a Dragon, and made the sky to look dark with his roaring: He also sware that he would try to be revenged on *Mansoul* for this. *So they, both he and his old friend* Incredulity *concluded to enter into great consultation, how they might get the Town of* Mansoul *again.*

Rom. 8.13. & 6. 12, 13, 14.

Now before this time the day was come in which the Prisoners in *Mansoul* were to be Executed: so they were brought to the Cross, and that by *Mansoul*, in most solemn manner: for the Prince said that this should be done by the hand of the Town of *Mansoul*, that I may see, said he, the forwardness of my now redeemed *Mansoul* to keep my word, and to do my Commandments; and that I may bless *Mansoul* in doing *this* deed. Proof of sincerity pleases me well, let *Mansoul* therefore first lay their hands upon these *Diabolonians* to destroy them.

Gal. 5. 24.

So the Town of *Mansoul* slew them according to the word of their Prince: but when the Prisoners were brought to the Cross to die, you can hardly believe what troublesome work *Mansoul* had of it to put the *Diabolonians* to death, (for the men knowing that they must die, and every of them having implacable enmity in their heart to *Mansoul*) what did they but took courage at the Cross, and there resisted the men of the Town of *Mansoul*? Wherefore the men of *Mansoul* were forced to cry out for help to the Captains and men of war. Now the great *Shaddai* had a *Secretary* in the Town, and he was a great lover of the men of *Mansoul*, and he was at the place of Execution also; so he hearing the men of *Mansoul* cry out against the struglings and unruliness of the Prisoners, rose up from his place, and came and put his hands upon the hands of the men of *Mansoul*. So they crucified the *Diabolonians* that had been a plague, a grief, and an offence to the Town of *Mansoul*.

The assistance of more Grace

Execution done. Rom. 8. 13.

Now when this good work was done, the Prince came down to see, to visit, and to speak comfortably to the men of *Mansoul*, and to strengthen their hands in such work. And he said to them, that by this act of theirs he had proved them, and found them to be lovers of his person, observers of his Laws, and such as had also respect to his honour. He said moreover, (to shew them that they by this should not be losers, nor their Town weakened by the loss of them) that he would make them another Captain, and that of one of themselves. And that this Captain should be the ruler of a thousand, for the good and benefit of the now flourishing Town of *Mansoul*.

The Prince comes down to congratulate them.

He promises to make them a new Captain.

So he called one to him whose name was *Waiting*, and bid him go quickly up to the Castle-gate, and enquire there for one Mr. *Experience* that waiteth upon that noble Captain, the Captain *Credence*, and bid him come hither to me. So the messenger that waited upon the good Prince *Emanuel* went & said as he was commanded. Now the young Gentleman was waiting to see the Captain train and muster his men in the Castle-yard. Then said Mr. *Waiting* to him, *Sir*, the Prince would that you should come down to his Highness forthwith. So he brought him down to *Emanuel*, and he came and made obeisance before him. Now the men of the Town knew Mr. *Experience* well, for he was born and bred in *Mansoul*; they also knew him to be a man of conduct, of valour, and a person

Experience must be the new Captain.

The qualifications of their new Captain.

prudent in matters; he was also a comely person, well spoken, and very successful in his undertakings.

Mansoul takes it well.

Wherefore the hearts of the Townsmen were transported with joy, when they saw that the Prince himself was so taken with Mr. *Experience*, that he would needs make him a *Captain* over a band of men.

So with one consent they bowed the knee before *Emanuel*, and with a shout said, *Let Emanuel live for ever*. Then said the Prince to the young Gentleman, whose name was Mr. *Experience*, I have thought good to confer upon thee a place of trust and honour in this my Town of *Mansoul*, (then the young man bowed his head and worshipped), It is, said *Emanuel*, that thou shouldest be a *Captain*, a Captain over a thousand men in my beloved Town of *Mansoul*. Then said the Captain, *Let the King live*. So the Prince gave out orders forthwith to the Kings Secretary, that he should draw up for Mr. *Experience* a Commission to make him a Captain over a thousand men, and let it be brought to me, said he, that I may set to my seal. So it was done as it was commanded. The Commission was drawn up, brought to *Emanuel*, and he set his seal thereto. Then by the hand of Mr. *Waiting* he sent it away to the Captain.

The thing told to Mr. *Experience*.

His Commission sent him.

Now so soon as the Captain had received his Commission, he sounded his Trumpet for Voluntiers, and young men come to him apace; yea the greatest and chiefest men in the Town sent their sons to be listed under his command. Thus Captain *Experience* came under command to *Emanuel*, for the good of the Town of *Mansoul*. He had for his *Lieutenant* one Mr. *Skilful*, and for his Cornet one Mr. *Memory*. His under Officers I need not name. His Colours were the *White Colours* for the Town of *Mansoul*; and his Scutcheon was *the dead Lion*, and *dead Bear*. So the Prince returned to his Royal Palace again.

His Under-Officers.

1 Sam. 17. 36, 37.

Now when he was returned thither, the Elders of the Town of *Mansoul*, to wit, the Lord *Mayor*, the *Recorder*, and the Lord *Wilbewill* went to *congratulate* him, and in special way to thank him for his love, care, and the tender compassion which

The Elders of *Mansoul* congratulate him.

he shewed to his ever obliged Town of *Mansoul*. So after a while, and some sweet Communion between them, the Towns-men having solemnly ended their Ceremony, returned to their place again.

Emanuel also at this time appointed them a day wherein he would renew their Charter, yea wherein he would renew and enlarge it, mending several *faults* therein, that *Mansouls* yoke might be yet more easie. And this he did without any desire of theirs, even of his own frankness, and noble mind. So when he had sent for and seen their old one, he laid it by, and said, *Now that which decayeth and waxeth old is ready to vanish away*. He said moreover, the Town of *Mansoul* shall have another, a better, a new one, more steady and firm by far. An Epitome hereof take as follows.

He renews their Charter. Heb. 8. 13. Mat. 11.

Emanuel, *Prince of Peace, and a great lover of the Town of* Mansoul, *I do in the name of my Father, and of mine own clemency, give, grant, and bequeath to my beloved Town of* Mansoul,

An Epitome of their new Charter.

First, free, full, and everlasting forgiveness of all wrongs, injuries, and offences done by them against my Father, me, their neighbour, or themselves.

Heb. 8. 12. Joh. 17. 8, 14. 2 Pet. 1. 4. 2 Cor. 7. 1. 1 John. 1. 16.

Secondly, *I do give them the holy Law, and my Testament, with all that therein is contained, for their everlasting comfort and consolation.*

Thirdly, *I do also give them a portion of the self-same grace and goodness that dwells in my Fathers heart and mine.*

Fourthly, *I do give, grant and bestow upon them freely the world, and what is therein for their good, and they shall have that power over them, as shall stand with the honour of my Father, my glory, and their comfort, yea, I grant them the benefits of life and death, and of things present, and things to come. This priviledg, no other City, Town or Corporation shall have but my* Mansoul *only.*

1 Cor. 3. 21, 22.

Fifthly, *I do give and grant them leave, and free access to me in my Palace at all seasons (to my Palace above or below) there to make known their wants to me, and I give them moreover a promise that I will hear and redress all their grievances.*

Heb. 10. 19, 20. Mat. 7. 7.

Sixthly, *I do give, grant to, and invest the Town of* Mansoul *with full power and authority to seek out, take, inslave, and destroy all,*

No man to die for killing of sin.

and all manner of Diabolonians *that at any time from whence soever shall be found stragling in, or about the Town of* Mansoul.

No lust has any grant by Christ, or any liberty to act in the Town of *Mansoul.* Eph. 4. 22. Col. 3. 5, 6, 7, 8, 9.

Seventhly, *I do further grant to my beloved Town of* Mansoul *that they shall have authority not to suffer any foreigner or stranger, or their seed, to be free in, and of the blessed Town of* Mansoul, *nor to share in the excellent priviledges thereof. But that all the grants, priviledges, and immunities that I bestow upon the famous Town of* Mansoul, *shall be for those the old natives, and true inhabitants thereof, to them I say, and to their right seed after them.*

But all Diabolonians *of what sort, birth, Country, or Kingdom soever, shall be debarred a share therein.*

2 Cor. 3. 3. Jer. 31. 33. Heb. 8. 10. Their Charter set upon their Castle gates.

So when the Town of *Mansoul* had received at the hand of *Emanuel* their gracious *Charter*, (which in it self is infinitely more large than by this lean Epitome is set before you) they carried it to *audience*, that is to the Market place, and there Mr. *Recorder* read it in the presence of all the people. This being done, it was had back to the Castle gates, and there fairly engraven upon the doors thereof, and laid in Letters of Gold, to the end that the Town of *Mansoul*, with all the people thereof, might have it always in their view, or might go where they might see what a blessed freedom their Prince had bestowed upon them, that their joy might be increased in themselves, and their love renewed to their great and good *Emanuel*.

Joy renewed in *Mansoul.*

But what joy! what comfort! what consolation think you, did now possess the hearts of the men of *Mansoul*; the Bells ringed, the Minstrils played, the people danced, the Captains shouted, the Colours waved in the wind, and the silver Trumpets sounded, and the *Diabolonians* now were glad to hide their heads, for they looked like them that had been long dead.

When this was over, the Prince sent again for the Elders of the Town of *Mansoul*, and communed with them about a Ministry that he intended to establish among them; such a Ministry that might open unto them, and that might instruct them in the things that did concern their present and future state.

Jer. 10. 23. 1 Cor. 2. 14

For said he, You of your selves, without you have Teachers

and Guides, will not be able to *know*, and if not to know, to be sure, not to *do* the will of my father.

The common good thoughts.

At this news when the Elders of *Mansoul* brought it to the people, the whole Town came running together, (for it pleased them well, as whatever the Prince now did, pleased the people) and all with one consent implored his Majesty that he would forthwith establish such a Ministry among them as might teach them both law and judgment, statute and commandment; that they might be documented in all good and wholsome things. So he told them that he would grant them their requests; and would establish two among them; one that was of his Fathers Court, and one that was a native of *Mansoul*.

2 Pet. 1 . 21. 1 Cor. 2. 10. Joh. 1. 1. 1 Joh. 5. 7.

He that is from the Court, said he, is a person of no less quality and dignity than is my Father and I: and he is the Lord chief *Secretary* of my Fathers house, for he is, and always has been the chief dictator of all my Fathers Laws, a person altogether well skill'd in all mysteries, and knowledg of mysteries as is my Father, or as my self is. Indeed he is one with us in nature, and also as to loving of, and being faithful to, and in, the eternal concerns of the Town of *Mansoul*.

Joh. 14. 26. Ch. 16. 13. 1 Joh. 2. 27.

And this is he, said the Prince, that must be your chief Teacher: for 'tis he, and he only that can teach you clearly in all high and supernatural things. He and he only it is that knows the ways and methods of my Father at Court, nor can any like him shew how the heart of my Father is at all times, in all things, upon all occasions towards *Mansoul*, (for as no man knows the things of a man but that spirit of a man which is in him: so the things of my Father knows no man but this his high and mighty *Secretary*. Nor can any (as he) tell *Mansoul*, how and what they shall do to keep themselves in the love of my Father.) He also it is that can bring lost things to your remembrance, and that can tell you things to come. This Teacher therefore must of necessity have the preheminence (both in your affections and judgment) before your other Teacher; his personal dignity, the excellency of his teaching, also the great dexterity that he hath to help you to make and draw up Petitions to my Father for your help, and to his pleasing, must lay obligations upon you to love him, fear him, and to take heed that you grieve him not.

1 Thes. 1. 5, 6. Act. 21. 10, 11. Jud. *v.* 20. Eph. 6. 18. Rom. 8. 26. Rev. 2. 7, 11, 17, 29. Eph. 4. 30. Isa. 63. 10.

This person can put life and vigor into all he says; yea, and can also put it into your heart. This person can make Seers of you, and can make you tell what shall be hereafter. By this person you must frame all your Petitions to my Father and me; and without his advice and counsel first obtained, let nothing enter into the Town or Castle of *Mansoul*, for that may disgust and grieve this noble person.

Take heed, I say, that you do not grieve this Minister, for if you do, he may fight against you; and should he once be moved by you, to set himself against you, against you in battel array, that will distress you more than if twelve legions should from my Fathers Court be sent to make war upon you.

1 Cor. 13. 14. Rom. 5. 5.

But (as I said) if you shall hearken unto him, and shall love him; if you shall devote you selves to his teaching, and shall seek to have converse, and to maintain Communion with him, you shall find him ten times better than is the whole world to any: yea, he will shed abroad the love of my Father in your hearts, and *Mansoul* will be the wisest, and most blessed of all people.

Conscience made a Minister.

Then did the Prince call unto him the *Old Gentleman*, who afore had been the *Recorder* of *Mansoul*, Mr. *Conscience* by name, and told him, That for as much as he was well skilled in the Law and Government of the Town of *Mansoul*, and was also well spoken, and could pertinently deliver to them his Masters will in all terrene & domestick matters, therefore he would also make him a Minister *for*, *in*, and *to* the goodly Town of *Mansoul*; in all the Laws, Statutes and Judgments of the famous

His limits.

Town of *Mansoul*. And thou must (said the Prince) confine thy self to the teaching of Moral Vertues, to Civil and Natural duties, but thou must not attempt to presume to be a revealer of those high and supernatural Mysteries that are

His Caution.

kept close in the bosome of *Shaddai* my Father: for those things know no man, nor can any reveal them but my Fathers *Secretary* only.

Thou art a native of the Town of *Mansoul*, but the Lord

Secretary is a native with my Father, wherefore as thou hast knowledg of the Laws and customs of the Corporation, so he of the things and will of my Father.

Wherefore, Oh! Mr. *Conscience*, although I have made thee a Minister and a Preacher to the Town of *Mansoul*, yet as to the things which the Lord *Secretary* knoweth, and shall teach to this people, there thou must be his scholar, and a learner, even as the rest of *Mansoul* are.

Thou must therefore in all high and supernatural things, go to him for information and knowledg; for though there be a spirit in man, this Persons inspiration must give him understanding. Wherefore, Oh thou Mr. *Recorder*, keep low and be humble, and remember that the *Diabolonians* that kept not their first charge, but left their own standing, are now made prisoners in the pit; be therefore content with thy station.

Job 33. 8.

I have made thee my Fathers Vicegerent on Earth, in such things of which I have made mention before: and thou, take thou power to teach them to *Mansoul*, yea, and to impose them with whips and chastisements, if they shall not willingly hearken to do thy Commandments.

His power in *Mansoul.*

And, Mr. *Recorder*, because thou art old, and through many abuses made feeble; therefore I give leave and licence to go when thou wilt to my fountain, my conduit, and there to drink freely of the blood of my Grape, for my conduit doth always run Wine. Thus doing, thou shalt drive from thy heart and stomach all foul, gross, and hurtful humours. It will also lighten thine eyes, and will strengthen thy memory for the reception and keeping of all that the Kings most noble *Secretary* teacheth.

His Liberty.

Body.
Heb. 9. 14.

When the Prince had thus put Mr. *Recorder* (that once so was) into the place and office of a Minister to *Mansoul*; and the man had thankfully accepted thereof: then did *Emanuel* address himself in a particular speech to the Townsmen themselves.

'Behold, (said the Prince to *Mansoul*) my love and care towards you, I have added to all that is past, this mercy, to appoint you Preachers: the most noble *Secretary* to teach you

The Princes speech to *Mansoul.*

A licence to *Mansoul.*

in all high and sublime Mysteries; and this Gentleman (pointing to Mr. *Conscience*) is to teach you all things humane and domestick, for therein lyeth his work. He is not by what I have said, debarred of telling to *Mansoul* any thing that he hath heard, and received at the mouth of the Lord high *Secretary*; only he shall not attempt to presume to pretend to be a revealer of those high Mysteries himself; for the breaking of them up, and the discovery of them to *Mansoul* lyeth only in the power, authority and skill of the Lord high *Secretary* himself. Talk of them he may, and so may the rest of the Town of *Mansoul*; yea, and may as occasion gives them opportunity, press them upon each other for the benefit of the whole. These things therefore I would have you observe and do, for it is for your life, and the lengthening of your days.

A world to come promised to *Mansoul.*

'And one thing more to my beloved Mr. *Recorder*, and to all the Town of *Mansoul*, you must not dwell in, nor stay upon any thing of that which he hath in Commission to teach you, as to your trust and expectation of the next world; (of the next world (I say) for I purpose to give another to *Mansoul*, when this with them is worn out) but for that you must wholly and solely have recourse to, and make stay upon his Doctrine, that is your teacher after the first order. Yea, Mr. *Recorder* himself must not look for life from that which he himself revealeth, his dependance for that must be founded in the Doctrine of the other Preacher. Let Mr. *Recorder* also take heed that he receive not any Doctrine, or point of Doctrine, that are not communicated to him by his superiour teacher, nor yet within the precincts of his own formal knowledg.'

He gives them caution about the Captains.

Now after the Prince had thus setled things in the famous Town of *Mansoul*, he proceeded to give to the Elders of the Corporation a necessary caution, to wit how they should carry it to the high and noble Captains that he had, from his Fathers Court, sent or brought with him to the famous Town of *Mansoul*.

Graces pickt from common Vertues.

'These Captains, said he, do love the Town of *Mansoul*, and they are pickt men, pickt out of abundance, as men that best suit, and that will most faithfully serve in the wars of *Shaddai* against the *Diabolonians*, for the preservation of the Town of *Mansoul*. I charge you therefore, said he, O ye inhabitants of the now flourishing Town of *Mansoul*, that you carry it not ruggedly, or untowardly to my Captains, or their men; since, as I said, they are pickt and choise men, men chosen out of many for the good of the Town of *Mansoul*. I say, I charge you that you carry it not untowardly to them; for though they have the hearts and faces of Lions, when at any time they shall be called forth to ingage and fight with the Kings foes, and the enemies of the Town of *Mansoul*; yet a little discountenance cast upon them from the Town of *Mansoul*, will deject and cast down their faces, will weaken and take away their courage. Do not therefore, Oh my beloved, carry it unkindly to my valiant Captains, and couragious men of war, but love them, nourish them, succour them, and lay them in your bosoms, and they will not only fight for you, but cause to fly from you all those the *Diabolonians* that seek, and will if possible be your utter destruction.

Satan cannot weaken our Graces as we our selves may.

Words.

'If therefore any of them should at any time be sick or weak, and so not able to perform that office of love, which with all their hearts they are willing to do, (and will do also when well and in health) slight them not, nor despise them, but rather strengthen them, and incourage them though weak and ready to die, for they are your fence, and your guard, your wall, your gates, your locks, and your bars. And although when they are weak, they can do but little, but rather need to be helped by you, (than that you should then expect great things from them) yet when well, you know what exploits, what feats and warlike Atchievements they are able to do, and will perform for you.

Heb. 12. 12.
Isa. 35. 3.
Rev. 3. 2.
I Thes. 5. 14.

'Besides, if they be weak, the Town of *Mansoul* cannot be strong; if they be strong, then *Mansoul* cannot be weak: your safety therefore doth lye in their health, and in your countenancing of them. *Remember also that if they be sick, they catch that disease of the Town of* Mansoul *it self.*

'These things I have said unto you, because I love your welfare, and your honour: Observe therefore Oh my *Mansoul*, to be punctual in all things that I have given in charge unto you, and that not only as a Town corporate, and so to your officers and guard, and guides in chief, but to you as you are a people whose well-being, as single persons, depends on the observation of the Orders and Commandments of their Lord.

A Caution about the *Diabolonians* that yet remain in *Marsoul.*

'Next, Oh my *Mansoul*, I do warn you of that of which notwithstanding that reformation that at present is wrought among you, you have need to be warn'd about: wherefore hearken diligently unto me. I am *now* sure, and you will know *hereafter* that there are yet of the *Diabolonians* remaining in the Town of *Mansoul*; *Diabolonians* that are sturdy and implacable, and that do already while I am with you, and that will yet more when I am from you, study, plot, contrive, invent, and jointly attempt to bring you to desolation, and so to a state far worse than that of the *Egyptian* bondage; they are the avowed friends of *Diabolus*, therefore look about you: they used heretofore to lodg with their Prince in the Castle, when *Incredulity* was the Lord *Mayor* of this Town, but since my coming hither, they lye more in the outsides, and walls, and have made themselves dens, and caves, and holes, and strong holds therein. Wherefore, Oh *Mansoul*! thy work as to this, will be so much the more difficult and hard. That is, to take, mortifie, and put them to death according to the will of my Father. Nor can you utterly rid your selves of them, unless you should pull down the walls of your Town, the which I am by no means willing you should. Do you ask me, *What shall we do then*? Why, be you diligent, and quit you like men, observe their holds, find out their haunts, assault them, and make no peace with them. Where ever they haunt, lurk, or abide, and what terms of peace soever they offer you abhor, and all shall be well betwixt you and me. And that you may the better know them from those that are the natives of *Mansoul*, I will give you this brief Schedule of the names of the chief of them; and they are these that follow: The Lord *Fornication*, the Lord *Adultery*, the Lord *Murder*, the Lord *Anger*, the Lord *Lasciviousness*, the Lord *Deceit*, the Lord *Evileye*, Mr. *Drunkenness*, Mr. *Reveling*, Mr. *Idolatry*, Mr. *Witch-*

Mar. 7. 21, 22.

Rom. 7. 18.

Christ would not have us destroy our selves thereby to destroy our sins.

The names of some of the *Diabolonians* in *Mansoul.*

craft, Mr. *Variance*, Mr. *Emulation*, Mr. *Wrath*, Mr. *Strife*, Mr. *Sedition*, and Mr. *Heresie*. These are some of the chief, Oh *Mansoul*! of those that will seek to overthrow thee for ever: these I say are the *Sculkers* in *Mansoul*, but look thou well into the Law of thy King, and there thou shalt find their *Physiognomy*, and such other characteristical notes of them, by which they certainly may be known.

'These, O my *Mansoul*, (and I would gladly that you should certainly know it) if they be suffered to run and range about the Town as they would, will quickly like Vipers eat out your bowels, yea poyson your Captains, cut the sinews of your souldiers, break the bar and bolts of your Gates, and turn your now most flourishing *Mansoul* into a barren and desolate wilderness, and ruinous heap. Wherefore that you may take courage to your selves to apprehend these Villains where ever you find them, *I give to you my Lord* Mayor, *my Lord* Wilbewill, *and* Mr. Recorder, *with all the inhabitants of the Town of* Mansoul, *full power and commission to seek out, to take, and to cause to be put to death by the Cross, all, and all manner of* Diabolonians, *when and where ever you shall find them to lurk within, or to range without the walls of the Town of* Mansoul.

A Commission to destroy the *Diabolonians* in *Mansoul*.

'I told you before, that I had placed a standing Ministry among you, not that you have but these with you, for my four first Captains who came against the Master and Lord of the *Diabolonians* that was in *Mansoul*, they can and (if need be, and) if they be required, will not only privately inform, but publickly Preach to the Corporation both good and wholsome Doctrine, and such as shall lead you in the way. Yea, they will set up a weekly, yea, if need be a daily Lecture in thee, Oh *Mansoul*! and will instruct thee in such profitable lessons, that if heeded will do thee good at the end. *And take good heed that you spare not the men that you have a Commission to take and crucifie.*

More Preachers if need be for *Mansoul*.

'Now as I have set out before your eyes the vagrants & runnagates by name, so I will tell you that among your selves some of them shall creep in to beguile you, even such as would seem, and that in appearance are, very rife and hot for

A Caution. Religion. And they if you watch not, will do you a mischief, such an one as at present you cannot think of.

'These, as I said, will shew themselves to you in another hue than those under description before. *Wherefore* Mansoul *watch and be sober, and suffer not thy self to be betrayed.*'

When the Prince had thus far new modelled the Town of *Mansoul*, and had instructed them in such matters as were profitable for them to know: then he appointed another day in which he intended when the Townsfolk came together to bestow a further badg of honour upon the Town of *Mansoul*. A badg that should distinguish them from all the people, kindreds and tongues that dwell in the Kingdom of *Universe*. Now it was not long before the day appointed was come, and the Prince and his people met in the Kings Palace, where first, *Emanuel* made a short speech unto them, and then did for them as he had said, and unto them as he had promised.

Another priviledg for *Mansoul*.

His speech to *Mansoul*.

'My *Mansoul*, said he, that which I now am about to do is to make you known to the world to be mine, and to distinguish you also in your own eyes, from all false Traytors that may creep in among you.'

Then he commanded that those that waited upon him should go and bring forth out of his treasury those white and glistering robes that I, said he, have provided and laid up in store for my *Mansoul*. So the white garments were fetched out of his treasury, and laid forth to the eyes of the people. Moreover, it was granted to them that they should take them and put them on, according, said he, to your sizse and stature. So the people were put into white, into fine linnen, white and clean.

White Robes.

Rev. 19. 8.

Then said the Prince unto them, 'This, O *Mansoul*, is my livery, and the badg by which mine are known from the servants of others. Yea, it is that which I grant to all that are mine, and without which no man is permitted to see my face. Wear them therefore for my sake who gave them unto you; and also if you would be known by the world to be mine.'

But now! can you think how *Mansoul* shone? it was fair as

the Sun, clear as the Moon, and terrible as an Army with banners.

The Prince added further, and said, 'No Prince, Potentate, or mighty one of *Universe*, giveth this livery but my self: Behold therefore, as I said before, you shall be known by it to be mine.

That which distinguisheth *Mansoul* from other people.

'And now, said he, I have given you my livery, let me give you also in commandment concerning them: and be sure that you take good heed to my words.

First, *Wear them daily, day by day, lest you should at sometimes appear to others, as if you were none of mine.*

Eccl. 9. 8. Rev. 3. 2.

Secondly, *Keep them always white, for if they be soiled, 'tis dishonour to me.*

Thirdly, *Wherefore gird them up from the ground, and let them not lag with dust and* dirt.

Fourthly, *Take heed that you lose them not, lest you walk naked, and they see your shame.*

Rev. 7. 15, 16, 17.

Fifthly, *But if you should sulley them, if you should defile them (the which I am greatly unwilling you should, and the Prince* Diabolus *will be glad if you would) then speed you to do that which is written in my Law, that yet you may stand, and not fall before me, and before my Throne. Also this is the way to cause that I may not leave you nor forsake you while here, but may dwell in this Town of* Mansoul *for ever.*

Luk. 21. 36.

And now was *Mansoul*, and the inhabitants of it as the signet upon *Emanuels* right hand; where was there now a Town, a City, a Corporation that could compare with *Mansoul*! A Town redeemed from the hand and from the power of *Diabolus*! A Town that the King *Shaddai* loved, and that he sent *Emanuel* to regain from the Prince of the *Infernal Cave*: yea, a Town that *Emanuel* loved to dwell in, and that he chose for his Royal habitation; a Town that he fortified for himself, and made strong by the force of his Army. What shall I say, *Mansoul* has now a most excellent Prince, Golden Captains and men of war, weapons proved, and garments as white as snow. Nor are these benefits to be counted little but great; can the Town of *Mansoul* esteem them so, and improve them

The glorious state of *Mansoul*.

to that end and purpose for which they are bestowed upon them?

When the Prince had thus compleated the modelling of the Town, to shew that he had great delight in the work of his hands, and took pleasure in the good that he had wrought for the famous and flourishing *Mansoul*, he commanded, and they set his standard upon the Battlements of the Castle. And then,

First, He gave them frequent visits, not a day now but the 2 Cor. 6. 16. Elders of *Mansoul* must come to him (or he to them) into his Palace. Now they must walk and talk together of all the great things that he had done, and yet further promised to do for the Town of *Mansoul*. Thus would he often do with the Lord Understanding. *Mayor*, my Lord The Will. *Wilbewill*, and the honest subordinate Preacher Mr. *Conscience*, and Mr. *Recorder*. But Oh! how graciously! how lovingly! how courteously! and tenderly did this blessed Prince now carry it towards the Town of *Mansoul*! in all the Streets, Gardens, Orchards, and other places where Hungry thoughts. he came, to be sure the *Poor* should have his blessing and benediction: yea, he would kiss them, and if they were ill, he would lay hands on them, and make them well. The *Captains* also he would daily, yea sometimes hourly incourage with his presence and goodly words. For you must know that a smile from him upon them would put more vigor, more life and stoutness into them, than would any thing else under Heaven.

The Prince would now also feast them, and with them continually: hardly a week would pass but a Banquet must 1 Cor. 5. 8. be had betwixt him and them. You may remember that some Pages before we make mention of *one* feast that they had together, but now to feast them was a thing more common, A token of Marriage. every day with *Mansoul* was a feast-day now. Nor did he when A token of Honour. they returned to their places, send them empty away, either A token of Beauty. they must have a *Ring*, a *Gold-chain*, a *Bracelet*, a *white stone*, A token of Pardon. or something; so dear was *Mansoul* to him now; so lovely was *Mansoul* in his eyes.

Secondly, When the Elders and Townsmen did not come to him, he would send in much plenty of provision unto them; meat that came from Court, wine and bread that were prepared for his Fathers Table: yea, such delicates would he send unto them, and therewith would so cover their Table, that whoever saw it confessed that the like could not be seen in any Kingdom.

Thirdly, If *Mansoul* did not frequently visit him as he desired they should, he would walk out to them, knock at their doors and desire entrance, that amity might be maintained betwixt them and him; if they did hear and open to him, as commonly they would *if they were at home*, then would he renew his former love, and confirm it too with some new tokens, and signs of continued favour.

The danger of wandring thoughts: Rev. 3. 20: Cant. 5. 2.

And was it not now amazing to behold, that in that very place where sometimes *Diabolus* had his abode, and entertained his *Diabolonians* to the almost utter destruction of *Mansoul*, the Prince of Princes should sit eating and drinking with them, while all his mighty Captains, men of War, Trumpeters, with the singing-men and singing-women of his Father stood round about to wait upon them! Now did *Mansouls* cup run over, now did her Conduits run sweet wine, now did she eat the finest of the wheat, and drink milk and hony out of the rock! Now she said, how great is his goodness! for since I found favour in his eyes, how honourable have I been!

Mansouls Glory.

The blessed Prince did also ordain a new Officer in the Town, and a goodly person he was, his name was Mr. *Gods peace*; this man was set over my Lord *Wilbewill*, my Lord *Mayor*, Mr. *Recorder*, the Subordinate Preacher, Mr. *Mind*, and over all the *Natives* of the Town of *Mansoul*. Himself was not a Native of it, but came with the Prince *Emanuel* from the Court. He was a great acquaintance of Captain *Credence*, and Captain *Goodhope*; some say they were kin, and I am of that opinion too. This man, as I said, was made Governour of the Town in general, specially over the Castle, and Captain *Credence* was to help him there. And I made great observation of it, that so long as all things went in *Mansoul* as this sweet natured *Gentleman* would, the Town was in most happy condition. Now there were no jars, no chiding, no interferings, no unfaithful doings in all the Town of *Mansoul*; every man

Col. 3. 15.

Rom. 15. 13.

in *Mansoul* kept close to his own imployment. The Gentry, the Officers, the Soldiers, and all in place observed their order. And as for the Women and Children of the Town, they followed their business joyfully, they would *work* and *sing*, *work* and *sing* from morning till night; so that quite through the Town of *Mansoul* now, nothing was to be found but harmony, quietness, joy and health. And this lasted all that Summer.

Holy Conceptions. Good Thoughts.

The story of Mr. *Carnal Security*.

But there was a man in the Town of *Mansoul*, and his name was Mr. *Carnal Security*, this man did after all this mercy bestowed on this Corporation, bring the Town of *Mansoul* into great and grievous slavery and bondage. A brief account of him and of his doings take as followeth.

Mr. *Self-conceit*.

When *Diabolus* at first took possession of the Town of *Mansoul*, he brought thither with himself, a great number of *Diabolonians*, men of his own conditions. Now among these these there was one whose name was Mr. *Self-conceit*, and a notable brisk man he was, as any that in those days did possess the Town of *Mansoul*. *Diabolus* then perceiving this man to be *active* and *bold* sent him upon many desperate designs, the which he managed better, and more to the pleasing of his Lord than most that came with him from the dens could do. Wherefore finding of him so fit for his purpose he preferred him, and made him next to the great Lord *Wilbewill*, of whom we have written so much before. Now the Lord *Wilbewill* being in those days very well pleased with him, and with his atchievements, gave him his daughter, the Lady *Fear-nothing*, to wife. Now of my Lady *Fear-nothing* did this Mr. *Self-conceit* beget this Gentleman Mr. *Carnal Security*. Wherefore there being then in *Mansoul* those strange kind of mixtures, 'twas hard for them in some cases to find out who were Natives, who not; for Mr. *Carnal Security* sprang from my Lord *Wilbewill* by mothers side, though he had for his Father a *Diabolonian* by nature.

Carnal Securities Original.

His Qualities.

Well, this *Carnal Security* took much after his Father and mother, he was *Self-conceited*, he *feared nothing*, he was also a very busie man; nothing of news, nothing of doctrine, nothing of alteration, or talk of alteration could at any time be on foot in *Mansoul*, but be sure Mr. *Carnal Security* would be at the *head* or *tayl* of it: but to be sure he would decline those that he deemed the weakest, and stood always with them (in his way of standing) that he supposed was the strongest side.

He is always for the strongest side.

Now when *Shaddai* the mighty, and *Emanuel* his Son made war upon *Mansoul* to take it, this Mr. *Carnal Security* was then in Town, and was a great doer among the people, incouraging them in their rebellion, putting of them upon hardning of themselves in their resisting of the Kings forces; but when he saw that the Town of *Mansoul* was taken and converted to the use of the glorious Prince *Emanuel*; and when he also saw what was become of *Diabolus*, and how he was unroosted, and made to quit the Castle in the greatest contempt and scorn, and that the Town of *Mansoul* was well lined with *Captains*, *Engins* of War, and *men*, and also provision, what doth he but sliely wheel about also; and as he had served *Diabolus* against the good Prince, so he feigned that he would serve the Prince against his foes.

And having got some little smattering of *Emanuels* things by the end (being bold) he ventures himself into the company of the Townsmen, and attempts also to chat among them. *Now he knew that the power and strength of the Town of* Mansoul *was great, and that it could not but be pleasing to the people if he cried up their might and their glory*. Wherefore he beginneth his tale with the power and strength of *Mansoul*, and affirmed that it was impregnable. *Now magnifying their Captains, and their slings, and their rams; then crying up their fortifications, and strong holds; and lastly the assurances that they had from their Prince, that* Mansoul *should be happy for ever*. But when he saw that some of the men of the Town were tickled and taken with his discourse, he makes it his business, and walking from street to street, house to house, and man to man, he at last brought *Mansoul* to dance after his pipe, and to grow almost as *carnally secure* as himself; so from talking they went to feasting, and from feasting to sporting; and so to some other matters (now *Emanuel* was yet in the Town of *Mansoul*, and he wisely observed their doings) My Lord *Mayor*, my Lord *Wilbewill*,

How Mr. *Carnal Security* begins the misery of *Mansoul*

'Tis not Grace received, but Grace improved, that preserves the soul from temporal dangers.

and Mr. *Recorder*, were also all taken with the words of this tatling *Diabolonian* Gentleman; forgetting that their Prince had given them warning before to take heed that they were not beguiled with any *Diabolonian* sleight: He had further told them that the security of the now flourishing Town of *Mansoul* did not so much lye in her present fortifications and force, as in her so using of what she had, as might oblige her *Emanuel* to abide within her Castle. For the right Doctrine of *Emanuel* was, that the Town of *Mansoul* should take heed that they forgot not his Fathers love and his; also that they should so demean themselves as to continue to keep themselves therein. Now this was not the way to do it, namely, to fall in love with one of the *Diabolonians*, and with such an one too as Mr *Carnal Security* was, and to be led up and down by the nose by him: They should have heard their Prince, fear'd their Prince, loved their Prince, and have ston'd this *naughty-pack* to death, and took care to have walked in the ways of their Princes prescribing, for then should their peace have been as a river, when their righteousness had been like the waves of the Sea.

Now when *Emanuel* perceived that through the policy of Mr. *Carnal Security*, the hearts of the men of *Mansoul* were chill'd and abated in their practical love to him:

Emanuel bemoans *Mansoul.*

First, he bemoans them, and condoles their state with the *Secretary*, saying, *Oh that my people had hearkened unto me, and that* Mansoul *had walked in my ways! I would have fed them with the finest of the wheat, and with hony out of the rock would I have sustained them.* This done, he said in his heart, *I will return to the Court and go to my place till* Mansoul *shall consider and acknowledg their offence.* And he did so, and the cause and manner of his going away from them was thus:

The cause was for that,

First, *Mansoul* declined him, as is manifest in these Particulars.

The way of *Mansouls* backsliding.

1. *They left off their former way of visiting of him, they came not to his Royal Palace as afore.*

2. *They did not regard, nor yet take notice that he came, or came not to visit them.*

3. *The love-feasts that had wont to be between their Prince and them, though he made them still, and called them to them, yet they neglected to come at them, or to be delighted with them.*

4. *They waited not for his counsels, but began to be head strong and confident in themselves, concluding that now they were strong and invincible, and that* Mansoul *was secure, and beyond all reach of the foe, and that her state must needs be unalterable for ever.*

Now, as was said, *Emanuel* perceiving that by the craft of Mr. *Carnal Security*, the Town of *Mansoul* was taken off from their dependance upon him, and upon his Father by him, and set upon what by them was bestowed upon it; He first, as I said, bemoaned their state, then he used means to make them understand that the way that they went on in was dangerous. For he sent my Lord High *Secretary* to them, to forbid them such ways; but twice when he came to them he found them at dinner in Mr. *Carnal Securities* Parlour, and perceiving also that they were not willing to reason about matters concerning their good, he took grief and went his way. The which when he had told to the Prince *Emanuel*, he took offence, and was grieved also, and so made provision to return to his Fathers Court.

They grieve the Holy Ghost and Christ.

Now the methods of his withdrawing, as I was saying before, were thus:

Christ withdraws not all at once.

1. *Even while he was yet with them in* Mansoul *he kept himself close, and more retired than formerly.*

2. *His speech was not now, if he came in their company, so pleasant and familiar as formerly.*

3. *Nor did he as in times past, send to* Mansoul *from his Table, those dainty bits which he was wont to do.*

4. *Nor when they came to visit him, as now and then they would, would he be so easily spoken with as they found him to be in times past. They might now knock once, yea twice, but he would seem not at all to regard them; whereas formerly at the sound of their feet he would up and run, and meet them half way, and take them too, and lay them in his bosom.*

The working of their affections.

But thus *Emanuel* carried it now, and by this his carriage he

He is gone.

Ezek. 11. 21. Hos. 5. 15. Lev. 26. 21, 22, 23, 24.

sought to make them bethink themselves and return to him. But alas they did not consider, they did not know his ways, they regarded not, they were not touched with these, nor with the true remembrance of former favours. Wherefore what does he but in private manner withdraw himself, first from his Palace, then to the Gate of the Town, and so away from *Mansoul* he goes, till they should acknowledg their offence, and more earnestly seek his face. Mr. *Godspeace* also laid down his Commission, and would for the present act no longer in the Town of *Mansoul*.

Jer. 2. 32.

Thus they walked contrary to him, and he again by way of retaliation, walked contrary to them. But alas by this time they were so hardened in their way, and had so drunk in the Doctrine of Mr. *Carnal Security*, that the departing of their Prince touched them not, nor was he remembered by them when gone; and so of consequence his absence not condoled by them.

A trick put upon Mr. *Godly-fear*, he goes to the feast and sits there like a stranger.

Now there was a day wherein this old Gentleman Mr. *Carnal Security* did again make a feast for the Town of *Mansoul*, and there was at that time in the Town one Mr. *Godlyfear*, one *now* but little set by, though formerly one of great request. This man old *Carnal Security* had a mind, if possible, to gull and debauch, and abuse as he did the rest, and therefore he now bids him to the feast with his neighbours: so the day being come they prepare, and he goes and appears with the rest of the guests; and being all set at the Table, they did eat and drink, and were merry even all but this one man. For Mr. *Godlyfear* sat like a stranger, and did neither eat, nor was merry. The which when Mr. *Carnal Security* perceived, he presently addrest himself in a speech thus to him:

Talk betwixt Mr. *Carnal Security*, and Mr. *Godly-fear*.

Carn. Mr. *Godlyfear*, are you not well? you seem to be ill of body or mind, or both. I have a cordial of Mr. *Forgetgoods* making, the which, *Sir*, if you will take a dram of, I hope, it may make you bonny and blith, and so make you more fit for we feasting companions.

Godly. *Unto whom the good old Gentleman discreetly replied*, Sir, *I thank you for all things courteous and civil, but for your cordial*

I have no list thereto. But a word to the natives of Mansoul*: You the* Elders *and* chief *of* Mansoul, *to me it is strange to see you so jocund and merry, when the Town of* Mansoul *is in such woful case.*

Carn. Then said Mr. *Carnal Security*, You want sleep, good Sir, I doubt. If you please lye down and take a nap, and we mean while will be merry.

Godly. Then said the good man as follows, *Sir, if you were not destitute of an honest heart, you could not do as you have done, and do.*

Carn. Then said Mr. *Carnal Security*, Why?

Godly. *Nay pray interrupt me not. 'Tis true, the Town of* Mansoul *was strong, and (with a* proviso) *impregnable; but you, the Townsmen have weakened it, and it now lyes obnoxious to its foes; nor is it a time to flatter, or be silent, 'tis you* Mr. Carnal Security *that have wilily stripped* Mansoul, *and driven her glory from her; you have pulled down her Towers, you have broken down her Gates, you have spoiled her locks and bars.*

And now to explain my self, from that time that my Lords of Mansoul *and you, Sir, grew so great, from that time the strength of* Mansoul *has been offended, and now he is arisen and is gone. If any shall question the truth of my words, I will answer him by this, and such like questions.* Where is the Prince *Emanuel*? When did a man or woman in *Mansoul* see him? When did you hear from him, or taste any of his dainty bits? *You are now a feasting with this* Diabolonian *monster, but he is not your Prince. I say therefore, though enemies from without, had you taken heed, could not have made a prey of you, yet since you have sinned against your Prince, your enemies within have been too hard for you.*

Carn. Then said Mr. *Carnal Security*, Fie, fie, Mr. *Godlyfear*, fie; will you never shake off your *timorousness*? are you afraid of being sparrow-blasted? who hath hurt you? behold I am on your side, only you are for doubting, and I am for being confident. Besides, is this a time to be sad in? A feast is made for mirth, why then do you now, to your shame, and our trouble, break out into such passionate melancholy language when you should eat and drink, and be merry?

Godly. *Then said* Mr. Godlyfear *again, I may well be sad, for* Emanuel *is gone from* Mansoul. *I say again he is gone, and you, Sir, are the man that has driven him away; yea, he is gone without so much as acquainting the Nobles of* Mansoul *with his going, and if that is not a sign of his anger, I am not acquainted with the methods of Godliness.*

His speech to the Elders of *Mansoul.*

And now my Lords and Gentlemen, for my speech is still to you, your gradual declining from him did provoke him gradually to depart from you, the which he did for some time, if perhaps you would have been made sensible thereby, and have been renewed by humbling of your selves; but when he saw that none would regard, nor lay these fearful beginnings of his anger and judgment to heart, he went away from this place, and this I saw with mine eye. Wherefore now while you boast, your strength is gone, you are like the man that had lost his locks that before did wave about his shoulders. You may with this Lord of your feast shake your selves, and conclude to do as at other times; but since without him you can do nothing, and he is departed from you, turn your feast into a sigh, and your mirth into lamentation.

Conscience startled.

Then the *Subordinate Preacher*, old Mr. *Conscience* by name, he that of old was *Recorder* of *Mansoul*, being startled at what was said, began to second it thus.

Con. Indeed, my Brethren, quoth he, I fear that Mr. *Godlyfear* tells us true: I, for my part, have not seen my Prince a long season. I cannot remember the day for my part. Nor can I answer Mr. *Godlyfears* question. I doubt, I am afraid that all is naught with *Mansoul.*

Godly. *Nay, I know that you shall not find him in* Mansoul, *for he is departed and gone; yea, and gone for the faults of the Elders, and for that they rewarded his grace with unsufferable unkindnesses.*

They are all agast.

Then did the *Subordinate Preacher* look as if he would fall down dead at the Table, also all there present, except the man of the house, began to look *pale* and *wan.* But having a little recovered themselves, and jointly agreeing to believe Mr. *Godlyfear* and his sayings, they began to consult was what best to be done (now Mr. *Carnal Security* was gone into his with-drawing room, for he liked not such dumpish doings) both to the man of the house for drawing them into evil, and also to recover *Emanuels* love.

And with that, that saying of their Prince came very hot

into their minds, which he had bidden them do to such as were false Prophets that should arise to delude the Town of *Mansoul*. So they took Mr. *Carnal Security* (concluding that he must be he) and burned his house upon him with fire, for he also was a *Diabolonian* by nature. They consult and burn their Feast-master.

So when this was past and over, they bespeed themselves to look for *Emanuel* their Prince, and they sought him, but they found him not; then were they more confirmed in the truth of Mr. *Godlyfears* sayings, and began also severely to reflect upon themselves for their so vile and ungodly doings; for they concluded now that it was through them that their Prince had left them. Cant. 5. 6.

Then they agreed and went to my Lord *Secretary*, (him whom before they refused to hear, him whom they had grieved with their doings) to know of him, for he was a Seer, and could tell where *Emanuel* was, and how they might direct a Petition to him. But the Lord *Secretary* would not admit them to a conference about this matter, nor would admit them to his Royal place of abode, nor come out to them to shew them his face, or intelligence. They apply themselves to the Holy Ghost, but he is grieved, &c. Isa. 63. 10. Eph. 4. 30. 1 Thess. 5. 19.

And now was it a day gloomy and dark, a day of clouds and of thick darkness with *Mansoul*. Now they saw that they had been foolish, and began to perceive what the company and prattle of Mr. *Carnal Security* had done, and what desperate damage his swaggering words had brought poor *Mansoul* into. But what further it was like to cost them, that they were ignorant of. Now Mr. *Godlyfear* began again to be in repute with the men of the Town; yea, they were ready to look upon him as a Prophet.

Well, when the Sabbath-day was come, they went to hear their *Subordinate Preacher*; but Oh how he did thunder and lighten this day! His Text was that in the Prophet *Jonah*, *They that observe lying vanities, forsake their own mercies*. But there was then such power and authority in that Sermon, and such a dejection seen in the countenances of the people that day, that the like hath seldom been heard or seen. The people when Sermon was done, were scarce able to go to their homes, or to A thundring Sermon. Jon. 2. 8.

Hos. 6. 5.

betake themselves to their imploys the week after; they were so Sermon-smitten, and also so Sermon-sick by being smitten, that they knew not what to do.

The *Sub-ordinate Preacher* doth acknowledg his fault, and bewails his compliance with Mr. *Carnal Security*.

Psal. 88.

He did not only shew to *Mansoul* their sin, but did tremble before them, under the sense of his *own*, still crying out of himself, as he Preached to them, *Unhappy man that I am! that I should do so wicked a thing*! That I! a Preacher! whom the Prince did set up to teach to *Mansoul* his Law, should my self live sensless, and sottishly here, and be one of the first found in transgression. This transgression also fell within my precincts, I should have cried out against the wickedness, but I let *Mansoul* lye wallowing in it, until it had driven *Emanuel* from its borders. With these things he also charged all the Lords and Gentry of *Mansoul*, to the almost distracting of them.

A great sickness in *Mansoul*.

Heb. 12. 12, 13. Rev. 3. 2. Isa. 3. 24.

Sin doth cause to be *weak*, both *body*, and *soul*, and *graces*.

About this time also there was a great sickness in the Town of *Mansoul*; and most of the inhabitants were greatly afflicted. Yea the Captains also, and men of war were brought thereby to a languishing condition, and that for a long time together; so that in case of an invasion, nothing could to purpose now have been done, either by the Townsmen, or Field-officers. Oh how many *pale* faces, *weak* hands, *feeble* knees, and staggering men were now seen to walk the streets of *Mansoul*. Here were groans, there pants, and yonder lay those that were ready to faint.

The garments too which *Emanuel* had given them were but in a sorry case; some were rent, some were torn, and *all* in a nasty condition; some also did hang so loosely upon them, that the next bush they came at was ready to pluck them off.

After some time spent in this sad and desolate condition the *Subordinate Preacher* called for a day of fasting, and to humble themselves for being so wicked against the great *Shaddai*, and his Son. And he desired that Captain *Boanerges* would Preach. So he consented to do it, and the day was come, and his Text was this, *Cut it down, why cumbreth it the ground?* And a very smart Sermon he made upon the place. First, he

2 marg. Hos. *6.* 5] Hos. *6.* 13

Boanerges doth Preach to *Mansoul.*

shewed what was the occasion of the words, to wit, *because the fig-tree was barren*; then he shewed what was contained in the sentence, to wit, *repentance, or utter desolation.* He then shewed also by whose authority this sentence was pronounced, and that was by *Shaddai* himself. And lastly, he shewed the *reasons of the point*, and then concluded his *Sermon.* But he was very pertinent in the application, insomuch that he made poor *Mansoul* tremble. For this Sermon as well as the former, wrought much upon the hearts of the men of *Mansoul*; yea it greatly helped to keep awake those that were roused by the Preaching that went before. So that now throughout the whole Town there was little or nothing to be heard or seen but sorrow and mourning, and wo.

The men of *Mansoul* much affected.

Now after Sermon they got together and consulted what was best to be done. But said the *Subordinate Preacher*, I will do nothing of mine own head, without advising with my neighbour Mr. *Godlyfear.*

They consult what to do.

For if he had afore, and understood more of the mind of our Prince than we, I do not know but he also may have it now, even now we are turning again to vertue. So they called and sent for Mr. *Godlyfear*, and he forthwith appeared; then they desired that he would further shew his opinion about what they had best to do. Then said the old Gentleman as followeth, *It is my opinion that this Town of* Mansoul *should in this day of her distress draw up and send an humble Petition to their offended Prince* Emanuel, *that he in his favour and grace will turn again unto you, and not keep anger for ever.*

Mr. *Godlyfears* advice.

When the Townsmen had heard this Speech, they did with one consent agree to his advice; so they did presently draw up their request, and the next was, But who shall carry it? At last they did all agree to send it by my Lord *Mayor.* So he accepted of the service, and addressed himself to his journey; and went and came to the Court of *Shaddai*, whither *Emanuel* the Prince of *Mansoul* was gone. But the Gate was shut, and a strict watch kept thereat, so that the Petitioner was forced to stand without for a great while together. Then he desired that some would go into the Prince and tell him who stood at

They send the Lord *Mayor* to Court.

Lam. 3. 8, 44.

the Gate, and what his business was. So one went and told to *Shaddai*, and to *Emanuel* his Son, that the Lord *Mayor* of the Town of *Mansoul* stood without at the Gate of the Kings Court, desiring to be admitted into the presence of the Prince, the Kings Son. He also told what was the Lord Mayors Errand, both to the King and his Son *Emanuel*. But the Prince would not come down nor admit that the Gate should be opened to him, but sent him an answer to this effect: *They have turned the back unto me, and not their face, but now in the time of their trouble they say to me Arise and save us. But can they not now go to* Mr. Carnal Security *to whom they went when they turned from me, and make him their leader, their Lord, and their protection now in their trouble; why now in their trouble do they visit me, since in their prosperity they went astray?*

Jer. 2. 27, 28.

A dreadful answer.

This answer made my Lord *Mayor* look black in the face; it troubled, it perplexed, it rent him sore. And now he began again to see what it was to be familiar with *Diabolonians*, such as Mr. *Carnal Security* was. When he saw that at Court (as yet) there was little help to be expected, either for himself, or friends in *Mansoul*; he smote upon his breast and returned weeping, and all the way bewailing the lamentable state of *Mansoul*.

Lam. 4. 7, 8.

The Lord *Mayor* returns, and how.

Well, when he was come within sight of the Town, the Elders and chief of the people of *Mansoul* went out at the Gate to meet him, and to salute him, and to know how he sped at Court. But he told them his tale in so doleful a manner, that they all cried out, and mourned, and wept. Wherefore they threw ashes and dust upon their heads, and put sackcloth upon their loins, and went crying out through the Town of *Mansoul*; the which when the rest of the Townsfolk saw, they all mourned and wept. This therefore was a day of rebuke and trouble, and of anguish to the Town of *Mansoul*, and also of great distress.

The state of *Mansoul* now.

The whole Town cast down.

After some time, when they had somewhat refrained themselves, they came together to consult again what by them was yet to be done; and they asked advice, as they did before, of that reverend Mr. *Godlyfear*, who told them that there was

They consult again Mr. *Godlyfears* advice.

no way better than to do as they had done, nor would he that they should be discouraged at all with that they had met with at Court; yea, though several of their Petitions should be answered with nought but silence or rebuke: *For*, said he, *it is the way of the wise* Shaddai *to make men wait and to exercise patience, and it should be the way of them in want, to be willing to stay his leisure.*

Then they took courage, and sent again, and again, and again, and again; for there was not now one day, nor an hour that went over *Mansouls* head, wherein a man might not have met upon the road one or other riding post, sounding the horn from *Mansoul* to the *Court* of the King *Shaddai*; and all with Letters Petitionary in behalf of (and for the Princes return, to) *Mansoul*.

See now what's the work of a backsliding Saint awakened.

Groaning desires.

The road, I say, was now full of messengers, going and returning, and meeting one another; some from the Court, and some from *Mansoul*, and this was the work of the miserable Town of *Mansoul*, all that long, that sharp, that cold and tedious winter.

Now if you have not forgot, you may yet remember that I told you before, that after *Emanuel* had taken *Mansoul*, yea, and after that he had new modelled the Town, there remained in several lurking places of the Corporation many of the old *Diabolonians*, that either came with the Tyrant when he invaded and took the Town, or that had there by reason of unlawful mixtures, their birth and breeding, and bringing up. And their holes, dens and lurking places were in, under, or about the wall of the Town. Some of their names are the Lord *Fornication*, the Lord *Adultery*, the Lord *Murder*, the Lord *Anger*, the Lord *Lasciviousness*, the Lord *Deceit*, the Lord *Evileye*, the Lord *Blasphemy*, and that horrible Villain the old and dangerous Lord *Covetousness*. These, as I told you, with many more, had yet their abode in the Town of *Mansoul*, and that after that *Emanuel* had driven their Prince *Diabolus* out of the Castle.

A Memento.

Against these the good Prince did grant a Commission to the Lord *Wilbewill* and others, yea to the whole Town of

Mansoul heeded not

her Princes Caution, nor put his Commission into execution.

Mansoul, to seek, take, secure, and destroy any, or all that they could lay hands of, for that they were *Diabolonians* by nature, enemies to the Prince, and those that sought to ruin the blessed Town of *Mansoul*. But the Town of *Mansoul* did not pursue this warrant, but neglected to look after, to apprehend, to secure, and to destroy these *Diabolonians*. Wherefore what do these Villains but by degrees take courage to put forth their heads, and to shew themselves to the inhabitants of the Town. Yea, and as I was told, some of the men of *Mansoul* grew too familiar with some of them, to the sorrow of the Corporation, as you yet will hear more of in time and place.

The *Diabolonians* Plot.

Well, when the *Diabolonian* Lords that were left, perceived that *Mansoul* had through sinning offended *Emanuel* their Prince, and that he had with-drawn himself and was gone, what do they but plot the ruin of the Town of *Mansoul*. So upon a time they met together at the hold of one Mr. *Mischiefs*, who also was a *Diabolonian*, and there consulted how they might deliver up *Mansoul* into the hands of *Diabolus* again. Now some advised one way, and some another, every man according to his own liking. At last my Lord *Lasciviousness* propounded, whether it might not be best in the first place for some of those that were *Diabolonians* in *Mansoul* to adventure to offer themselves for servants to some of the Natives of the Town, for said he, if they do, and *Mansoul* shall accept of them, they may for us, and for *Diabolus* our Lord, make the taking of the Town of *Manso.* more easie than otherwise it will be. But then stood up the Lord *Murder*, and said, This may not be done at this time, for *Mansoul* is now in a kind of a rage, because by our friend Mr. *Carnal Security* she hath been once insnared already and made to offend against her Prince, and how shall she reconcile her self unto her Lord again, but by the heads of these men? Besides, we know that they have in commission to take and slay us where ever they shall find us, let us therefore be wise as Foxes, when we are dead we can do them no hurt, but while we live we may. Thus when they had tossed the matter to and fro, they jointly agreed that a

They send to Hell for advice.

Letter should forthwith be sent away to *Diabolus* in their

name, by which the state of the Town of *Mansoul* should be shewed him, and how much it is under the frowns of their Prince; we may also, said some, let him know our intentions, and ask of him his advice in the case.

So a Letter was presently framed, the Contents of which was this.

To our great Lord, the Prince *Diabolus*, dwelling below in the *Infernal Cave*.

The Copy of their Letter.

O Great Father, and mighty Prince Diabolus, *we, the true* Diabolonians, *yet remaining in the rebellious Town of* Mansoul, *having received our beings from thee, and our nourishment at thy hands, cannot with content and quiet endure to behold, as we do this day, how thou art dispraised, disgraced, and reproached among the inhabitants of this Town; nor is thy long absence at all delightful to us, because greatly to our detriment.*

The reason of this our writing unto our Lord, is for that we are not altogether without hope that this Town may become thy habitation again; for it is greatly declined from its Prince Emanuel, *and he is up-risen, and is departed from them; yea, and though they send, and send, and send, and send after him to return to them, yet can they not prevail, nor get good words from him.*

There has been also of late, and is yet remaining a very great sickness and faintings among them, and that not only upon the poorer sort of the Town, but upon the Lords, Captains, and chief Gentry of the place (we only who are of the Diabolonians *by nature remain well, lively, and strong) so that through their great transgression on the one hand, and their dangerous sickness on the other, we judg they lye open to thy hand and power. If therefore it shall stand with thy horrible cunning, and with the cunning of the rest of the Princes with thee, to come and make an attempt to take* Mansoul *again, send us word, and we shall to our utmost power be ready to deliver it into thy hand. Or if what we have said shall not by thy Fatherhood be thought best, and most meet to be done, send us thy mind in a few words, and we are all ready to follow thy counsel to the hazarding of our lives, and what else we have.*

Given under our hands the day and date above written, after a close consultation at the house of Mr. Mischief, *who yet is alive, and hath his place in our desirable Town of* Mansoul.

Mr. *Profane* is Carrier, he brings the Letter to *Hellgate-hill*, and there presents it to *Cerberus* the Porter.

When Mr. *Profane* (for he was the Carrier) was come with his Letter to *Hellgate hill*, he knocked at the Brazen gates for entrance. Then did *Cerberus* the Porter, for he is the keeper of that Gate, open to Mr. *Profane*, to whom he delivered his Letter, which he had brought from the *Diabolonians* in *Mansoul*. So he carried it in and presented it to *Diabolus* his Lord; and said, Tidings my Lord, from *Mansoul*; from our trusty friends in *Mansoul*.

Dead-mans bell, and how it went.

Then came together from all places of the den *Beelzebub*, *Lucifer*, *Apollyon*, with the rest of the rabblement there, to hear what news from *Mansoul*. So the Letter was broken up and read, and *Cerberus* he stood by. When the Letter was openly read, and the Contents thereof spread into all the corners of the den, command was given that without let or stop, *Dead-mans-bell* should be rung for joy. So the Bell was rung, and the Princes rejoiced that *Mansoul* was like to come to ruin. Now the Clapper of the Bell went, *The Town of* Mansoul *is coming to dwell with us, make room for the Town of* Mansoul. This Bell therefore they did ring, because they did hope that they should have *Mansoul* again.

Now when they had performed this their horrible ceremony, they got together again to consult what answer to send to their friends in *Mansoul*, and some advised one thing, and some another, but at length because the business required haste, they left the whole business to the Prince *Diabolus*, judging him the most proper Lord of the place. So he drew up a Letter as he thought fit, in answer to what Mr. *Profane* had brought, and sent it to the *Diabolonians* that did dwell in *Mansoul*, by the same hand that had brought theirs to him: And this was the Contents thereof,

To our off-spring the high and mighty Diabolonians, *that yet dwell in the Town of* Mansoul, Diabolus *the great Prince of* Mansoul, *wisheth a prosperous issue and conclusion of those*

many brave enterprizes, conspiracies, and designs that you of your love and respect to our honour, have in your hearts to attempt to do against Mansoul.

B*eloved children and disciples, my Lord* Fornication, Adultery, *and the rest, we have here in our desolate den received to our highest joy and content, your welcome Letter by the hand of our trusty Mr.* Profane, *and to shew how acceptable your tidings were, we rang out our Bell for gladness; for we rejoiced as much as we could, when we perceived that yet we had friends in* Mansoul, *and such as sought our honour and revenge in the ruin of the Town of* Mansoul. *We also rejoiced to hear that they are in a degenerated condition, and that they have offended their Prince, and that he is gone. Their sickness also pleaseth us, as does also your health, might and strength. Glad also would we be, right horribly beloved, could we get this Town into our clutches again. Nor will we be sparing of spending our wit, our cunning, our craft, and hellish inventions to bring to a wished conclusion this your brave beginning in order thereto.*

And take this for your comfort, (our birth, and our off spring) that shall we again surprize it and take it, we will attempt to put all your foes to the sword, and will make you the great Lords and Captains of the place. Nor need you fear (if ever we get it again) that we after that shall be cast out any more; for we will come with more strength, and so lay far more fast hold than at the first we did. Besides, it is the Law of that Prince that now they own, that if we get them a second time they shall be ours for ever. Mat. 12. 43, 44, 45.

Do you therefore our trusty Diabolonians, *yet more pry into, and endeavour to spie out the weakness of the Town of* Mansoul, *We also would that you your selves do attempt to weaken them more and more. Send us word also by what means you think we had best to attempt the regaining thereof: to wit, whether by perswasion to a vain and loose life; or, whether by tempting them to doubt and despair; or, whether by blowing up of the Town by the Gun-powder of pride, and self conceit. Do you also, O ye brave* Diabolonians, *and true sons of the Pit, be always in a readiness to make a most hideous assault within, when we shall be ready to storm it without. Now speed you in your project, and we in our desires, the utmost power of our Gates, which is the wish of your great* Diabolus, Mansouls *enemy, and him that trembles when he thinks of judgment to come, all the blessings of the Pit be upon you, and so we close up our Letter.*

Given at the Pits mouth by the joint consent of all the Princes of Darkness to be sent (to the force and power that we have yet remaining in Mansoul) *by the hand of Mr*. Profane.

By me Diabolus.

This Letter, as was said, was sent to *Mansoul*, to the *Diabolonians* that yet remained there, and that yet inhabited the wall, from the dark Dungeon of *Diabolus*, by the hand of Mr. *Profane*, by whom they also in *Mansoul* sent theirs to the Pit. Now when this Mr. *Profane* had made his return, and was come to *Mansoul* again, he went and came as he was wont to the house of Mr. *Mischief*, for there was the Conclave, and the place where the Contrivers were met. Now when they saw that their messenger was returned safe and sound, they were greatly gladded thereat. Then he presented them with his Letter which he had brought from *Diabolus* for them; the which when they had read and considered, did much augment their gladness. They asked them after the welfare of their friends, as how their Lord *Diabolus*, *Lucifer*, and *Beelzebub* did, with the rest of those of the Den. To which this *Profane* made answer, Well, well, my Lords, they are well, even as well as can be in their place. They also, said he, did ring for joy at the reading of your Letter, as you well perceived by this when you read it.

Flesh.

Profane comes home again.

Now, as was said, when they had read their Letter, and perceived that it incouraged them in their work, they fell to their way of contriving again, to wit, how they might compleat their *Diabolonian* design upon *Mansoul*. *And the first thing that they agreed upon was to keep all things from Mansoul as close as they could.* Let it not be known, let not *Mansoul* be acquainted with what we design against it. The next thing was, how, or by what means they should try to bring to pass the ruin and overthrow of *Mansoul*, and one said after this manner, and another said after that. Then stood up Mr. *Deceit*, and said, My right *Diabolonian* friends, our Lords, and

☞

the high ones of the deep Dungeon do propound unto us these three ways.

1. Whether we had best to seek its ruin by making of *Mansoul* loose and vain.

2. Or whether by driving them to doubt and despair.

3. Or whether by endeavouring to blow them up by the Gun-powder of pride and self conceit.

Take heed *Mansoul.*

Now I think if we shall tempt them to pride, that may do something; and it we tempt them to wantonness, that may help. But in my mind, if we could drive them into desperation, that would knock the nail on the head; for then we should have them in the first place question the truth of the love of the heart of their Prince towards them, and that will disgust him much. This if it works well, will make them leave off quickly their way of sending Petitions to him; then farewell earnest sollicitations for help and supply; for then this conclusion lies naturally before them, *As good do nothing as do to no purpose.* So to Mr. *Deceit* they unanimously did consent.

Then the next question was, but how shall we do to bring this our project to pass? and 'twas answered by the same Gentleman, That this might be the best way to do it, even let, quoth he, so many of our friends as are willing to venture themselves for the promoting of their Princes cause, disguise themselves with apparel, change their names, and go into the market like far Country men, and proffer to let themselves for servants to the famous Town of *Mansoul*, and let them pretend to do for their Masters as beneficially as may be; for by so doing they may, if *Mansoul* shall hire them, in little time so corrupt and defile the Corporation, that her now Prince shall be not only further offended with them, but in conclusion shall spue them out of his mouth. And when this is done our Prince *Diabolus* shall prey upon them with ease: *Yea, of themselves they shall fall into the mouth of the eater.*

Take heed *Mansoul.*

Take heed *Mansoul.*

This project was no sooner propounded, but was as highly accepted, and forward were all *Diabolonians* now to engage in so delicate an interprize; but it was not thought fit that all should do thus, wherefore they pitched upon two or three, namely, the Lord *Covetousness*, the Lord *Lasciviousness*, and the Lord *Anger*. The Lord *Covetousness* called himself by the name of *Prudent thrifty*; the Lord *Lasciviousness* called himself by the name of *Harmless-mirth*; and the Lord *Anger* called himself by the name of *Good-zeal*.

Take heed *Mansoul.*

So upon a Market-day they came into the Market-place, three lusty fellows they were to look on, and they were clothed in *sheepsrusset*, which was also now in a manner as white as were the white robes of the men of *Mansoul*. Now the men could speak the language of *Mansoul* well. So when they were come into the Market-place, and had offered to let themselves to the Townsmen, they were presently taken up, for they asked but little wages, and promised to do their Masters great service.

Take heed *Mansoul.*

Mr. *Mind* hired *Prudent-thrifty*, and Mr. *Godly-fear* hired *Good-zeal*. True, this fellow *Harmless-mirth* did hang a little in hand, and could not so soon get him a Master as the other did, because the Town of *Mansoul* was now in *Lent*, but after a while because *Lent* was almost out, the Lord *Wilbewill* hired *Harmless-mirth* to be both his *Waiting-man*, and his *Lacquy*, and thus they got them Masters.

Take heed *Mansoul.*

These Villains now being got thus far into the houses of the men of *Mansoul*, quickly began to do great mischief therein; for being filthy arch and slie, they quickly corrupted the families where they were; yea, they tainted their Masters much, especially this *Prudent-thrifty*, and him they call *Harmless-mirth*. True, he that went under the vizor of *Good-zeal*, was not so well liked of his Master, for he quickly found that he was but a counterfeit Rascal; the which when the fellow perceived, with speed he made his escape from the house, or I doubt not but his Master had hanged him.

Well, when these Vagabonds had thus far carried on their design, and had corrupted the Town as much as they could, in the next place they considered with themselves at what time their Prince *Diabolus* without, and themselves within the Town should make an attempt to seise upon *Mansoul*; and they all agreed upon this, that a Market-day would be best for that work; for why? then will the Townsfolk be busie in their ways: and always take this for a rule, *When people are most busie in the world, they least fear a surprize.* We also then, said they, shall be able with less suspicion to gather our selves together for the work of our friends, and Lords; yea, and in such a day, if we shall attempt our work, and miss it, we may when they shall give us the rout, the better hide our selves in the croud and escape.

A day of worldly cumber.

Take heed *Mansoul.*

These things being thus far agreed upon by them, they wrote another Letter to *Diabolus*, and sent it by the hand of Mr. *Profane*, the Contents of which was this:

The Lords of Looseness *send to the great and high* Diabolus *from our Dens, caves, holes, and strong holds, in, and about the wall of the Town of* Mansoul, *Greeting:*

Look to it *Mansoul.*

O*UR great Lord, and the nourisher of our lives,* Diabolus; *how glad we were when we heard of your fatherhoods readiness to comply with us, and help forward our design in our attempts to ruin* Mansoul! *none can tell but those who as we do set themselves against all appearance of good when and wheresoever we find it.*

Rom. 7. 21
Gal. 5. 17.

Touching the incouragement that your greatness is pleased to give us to continue to devise, contrive, and study the utter desolation of Mansoul, *that we are not sollicitous about, for we know right well that it cannot but be pleasing and profitable to us, to see our enemies and them that seek our lives, to die at our feet, or fly before us. We therefore are still contriving, and that to the best of our cunning, to make this work most facile and easie to your Lordships, and to us.*

First we considered of that most hellishly, cunning, compacted, three-fold project, that by you was propounded to us in your last; and have concluded, that though to blow them up with the Gun-powder of pride would do well, and to do it by tempting them to be loose and vain will help on, yet to contrive to bring them into the gulf of desperation, we think will do best of all. Now we who are at your beck, have thought of two ways to do this: First, we for our parts will make them as vile as we can, and then you with us, at a time appointed, shall be ready to fall upon them with the utmost force. And of all the Nations

Look to it *Mansoul.*

Take heed *Mansoul.*

that are at your whistle, we think that an army of Doubters *may be the most likely to attack and overcome the Town of* Mansoul. *Thus shall we overcome these enemies, else the Pit shall open her mouth upon them, and desperation shall thrust them down into it. We have also, to effect this so much by us desired design, sent already three of our trusty* Diabolonians *among them, they are disguised in garb, they have changed their names, and are now accepted of them, to wit,* Covetousness, Lasciviousness *and* Anger. *The name of* Covetousness *is changed to* Prudent-thrifty*; and him* Mr. Mind *has hired, and is almost become as bad as our friend.* Lasciviousness *has changed his name to* Harmless-mirth, *and he is got to be the Lord* Wilbewills *Lacquy, but he has made his master very wanton.* Anger *changed his name into* Good-zeal, *and was entertained by* Mr. Godly-fear, *but the peevish old Gentleman took pepper in the nose and turned our companion out of his house. Nay he has informed us since, that he ran away from him, or else his old master had hanged him up for his labour.*

Look to it *Mansoul.*

Now these have much helped forward our work and design upon Mansoul*; for notwithstanding the spite and quarrelsome temper of the old Gentleman last mentioned, the other two ply their business well, and are like to ripen the work apace.*

Take heed *Mansoul.*

Our next project is, that it be concluded that you come upon the Town upon a Market-day, and that when they are upon the heat of their business; for then to be sure they will be most secure, and least think that an assault will be made upon them. They will also at such a time be less able to defend themselves, and to offend you in the prosecution of our design. And we your trusty, (and we are sure your beloved) ones shall when you shall make your furious assault without, be ready to second the business within. So shall we in all likelihood be able to put Mansoul *to utter confusion, and to swallow them up before they can come to themselves. If your Serpentine heads, most subtil Dragons, and our highly esteemed Lords can find out a better way than this, let us quickly know your minds.*

To the Monsters of the Infernal Cave from the house of Mr. Mischief *in* Mansoul, *by the hand of Mr.* Profane.

Now all the while that the raging runnagates, and hellish *Diabolonians* were thus contriving the ruin of the Town of

Mansoul, they, to wit, the poor Town it self was in a sad and woful case, partly because they had so grievously offended *Shaddai* and his Son, and partly because that the enemies thereby got strength within them afresh, and also because though they had by many Petitions made suit to the Prince *Emanuel*, and to his Father *Shaddai* by him for their pardon and favour, yet hitherto obtained they not one smile; but contrariwise through the craft and subtilty of the Domestick *Diabolonians*, their cloud was made to grow blacker and blacker, and their *Emanuel* to stand at further distance.

The sad state of Mansoul.

The sickness also did still greatly rage in *Mansoul*, both among the Captains and the inhabitants of the Town their enemies, and their enemies only were now lively and strong, and like to become the head whilest *Mansoul* was made the tail.

By this time the Letter last mentioned, that was written by the *Diabolonians* that yet lurked in the Town of *Mansoul*, was conveyed to *Diabolus* in the *Black-den*, by the hand of Mr. *Profane*. He carried the Letter by *Hellgate-hill* as afore, and conveyed it by *Cerberus* to his Lord.

Profane arrives at Hellgate-hill.

But when *Cerberus* and Mr. *Profane* did meet, they were presently as great as beggers, and thus they fell into discourse about *Mansoul*, and about the project against her.

Cerb. Ah! old friend, quoth *Cerberus*, art thou come to *Hellgate-hill* again! By St. *Mary* I am glad to see thee.

Prof. Yes, my Lord, I am come again about the concerns of the Town of Mansoul.

Talk between him and Cerberus.

Cerb. Prithee tell me what condition is that Town of *Mansoul* in at present?

Prof. *In a brave condition, my Lord, for us, and for my Lords, the Lords of this place I trow; for they are greatly decayed as to Godliness, and that's as well as our heart can wish; their Lord is greatly out with them, and that doth also please us well. We have already also a foot in their dish, for our* Diabolonian *friends are laid in their bosomes, and what do we lack but to be masters of the place. Besides, our trusty friends in* Mansoul *are daily plotting to betray it to the Lords of this Town, also the sickness rages bitterly among them, and that which makes up all, we hope at last to prevail.*

Cerb. Then said the Dog of *Hellgate*, no time like this to assault them, I wish that the enterprize be followed close, and that the success desired may be soon effected: Yea, I wish it for the poor *Diabolonians* sakes that live in the continual fear of their lives in that Trayterous Town of *Mansoul*.

Prof. *The contrivance is almost finished, the Lords in* Mansoul *that are* Diabolonians *are at it day and night, and the other are like silly doves, they want heart to be concerned with their state, and to consider that ruin is at hand. Besides, you may, yea must think when you put all things together, that there are many reasons that prevail with* Diabolus *to make what hast he can.*

Cerb. Thou hast said as it is, I am glad things are at this pass. Go in my brave *Profane* to my Lords, they will give thee for thy welcome as good a *Coranto* as the whole of this Kingdom will afford. I have sent thy Letter in already.

Profane's Entertainment.

Then Mr. *Profane* went into the Den, and his Lord *Diabolus* met him, and saluted him with Welcome my trusty servant. I have been made glad with thy Letter. The rest of the Lords of the Pit gave him also their salutations. Then *Profane* after obeisance made to them all, said, Let *Mansoul* be given to my Lord *Diabolus*, and let him be her King for ever. And with that the hollow belly, and yauning gorge of Hell gave so loud and hideous a groan (for that is the musick of that place) that it made the mountains about it *totter*, as if they would fall in pieces.

Now after they had read and considered the Letter, they consulted what answer to return, and the first that did speak to it was *Lucifer*.

They consult what answer to give to the Letter.

Lucifer. Numb. 31. 16. Rev. 2. 14.

Lucif. Then said he, The first project of the *Diabolonians* in *Mansoul* is like to be lucky, and to take; to wit, that they will by all the ways and means they can, make *Mansoul* yet more vile and filthy; no way to destroy a *Soul* like this; this is *Probatum est*, our old friend *Balaam* went this way and prospered, many years ago, let this therefore stand with us for a maxim and be to *Diabolonians* for a general rule in all ages, for nothing can make this to fail but Grace, in which I would hope that this Town has no share. But whether to fall upon them on a

Market-day, because of their cumber in business; that I would should be under debate. And there is more reason why this head should be debated, than why some other should; because upon this will turn the whole of what we shall attempt. If we time not our business well, our whole project may fail. Our friends the *Diabolonians* say that a *Market-day* is best, for then will *Mansoul* be most busie, and have fewest thoughts of a surprize. But what if also they shall double their guards on those days, (and methinks nature and reason should teach them to do it) and what if they should keep such a watch on those days as the necessity of their present case doth require: yea, if their men should be always in arms on those days? then you may, my Lords, be disappointed in your attempts, and may bring our friends in the Town to utter danger of unavoidable ruin.

Cumberments are dangerous.

They had need do it.

Beel. Then said the great *Beelzebub*, There is something in what my Lord hath said, but his conjecture may, or may not fall out. Nor hath my Lord laid it down as that which must not be receded from, for I know that he said it only to provoke to a warm debate thereabout. Therefore we must understand if we can, whether the Town of *Mansoul* has such sense and knowledg of her decayed state, and of the design that we have on foot against her, as doth provoke her to set watch and ward at her Gates, and to double these on Market-days. But if after enquiry made, it shall be found that they are asleep, then any day will do, but a Market day is best; and this is my judgment in this case.

A Lesson for Christians.

Diab. Then quoth *Diabolus*, how should we know this? and 'twas answered, enquire about it at the mouth of Mr. *Profane*. So *Profane* was called in and asked the question, and he made his answer as follows.

Prof. *My Lords, so far as I can gather, this is at present the condition of the Town of* Mansoul, *they are decayed in their faith and love,* Emanuel *their Prince has given them the back; they send often by petition to fetch him again, but he maketh not hast to answer their request, nor is there much reformation among them.*

Profane's description of the present state of *Mansoul.*

Diab. I am glad that they are backward to a *reformation*, but yet I am afraid of their *Petitioning*. However their loosness of life is a sign that there is not much heart in what they do, and without the heart things are little worth. But go on my masters, I will divert you, my Lords, no longer.

Beel. If the case be so with *Mansoul*, as Mr. *Profane* has described it to be, 'twill be no great matter what day we assault it, not their prayers, nor their power will do them much service.

Dreadful advice against *Mansoul*.

Apoll. When *Beelzebub* had ended his Oration, then *Apollyon* did begin. My opinion said he concerning this matter, is, that we go on fair and softly, not doing things in an hurry. Let our friends in *Mansoul* go on still to pollute and defile it, by seeking to draw it yet more into sin (for there is nothing like sin to devour *Mansoul*.) If this be done, and it takes effect, *Mansoul* of it self will leave off to watch, to Petition, or any thing else that should tend to her security and safety; for she will forget her *Emanuel*, she will not desire his company, and can she be gotten thus to live, her Prince will not come to her in hast. Our trusty friend Mr. *Carnal Security*, with one of his tricks, did *drive* him out of the Town, and why may not my Lord *Covetousness*, and my Lord *Lasciviousness*, by what they may do, *keep* him out of the Town? And this I will tell you (not because you know it not) that two or three *Diabolonians*, if entertained and countenanced by the Town of *Mansoul*, will do more to the keeping of *Emanuel* from them, and towards making of the Town of *Mansoul* your own, than can an army of a legion that should be sent out from us to withstand him.

Dreadful advice against *Mansoul*.

Let therefore this first project that our friends in *Mansoul* have set on foot, be strongly and diligently carried on with all cunning and craft imaginable; and let them send continually under one guise or another, *more* and *other* of their men to play with the people of *Mansoul*; and then perhaps we shall not need to be at the charge of making a War upon them; or if that must of necessity be done, yet the more sinful they are, the more unable, to be sure, they will be to resist us, and then the more easily we shall overcome them. And besides, suppose (and that is the worst that can be supposed) that *Emanuel* should come to them again, why may not the same means (or the like) drive him from them once more? Yea, why may he not by their lapse into that sin again be driven from them for ever, for the sake of which he was at the first driven from them for a season? And if this should happen, then away go with him his *Rams*, his *Slings*, his *Captains*, his *Souldiers*, and he leaveth *Mansoul* naked and bare. Yea, will not this Town, when she sees her self utterly forsaken of her Prince, of her own accord open her Gates again unto you, and make of you as in the days of old? but this must be done by time, a few days will not effect so great a work as this.

Dreadful advice against *Mansoul.*

So soon as *Apollyon* had made an end of speaking, *Diabolus* began to blow out his own malice, and to plead his own cause, and he said, My Lords and Powers of the Cave, my true and trusty friends, I have with much impatience, as becomes me, given ear to your long and tedious Orations. But my furious gorge, and empty panch, so lusteth after a repossession of my famous Town of *Mansoul*, that whatever comes out I can wait no longer to see the events of lingering projects. I must, and that without further delay, seek by all means I can to fill my unsatiable gulf with the soul and body of the Town of *Mansoul*. Therefore lend me your heads, your hearts, and your help, now I am going to recover my Town of *Mansoul*.

Look to it *Mansoul.*

When the Lords and Princes of the Pit saw the flaming desire that was in *Diabolus* to devour the miserable Town of *Mansoul*, they left off to raise any more objections, but consented to lend him what strength they could: Though had *Apollyons* advice been taken, they had far more fearfully distressed the Town of *Mansoul*. But, I say, they were willing to lend him what strength they could, not knowing what need they might have of him, when they should engage for themselves, as he. Wherefore they fell to advising about the next thing propounded, to wit, what Souldiers they were, and also how many, with whom *Diabolus* should go against the Town of *Mansoul* to take it; and after some debate it was concluded, according as in the Letter the *Diabolonians* had suggested, that none was more fit for that Expedition than an Army of

An army of *Doubters* raised to go against the Town of *Mansoul.*

The Princes of the Pit go with them.

terrible *Doubters*. They therefore concluded to send against *Mansoul* an Army of sturdy *Doubters*. The number thought fit to be imployed in that service, was between twenty and thirty thousand. So then the result of that great counsel of those high and mighty Lords was, That *Diabolus* should even now out of hand beat up his Drum for men in the land of *Doubting*, (which land lyeth upon the confines of the place called *Hellgate hill*) for men that might be imployed by him against the miserable Town of *Mansoul*. It was also concluded that these Lords themselves should help him in the War, and that they would to that end head and manage his men. So they drew up a Letter and sent back to the *Diabolonians* that lurked in *Mansoul*, and that waited for the back-coming of Mr. *Profane*, to signifie to them into what method and forwardness they at present had put their design. The Contents whereof now followeth.

Another Letter from *Diabolus* to the *Diabolonians* in *Mansoul.*

From the dark and horrible Dungeon of Hell, *Diabolus* with all the Society of the Princes of Darkness, sends to our trusty ones, in and about the walls of the Town of *Mansoul*, now impatiently waiting for our most Devillish answer to their venomous, and most poysonous design against the Town of *Mansoul*.

OUR native ones, in whom from day to day we boast, and in whose actions all the year long we do greatly delight our selves: We received your welcome, because highly esteemed Letter, at the hand of our trusty and greatly beloved the old Gentleman Mr. Profane. *And do give you to understand, that when we had broken it up, and had read the Contents thereof (to your amazing memory be it spoken) our yauning hollow bellied place, where we are, made so hideous and yelling a noise for joy, that the mountains that stand round about* Hellgate-hill, *had like to have been shaken to pieces at the sound thereof.*

We could also do no less than admire your faithfulness to us, with the greatness of that subtilty that now hath shewed it self to be in your heads to serve us against the Town of Mansoul. *For you have invented for us so excellent a method for our proceeding against that rebellious people, a more effectual cannot be thought of by all the wits of* Hell. *The proposals therefore which now at last you have sent us, since we saw them, we have done little else but highly approved and admired them.*

Nay, we shall to incourage you in the profundity of your craft, let you know, that at a full assembly and conclave of our Princes, and Principalities of this place, your project was discoursed and tossed from one side of our Cave to the other by their mightinesses, but a better, and as was by themselves judged a more fit and proper way by all their wits could not be invented to surprize, take, and make our own, the rebellious Town of Mansoul.

Wherefore in fine, all that was said that varied from what you had in your Letter propounded, fell of it self to the ground, and yours only was stuck to by Diabolus *the Prince; yea, his gaping gorge, and yauning panch was on fire to put your invention into execution.*

We therefore give you to understand that our stout, furious, and unmerciful Diabolus, *is raising for your relief, and the ruin of the rebellious Town of* Mansoul *more than twenty thousand Doubters to come against that people. They are all stout and sturdy men, and men that of old have been accustomed to war, and that can therefore well endure the Drum, I say he is doing of this work of his with all the possible speed he can; for his heart and spirit is engaged in it. We desire therefore that as you have hitherto stuck to us, and given us both advice and incouragement thus far; that you still will prosecute our design, nor shall you lose but be gainers thereby; yea, we intend to make you the Lords of* Mansoul.

One thing may not by any means be omitted, that is, those with us do desire that every one of you that are in Mansoul *would still use all your power, cunning and skill, with delusive perswasions, yet to draw the Town of* Mansoul *into more sin and wickedness, even that sin may be finished and bring forth death.*

For thus it is concluded with us, that the more vile, sinful, and debauched the Town of Mansoul *is, the more backward will be their* Emanuel *to come to their help, either by presence, or other relief; yea, the more sinful, the more weak, and so the more unable will they be to make resistance when we shall make our assault upon them to swallow them up. Yea, that may cause that their mighty* Shaddai *himself may*

Take heed Mansoul. *cast them out of his protection; yea, and send for his Captains and Souldiers home, with his Slings and Rams, and leave them naked and bare, and then the Town of* Mansoul *will of it self open to us, and fall as the fig into the mouth of the eater. Yea, to be sure that we then with a great deal of ease shall come upon her and overcome her.*

As to the time of our coming upon Mansoul, *we as yet have not fully resolved upon that, though at present some of us think as you, that a Market-day, or a Market-day at night will certainly be the best. However do you be ready, and when you shall hear our roaring* 1 Pet. 5. 8. *Drum without, do you be as busie to make the most horrible confusion within. So shall* Mansoul *certainly be distressed before and behind, and shall not know which way to betake her self for help. My Lord* Lucifer, *my Lord* Beelzebub, *my Lord* Apollyon, *my Lord* Legion, *with the rest salute you, as does also my Lord* Diabolus, *and we wish both you, with all that you do or shall possess, the very self-same fruit and success for their doing, as we our selves at present enjoy for ours.*

From our dreadful Confines in the most fearful Pit, we salute you, and so do those many Legions here with us, wishing you may be as Hellishly prosperous as we desire to be our selves. By the Letter-Carrier Mr. *Profane*.

Then Mr. *Profane* addressed himself for his return to *Mansoul*, with his Errand from the horrible Pit to the *Diabolonians* that dwelt in that Town. So he came up the stairs from the deep to the mouth of the Cave where *Cerberus* was. Now when *Cerberus* saw him, he asked how matters did go below, about, and against the Town of *Mansoul*.

More talk between *Profane & Cerberus*.

Prof. *Things go as well as we can expect. The Letter that I carried thither was highly approved, and well liked by all my Lords, and I am returning to tell our* Diabolonians *so. I have an answer to it here in my bosom, that I am sure will make our masters that sent me glad; for the Contents thereof is to encourage them to pursue their design to the utmost, and to be ready also to fall on within when they shall see my Lord* Diabolus *beleaguring of the Town of* Mansoul.

Cerb. But does he intend to go against them himself?

Prof. *Does he! Ay, and he will take along with him more than twenty thousand, all sturdy* Doubters, *and men of war, pickt men, from the land of* Doubting, *to serve him in the Expedition.*

The land from the which the *Doubters* come.

Cerb. Then was *Cerberus* glad, and said, And is there such brave preparations a making to go against the miserable Town of *Mansoul*; and would I might be put at the head of a thousand of them, that I might also shew my valour against the famous Town of *Mansoul.*

Prof. *Tour wish may come to pass, you look like one that has mettle enough, and my Lord will have with him those that are valiant and stout. But my business requires hast.*

Cerb. Ay, so it does. Speed thee to the Town of *Mansoul*, with all the deepest mischiefs that this place can afford thee. And when thou shalt come to the house of Mr. *Mischief*, the place where the *Diabolonians* meet to plot, tell them that *Cerberus* doth wish them his service, and that if he may, he will with the army come up against the famous Town of *Mansoul.*

Prof. *That I will. And I know that my Lords that are there, will be glad to hear it, and to see you also.*

So after a few more such kind of Complements, Mr. *Profane* took his leave of his friend *Cerberus*, and *Cerberus* again with a thousand of their Pit-wishes, bid him hast with all speed to his Masters. The which when he had heard he made obeisance, and began to gather up his heels to run.

Thus therefore he returned, and went and came to *Mansoul*, and going as afore to the house of Mr. *Mischief*, there he found the *Diabolonians* assembled, and waiting for his return. Now when he was come and had presented himself, he also delivered to them his Letter, and adjoined this Complement to them therewith: My Lords from the Confines of the Pit, the high and mighty Principalities and powers of the *Den* salute you here, the true *Diabolonians* of the Town of *Mansoul.* Wishing you always the most proper of their benedictions, for the great service, high attempts, and brave atchievements that you have put your selves upon, for the restoring to our Prince *Diabolus* the famous Town of *Mansoul.*

Profane returned again to *Mansoul.*

This was therefore the present state of the miserable Town

of *Mansoul*: she had offended her Prince, and he was gone; she had incouraged the powers of Hell by her foolishness, to come against her to seek her utter destruction.

True, the Town of *Mansoul* was somewhat made sensible of her sin, but the *Diabolonians* were gotten into her bowels; she cried, but *Emanuel* was gone, and her cries did not fetch him as yet again. Besides she knew not now whether *ever* or *never*, he would return and come to his *Mansoul* again, nor did they know the power and industry of the enemy nor how forward they were to put in Execution that plot of Hell that they had devised against her.

They did indeed still send Petition after Petition to the Prince, but he answered all with silence. They did neglect reformation, and that was as *Diabolus* would have it, for he knew, if they regarded iniquity in their heart, their King would not hear their prayer; they therefore did still grow weaker and weaker, and were as a rouling thing before the whirlwind. They cried to their King for help, and laid *Diabolonians* in their bosoms, what therefore should a King do to them? Yea, there seemed now to be a mixture in *Mansoul*, the *Diabolonians* and the *Mansoulians* would walk the streets together. Yea, they began to seek their peace, for they thought that since the sickness had been so mortal in *Mansoul*, 'twas in vain to go to handigripes with them. Besides, the weakness of *Mansoul* was the strength of their enemies; and the sins of *Mansoul* the advantage of the *Diabolonians*. The foes of *Mansoul* did also now begin to promise themselves the Town for a possession, there was no great difference now betwixt *Mansoulians* and *Diabolonians*, both seemed to be Masters of *Mansoul*. Yea, the *Diabolonians* increased and grew, but the Town of *Mansoul* diminished greatly. There was more than eleven thousand of men, women and children that died by the sickness in *Mansoul*.

Good Thoughts. Good conceptions, and good desires.

But now as *Shaddai* would have it, there was one whose name was Mr. *Prywell*, a great lover of the people of *Mansoul*. And he as his manner was did go listning up and down in *Mansoul* to see, and to hear if at any time he might, whether there was any design against it or no. For he was always a jealous man, and feared some *mischief* sometime would befall it, either from the *Diabolonians* within, or from some power without. Now upon a time it so happened as Mr. *Prywell* went listning here and there, that he lighted upon a place called *Vile-hill* in *Mansoul*, where *Diabolonians* used to meet; so hearing a muttering (you must know that it was in the night) he softly drew near to hear, nor had he stood long under the house-end, (for there stood a house there) but he heard one confidently affirm, That it was not, or would not be long before *Diabolus* should possess himself again of *Mansoul*, and that then the *Diabolonians* did intend to put all *Mansoulians* to the sword, and would kill and destroy the Kings Captains, and drive all his Souldiers out of the Town.

The story of Mr. *Prywell.*

The *Diabolonian* Plot discovered, and by whom.

He said moreover, That he knew there were above twenty thousand fighting men prepared by *Diabolus* for the accomplishing of this design, and that it would not be months before they all should see it. When Mr. *Prywell* had heard this story, he did quickly believe it was true, wherefore he went forthwith to my Lord *Mayors* house, and acquainted him therewith; who sending for the *Subordinate Preacher*, brake the business to him, and he as soon gave the alarm to the Town, for he was now the chief Preacher in *Mansoul*, because as yet my Lord *Secretary* was *ill at ease*. And this was the way that the *Subordinate Preacher* did take to alarm the Town therewith: The same hour he caused the *Lecture-bell* to be rung, so the people came together, he gave them then a short Exhortation to watchfulness, and made Mr. *Prywels* news the argument thereof. For, said he, an horrible plot is contrived against *Mansoul* even to *massacre* us all in a day; nor is this story to be slighted, for Mr. *Prywell* is the author thereof. Mr. *Prywell* was always a lover of *Mansoul*, a sober and judicious man, a man that is no tatler, nor raiser of false reports, but one that loves to look into the very bottom of matters, and talks nothing of news but by very solid arguments.

Understanding. Conscience.

The *Subordinate Preacher* awakened.

I will call him, and you shall hear him your own selves; so he called him, and he came and told his tale so punctually,

Prywell tells his news to *Mansoul.*

and affirmed its truth with such ample grounds, that *Mansoul* fell presently under a conviction of the truth of what he said. The Preacher did also back him, saying, Sirs, it is not irrational for us to believe it, for we have provoked *Shaddai* to anger, and have sinned *Emanuel* out of the Town; we have had too much correspondence with *Diabolonians*, and have forsaken our former mercies; no marvel then if the enemy both within and without should design and plot our ruin; and what time like this to do it? The sickness is now in the Town, and we have been made weak thereby. Many a good meaning man is dead, and the *Diabolonians* of late grow stronger and stronger.

Good desires.

They take the alarms.

Besides, quoth the *Subordinate Preacher*, I have received from this good Truth-teller this one inkling further, that he understood by those that he over-heard, that several Letters have lately passed between the *Furies* and the *Diabolonians* in order to our destruction. When *Mansoul* heard all this, and not being able to gain-say it, they lift up their voice and wept. Mr. *Prywell* did also in the presence of the Townsmen, confirm all that their *Subordinate Preacher* had said. Wherefore they now set afresh to bewail their folly, and to a doubling of Petitions to *Shaddai* and his Son. They also brake the business to the Captains, high Commanders, and men of War in the Town of *Mansoul*, entreating of them to use the means to be strong, and to take good courage, and that they would look after their harness, and make themselves ready to give *Diabolus* battel by night and by day, shall he come, as they are inform'd he will, to beleaguer the Town of *Mansoul*.

They tell the thing to the Captains.

They come together to consult.

When the Captains heard this, they being always true lovers of the Town of *Mansoul*, what do they but like so many *Sampsons* they shake themselves, and come together to consult and contrive how to defeat those bold and hellish contrivances that were upon the wheel by the means of *Diabolus* and his friends against the now sickly, weakly, and much impoverished Town of *Mansoul*; and they agreed upon these following Particulars.

Their agreement.

1. That the Gates of *Mansoul* should be kept shut, and made fast with bars and locks, and that all persons that went

out, or came in, should be very strictly examined by the Captains of the Guards. To the end, said they, that those that are managers of the Plot amongst us, may either coming or going be taken; and that we may also find out who are the great contrivers (amongst us) of our ruin.

1 Cor. 16. 13.
Lam. 3. 40.

2. The next thing was, that a strict search should be made for all kind of *Diabolonians* throughout the whole Town of *Mansoul*; and that every mans house from top to bottom should be looked into, and that too, house by house, that if possible a further discovery might be made of all such among them as had a hand in these designs.

Heb. 12. 15, 16.

3. It was further concluded upon, that *wheresoever* or with *whomsoever* any of the *Diabolonians* were found, that even those of the Town of *Mansoul* that had given them house and harbour, should to their shame, and the warning of others take penance in the open place.

Jer. 2. 34.
Chap. 5. 26.
Ezek. 16. 52.

4. It was moreover resolved by the famous Town of *Mansoul*, that a publick fast, and a day of humiliation should be kept throughout the whole Corporation to the justifying of their Prince, the abasing of themselves before him for their transgressions against him, and against *Shaddai* his Father. It was further resolved that all such in *Mansoul* as did not on that day endeavour to keep that fast, and to humble themselves for their faults, but that should mind their worldly imploys, or be found wandring up and down the streets, should be taken for *Diabolonians*, and should suffer as *Diabolonians* for such their wicked doings.

Joel 1. 14.
Chap. 2. 15, 16.

5. It was further concluded then that with what speed, and with what warmth of mind they could, they would renew their humiliation for sin, and their Petitions to *Shaddai* for help; they also resolved to send tidings to the Court of all that Mr. *Prywell* had told them.

Jer. 37. 4.

6. It was also determined that thanks should be given by the Town of *Mansoul* to Mr. *Prywell* for his diligent seeking of the welfare of their Town; and further, that forasmuch as he was so naturally inclined to seek their good, and also to undermine their foes, they gave him a Com-

Mr. *Prywel* is made Scout-master General.

mission of *Scoutmaster-general*, for the good of the Town of *Mansoul*.

When the Corporation with their Captains had thus concluded, they did as they had said, they shut up their Gates, they made for *Diabolonians* strict search, they made those with whom any was found to take penance in the open place. They kept their Fast, and renewed their Petitions to their Prince, and Mr. *Prywell* managed his charge, and the trust that *Mansoul* had put in his hands with great Conscience, and good fidelity; for he gave himself wholly up to his imploy, and that not only within the Town, but he went out to *pry*, to *see*, and to *hear*.

Mr. *Prywel* goes a-scouting.

And not many days after he provided for his Journey, and went towards *Hellgate-hill* into the Country where the *Doubters* were, where he heard of all that had been talked of in *Mansoul*, and he perceived also that *Diabolus* was almost ready for his march, *&c.* so he came back with speed, and calling the Captains and Elders of *Mansoul* together, he told them where he had been, what he had heard, and what he had seen.

He returns with great news.

Particularly he told them that *Diabolus* was almost ready for his march, and that he had made old Mr. *Incredulity* that once brake prison in *Mansoul*, the General of his Army; that his Army consisted all of *Doubters*, and that their number was above twenty thousand. He told moreover that *Diabolus* did intend to bring with him the chief Princes of the *Infernal Pit*, and that he would make them chief Captains over his *Doubters*. He told them moreover that it was certainly true that several of the Black-den would with *Diabolus* ride *Reformades* to reduce the Town of *Mansoul* to the obedience of *Diabolus* their Prince.

He said moreover that he understood by the *Doubters* among whom he had been, that the reason why old *Incredulity* was made General of the whole Army, was because none truer than he to the Tyrant; and because he had an implacable spite against the welfare of the Town of *Mansoul*. Besides, said he, he remembers the affronts that *Mansoul* has given, and he is resolved to be revenged of them.

But the black Princes shall be made high Commanders, only *Incredulity* shall be over them all, because (which I had almost forgot) he can more easily, and more dextrously beleaguer the Town of *Mansoul*, than can any of the Princes besides.

Heb. 12. 1.

Now when the Captains of *Mansoul* with the Elders of the Town, had heard the tidings that Mr. *Prywell* did bring, they thought it expedient without further delay to put into execution the Laws that against the *Diabolonians*, their Prince had made for them, and given them in commandment to manage against them. Wherefore forthwith a diligent and impartial search was made in all houses in *Mansoul* for all and all manner of *Diabolonians*. Now in the house of Mr. *Mind*, and in the house of the great Lord *Wilbewill* were two *Diabolonians* found. In Mr. *Minds* house was one Lord *Covetousness* found, but he had changed his name to *Prudent thrifty*. In my Lord *Wilbewills* house, one *Lasciviousness* was found; but he had changed his name to *Harmless mirth*. These two the Captains and Elders of the Town of *Mansoul* took, and committed them to custody under the hand of Mr. *Trueman* the Gaoler; and this man handled them so severely, and loaded them so well with irons, that in time they both fell into a very deep Consumption, and died in the Prison-house; their masters also according to the agreement of the Captains and Elders, were brought to take penance in the open place to *their* shame, and for a warning to the rest of the Town of *Mansoul*.

Some *Diabolonians* taken in *Mansoul* and committed to Prison.

The Lord *Wilbewill* and Mr. *Mind* take penance.

Now this was the manner of penance in those days. The persons offending being made sensible of the evil of their doings, were injoined open confession of their faults, and a strict amendment of their lives.

Penance what.

After this the *Captains* and *Elders* of *Mansoul* sought yet to find out more *Diabolonians*, where ever they lurked, whether in dens, caves, holes, vaults, or where else they could, in, or about the wall, or Town of *Mansoul*. But though they could plainly see their footing, and so follow them by their tract, and smell to their holds, even to the mouths of their caves and dens, yet take them, hold them, and do justice upon them they could not, their ways were so crooked, their holds so strong, and they so quick to take sanctuary there.

But *Mansoul* did now with so stiff an hand rule over the *Diabolonians* that were left, that they were glad to shrink into corners: time was when they durst walk openly, and in the day, but now they were forced to imbrace privacy and the night: time was when a *Mansoulian* was their companion, but now they counted them deadly enemies. This good change did Mr. *Prywells* intelligence make in the famous Town of *Mansoul*.

By this time *Diabolus* had finished his Army which he intended to bring with him for the ruin of *Mansoul*, and had set over them Captains, and other Field-officers, such as liked his furious stomach best, himself was Lord paramount, *Incredulity* was General of his Army. Their highest Captains shall be named afterwards, but now for their Officers, Colours and Scutcheons.

Diabolus's Army.

Rev. 12. 3, 4, 13, 15, 17.

1. Their first Captain was Captain *Rage*, he was Captain over the *Election-Doubters*, his were the Red Colours; his Standard-bearer was Mr. *Destructive*, and the great Red Dragon he had for his Scutcheon.

Num. 21. 6.

2. The second Captain was Captain *Fury*, he was Captain over he *Vocation-doubters*; his Standard-bearer was Mr. *Darkness*, his Colours were those that were pale, and he had for his Scutcheon the fiery flying Serpent.

Mat. 22. 13. Revel. 9. 1.

3. The third Captain was Captain *Damnation*, he was Captain over the *Grace-doubters*, his were the Red Colours, Mr. *No-life* bare them, and he had for his Scutcheon the Black-den.

Pro. 27. 20.

4. The fourth Captain was the Captain *Insatiable*, he was Captain over the *Faith-doubters*, his were the Red Colours, Mr. *Devourer* bare them, and he had for a Scutcheon the *yawning Jaws*.

Psal. 11. 6. Rev. 14. 11.

5. The fifth Captain was Captain *Brimstone*, he was Captain over the *Perseverance-doubters*, his also were the Red Colours, Mr. *Burning* bare them, and his Scutcheon was the Blue and stinking flame.

26 marg. Mat. 22. 13] Mat. 3. 22, 13   35 bare] bear *1682 first state*

6. The sixth Captain was Captain *Torment*, he was Captain over the *Resurrection-doubters*, his Colors were those that were pale, Mr. *Gnaw* was his Ancient bearer, and he had the *Black worm* for his Scutcheon.
Mar. 9. 44, 46, 48.

7. The seventh Captain was Captain *No-ease*, he was Captain over the *Salvation-doubters*, his were the Red Colours, Mr. *Restless* bare them, and his Scutcheon was the gastly picture of death.
Rev. 4. 11. Chap. 6. 8.

8. The eighth Captain was the Captain *Sepulcher*, he was Captain over the *Glory-doubters*, his also were the pale Colours, Mr. *Corruption* was his Ancient-bearer, and he had for his Scutcheon a Scull, and dead mens bones.
Jer. 5. 16. Ch. 2. 25.

9. The ninth Captain was Captain *Past-hope*, he was Captain of those that are called the *Felicity-doubters*, his Ancient-bearer was Mr. *Despair*; his also were the Red Colours, and his Scutcheon was the hot iron, and the hard heart.
1 Tim. 4. 2. Rom. 2. 5.

These were his Captains, and these were their forces, these were their Ancients, these were their Colours, and these were their Scutcheons. Now over these did the great *Diabolus* make superiour Captains, and they were in number seven: as namely the Lord *Beelzebub*, the Lord *Lucifer*, the Lord *Legion*, the Lord *Apollyon*, the Lord *Python*, the Lord *Cerberus*, and the Lord *Belial*; these seven he set over the Captains, and *Incredulity* was Lord General, and *Diabolus* was *King*.

The *Reformades* also, such as were like themselves, were made some of them Captains of hundreds, and some of them Captains of more: and thus was the army of *Incredulity* compleated.
Diabolus his army compleated

So they set out at *Hellgate-hill* (for there they had their Randezvouz) from whence they came with a straight course upon their march toward the Town of *Mansoul*. Now as was hinted before, the Town had, as *Shaddai* would have it, received from the mouth of Mr. *Prywell* the alarm of their

3 Ancient] standard *1682 third state* 11 Ancient-bearer] Standard-bearer *1682 third state* 14–15 *Felicity-doubters*, his Ancient-bearer] *Felicity-doubters*; his Standard-bearer *1682 third state* 19 Ancients] Standards *1682 third state*

coming before. Wherefore they set a strong watch at the Gates, and had also doubled their guards, they also mounted their slings in good places where they might conveniently cast out their great stones to the annoyance of the furious enemy.

Nor could those *Diabolonians* that were in the Town do that hurt as was designed they should; for *Mansoul* was now awake. But alas poor people, they were sorely affrighted at the first appearance of their foes, and at their sitting down before the Town, especially when they heard the roaring of their *DRUM*. This, to speak truth, was amazingly hideous to hear, it frighted all men seven miles round if they were but awake and heard it. The streaming of their Colours were also terrible, and dejecting to behold.

1 Pet. 5. 8

He makes an assault upon *Eargate*, and is repelled.

When *Diabolus* was come up against the Town, first he made his approach to *Ear-gate*, and gave it a furious assault, supposing as it seems that his friends in *Mansoul* had been ready to do the work within; but care was taken of that before, by the vigilance of the Captains. Wherefore missing of the help that he expected from them, and finding of his Army warmly attended with the stones that the slingers did sling (for that I will say for the Captains, that considering the weakness that yet was upon them by reason of the long sickness that had annoyed the Town of *Mansoul*, they did gallantly behave themselves), he was forced to make some retreat from *Mansoul*, and to intrench himself and his men in the field without the reach of the slings of the Town.

Jam. 4. 7. He retreats and intrenches himself.

He casts up Mounts against the Town.

Now having intrenched himself, he did cast up four Mounts against the Town; the first he called Mount *Diabolus*, putting his own name thereon, the more to affright the Town of *Mansoul*; the other three he called thus, Mount *Alecto*, Mount *Megæra*, and Mount *Tisiphone*; for these are the names of the dreadful Furies of Hell. Thus he began to play his game with *Mansoul*, and to serve it as doth the Lion his prey, even to make it fall before his terrour. But, as I said, the Captains and Souldiers resisted so stoutly, and did do such execution with their stones, that they made him, though against stomach, to retreat: wherefore *Mansoul* began to take courage.

Now upon Mount *Diabolus*, which was raised on the North-side of the Town, there did the Tyrant set up his *Standard*, and a fearful thing it was to behold, for he had *wrought* in it by Devillish art, after the manner of a Scutcheon, a flaming flame fearful to behold, and the picture of *Mansoul* burning in it.

Diabolus his standard set up.

When *Diabolus* had thus done, he commanded that his *Drummer* should every night approach the walls of the Town of *Mansoul*, and so to beat a parley; the command was to do it a nights, for in the day time they annoyed him with their slings; for the Tyrant said that he had a mind to parley with the now trembling Town of *Mansoul*, and he commanded that the Drums should beat every night, that through weariness they might at last (if possibly, at the first they were unwilling) yet be forced to do it.

He bids his Drummer to beat his Drum.

So this Drummer did as commanded, he arose and did beat his Drum. But when his Drum did go, if one looked toward the Town of *Mansoul*, *Behold darkness and sorrow, and the light was darkened in the heaven thereof.* No noise was ever heard upon earth more terrible, except the voice of *Shaddai* when he speaketh. But how did *Mansoul* tremble! it now looked for nothing but forthwith to be swallowed up.

Mansoul trembles at the noise of his Drum. Isa. 5. 30.

When this Drummer had beaten for a Parley, he made this speech to *Mansoul*, *My Master has bid me tell you, That if you will willingly submit, you shall have the good of the earth, but if you shall be stubborn, he is resolved to take you by force.* But by that the fugitive had done beating of his Drum, the people of *Mansoul* had betaken themselves to the *Captains* that were in the Castle, so that there was none to regard, nor to give this Drummer an answer; so he proceeded no further that night, but returned again to his Master to the Camp.

Diabolus calls back his Drum.

When *Diabolus* saw that by *Drumming* he could not work out *Mansoul* to his will, the next night he sendeth his Drummer without his Drum still to let the *Townsmen* know that he had a mind to Parley with them. But when all came to all, his Parley was turned into a Summons to the Town to deliver up themselves; but they gave him neither heed nor hearing, for they remembered what at first it cost them to hear him a few words.

The next night he sends again, and then who should be his messenger to *Mansoul* but the terrible Captain *Sepulcher*; so Captain *Sepulcher* came up to the walls of *Mansoul*, and made this Oration to the Town.

Mansoul summoned by Captain *Sepulcher*.

O ye inhabitants of the rebellious Town of Mansoul! *I summon you in the name of the Prince* Diabolus, *that without any more ado, you set open the Gates of your Town, and admit the great Lord to come in. But if you shall still rebel, when we have taken to us the Town by force, we will swallow you up as the grave; wherefore if you will hearken to my Summons, say so, and if not, then let me know.*

The reason of this my Summons, quoth he, is, for that my Lord is your undoubted Prince and Lord, as you your selves have formerly owned. Nor shall that assault that was given to my Lord, when Emanuel *dealt so dishonourably by him, prevail with him to lose his right, and to forbear to attempt to recover his own. Consider then O* Mansoul, *with thy self, wilt thou shew thy self peaceable, or no? If thou shalt quietly yield up thy self, then our old friendship shall be renewed; but if thou shalt yet refuse and rebell, then expect nothing but fire and sword.*

They answer him not a word.

When the languishing Town of *Mansoul* had heard this Summoner, and his Summons, they were yet more put to their dumps, but made to the Captain no answer at all, so away he went as he came.

They address themselves to their good Lord *Secretary*.

But after some consultation among themselves, as also with some of their Captains, they applied themselves afresh to the Lord *Secretary* for counsel and advice from him; for this Lord *Secretary* was their chief Preacher (as also is mentioned some pages before) only now he was *ill at ease*; and of him they begged favour in these two or three things.

1. That he would look comfortably upon them, and not keep himself so much retired from them as formerly. Also that he would be prevailed with to give them a hearing while they should make known their miserable condition to him.

But to this he told them as before, *That as yet he was but ill at ease, and therefore could not do as he had formerly done.*

2. The second thing that they desired, was, that he would be pleased to give them his advice about their *now* so important affairs, for that *Diabolus* was come and set down before the Town with no less than twenty thousand *Doubters.* They said moreover, that both he and his Captains were cruel men, and that they were afraid of them. But to this he said, *You must look to the Law of the Prince, and there see what is laid upon you to do.*

3. Then they desired that his Highness would help them to frame a Petition to *Shaddai*, and unto *Emanuel* his son, and that he would set his own hand thereto as a token that he was one with them in it: *For*, said they, *my Lord*, *many a one have we sent, but can get no answer of peace; but now surely one with thy hand unto it, may obtain good for* Mansoul.

But all the answer that he gave to this, was, *That they had offended their* Emanuel, *and had also grieved himself, and that therefore they must as yet partake of their own devices.*

The cause of his being ill at ease.

This answer of the Lord *Secretary* fell like a milstone upon them; yea, it crushed them so that they could not tell what to do, yet they durst not comply with the demands of *Diabolus*, nor with the demands of his Captain. So then here were the straights that the Town of *Mansoul* was betwixt, when the enemy came upon her: Her foes were ready to swallow her up, and her friends did forbear to help her.

Lam. 1. 3. The sad straights of Mansoul.

Then stood up my Lord *Mayor*, whose name was my Lord *Understanding*, and he began to pick and pick, until he had pickt comfort out of that seemingly bitter saying of the Lord *Secretary*; for thus he descanted upon it: First, said he, This unavoidably follows upon the saying of my Lord, *That we must suffer for our sins.* 2. *But*, quoth he, *the words yet sound as if at last we should be saved from our enemies, and that after a few more sorrows* Emanuel *will come and be our help.* Now the Lord *Mayor* was the more critical in his dealing with the *Secretaries* words, because my Lord was more than a Prophet, and because none

A Comment upon the Lord Secretaries Speech.

of his words were *such*, but that at all times they were most exactly significant, and the Townsmen were allowed to pry into them, and to expound them to their best advantage.

So they took their leaves of my Lord, and returned, and went, and came to the Captains, to whom they did tell what my Lord high *Secretary* had said, who when they had heard it, were all of the same opinion as was my Lord *Mayor* himself; the *Captains* therefore began to take some courage unto them, and to prepare to make some brave attempt upon the Camp of the enemy, and to destroy all that were *Diabolonians*, with the roving *Doubters* that the Tyrant had brought with him to destroy the poor Town of *Mansoul*.

The Town of *Mansoul* in order.

So all betook themselves forthwith to their places, the *Captains* to theirs, the Lord *Mayor* to his, the *Subordinate Preacher* to his, and my Lord *Wilbewill* to his. The *Captains* longed to be at some work for their Prince, for they delighted in Warlike Atchievements. The next day therefore they came together and consulted, and after consultation had, they resolved to give an answer to the Captain of *Diabolus* with slings; and so they did at the rising of the Sun on the morrow; for *Diabolus* had adventured to come nearer again, but the sling-stones were to him and his like Hornets. For as there is nothing to the Town of *Mansoul* so terrible as the roaring of *Diabolus*'s Drum, so there is nothing to *Diabolus* so terrible as the well playing of *Emanuels* slings. Wherefore, *Diabolus* was forced to make another retreat, yet further off from the famous Town of *Mansoul*. Then did the Lord Mayor of *Mansoul* cause the Bells to be rung, *and that thanks should be sent to the Lord high* Secretary *by the mouth of the* Subordinate Preacher; *for that by his words the Captains and Elders of* Mansoul *had been strengthened against* Diabolus.

Words applied against him by faith. Zach. 9. 15

When *Diabolus* saw that his Captains and Souldiers, high Lords, and renowned, were frightened, and beaten down by the stones that came from the Golden slings of the Prince of the Town of *Mansoul*, he bethought himself, and said, *I will try to catch them by fawning, I will try to flatter them into my net.*

Wherefore after a while he came down again to the wall,

not now with his Drum, nor with Captain *Sepulcher*, but having all to be sugared his lips, he seemed to be a very sweet-mouthed, peaceable Prince, designing nothing for humours sake, nor to be revenged on *Mansoul* for injuries by them done to him, but the welfare, and good, and advantage of the Town and people therein, was now, as he said, his only design. Wherefore after he had called for audience, and desired that the Townsfolk would give it to him, he proceeded in his Oration: And said,

Diabolus changes his way.

O! the desire of my heart, the famous Town of Mansoul! *how many nights have I watched, and how many weary steps have I taken, if perhaps I might do thee good: Far be it, far be it from me to desire to make a war upon you; if ye will but willingly and quietly deliver up your selves unto me. You know that you were mine of old. Remember also, that so long as you enjoyed me for your Lord, and that I enjoyed you for my subjects, you wanted for nothing of all the delights of the earth, that I your Lord and Prince could get for you; or that I could invent to make you bonny and blith withal. Consider, you never had so many hard, dark, troublesome and heart-afflicting hours, while you were mine, as you have had since you revolted from me; nor shall you ever have peace again until you and I become one as before. But be but prevailed with to imbrace me again, and I will grant, yea inlarge your old Charter with abundance of priviledges; so that your licence and liberty shall be to take, hold, enjoy, and make your own all that is pleasant from the East to the West. Nor shall any of those incivilities wherewith you have offended me, be ever charged upon you by me, so long as the Sun and Moon endureth. Nor shall any of those dear friends of mine that now for the fear of you, lye lurking in dens, and holes, and caves in* Mansoul, *be hurtful to you any more, yea, they shall be your servants, and shall minister unto you of their substance, and of whatever shall come to hand. I need speak no more, you know them, and have sometime since been much delighted in their company, why then should we abide at such odds? let us renew our old acquaintance and friendship again.*

1 Pet. 5. 8. Rev. 12. 10.

Mat. 4. 8. Luk. 4. 6, 7.

Satan reads all backwards.

Take heed *Mansoul.*

Sins.

The pleasure of sin.

No, no, no, not upon pain of eternal damnation.

Bear with your friend, I take the liberty at this time to speak thus freely unto you. The love that I have to you presses me to do it, as also does the zeal of my heart for my friends with you; put me not therefore to further trouble, nor your selves to further fears and frights. Have you I will in a way of peace or war; nor do you flatter your selves with the power and force of your Captains, *or that your* Emanuel *will shortly come in to your help; for such strength will do you no pleasure.*

I am come against you with a stout and valiant army, and all the chief Princes of the den, are even at the head of it. Besides, my Captains are swifter then Eagles, *stronger than* Lions, *and more greedy of prey than are the evening-wolves. What is* Og *of* Bashan! *what's* Goliah *of* Gath! *and what's an hundred more of them to one of the least of my Captains! how then shall* Mansoul *think to escape my hand and force?*

Diabolus having thus ended his flattering, fawning, deceitful and lying speech to the famous Town of *Mansoul*, the Lord Mayor replied upon him as follows.

The Lord Mayors answer.

O Diabolus, *Prince of darkness, and master of all deceit; thy lying flatteries we have had and made sufficient probation of, and have tasted too deeply of that destructive cup already; should we therefore again hearken unto thee, and so break the Commandments of our great* Shaddai, *to join in affinity with thee; would not our Prince reject us, and cast us off for ever; and being cast off by him, can the place that he has prepared for thee be a place of rest for us! Besides, O thou that art empty and void of all truth, we are rather ready to die by thy hand than to fall in with thy flattering and lying deceits.*

When the Tyrant saw that there was little to be got by parleying with my Lord Mayor, he fell into an Hellish rage, and resolved that again with his army of *Doubters*, he would another time assault the Town of *Mansoul*.

So he called for his *Drummer*, who beat up for his men (and while he did *beat*, Mansoul *did shake*) to be in a readiness to give battel to the Corporation; then *Diabolus* drew near with his army, and thus disposed of his men. Captain *Cruel*, and

Feelgate.

Captain *Torment*, these he drew up and placed against *Feelgate*, and commanded them to sit down there for the war. And he also appointed, that if need were, Captain *Noease* should come

Nosegate. — *Eyegate.*

in to their relief. At *Nosegate* he placed the Captain *Brimstone*, and Captain *Sepulcher*, and bid them look well to their Ward, on that side of the Town of *Mansoul*. But at *Eyegate* he placed that grim-faced one the Captain *Pasthope*, and there also *now* he did set up his terrible standard.

Now Captain *Insatiable* he was to look to the Carriages of *Diabolus*, and was also appointed to take into custody, that, or those persons and things that should at any time as prey be taken from the enemy.

Mouthgate. — The use of *Mouthgate*.

Now *Mouthgate* the inhabitants of *Mansoul* kept for a *Sally-port*, wherefore *that* they kept strong, for that was it, by, and out at which the Townsfolk did send their Petitions to *Emanuel* their Prince, that also was the Gate from the top of which the Captains did play their slings at the enemies, for that Gate stood somewhat ascending, so that the placing of them there, and the letting of them fly from that place did much execution against the Tyrants army; wherefore for these causes with others, *Diabolus* sought, if possible, to land up *Mouthgate* with durt.

The Lord *Wilbewill* plays the man. — *Jolley* and *Grigish* taken and executed.

Now as *Diabolus* was busie and industrious in preparing to make his assault upon the Town of *Mansoul* without, so the Captains and Souldiers in the Corporation were as busie in preparing within; they mounted their Slings, they set up their Banners, they sounded their Trumpets, and put themselves in such order as was judged most for the annoyance of the enemy, and for the advantage of *Mansoul*, and gave to their Souldiers orders to be ready at the sound of the Trumpet for war. The Lord *Wilbewill* also, he took the charge of watching against the Rebels within, and to do what he could to take them while without, or to stifle them within their caves, dens and holes in the Town wall of *Mansoul*. And to speak the truth of him, ever since he took penance for his fault, he has shewed as much honesty and bravery of spirit as any *he* in *Mansoul*; for he took one *Jolley*, and his brother *Griggish*, the two sons of his servant *Harmless-mirth* (for to that day, though the father was committed to Ward, the sons had a dwelling in the house of my Lord) I say he took them, and with his own hands put them to the Cross. And this was the reason why he hanged them up, after their father was put into the hands of Mr. *Trueman* the Gaoler; they his sons began to play his pranks, and to be ticking and toying with the daughters of their Lord; nay, it was jealoused that they were too familiar with them, the which was brought to his Lordships ear. Now his Lordship being unwilling unadvisedly to put any man to death, did not suddenly fall upon them, but set watch and spies to see if the thing was true; of the which he was soon informed, for his two servants, whose names were *Find-out*, and *Tell-all*, catcht them together in uncivil manner more than *once or twice*, and went and told their Lord. So when my Lord *Wilbewill* had sufficient ground to believe the thing was true, he takes the two young *Diabolonians*, for such they were (for their father was a *Diabolonian* born) and has them to *Eyegate*, where he raised a very high Cross just in the face of the army of *Diabolus*, and of his army, and there he hanged the young Villains in defiance to Captain *Pasthope*, and of the horrible standard of the Tyrant.

The place of their Execution.

Mortification of sin is a sign of hope of life.

Now this *Christian* act of the brave Lord *Wilbewill* did greatly abash Captain *Past-hope*, discourage the army of *Diabolus*, put fear into the *Diabolonian* runnagates in *Mansoul*, and put strength and courage into the Captains that belonged to *Emanuel* the Prince; for they without did gather, and that by this very act of my Lord, that *Mansoul* was resolved to fight, and that the *Diabolonians* within the Town could not do such things as *Diabolus* had hopes they would. Nor was this the only proof of the brave Lord *Wilbewills* honesty to the Town, nor of his loyalty to his Prince, as will afterwards appear.

Mr. *Mind* plays the man.

Now when the children of *Prudent-thrifty* who dwelt with Mr. *Mind*, (for *Thrift* left children with Mr. *Mind*, when he was also committed to prison, and their names were *Gripe* and *Rake-all*, these he begat of Mr. *Mind's Bastard-daughter*, whose name was Mrs. *Holdfastbad*) I say when his children perceived how the Lord *Wilbewill* had served them that dwelt with him, what do they but (lest they should drink of the same cup) endeavour to make their escape? But Mr. *Mind* being wary of it, took them and put them in hold in his house till morning (for this was done over night) and remembring that by the Law of *Mansoul* all *Diabolonians* were to die, and to be sure they were at least by fathers side such, and some say by mothers side too; what does he but takes them and puts them in chains, and carries them to the self-same place where my Lord hanged his two before, and there he hanged them.

Mansoul set against the *Diabolonians*.

The Townsmen also took great incouragement at this act of Mr. *Mind*, and did what they could to have taken some more of these *Diabolonian* troublers of *Mansoul*; but at that time the rest lay so quat and close that they could not be apprehended; so they set against them a diligent watch, and went every man to his place.

Diabolus his kindness turned into furious madness.

I told you a little before that *Diabolus* and his army were somewhat abasht and discouraged at the sight of what my Lord *Wilbewill* did, when he hanged up those two young *Diabolonians*; but his discouragement quickly turned itself into furious madness and rage against the Town of *Mansoul*, and fight it he would. Also the Townsmen, and Captains within, they had their hopes and their expectations heightened, believing at last the day would be theirs, so they feared them the less. Their *Subordinate Preacher* too made a Sermon about it, and he took that theme for his Text, *Gad, a troop shall overcome him, but he shall overcome at the last*. Whence he shewed that though *Mansoul* should be sorely put to it at the first, yet the victory should most certainly be *Mansouls* at the last.

Gen. 49. 19.

With heart and mouth.

So *Diabolus* commanded that his *Drummer* should beat a Charge against the Town, and the Captains also that were in the Town sounded a Charge against them, but they had no Drum, they were Trumpets of Silver with which they sounded against them. Then they which were of the Camp of *Diabolus* came down to the Town to take it, and the Captains in the Castle, with the slingers at *Mouthgate* played upon them *amain*. And now there was nothing heard in the Camp of *Diabolus* but horrible rage and blasphemy; but in the Town good words,

Prayer and singing of Psalms: the enemy replied with horrible objections, and the terribleness of their *Drum*; but the Town made answer with the slapping of their slings, and the melodious noise of their Trumpets. And thus the fight lasted for several days together, only now and then they had some small intermission, in the which the Townsmen refreshed themselves, and the Captains made ready for another assault.

The Captains of *Emanuel* were clad in *Silver* armour, and the Souldiers in that which was of Proof; the Souldiers of *Diabolus* were clad in *Iron*, which was made to give place to *Emanuels* Engine-shot. In the Town some were hurt, and some were greatly wounded. Now the worst on 't was, a Chirurgeon was scarce in *Mansoul*, for that *Emanuel* at present was absent.

Rev. 22. 2.
Psal. 38. 5.

Howbeit, with the leaves of a tree the wounded were kept from dying; yet their wounds did greatly putrifie, and some did grievously stink. Of the Townsmen these were wounded, to wit,

Who of *Mansoul* were wounded.

My Lord *Reason*, he was wounded in the *head*.

Another that was wounded was the brave Lord *Mayor*, he was wounded in the *Eye*.

Another that was wounded was Mr. *Mind*, he received his wound about the *Stomach*.

The honest *Subordinate Preacher* also, he received a shot not far off the heart, but none of these were mortal.

Hopeful thoughts.

Many also of the inferiour sort, were not only wounded, but slain out-right.

Who in the Camp of *Diabolus* were wounded and slain.

Now in the Camp of *Diabolus* were wounded, and slain a considerable number. For instance,

Captain *Rage* he was wounded, and so was Captain *Cruel*.

Captain *Damnation* was made to retreat, and to intrench himself further off of *Mansoul*; the standard also of *Diabolus* was beaten down, and his standard-bearer Captain *Much-hurt*, had his brains beat out with a sling-stone, to the no little grief and shame of his Prince *Diabolus*.

Many also of the *Doubters* were slain out-right, though enough of them are left alive to make *Mansoul* shake and totter.

The Victory

Now the Victory that day being turned to *Mansoul*,

did put great valour into the Townsmen and Captains, and did cover *Diabolus*'s camp with a cloud, but withal it made them far more furious. So the next day *Mansoul* rested, and commanded that the Bells should be rung; the Trumpets also joyfully sounded, and the *Captains* shouted round the Town.

did turn that day to *Mansoul* &c.

My Lord *Wilbewill* taketh one *Anything*, and one *Loosefoot*, and committeth them to Ward.

My Lord *Wilbewill* also was not idle, but did notable service within against the Domesticks, or the *Diabolonians* that were in the Town, not only by keeping of them in awe, for he lighted on one at last whose name was Mr. *Any-thing*, a fellow of whom mention was made before; for 'twas he, if you remember, that brought the three fellows to *Diabolus*, whom the *Diabolonians* took out of Captain *Boanerges* Companies; and that perswaded them to list themselves under the Tyrant, to fight against the army of *Shaddai*; my Lord *Wilbewill* did also take a notable *Diabolonian* whose name was *Loosefoot*; this *Loosefoot* was a scout to the vagabonds in *Mansoul*, and that did use to carry tidings out of *Mansoul* to the camp, and out of the camp to those of the enemies in *Mansoul*; both these my Lord sent away safe to Mr. *Trueman* the Gaoler, with a commandment to keep them in irons; for he intended *then* to have them out to be crucified, *when* 'twould be for the best to the Corporation, and most for the discouragement of the camp of the enemies.

The Captains consult to fall upon the enemy.

My Lord *Mayor* also, though he could not stir about so much as formerly, because of the wound that he lately received, yet gave he out orders to all that were the Natives of *Mansoul*, to look to their watch, and stand upon their guard, and as occasion should offer to prove themselves men.

Mr. *Conscience* the Preacher, he also did his utmost to keep all his good documents alive upon the hearts of the people of *Mansoul*.

Well, a while after the *Captains* and stout ones of the Town of *Mansoul* agreed, and resolved upon a time to make a salley out upon the camp of *Diabolus*, and this must be done in the night, and there was the folly of *Mansoul* (for the night is always the best for the enemy, but the worst for *Mansoul* to fight in) but yet they would do it, their courage was so high; their last victory also still stuck in their memories.

They fight in the night. Who do lead the Van.

So the night appointed being come, the Princes brave *Captains* cast lots who should lead the Van in this new and desperate Expedition against *Diabolus*, and against his *Diabolonian* army, and the lot fell to *Captain Credence*, to *Captain Experience*, and to *Captain Goodhope* to lead the *Forlorn hope*. (The *Captain Experience* the Prince created such when himself did reside in the Town of *Mansoul*); so as I said, they made their Salley out upon the army that lay in the siege against them; and their hap was to fall in with the main body of their enemies. Now *Diabolus* and his men being expertly accustomed to night-work, took the alarm presently, and were as ready to give them battel, as if they had sent them word of their coming. Wherefore to it they went amain, and blows were hard on every side; the *Hell-drum* also was beat most furiously, while the Trumpets of the Prince most sweetly sounded. And thus the battel was joined, and *Captain Insatiable* looked to the enemies carriages, and waited when he should receive some prey.

How they fall on.

They fight bravely.

The Princes *Captains* fought it stoutly, beyond what indeed could be expected they should; they wounded many; they made the whole army of *Diabolus* to make a retreat. But I cannot tell how, but the brave *Captain Credence*, *Captain Goodhope*, and *Captain Experience*, as they were upon the pursuit, cutting down, and following hard after the enemy in the Rere, *Captain Credence* stumbled and fell, by which fall he caught so great a hurt that he could not rise till *Captain Experience* did help him up, at which their men were put in disorder; the *Captain* also was so full of pain that he could not forbear but aloud to cry out; at this the other two *Captains* fainted, supposing that *Captain Credence* had received his mortal wound: their men also were more disordered, and had no list to fight. Now *Diabolus* being very observing, though at this time as yet he was put to the worst, perceiving that an *hault* was made among the men that were the pursuers, what does he but taking it for granted that the *Captains* were either

Captain *Credence* hurt.

The rest of the Captains faint.

wounded or dead, he therefore makes at first a stand, then faces about, and so comes up upon the Princes army with as much of his fury as Hell could help him to, and his hap was to fall in just among the three *Captains*, *Captain Credence*, *Captain Goodhope*, and *Captain Experience*, and did cut, wound, and pierce them so dreadfully, that what through discouragement, what through disorder, and what through the wounds that now they had received, and also the loss of much blood, they scarce were able, though they had for their power the three best bands in *Mansoul*, to get safe into the hold again.

Diabolus takes courage.

The Princes forces beaten.

Now when the body of the Princes army saw how these three *Captains* were put to the worst, they thought it their wisdom to make as safe and good a retreat as they could, and so returned by the Salley-port again, and so there was an end of this present action. But *Diabolus* was so flusht with this nights-work, that he promised himself in few days, an easie and compleat conquest over the Town of *Mansoul*; wherefore on the day following he comes up to the sides thereof with great boldness, and demands entrance, and that forthwith they deliver themselves up to his Government. (The *Diabolonians* too that were within, they began to be somewhat brisk, as we shall shew afterward.)

Satan sometimes makes Saints eat their words.

Diabolus flusht.

He demands the Town.

But the valiant Lord *Mayor* replied, *That what he got he must get by force, for as long as* Emanuel *their Prince was alive (though he at present was not so with them as they wisht) they should never consent to yield* Mansoul *up to another.*

The Lord *Mayors* answer.

And with that the Lord *Wilbewill* stood up and said, Diabolus, *thou master of the den, and enemy to all that is good; we poor inhabitants of the Town of* Mansoul, *are too well acquainted with thy rule and government, and with the end of those things that for certain will follow submitting to thee, to do it. Wherefore though while we were without knowledg we suffered thee to take us (as the bird that saw not the snare, fell into the hands of the fowler) yet since we have been turned from darkness to light; we have also been turned from the power of Satan to God. And though through thy subtilty, and also the subtilty of the* Diabolonians *within, we have sustained much*

Brave *Wilbewills* Speech.

loss, and also plunged our selves into much perplexity, yet give up our selves, lay down our arms, and yield to so horrid a Tyrant as thou, we shall not; die upon the place we chuse rather to do. Besides, we have hopes that in time deliverance will come from Court unto us, and therefore we yet will maintain a war against thee.

The Captains incouraged.

This brave Speech of the Lord *Wilbewill*, with that also of the Lord *Mayor*, did somewhat abate the boldness of *Diabolus*, though it kindled the fury of his rage. It also succoured the Townsmen and Captains; yea, it was as a plaister to the brave *Captain Credence* his wound; for you must know that a brave speech *now*, when the Captains of the Town with their men of war came home routed, and when the enemy took courage and boldness at the success that he had obtained to draw up to the walls, and demand entrance, as he did, was in season, and also advantageous.

Wilbewills Galantry.

The Lord *Wilbewill* also did play the man within, for while the *Captains* and Soldiers were in the field, he was in arms in the Town, and where ever by him there was a *Diabolonian* found, they were forced to feel the weight of his heavy hand, and also the edg of his penetrating sword; many therefore of the *Diabolonians* he wounded, as the Lord *Cavel*, the Lord *Brisk*, the Lord *Pragmatick*, and the Lord *Murmur*; several also of the meaner sort he did sorely maim; though there cannot at this time an account be given you of any that he slew out-right. The cause, or rather the advantage that my Lord *Wilbewill* had at this time to do thus, was for that the *Captains* were gone out to fight the enemy in the field. For now, thought the *Diabolonians* within, is our time to stir and make an uproar in the Town; what do they therefore but quickly get themselves into a *body*, and fall forthwith to *hurricaning* in *Mansoul*, as if now nothing but whirlwind and tempest should be there; wherefore, as I said, he takes this opportunity to fall in among them with his men, cutting and slashing with courage that was undaunted; at which the *Diabolonians* with all hast dispersed themselves to their holds, and my Lord to his place as before.

Nothing like faith to crush *Diabolus*.

This brave act of my Lord did somewhat *revenge* the wrong done by *Diabolus* to the *Captains*, and also did let them know that *Mansoul* was not to be parted with, for the loss of a victory or two; wherefore the wing of the Tyrant was clipt again, as to boasting, I mean in comparison of what he would have done if the *Diabolonians* had put the Town to the same plight, to which he had put the *Captains*.

Well, *Diabolus* yet resolves to have the other bout with *Mansoul*; for thought he, since I beat them once, I may beat them twice: wherefore he commanded his men to be ready at such an hour of the night to make a fresh assault upon the Town, and he gave it out in special that they should bend all their force against *Feelgate*, and attempt to break into the Town through that: The word that then he did give to his Officers and Souldiers was *Hellfire*. And, said he, if we break in upon them, as I wish we do, either with some, or with all our force, let them that break in look to it, that they forget not the word. And let nothing be heard in the Town of *Mansoul* but *Hell-fire*, *Hell-fire*, *Hell-fire*. The *Drummer* was also to beat without ceasing, and the Standard bearers were to display their Colours; the Souldiers too were to put on what courage they could, and to see that they played manfully their parts against the Town.

He trys what he can do upon the sense and feeling of the Christian.

So the night was come, and all things by the Tyrant made ready for the work, he suddenly makes his assault upon *Feelgate*, and after he had a while strugled there, he throws the Gates wide open. For the truth is, those Gates were but weak, and so most easily made to yield. When *Diabolus* had thus *far* made his attempt, he placed his *Captains*, to wit, *Torment* and *No ease* there; so he attempted to press forward, but the Princes *Captains* came down upon him and made his entrance more difficult than he desired. And to speak truth, they made what resistance they could; but the three of their best and most valiant *Captains* being wounded, and by their wounds made much uncapable of doing the Town that service they would (and all the rest having more than their hands full of the *Doubters*, and their *Captains* that did follow *Diabolus*) they were over-powered with force, nor could they keep them out of the Town. Wherefore the Princes men and their

Feelgate but weak.

When these three Captains are disabled, what can the rest do for the Town of *Mansoul*?

Captains betook themselves to the Castle, as to the strong hold of the Town: and this they did partly for their own security, partly for the security of the Town, and partly, or rather chiefly to preserve to *Emanuel* the Prerogative-royal of *Mansoul*, for so was the Castle of *Mansoul*.

The *Captains* therefore being fled into the Castle, the enemy without much resistance, possess themselves of the rest of the Town, and spreading themselves as they went into every corner, they cried out as they marched according to the command of the Tyrant, *Hell-fire*, *Hell-fire*, *Hell-fire*, so that nothing for a while throughout the Town of *Mansoul* could be heard but the direful noise of *Hell fire*; together with the roaring of *Diabolus*'s Drum.

The sad fruits of Apostasy.

And now did the clouds hang black over *Mansoul*, nor to reason did any thing but ruin seem to attend it. *Diabolus* also quartered his Souldiers in the houses of the inhabitants of the Town of *Mansoul*. Yea, the *Subordinate Preachers* house was as full of these outlandish *Doubters* as ever it could hold; and so was my Lord *Mayors*, and my Lord *Wilbewills* also. Yea, where was there a corner, a Cottage, a Barn, or a Hogstie that now were not full of these vermin? yea, they turned the men of the Town out of their houses, and would lye in their beds, and sit at their tables themselves. Ah poor *Mansoul*! now thou feelest the fruits of sin, and what venom was in the flattering words of Mr. *Carnal Security*!

Guilt. Good and tender thoughts.

They made great havock of what ever they laid their hands on; yea, they fired the Town in several places; many young children also were by them dashed in pieces; yea, those that were yet unborn they destroyed in their mothers wombs: for you must needs think that it could not now be otherwise; for what conscience, what pity, what bowels or compassion can any expect at the hands of outlandish *Doubters*?

Holy conceptions of good.

Many in *Mansoul* that were *women*, both young and old, they forced, ravished, and beastlike abused, so that they swooned, miscarried, and many of them died, and so lay at the top of every street, and in all by-places of the Town.

And now did *Mansoul* seem to be nothing but a den of Dragons, an emblem of Hell, and a place of total darkness.

Now did *Mansoul* lye (almost) like the barren wilderness; nothing but nettles, briers, thorns, weeds, and stinking things seemed now to cover the face of *Mansoul*. I told you before, how that these *Diabolonian* Doubters turned the men of *Mansoul* out of their Beds, and now I will add, they wounded them, they mauled them, yea, and almost brained many of them. Many, did I say, yea most, if not all of them. Mr. *Conscience* they so wounded, yea, and his wounds so festered, that he could have no ease day nor night, but lay as if continually upon a rack, (but that *Shaddai* rules all, certainly they had slain him out-right). Mr. Lord *Mayor* they so abused that they almost put out his eyes; and had not my Lord *Wilbewill* got into the Castle, they intended to have chopt him all to pieces, for they did look upon him (as his *heart* now stood) to be one of the very worst that was in *Mansoul* against *Diabolus* and his crew. And indeed he hath shewed himself a man, and more of his Exploits you will hear of afterwards.

Rest.

Sad work among the Townsmen.

Satan has a particular spite against a sanctified *will*.

Now a man might have walked for days together in *Mansoul*, and scarce have seen one in the Town that lookt like a Religious man. Oh the fearful state of *Mansoul* now! now every corner swarmed with outlandish *Doubters*; Red-coats, and Black-coats, walked the Town by clusters, and filled up all the houses with hideous noises, vain Songs, lying stories and blasphemous language against *Shaddai* and his Son. Now also those *Diabolonians* that lurked in the walls and dens, and holes that were in the Town of *Mansoul*, came forth and shewed themselves; yea, walked with open face in company with the *Doubters* that were in *Mansoul*. Yea, they had more boldness now to walk the streets, to haunt the houses, and to shew themselves abroad, than had any of the honest inhabitants of the now woful Town of *Mansoul*.

Thought.

The soul full of idle thoughts and blasphemies.

But *Diabolus* and his outlandish men were not at peace in *Mansoul*, for they were not there entertained as were the Captains and forces of *Emanuel*; the Townsmen did brow-beat them what they could: nor did they partake or make stroy of any of the Necessaries of *Mansoul*, but that which they seised on against the Townsmens *will*; what they could they hid from them, and what they could not, they had with an ill will. They, poor hearts, had rather have had their room than Rom. 7. their company, but they were at present their *Captives*, and their *Captives* for the present they were forced to be. But, I say, they discountenanced them as much as they were able, and shewed them all the dislike that they could.

The Captains also from the *Castle* did hold them in continual play with their slings, to the chafing and fretting of the minds of the enemies. True, *Diabolus* made a great many attempts to have broken open the Gates of the *Castle*, but Mr. *Godlyfear* was made the Keeper of that; and he was a man of that courage, conduct and valour, that 'twas in vain as long as life lasted within him, to think to do that work though mostly desired, wherefore all the attempts that *Diabolus* made against him were fruitless; (I have wished sometimes that that man had had the whole rule of the Town of *Mansoul*.)

Mr. *Godlyfear* is made keeper of the Castle gates

The Town of *Mansoul* the seat of War.

Well, this was the condition of the Town of *Mansoul* for about two years and an half; the *body* of the Town was the seat of war; the people of the Town were driven into holes, and the glory of *Mansoul* was laid in the dust; what rest *then* could be to the inhabitants, what peace could *Mansoul* have, and what Sun could shine upon it? Had the enemy lain so long without in the plain against the Town, it had been enough to have famished them; but now when they shall be within, when the Town shall be their Tent, their Trench, and Fort against the Castle that was in the Town, when the Town shall be against the Town, and shall serve to be a defence to the enemies of her strength and life: I say when they shall make use of the Forts, and Town holds, to secure Heart. themselves in even till they shall take, spoil, and demolish the Castle, this was terrible; and yet this was now the state of the *Town* of *Mansoul*.

After the Town of *Mansoul* had been in this sad and lamentable condition for so long a time as I have told you, and no Petitions that they presented their Prince with (all this while) could prevail; the inhabitants of the Town, to wit, the Elders and chief of *Mansoul* gathered together, and after some time spent in condoling their miserable state, and this miserable judgment coming upon them, they agreed together to draw up yet another Petition, and to send it away to *Emanuel* for relief. But Mr. *Godlyfear* stood up, and answered, that he knew that his Lord the Prince never did, nor ever would receive a Petition for these matters from the hand of any whoever, unless the Lord *Secretaries* hand was to it, (and this, quoth he, is the reason that you prevailed not all this while.) Then they said, they would draw up one, and get the Lord *Secretaries* hand unto it. But Mr. *Godlyfear* answered again, that he knew also that the Lord *Secretary* would not set his hand to any Petition that himself had not an hand in composing and drawing up; and besides, said he, the Prince doth know my Lord *Secretaries* hand from all the hands in the world; wherefore he cannot be deceived by any pretence whatever; wherefore my advice is, that you go to my Lord, and implore him to lend you his aid (now he did yet abide in the Castle where all the Captains and men at arms were).

Mr. *Godlyfears* advice about drawing up of a Petition to the Prince.

So they heartily thanked Mr. *Godlyfear*, took his counsel, and did as he had bidden them; so they went and came to my Lord, and made known the cause of their coming to him, to wit, that since *Mansoul* was in so deplorable a condition, his Highness would be pleased to undertake to draw up a Petition for them to *Emanuel*, the son of the mighty *Shaddai*, and to their King and his Father by him.

Then said the *Secretary* to them, *What Petition is it that you would have me draw up for you?* But they said, Our Lord knows best the state and condition of the Town of *Mansoul*; and how we are backsliden and degenerated from the Prince; thou also knowest who is come up to war against us, and how *Mansoul* is now the seat of war. My Lord knows moreover what barbarous usages our men, women and children have suffered at ther hands, and how our home-bred *Diabolonians* do walk now with more boldness than dare the Townsmen in the streets of *Mansoul*. Let our Lord therefore according to the wisdom of God that is in him, draw up a Petition for his poor servants to our Prince *Emanuel*. *Well*, said the Lord

The *Secretary* imployed to draw up a Petition for *Mansoul*.

Secretary, I will draw up a Petition for you, and will also set my hand thereto. Then said they, But when shall we call for it at the hands of our Lord? But he answered, *Your selves must be present at the doing of it. Yea, you must put your desires to it. True, the hand and pen shall be mine, but the ink and paper must be yours, else how can you say it is your Petition? nor have I need to Petition for my self, because I have not offended.*

He also added as followeth, *No Petition goes from me in my name to the Prince, and so to his Father by him, but when the people that are chiefly concerned therein do join in* heart and soul *in the matter, for that must be inserted therein.*

So they did heartily agree with the sentence of the Lord, and a Petition was forthwith drawn up for them. But now who should carry it, that was next. But the *Secretary* advised that Captain *Credence* should carry it, for he was a well-spoken man. They therefore called for him, and propounded to him the business. Well, said the Captain, I gladly accept of the motion; and though I am lame, I will do this business for you, with as much speed, and as well as I can.

The Petition drawn up and sent to *Emanuel* by the hand of Captain *Credence*.

The Contents of the Petition were to this purpose:

O our Lord, and Sovereign Prince Emanuel, *the potent, the long-suffering Prince: Grace is poured into thy lips, and to thee belongs mercy and forgiveness, though we have rebelled against thee. We who are no more worthy to be called thy* Mansoul, *nor yet fit to partake of common benefits, do beseech thee, and thy Father by thee to do away our transgressions. We confess that thou mightest cast us away for them, but do it not for thy names sake; let the Lord rather take an opportunity at our miserable condition, to let out his bowels and compassions to us; we are compassed on every side, Lord, our own back-slidings reprove us; our* Diabolonians *within our Town fright us, and the army of the Angel of the bottomless pit distresses us. Thy grace can be our salvation, and whither to go but to thee we know not.*

The Contents of their Petition.

Furthermore, O Gracious Prince, we have weakened our Captains, and they are discouraged, sick, and of late some of them grievously worsted and beaten out of the field by the power and force of the Tyrant. Yea, even those of our Captains in whose valour we did formerly use to put most of our confidence, they are as wounded men.

Besides, Lord, our enemies are lively, and they are strong, they vaunt and boast themselves, and do threaten to part us among themselves for a booty. They are fallen also upon us, Lord, with many thousand Doubters, *such as with whom we cannot tell what to do; they are all grim-looked, and unmerciful ones, and they bid defiance to us and thee.*

Our wisdom is gone, our power is gone, because thou art departed from us, nor have we what we may call ours but sin, shame and confusion of face for sin. Take pity upon us, O Lord, take pity upon us thy miserable Town of Mansoul, *and save us out of the hands of our enemies.* Amen.

This Petition as was touched afore, was handed by the Lord *Secretary*, and carried to the Court by the brave and most stout Captain *Credence*. Now he carried it out at *Mouthgate*, for that, as I said, was the salli-port of the Town; and he went and came to *Emanuel* with it. Now how it came out, I do not know, but for certain it did, and that so far as to reach the ears of *Diabolus*. Thus I conclude, because that the Tyrant had it presently by the end, and charged the Town of *Mansoul* with it, saying, *Thou rebellious and stubborn-hearted* Mansoul, *I will make thee to leave off Petitioning; art thou yet for Petitioning? I will make thee to leave*. Yea, he also knew who the messenger was that carried the Petition to the Prince, and it made him both to fear and rage.

Satan cannot abide Prayer.

Wherefore he commanded that his *Drum* should be beat again, a thing that *Mansoul* could not abide to hear; but when *Diabolus* will have his *Drum* beat, *Mansoul* must abide the noise. Well, the Drum was beat, and the *Diabolonians* were gathered together.

Then said *Diabolus*, *O ye stout* Diabolonians, *be it known unto you, that there is treachery hatcht against us in the rebellious Town of* Mansoul; *for albeit the Town is in our possession, as you see, yet these miserable* Mansoulians *have attempted to dare, and have been so hardy as yet to send to the Court to* Emanuel *for help. This I give you to understand, that ye may yet know how to carry it to the wretched Town of* Mansoul. *Wherefore, O my trusty* Diabolonians, *I command that yet more and more ye distress this Town of* Mansoul, *and vex it with your* wiles, *ravish their women, deflower their*

Poor *Mansoul*.

virgins, slay their children, brain their Ancients, fire their Town, and what other mischief you can; and let this be the reward of the Mansoulians *from me, for their desperate rebellions against me.*

This you see was the charge, but something stept in betwixt that and execution for as yet there was but little more done than to rage.

Moreover, when *Diabolus* had done thus, he went the next way up to the Castle-gates, and demanded that upon pain of death, the Gates should be opened to him, and that entrance should be given him and his men that followed after. To whom Mr. *Godlyfear* replied, (for he it was that had the charge of that Gate), *That the Gate should not be opened unto him, nor to the men that followed after him.* He said moreover, *That* Mansoul *when she had suffered a while should be made perfect, strengthened, setled.*

Satan cannot abide Faith.

Then said *Diabolus, Deliver me then the men that have Petitioned against me, especially Captain* Credence *that carried it to your Prince, deliver that Varlet into my hands, and I will depart from the Town.*

Mr. *Fooling*.

Then up starts a *Diabolonian*, whose name was Mr. *Fooling*, and said, *My Lord offereth you fair, 'tis better for you that one man perish, than that your whole* Mansoul *should be undone.*

But Mr. *Godlyfear* made him this replication, *How long will* Mansoul *be kept out of the dungeon, when she hath given up her faith to* Diabolus? *As good lose the Town as lose Captain* Credence; *for if one be gone, the other must follow.* But to that Mr. *Fooling* said nothing.

Then did my Lord *Mayor* reply, and said, *O thou devouring Tyrant, be it known unto thee, we shall hearken to none of thy words, we are resolved to resist thee as long as a Captain, a man, a sling, and a stone to throw at thee, shall be found in the Town of Mansoul.* But

Diabolus rages.

Diabolus answered, *Do you hope, do you wait, do you look for help and deliverance? you have sent to* Emanuel, *but your wickedness sticks too close in your skirts, to let innocent prayers come out of your lips. Think you, that you shall be prevailers and prosper in this design? you will fail in your wish, you will fail in your attempts; for 'tis not only I, but your* Emanuel *is against you. Yea, it is he that hath sent me against you to subdue you; for what then do you hope, or by what means will you escape?*

Then said the Lord *Mayor*, *We have sinned indeed, but that shall be no help to thee, for our* Emanuel *hath said it, and that in great faithfulness. And him that cometh to me I will in no wise cast out. He hath also told us (O our enemy) that all manner of sin and blasphemy shall be forgiven to the sons of men. Therefore we dare not despair, but will look for, wait for, and hope for deliverance still.*

The Lord *Mayors* Speech just at the time of the return of Captain *Credence*.

Now by this time Captain *Credence* was returned and come from the Court from *Emanuel* to the Castle of *Mansoul*, and he returned to them with a Pacquet. So my Lord *Mayor* hearing that Captain *Credence* was come, withdrew himself from the noise of the roaring of the Tyrant, and left him to yell at the wall of the Town, or against the Gates of the Castle. So he came up to the Captains Lodgings, and saluting him, he asked him of his welfare, and what was the best news at Court? but when he asked Captain *Credence* that, the water stood in his eyes. Then said the *Captain*, Cheer up, my Lord, for all will be well in time. And with that he first produced his Pacquet, and laid it by, but that the Lord *Mayor*, and the rest of the Captains took for a sign of good tidings. (Now a season of Grace being come, he sent for all the Captains and Elders of the Town that were here and there in their lodgings in the Castle, and upon their guard, to let them know that Captain *Credence* was returned from the Court, and that he had something in general, and something in special to communicate to them.) So they all came up to him, and saluted him, and asked him concerning his journey, and what was the best news at the Court? And he answered them as he had done the Lord *Mayor* before, that all would be well at last. Now when the Captain had thus saluted them, he opened his *Pacquet*, and thence did draw out his several Notes for those that he had sent for. And the first Note was for my Lord *Mayor*, wherein was signified:

A sign of Goodness.

The Pacquet opened.

That the Prince Emanuel *had taken it well that my Lord Mayor had been so true and trusty in his office, and the great concerns that lay upon him for the Town and people of* Mansoul. *Also he bid him to know that he took it well that he had been so bold for his Prince* Emanuel, *and had engaged so faithfully in his cause against*

A Note for my Lord *Mayor*.

Diabolus. *He also signified at the close of his Letter, that he should shortly receive his reward.*

A Note for the Lord *Wilbewill.*

The second note that came out, was for the noble Lord *Wilbewill*, wherein there was signified, *That his Prince* Emanuel *did well understand how valiant and courageous he had been for the honour of his Lord, now in his absence, and when his name was under contempt by* Diabolus. *There was signified also that his Prince had taken it well that he had been so faithful to the Town of* Mansoul *in his keeping of so strict a hand and eye over, and so strict a rein upon the necks of the* Diabolonians *that did still lye lurking in their several holes in the famous Town of* Mansoul.

He signified moreover, how that he understood that my Lord had with his own hand done great execution upon some of the chief of the rebells there, to the great discouragement of the adverse party, and to the good example of the whole Town of Mansoul, *and that shortly his Lordship should have his reward.*

A Note for the *Subordinate Preacher.*

The third Note came out for the *Subordinate Preacher*, wherein was signified, *That his Prince took it well from him that he had so honestly, and so faithfully performed his office, and executed the trust committed to him by his Lord, while he exhorted, rebuked, and fore-warned* Mansoul *according to the Laws of the Town. He signified moreover, that he took well at his hand that he called to fasting, to sackcloth and ashes, when* Mansoul *was under her revolt. Also that he called for the aid of the Captain* Boanerges *to help in so weighty a work, and that shortly he also should receive his reward.*

A Note for Mr. *Godlyfear.*

The fourth Note came out for Mr. *Godlyfear*, wherein his Lord thus signified, *That his Lordship observed that he was the first of all the men in* Mansoul, *that detected* Mr. Carnal Security *as the only one that through his subtilty and cunning had obtained for* Diabolus *a defection and decay of goodness in the blessed Town of* Mansoul. *Moreover, his Lord gave him to understand that he still remembred his tears and mourning for the state of* Mansoul. *It was also observed by the same Note that his Lord took notice of his detecting of this* Mr. Carnal Security, *at his own table among his guests, in his own house, and that in the midst of his jolliness, even while he was seeking to perfect his villanies against the Town of* Mansoul. Emanuel *also took notice that this reverend person,* Mr.

Godlyfear, *stood stoutly to it at the Gates of the Castle against all the threats and attempts of the Tyrant, and that he had put the Townsmen in a way to make their Petition to their Prince, so as that he might accept thereof, and as that they might obtain an answer of peace; and that therefore shortly he should receive his reward.*

After all this, there was yet produced a Note which was written to the whole Town of *Mansoul*, whereby they *perceived that their Lord took notice of their so often repeating of Petitions to him, and that they should see more of the fruits of such their doings in time to come. Their Prince did also therein tell them, That he took it well that their heart and mind, now at last, abode fixed upon him and his ways, though* Diabolus *had made such inroads upon them, and that neither flatteries on the one hand, nor hardships on the other, could make them yield to serve his cruel designs.* There was also inserted at the bottom of this Note, *That his Lordship had left the Town of* Mansoul *in the hands of the Lord* Secretary, *and under the conduct of Captain* Credence, *saying, Beware that you yet yield your selves unto their governance, and in due time you shall receive your reward.*

A Note for the Town of *Mansoul.*

So after the brave Captain *Credence* had delivered his Notes to those to whom they belonged, he retired himself to my Lord *Secretaries* Lodgings, and there spends time in conversing with him; for they two were very great one with another, and did indeed know more how things would go with *Mansoul* than did all the Townsmen besides. The Lord *Secretary* also loved the Captain *Credence* dearly; yea, many a good bit was sent him from my Lords table; also he might have a shew of countenance when the rest of *Mansoul* lay under the clouds; so after some time for converse was spent, the *Captain* betook himself to his Chambers to rest. But it was not long after but my Lord did send for the *Captain* again; so the *Captain* came to him, and they greeted one another with usual salutations. Then said the *Captain* to the Lord *Secretary*, What hath my Lord to say to his servant? So the Lord *Secretary* took him, and had him a to side, and after a sign or two of more favour, he said, *I have made thee the Lords Lieutenant over all the forces in* Mansoul*; so that from this day forward, all men in* Mansoul *shall*

Captain *Credence* retires to the Lord *Secretaries* Lodgings.

Captain *Credence* made the Lords *Lieutenant* over all the forces in *Mansoul.*

be at thy word, and thou shalt be he that shall lead in, and that shall lead out Mansoul. *Thou shalt therefore manage according to thy place, the war for thy Prince, and for the Town of* Mansoul, *against the force and power of* Diabolus, *and at thy command shall the rest of the Captains be.*

Now the Townsmen began to perceive what interest the Captain had, both with the Court, and also with the Lord *Secretary* in *Mansoul*; for no man before could speed when sent, nor bring such good news from *Emanuel* as he. Wherefore what do they, after some lamentation that they made no more use of him in their distresses, but send by their *Subordinate Preacher* to the Lord *Secretary*, to desire him that all that ever they were and had, might be put under the Government, care, custody, and conduct of Captain *Credence*.

The Town of *Mansoul* craves that she may be under the conduct of Captain *Credence.*

So their Preacher went and did his Errand, and received this answer from the mouth of his Lord, that Captain *Credence* should be the great doer in all the Kings Army, against the Kings enemies, and also for the welfare of *Mansoul*. So he bowed to the ground, and thanked his Lordship, and returned and told his news to the Townsfolk. But all this was done with all imaginable secresie, because the foes had yet great strength in the Town. But,

Diabolus rages.

To return to our story again: When *Diabolus* saw himself thus boldly confronted by the Lord *Mayor*, and perceived the stoutness of Mr. *Godlyfear*, he fell into a rage, and forthwith called a Council of War that he might be revenged on *Mansoul*. So all the Princes of the Pit came together, and old *Incredulity* in the head of them, with all the Captains of his Army. So they consult what to do, now the effect and conclusion of the Council that day, was how they might take the Castle, because they could not conclude themselves masters of the Town so long as *that* was in the possession of their enemies. So one advised this way, and another advised that; but when they could not agree in their verdict, *Apollyon* that President of the Council stood up, and thus he began: *My Brotherhood*, quoth he, *I have two things to propound unto you; and my first is this, let us withdraw our selves from the Town into the Plain again, for our presence here will do us no good, because the Castle is yet in our enemies hands; nor is it possible that we should take that so long as so many brave Captains are in it, and that this bold fellow* Godlyfear *is made the Keeper of the Gates of it.*

Now when we have withdrawn our selves into the Plain, they of their own accord will be glad of some little ease, and it may be of their own accord they again may begin to be remiss, and even their so being will give them a bigger blow than we can possibly give them ourselves. But if that should fail, our going forth of the Town may draw the Captains out after us, and you know what it cost them when we fought them in the field before. Besides, can we but draw them out into the field, we may lay an ambush behind the Town, which shall, when they are come forth abroad, rush in and take possession of the Castle. But *Beelzebub* stood up and replied, saying, 'Tis impossible to draw them all off from the Castle; some you may be sure will lye there to keep that; wherefore it will be but in vain *thus* to attempt, unless we were sure that they will all come out. He therefore concluded that what was done, must be done by some other means. And the most likely means that the greatest of their heads could invent was that which *Apollyon* had advised to before, to wit, to get the Towns-men again to *sin*. For, said he, it is not our being in the Town, nor in the field, nor our fighting nor our killing of their men, that can make us the Masters of *Mansoul*; for so long as one in the Town is able to lift up his finger against us, *Emanuel* will take their parts, and if he shall take their parts, we know what time a day it will be with us. Wherefore for my part, quoth he, there is in my judgment no way to bring them into bondage to us, like inventing a way to make them sin. Had we, said he, left all our *Doubters* at home, we had done as well as we have done now, unless we could have made them the Masters and Governours of the Castle; for *Doubters* at a distance are but like Objections refell'd with arguments. Indeed can we but get them into the hold, and make them possessors of that, the day will be our own. Let us therefore withdraw our selves into the Plain (not expecting that the Captains in *Mansoul*

Look to it *Mansoul.*

Look to it *Mansoul.*

2 Pet. 2. 18, 19, 20, 21.

Look to it *Mansoul.*

should follow us) but yet I say let us do this, and before we so do, let us advise again with our trusty *Diabolonians* that are yet in their holds of *Mansoul*, and set them to work to betray the Town to us; for they indeed must do it, or it will be left undone for ever. By these sayings of *Beelzebub* (for I think 'twas he that gave this counsel) the whole Conclave was forced to be of his opinion, to wit, that the way to get the Castle was to get the Town to sin. Then they fell to inventing by what means they might do this thing.

Look to it *Mansoul.*

Then *Lucifer* stood up and said, *The counsel of* Beelzebub *is pertinent; now the way to bring this to pass, in mine opinion is this: Let us withdraw our force from the Town of* Mansoul, *let us do this, and let us terrifie them no more, either with Summons, or threats, or with the noise of our* Drum, *or any other awakening means. Only let us lye in the field at a distance, and be as if we regarded them not (for frights I see do but awaken them, and make them more stand to their arms.) I have also another stratagem in my head, you know* Mansoul *is a Market-Town, and a Town that delights in commerce, what therefore if some of our* Diabolonians *shall feign themselves far-country men, and shall go out and bring to the Market of* Mansoul *some of our wares to sell; and what matter at what rates they sell their wares, though it be but for half the worth. Now let those that thus shall trade in their market, be those that are witty and true to us, and I will lay my* Crown *to pawn, it will do. There are two that are come to my thoughts already, that I think will be arch at this work, and they are* Mr. Penniwise-Pound-foolish, *and* Mr. Get ith'-hundred-and lose-ith'-shire; *nor is this man with the long name at all inferior to the other. What also if you join with them* Mr. Sweet world, *and* Mr. Present-good, *they are men that are civil and cunning, but our true friends and helpers. Let these with as many more engage in this business for us, and let* Mansoul *be taken up in much business, and let them grow full and rich, and this is the way to get ground of them; remember ye not that thus we prevailed upon* Laodicea, *and how many at present do we hold in this snare? Now when they begin to grow full they will forget their misery, and if we shall not affright them, they may happen to fall asleep, and so be got to neglect their Townwatch, their Castle-watch, as well as their watch at the Gates.*

Look to it.
Rev. 3. 17.
Heart.

Yea, may we not by this means, so cumber Mansoul *with abundance, that they shall be forced to make of their Castle a* Warehouse *instead of a Garrison fortified against us, and a receptacle for men of war. Thus if we get our goods and commodities thither, I reckon that the Castle is more than half ours. Besides, could we so order it that that shall be filled with such kind of wares, then if we made a sudden assault upon them, it would be hard for the Captains to take shelter there. Do you not know that of the Parable,* The deceitfulness of riches choak the word; *and again,* When the heart is over charged with surfeiting and drunkenness, and the cares of this life, *all mischief comes upon them at unawares.*

Luk. 8. 14.
Chap. 21. 34, 35, 36.

Furthermore, my Lords, quoth he, *you very well know that it is not easie for a people to be filled with our things, and not to have some of our* Diabolonians *as retainers to their houses and services. Where is a* Mansoulian *that is full of this world that has not for his servants, and waiting-men* Mr. Profuse, *or* Mr. Prodigality, *or some other of our* Diabolonian *gang, as* Mr. Voluptuous, Mr. Pragmatical, Mr. Ostentation, *or the like? Now these can take the Castle of* Mansoul, *or blow it up, or make it unfit for a Garrison for* Emanuel, *and any of these will do. Yea, these for ought I know may do it for us sooner than an army of twenty thousand men. Wherefore to end as I began, my advice is that we quietly withdraw our selves, not offering any further force, or forcible attempts upon the Castle, at least at this time, and let us set on foot our new project, and lets see if that will not make them destroy themselves.*

Look to it *Mansoul.*

This advice was highly applauded by them all, and was accounted the very masterpiece of Hell, to wit, to choak *Mansoul* with a fulness of this world, and to surfeit her heart with the good things thereof. But see how things meet together, just as this *Diabolonian* counsel was broken up, Captain *Credence* received a Letter from *Emanuel*, the Contents of which was this, *That upon the third day he would meet him in the field in the Plains about Mansoul.* Meet *me* in the field, quoth the Captain? what meaneth my Lord by this? I know not what he meaneth by meeting of me in the field. So he took the Note in his hand, and did carry it to my Lord *Secretary* to ask his thoughts thereupon, (for my Lord was a Seer in all

Captain *Credence* receives that from his Prince which he understandeth not.

matters concerning the King, and also for the good and comfort of the Town of *Mansoul*.) So he shewed my Lord the Note, and desired his opinion thereof: For my part, quoth Captain *Credence*, I know not the meaning thereof. So my Lord did take and read it, and after a little pause he said, *The* Diabolonians *have had against* Mansoul *a great consultation to day; they have I say, this day been contriving the utter ruin of the Town; and the result of their counsel is, to set* Mansoul *into such a way, which if taken, will surely make her destroy her self. And to this end they are making ready for their own departure out of the Town, intending to betake themselves to the field again, and there to lye till they shall see whether this their project will take or no. But be thou ready with the men of thy Lord (for on the third day they will be in the Plain) there to fall upon the* Diabolonians*; for the Prince will by that time be in the field; yea, by that it is break of day, Sun-rising, or before, and that with a mighty force against them. So he shall be before them, and thou shalt be behind them, and betwixt you both their army shall be destroyed.*

The riddle expounded to Captain *Credence*.

The Captains are gladed to hear.

When Captain *Credence* heard this, away goes he to the rest of the Captains, and tells them what a Note he had a while since, received from the hand of *Emanuel*. And, said he, that which was dark therein has my Lord the Lord *Secretary* expounded unto me. He told them moreover, what by himself and by them must be done to answer the mind of their Lord. Then were the Captains glad, and Captain *Credence* commanded that all the Kings Trumpeters should ascend to the battlements of the Castle, and there in the audience of *Diabolus*, and of the whole Town of *Mansoul*, make the best musick that heart could invent. The Trumpeters then did as they were commanded. They got themselves up to the top of the Castle, and thus they began to sound; then did *Diabolus* start, and said, What can be the meaning of this, they neither sound *Boot and saddle*, nor *horse and away*, nor a *Charge*. What do these mad men mean, that yet they should be so merry and glad? Then answered him one of themselves and said, this is for joy that their Prince *Emanuel* is coming to relieve the Town of *Mansoul*; that to this end he is at the head of an Army, and that this relief is near.

Curious Musick made by the Trumpeters.

The men of *Mansoul* also were greatly concerned at this melodious charm of the Trumpets; they said, yea, they answered one another saying, This can be no harm to us; surely this can be no harm to us. Then said the *Diabolonians*, what had we best to do? and it was answered, It was best to quit the Town; and that said one, Ye may do in pursuance of your last counsel, and by so doing also be better able to give the enemy battel, should an army from without come upon us. So on the second day they withdrew themselves from *Mansoul*, and abode in the Plains without, but they incamped themselves before *Eyegate*, in what terrene and terrible manner they could. The reason why they would not abide in the Town (besides the reasons that were debated in their late Conclave,) was for that they were not possessed of the strong hold, and because, said they, we shall have more convenience to fight, and also to fly if need be when we are incamped in the open Plains. Besides, the Town would have been a pit for them rather than a place of defence, had the Prince come up and enclosed them fast therein. Therefore they betook themselves to the field, that they might also be out of the reach of the slings, by which they were much annoyed all the while that they were in the Town.

Diabolus withdraws from the Town, and why.

Well, the time that the Captains were to fall upon the *Diabolonians* being come, they eagerly prepared themselves for action, for Captain *Credence* had told the Captains over night, that they should *meet their Prince in the field to morrow*. This therefore made them yet far more desirous to be engaging the enemy: *for you shall see the Prince in the Field to morrow*, was like oyl to a flaming fire; for of a long time they had been at a distance: they therefore were for this the more earnest and desirous of the work. So, as I said, the hour being come, Captain *Credence* with the rest of the men of war, drew out their forces before it were day by the Salliport of the Town. And being *all* ready, Captain *Credence* went up to the head of the Army, and gave to the rest of the *Captains* the *word*, and so they to their Under-officers and Souldiers, the word was, *The Sword of the Prince* Emanuel, *and the Shield of Captain* Credence,

The time come for the Captains to fight them.

They draw out into the field.

The Word.

which is in the *Mansoulian* tongue, *The word of God and faith*. Then the Captains fell on and began roundly to front, and flank, and rere *Diabolus*'s Camp.

Captain *Experience* will fight for his Prince upon his Crutches

Now they left Captain *Experience* in the Town because he was yet ill of his wounds which the *Diabolonians* had given him in the last fight. But when he perceived that the Captains were at it, what does he but calling for his *Crutches* with hast, gets up, and away he goes to the battel, saying, Shall I lye here when my brethren are in the fight, and when *Emanuel* the Prince will shew himself in the field to his servants? But when the enemy saw the man come with his *Crutches* they were daunted yet the more, for thought they, what spirit has possessed these *Mansoulians* that they fight me upon their Crutches. Well, the Captains as I said fell on, and did bravely handle their weapons, still crying out, and shouting as they laid on blows, *The Sword of the Prince* Emanuel, *and the Shield of Captain* Credence.

Now when *Diabolus* saw that the Captains were come out, and that so valiantly they surrounded his men, he concluded (that for the present) nothing from them was to *be* looked for but blows, and the dints of their *two-edged sword*.

The battel joined.

Wherefore he also falls on upon the Princes army, with all his deadly force. So the battel was joined. Now who was it that at first *Diabolus* met with in the fight, but Captain *Credence* on the one hand, and the Lord *Wilbewill* on the other; now *Wilbewills* blows were like the blows of a Giant, for that man had a strong arm, and he fell in upon the *Election-doubters*, for they were the life-guard of *Diabolus*, and he kept them in play a good while, cutting and battering shrewdly. Now when Captain *Credence* saw my Lord engaged, he did stoutly fall on, on the other hand upon the same company also; so they put them to great disorder. Now Captain *Good hope* had engaged the *Vocation-doubters*, and they were sturdy men; but the Captain was a valiant man: Captain *Experience* did also send him some aid, so he made the *Vocation-doubters* to retreat. The rest of the Armies were hotly engaged, and that on every side, and the *Diabolonians* did fight stoutly. Then did my Lord

Wilbewill ingaged.

Credence ingaged.

Goodhope ingaged.

Secretary command that the slings from the Castle should be plaid, and his men could throw stones at an hairs bredth. But after a while those that were made to fly before the Captains of the Prince, did begin to ralley again, and they came up stoutly upon the Rere of the Princes Army: wherefore the Princes Army began to faint; but remembring that they should see the face of their Prince by and by, they took courage, and a very fierce battel was fought. Then shouted the Captains, saying, *The Sword of the Prince* Emanuel, *and the Shield of Captain Credence*; and with that *Diabolus* gave back, thinking that more aid had been come. But no *Emanuel* as yet appeared. Moreover the battel did hang in doubt; and they made a little retreat on both sides. Now in the time of respite Captain *Credence* bravely incouraged his men to stand to it, and *Diabolus* did the like as well as he could. But Captain *Credence* made a brave Speech to his Souldiers, the Contents whereof here follow.

The Lord *Secretary* ingaged.

The battel renewed.

A fierce fight.

They both retreat, and in the time of respite Captain *Credence* makes a Speech to his Souldiers.

Gentlemen Souldiers, and my Brethren in this design, it rejoiceth me much to see in the field for our Prince this day, so stout and so valiant an Army, and such faithful lovers of Mansoul. *You have hitherto as hath become you, shewn your selves men of truth and courage against the* Diabolonian *forces, so that for all their boast, they have not yet cause much to boast of their gettings. Now take to your selves your wonted courage, and shew your selves men even this once only; for in a few minutes after the next engagement this time, you shall see your Prince shew himself in the field; for we must make this second assault upon this Tyrant* Diabolus, *and then* Emanuel *comes.*

No sooner had the Captain made this Speech to his Souldiers, but one Mr. *Speedy* came post to the Captain from the Prince, to tell him that *Emanuel* was at hand. This news when the Captain had received, he communicated to the other Field-officers, and they again to their Souldiers and men of war. Wherefore like men raised from the dead, so the Captains and their men arose, made up to the enemy, and cried as before, *The Sword of the Prince* Emanuel, *and the shield of Captain* Credence.

The *Diabolonians* also bestirred themselves, and made

resistance as well as they could, but in this last engagement the *Diabolonians* lost their courage, and many of the *Doubters* fell down dead to the ground. Now when they had been in heat of battel about an hour or more, *Captain Credence* lift up his eyes and saw, and behold *Emanuel* came, and he came with Colours flying, Trumpets sounding, and the feet of his men scarce toucht the ground, they hasted with that celerity towards the *Captains* that were engaged. Then did *Credence* winde with his men to the Town-ward, & gave to *Diabolus* the field. So *Emanuel* came upon him on the one side, and the enemies place was betwixt them both; then again they fell to it afresh, and now it was but a little while more but *Emanuel* and *Captain Credence* met, still trampling down the slain as they came.

When the enemy is betwixt Christ and faith, then down they go to be sure.

But when the *Captains* saw that the Prince was come, and that he fell upon the *Diabolonians* on the other side, and that *Captain Credence* and his Highness had got them up betwixt them, they shouted, (they so shouted that the ground rent again) saying, *The Sword of* Emanuel, *and the Shield of Captain Credence*. Now when *Diabolus* saw that he and his forces were so hard beset by the Prince and his Princely Army, what does he and the Lords of the Pit that were with him, but make their escape, and forsake their Army, and leave them to fall by the hand of *Emanuel*, and of his noble *Captain Credence*: so they fell all down slain before them, before the Prince, and before his Royal Army; there was not left so much as one *Doubter* alive, they lay spread upon the ground dead men, as one would spread dung upon the land.

The Victory falls to *Emanuel*, and to his men, who slay all.

When the battel was over, all things came into order in the Camp; then the Captains and Elders of *Mansoul* came together to salute *Emanuel*, while without the Corporation; so they saluted him, and welcomed him, and that with a thousand welcomes, for that he was come to the borders of *Mansoul* again: So he smiled upon them, and said, *Peace be to you*. Then they addressed themselves to go to the Town; they went then to go up to *Mansoul*, they, the Prince with all the new forces that now he had brought with him to the war. Also all the

Song. 8. 1. *Mansoul* salutes the Prince without, he addresses himself to go into the Town.

Gates of the Town were set open for his reception, so glad were they of his blessed return. And this was the manner and order of this going of his into *Mansoul.*

First, (as I said) all the Gates of the Town were set open, yea the Gates of the Castle also; the Elders too of the Town of *Mansoul* placed themselves at the Gates of the Town to salute him at his entrance thither: And so they did, for as he drew neer, and approached towards the Gates, they said, *Lift up your heads, O ye Gates, and be ye lift up ye everlasting doors, and the King of Glory shall come in.* And they answered again, *Who is the King of Glory*? and they made return to themselves, *The Lord strong and mighty, the Lord mighty in battel. Lift up your heads, O ye Gates, even lift them up ye everlasting doors, &c.*

The manner of his going in.

Secondly, It was ordered also by those of *Mansoul*, that all the way from the Town-gates to *those* of the Castle his blessed Majesty should be entertained with the *Song*, by them that could best skill in musick in all the Town of *Mansoul*; then did the Elders, and the rest of the men of *Mansoul* answer one another as *Emanuel* entered the Town, till he came at the Castle-gates with Songs and sound of Trumpets, saying, *They have seen thy goings O God, even the goings of my God, my King in the Sanctuary. So the Singers went before, the players on instruments followed after, and among them were the damsels playing on timbrels.*

Thirdly. Then the Captains (for I would speak a word of them) they in their order waited on the Prince as he entred into the Gates of *Mansoul.* Captain *Credence* went before, and Captain *Goodhope* with him; Captain *Charity* came behind with other of his companions, and Captain *Patience* followed after all, and the rest of the Captains, some on the right hand, and some on the left accompanied *Emanuel* into *Mansoul.* And all the while the Colours were displayed, the Trumpets sounded, and continual shoutings were among the Souldiers. *The Prince himself rode into the Town in his Armour, which was all of beaten Gold, and in his Chariot, the pillars of it were of Silver, the bottom thereof of Gold, the covering of it were of purple; the midst thereof being paved with love for the daughters of the Town of* Mansoul.

Fourthly, When the Prince was come to the entrance of

Mansoul, he found all the streets strewed with lillies and flowers, curiously decked with boughs and branches from the green trees that stood round about the Town. Every door also was filled with persons who had adorned every one their fore-part against their house with something of variety, and singular excellency to entertain him withal as he passed in the streets; they also themselves as *Emanuel* passed by, did welcome him with shouts and acclamations of joy, saying, *Blessed be the Prince that cometh in the name of his Father* Shaddai.

Good and joyful Thoughts.

Fifthly, At the Castle-gates the Elders of *Mansoul*, to wit, the Lord *Mayor*, the Lord *Wilbewill*, the *Subordinate Preacher*, Mr. *Knowledg*, and Mr. *Mind*, with other of the Gentry of the place saluted *Emanuel* again. They bowed before him, they kissed the dust of his feet, they thanked, they blessed, and praised his Highness for not taking advantage against them for their sins, but rather had pity upon them in their misery, and returned to them with mercies, and to build up their *Mansoul* for ever. Thus was he had up straightway to the Castle; for that was the Royal Palace, and the place where his Honour was to dwell; the which was ready prepared for his Highness by the presence of the Lord *Secretary*, and the work of Captain *Credence*. So he entred in.

Sixthly, Then the people and commonalty of the Town of *Mansoul* came to him into the Castle to mourn, and to weep, and to lament for their wickedness, by which they had forced him out of the Town. So they when they were come, bowed themselves to the ground seven times; they also wept, they wept aloud, and asked forgiveness of the Prince, and prayed that he would again, as of old, confirm his love to *Mansoul*.

To the which the great Prince replied, *Weep not, but go your way, eat the fat, and drink the sweet, and send portions to them for whom nought is prepared, for the joy of your Lord is your strength. I am returned to* Mansoul *with mercies, and my name shall be set up, exalted and magnified by it.* He also took these inhabitants and kissed them, and laid them in his bosom.

The holy Conceptions of *Mansoul*.

Moreover, he gave to the Elders of *Mansoul*, and to each Town-officer a chain of Gold, and a Signet. He also sent to their *wives* ear-rings and jewels, and bracelets, and other things. He also bestowed upon the *true-born* children of *Mansoul*, many precious things. Young and tender holy Thoughts.

When *Emanuel* the Prince had done all these things for the famous Town of *Mansoul*, then he said unto them, first, *Wash your garments, then put on your ornaments, and then come to me into the Castle of Mansoul.* So they went to the fountain that was set open for *Judah* and *Jerusalem* to wash in; and there they washed, and there they made their *garments white*, and came again to the Prince into the Castle, and thus they stood before him. Eccle. 9. 8. Zach. 13. 1. Rev. 7. 14, 15.

And now there was musick and dancing throughout the whole Town of *Mansoul*; and that because their Prince had again granted to them his presence, and the light of his countenance; the Bells also did ring, and the Sun shone comfortably upon them for a great while together.

The Town of *Mansoul* did also *now* more throughly seek the destruction and ruin of all remaining *Diabolonians* that abode in the walls, and the dens (that they had) in the Town of *Mansoul*; for there was of them that had to this day escaped with life and limb from the hand of their suppressors in the famous Town of *Mansoul*.

But my Lord *Wilbewill* was a greater terrour to them now than ever he had been before; forasmuch as his heart was yet more fully bent to seek, contrive, and pursue them to the death; he pursued them night and day, and did put them now to sore distress, as will afterwards appear. *Wilbewill* a greater terrour to the *Diabolonians* now, than he had been in former times.

After things were thus far put into order in the famous Town of *Mansoul*, care was taken, and order given by the blessed Prince *Emanuel*, that the Townsmen should without further delay appoint some to go forth into the Plain to bury the dead that were there; the dead that *fell by the sword of* Emanuel, *and by the shield of the Captain Credence*, lest the fumes and ill favours that would arise from them, might infect the air, and so annoy the famous Town of *Mansoul*. This also was a reason of this order, *to wit*, that as much as in *Mansoul* lay, they might cut off the name and being, and remembrance of Orders given out to bury the dead.

those enemies from the thought of the famous Town of *Mansoul*, and its inhabitants.

So order was given out by the Lord *Mayor*, that wise and trusty friend of the Town of *Mansoul*, that persons should be employed about this necessary business; and Mr. *Godlyfear*, and one Mr. *Upright* were to be Overseers about this matter; so persons were put under them to work in the fields, and to bury the slain that lay dead in the Plains. And these were their places of imployment, some were to make the graves, some to bury the dead, and some were to go to and fro in the Plains, and also round about the borders of *Mansoul* to see if a skull or a bone, or a piece of a bone of a *Doubter*, was yet to be found above ground any where near the Corporation; and if any were found, it was ordered that the Searchers that searched should set up a mark thereby, and a sign, that those that were appointed to bury them might find it, and bury it out of sight, that the name and remembrance of a *Diabolonian Doubter* might be blotted out from under Heaven. And that the children, and they that were to be born in *Mansoul* might not know (if possible) what a skull, what a bone, or a piece of a bone of a *Doubter* was. So the buriers, and those that were appointed for that purpose, did as they were commanded, they buried the *Doubters*, and all the skulls and bones, and pieces of bones of *Doubters*, where ever they found them, and so they cleansed the Plains. Now also Mr. *Godspeace* took up his Commission, and acted again as in former days.

Not a skul or a bone, or a piece of a bone of a *Doubter* to be left unburied.

Thus they buried in the Plains about *Mansoul*, the *Election-doubters*, the *Vocation-doubters*, the *Grace-doubters*, the *Perseverance-doubters*, the *Resurrection-doubters*, the *Salvation-doubters*, and the *Glory-doubters*; whose Captains were Captain *Rage*, Captain *Cruel*, Captain *Damnation*, Captain *Insatiable*, Captain *Brimstone*, Captain *Torment*, Captain *Noease*, Captain *Sepulcher*, and Captain *Past-hope*; and old *Incredulity* was under *Diabolus* their General; there were also the seven heads of their army, and they were the Lord *Beelzebub*, the Lord *Lucifer*, the Lord *Legion*, the Lord *Apollyon*, the Lord *Python*, the Lord *Cerberus*, and the Lord *Belial*. But the Princes, and the Captains with old *Incredulity* their General, did all of them make their escape; so their men fell down slain by the power of the Princes forces, and by the hands of the men of the Town of *Mansoul*. They also were buried as is afore related, to the exceeding great joy of the now famous Town of *Mansoul*. They that buried them, buried also with them their arms, which were cruel instruments of death, (their weapons were arrows, darts, mauls, fire-brands, and the like) they buried also their armour, their colours, banners, with the standard of *Diabolus*, and what else soever they could find that did but smell of a *Diabolonian Doubter*.

Their arms and armour buried with them.

Now when the Tyrant was arrived at *Hellgate-hill*, with his old friend *Incredulity*, they immediately descended the Den, and having there with their fellows for a while condoled their *misfortune*, and great loss that they sustained against the Town of *Mansoul*, they fell at length into a passion, and revenged they would be for the loss that they sustained before the Town of *Mansoul*; wherefore they presently call a Councel to contrive yet further what was to be done against the famous Town of *Mansoul*; for their yawning panches could not wait to see the result of their Lord *Lucifers*, and their Lord *Apollyons* counsel that they had given before, (for their raging gorge thought every day even as long as a *short-for-ever*) until they were filled with the body and soul, with the flesh and bones, and with all the delicates of *Mansoul*. They therefore resolve to make another attempt upon the Town of *Mansoul*, and that by an army mixed, and made up partly of *Doubters*, and partly of *Blood-men*. A more particular account now take of both.

The Tyrant resolves to have yet a bout with *Mansoul*.

The *Doubters* are such as have their *name* from their *nature*, as well as from the Lord and Kingdom where they are born; their nature is to put a question upon every one of the Truths of *Emanuel*, and their Country is called *the land of Doubting*, and that land lyeth off, and furthest remote to the *North*, between the land of *Darkness*, and that called the *Valley of the shadow of death*. For though *the land of Darkness*, and that called *the land of the shadow of death*, be sometimes called as if they were *one* and the self same place; yet indeed they are *two*, lying but a little way asunder, and the land of *Doubting* points

An army of *Doubters* and *Bloodmen*.

Of the Country of the *Doubters*, and of the *Bloodmen* where they lye.

in, and lyeth between them. *This is the land of Doubting*, and these that came with *Diabolus* to ruin the Town of *Mansoul*, are the natives of that Country.

The *Bloodmen* are a people that have their name derived from the *malignity* of their nature, and from the fury that is in them to execute it upon the Town of *Mansoul*; their land lyeth under the *Dog-star*, and by that they are governed as to their *Intellectuals*. The name of their Country is the Province of *Loathgood*, the remote parts of it are far distant from the land of *Doubting*, yet they do both *butt* and bound upon the Hill called *Hellgate-hill*. These people are always in league with the *Doubters* for they jointly do make question of the faith and fidelity of the men of the Town of *Mansoul*, and so are both alike qualified for the service of their Prince.

The number of his new army.

Now of these two Countries did *Diabolus* by the beating of his *Drum* raise another army against the Town of *Mansoul*, of five and twenty thousand strong. There were ten thousand *Doubters*, and fifteen thousand *Bloodmen*, and they were put under several Captains for the war; and old *Incredulity* was again made General of the Army.

As for the *Doubters*, their Captains were five of the seven that were heads of the last *Diabolonian* army, and these are their names, Captain *Beelzebub*, Captain *Lucifer*, Captain *Apollyon*, Captain *Legion*, and Captain *Cerberus*; and the Captains that they had before, were some of them made Lieutenants, and some Ensignes of the Army.

His chief strength lyes in the *Bloodmen*.

But *Diabolus* did not count that in this Expedition of his, these *Doubters* would prove his principal men, for their *manhood* had been tried before, also the *Mansoulians* had put them to the worst, only he did bring them to multiply a number, and to help if need was at a pinch, but his trust he put in his *Bloodmen*; for that they were all rugged Villains, and he knew that they had done feats heretofore.

The Captains of the *Bloodmen*.

As for the *Bloodmen* they also were under command, and the names of their Captains were Captain *Cain*, Captain *Nimrod*, Captain *Ishmael*, Captain *Esau*, Captain *Saul*, Captain *Absalom*, Captain *Judas*, and Captain *Pope*.

1. Captain *Cain* was over two bands, to wit, the *zealous* and the *angry* Bloodmen; his *Standard*-bearer bare the Red-colours, and his Scutcheon was the *Murdering Club*. Gen. 4. 8.

2. Captain *Nimrod* was Captain over two bands, to wit, the *Tyrannical* and *Incroaching Bloodmen*; his *Standard*-bearer bare the Red-colors, and his *Scutcheon* was the *Great Bloodhound*. Gen. 10. 8, 9.

3. *Captain Ishmael* was *Captain* over two bands, to wit, over the *Mocking* and *Scorning Bloodmen*; his *Standard*-bearer bare the Red-colours, and his *Scutcheon* was one *mocking* at *Abrahams Isaac*.

4. *Captain Esau* was *Captain* over two bands, to wit, the *Bloodmen* that *grudged* that another should have the blessing; also over the *Bloodmen* that are for *executing their private revenge upon others;* his *Standard*-bearer bare the Red-colours, and his *Scutcheon* was one *privately lurking to murder Jacob*. Gen. 21. 9, 10. Gen. 27. 42, 43, 44, 45.

5. *Captain Saul* was *Captain* over two bands, to wit, the *Groundlesly jealous*, and the *Devilishly furious Bloodmen*; his *Standard*-bearer bare the Red-colours, and his *Scutcheon* was *three bloody darts cast at harmless David*. 1 Sam. 18. 10. Ch. 19. 10. Ch. 20. 23.

6. *Captain Absalom* was *Captain* over two bands, to wit, over the *Bloodmen* that will *kill a father* or a friend, for the glory of this world; also over those *Bloodmen* that will *hold one fair in hand* with words, till they shall have pierced him with their swords; his *Standard*-bearer did bear the Red-colors, and his *Scutcheon* was the *Son a pursuing the fathers blood*. 2 Sam. 15, 16, 17. Chapters.

7. *Captain Judas* was over two bands, to wit, the *Bloodmen* that will sell a mans life for mony, and those also that will betray their friend with a kiss; his *Standard*-bearer bare the Red-colours, and his *Scutcheon* was thirty pieces of *Silver*, and the *Halter*. Mat. 26. 14, 15, 16.

8. *Captain Pope* was *Captain* over one band, for all these spirits are joined in one under him; his *Standard*-bearer bare the Red-colours, and his *Scutcheon* was the stake, the flame, and the *good man in it*. Rev. 13. 7, 8. Dan. 11. 33.

Now the reason why *Diabolus* did so soon rally another force after he had been beaten out of the field, were for that he put mighty confidence in this army of *Bloodmen*, for he put a great The conditions of the *Bloodmen*, their stoutness, and valor.

deal of more trust in them, than he did before in his army of *Doubters*; though they had also often done great service for him in the strengthening of him in his Kingdom. But these *Bloodmen*, he had proved them often, and their sword did seldom return empty. Besides, he knew that these like Mastiffs, would fasten upon any; upon father, mother, brother, sister, Prince, or Governour, yea, upon the Prince of Princes. And that which incouraged him the more, was for that they once did force *Emanuel* out of the Kingdom of *Universe*, and why thought he, may they not also drive him from the Town of *Mansoul*.

They sit down before *Mansoul*.

So this army of five and twenty thousand strong, was by their General the great Lord *Incredulity*, led up against the Town of *Mansoul*. Now Mr. *Prywell* the *Scout-master-general*, did himself go out to spie, and he did bring *Mansoul* tidings of their coming: wherefore they shut up their Gates, and put themselves in a posture of defence against these new *Diabolonians* that came up against the Town.

How they dispose of themselvs.

So *Diabolus* brought up his Army, and beleaguered the Town of *Mansoul*; the *Doubters* were placed about *Feetgate*, and the *Bloodmen* set down before *Eyegate* and *Eargate*.

They summon the Town with a threatning.

Now when this Army had thus incamped themselves, *Incredulity* did in the name of *Diabolus*, his own name, and in the name of the *Bloodmen*, and the rest that were with him, send a Summons as hot as a red hot iron to *Mansoul*, to yield to their demands; threatning that if they still stood it out against them, they would presently burn down *Mansoul* with fire. For you must know that as for the *Bloodmen*, they were not so much that *Mansoul* should be *surrenderd*, as that *Mansoul* should be *destroyed*, and cut off out of the land of the living. True, they send to them to surrender, but should they so do, that would not stench or quench the thirsts of these men. They must have blood, the blood of *Mansoul*, else they die; and it is from *hence that they have their name*. Wherefore these *Bloodmen* he reserved while now that they might when all his Engins proved ineffectual, as his last and sure card be played against the Town of *Mansoul*.

Psa. 29. 10. Isa. 59. 7. Jer. 22. 17.

Now when the Townsmen had received this red-hot Summons, it begat in them at present some changing and interchanging thoughts; but they jointly agreed in less than half an hour to carry the Summons to the Prince, the which they did when they had write at the bottom of it, *Lord save* Mansoul *from bloody men.*

Psal. 59. 2.

So he took it, and looked upon it, and considered it, and took notice also of that short Petition that the men of *Mansoul* had written at the bottom of it and called to him the noble *Captain Credence*, and bid him go and take *Captain Patience* with him, and go and take care of that side of *Mansoul* that was beleaguered by the *Bloodmen*. So they went and did as they were commanded, the *Captain Credence* went and took *Captain Patience*, and they both secured that side of *Mansoul* that was besieged by the *Bloodmen*.

Heb. 6. 12. Ver. 15.

Then he commanded that *Captain Goodhope* and *Captain Charity*, and my Lord *Wilbewill*, should take charge of the other side of the Town; and I, said the Prince, will set my standard upon the Battlements of your Castle, and do you three watch against the *Doubters*. This done, he again commanded that the brave *Captain* the *Captain Experience* should draw up his men in the Market-place, and that there he should exercise them day by day before the people of the Town of *Mansoul*. Now this siege was long, and many a fierce attempt did the enemy, especially those called the *Bloodmen*, make upon the Town of *Mansoul*, and many a shrewd brush did some of the Townsmen meet with from them; especially *C. Self-denial*; who, I should have told you before, was commanded to take the care of *Eargate* and *Eyegate* now against the *Bloodmen*. This Captain *Self-denial* was a young man, but stout, and a Townsman in *Mansoul*, as *Captain Experience* also was. And *Emanuel* at his second return to *Mansoul*, made him a Captain over a thousand of the *Mansoulians*, for the good of the Corporation. This Captain therefore being an hardy man, and a man of great courage, and willing to venture himself for the good of the Town of *Mansoul*, would now and then salley out upon the *Bloodmen*, and give them many notable alarms,

Captain *Self-denial* the last of those that were put in office in the Town of *Mansoul*.

His valor.

and entered several brisk skirmishes with them, and also did some execution upon them, but you must think that this could not easily be done, but he must meet with brushes himself, for he carried several of their marks in his face; yea, and some in some other parts of his body.

His signs of manhood.

Emanuel prepares to give the enemy battel. How he ordereth his men.

So after some time spent for the trial of the *faith*, and *hope*, and *love* of the Town of *Mansoul*; the Prince *Emanuel* upon a day calls his *Captains* and *men of war* together, and divides them into two Companies; this done, he commands them at a time appointed, and that in the morning very early to salley out upon the enemy: saying, Let half of you fall upon the *Doubters*, and half of you fall upon the *Bloodmen.* Those of you that go out against the *Doubters*, kill and slay, and cause to perish so many of them as by any means you can lay hands on; but for you that go out against the *Bloodmen*, slay them not, but take them alive.

The Captains go out.

So at the time appointed, betimes in the morning the Captains went out as they were commanded against the enemies: Captain *Goodhope*, Captain *Charity*, and those that were joined with them, as Captain *Innocent*, and Captain *Experience*, went out against the *Doubters*; and Captain *Credence*, and Captain *Patience*, with Captain *Self-denial*, and the rest that were to join with them, went out against the *Bloodmen.*

The *Doubters* put to flight.

Now those that went out against the *Doubters*, drew up into a body before the Plain, and marched on to bid them battel: But the *Doubters* remembring their last success, made a retreat, not daring to stand the shock, but fled from the Princes men; wherefore they pursued them, and in their pursuit slew many, but they could not catch them all. Now those that escaped went some of them home, and the rest by fives, nines, and seventeens, like wanderers, went stragling up and down the Country, where they upon the barbarous people shewed and exercised many of their *Diabolonian actions*; nor did these people rise up in arms against them, but suffered themselves to be enslaved by them. They would also after this shew themselves in companies before the Town of

The *unbeliever* never fights the *Doubters*.

Mansoul, but never to abide it; for if Captain *Credence*, Captain *Goodhope*, or Captain *Experience* did but shew themselves, they fled.

The *Bloodmen* are taken, and how.

Those that went out against the *Bloodmen*, did as they were commanded, they forbore to slay any, but sought to compass them about. But the *Bloodmen* when they saw that no *Emanuel* was in the field, concluded also that no *Emanuel* was in *Mansoul*; wherefore they looking upon what the Captains did, to be, as they called it, a fruit of the extravagancy of their wild and foolish fancies, rather despised them, than feared them, but the Captains minding their business, at last did compass them round, they also that had routed the *Doubters* came in amain to their aid; so in fine, after some little strugling, for the *Bloodmen* also would have run for it, only now it was too late, (for though they are mischievous and cruel, where they can overcome, yet all *Bloodmen* are chicken-hearted men, when they once come to see themselves matcht and equal'd) so the Captains took them, and brought them to the Prince.

They are brought to the Prince and found to be of 3 sorts.

Now when they were taken, had before the Prince, and examined, he found them to be of three several Countries, though they all came out of one land.

1. One sort of them came out of *Blindmanshire*, and they were such as did ignorantly what they did.

2. Another sort of them came out of *Blindzealshire*, and they did superstitiously what they did.

3. The third sort of them came out of the Town of *Malice* in the County of *Envy*, and they did what they did out of spite and implacableness.

1 Tim. 1. 13, 14, 15. Mat. 5. 44. Luk. 6. 22. Joh. 16. 1, 2. Act. 9. 5, 6. Revel. 9. 20, 21. Joh. 8. 40, 41, 42, 43, &c.

For the first of these, to wit, they that came out of *Blindmanshire*, when they *saw* where they were, and against whom they had fought, they trembled, and cried as they stood before him; and as many of these as asked him mercy, he touched their lips with his Golden Scepter.

They that came out of *Blindzealshire*, they did not as their fellows did, for they pleaded that they had right to do what they did, because *Mansoul* was a Town whose laws and customs were diverse from all that dwelt thereabouts; very few of these could be brought to see their evil but those that did, and asked mercy, they also obtained favour.

The *Bloodmen* are bound over to answer for what they have done at the Assizes. The day of Judgment.

Now they that came out of the Town of *Malice*, that is in the County of *Envy*, they neither *wept*, nor *disputed* nor *repented*, but stood gnawing of their tongues before him for anguish and madness, because they could not have their will upon *Mansoul*. Now these last, with all those of the other two sorts that did not unfeignedly ask pardon for their faults: *Those he made to enter into sufficient bond to answer for what they had done against* Mansoul, *and against her King, at the great and general Assizes to be holden for our Lord the King, where he himself should appoint for the Country and Kingdom of Universe.*

So they became bound each man for himself to come in when called upon to answer before our Lord the King for what they had done as before.

And thus much concerning this second army that were sent by *Diabolus* to overthrow *Mansoul*.

Three or four of the *Doubters* go into *Mansoul*, are entertained, and by whom.

But there were three of those that came from the land of *Doubting*, who after they had wandred and ranged the Country a while, and perceived that they had escaped, were so hardy as to thrust themselves, knowing that yet there were in the Town *Diabolonians*, I say they were so hardy as to thrust themselves into *Mansoul* among them. (Three did I say, I think there were four.) Now to whose house should these *Diabolonian Doubters* go, but to the house of an old *Diabolonian* in *Mansoul*, whose name was *Evil questioning*, a very great enemy he was to *Mansoul*, and a great doer among the *Diabolonians* there. Well, to this *Evil-questionings* house, as was said, did these *Diabolonians* come, (you may be sure that they had directions how to find the way thither) so he made them welcome, pitied their misfortune, and succoured them with the best that he had in his house. Now after a little acquaintance, and it was not long before they had that, this old *Evil-questioning* asked the *Doubters* if they were all of a *Town*, (he knew that they were all of one Kingdom)? and they answered no, nor not of one *Shire* neither; for I, said one, am an *Election-Doubter*. I, said another, am a *Vocation-Doubter*; then said the

What sort of *Doubters* they are.

third, I am a *Salvation-Doubter*; and the fourth said he was a *Grace-Doubter*. Well, quoth the old *Gentleman*, be of what shire you will, I am perswaded that you are down boys, you have the very length of my foot, are one with my heart, and shall be welcome to me. So they thanked him, and were glad that they had found themselves an harbour in *Mansoul*. Then said *Evil-questioning* to them, How many of your company might there be that came with you to the siege of *Mansoul*? and they answered, there were but ten thousand *Doubters* in all, for the rest of the Army consisted of fifteen thousand *Bloodmen*: These *Bloodmen*, quoth they, border upon our Country, but poor men, as we hear, they were every one taken by *Emanuels* forces. Ten thousand! quoth the old Gentleman, I'le promise you that's a round company. But how came it to pass since you were so mighty a number that you fainted, and durst not fight your foes? Our General, said they, was the first man that did run for't. Pray, quoth their Landlord, who was that your cowardly General? He was once the Lord *Mayor* of *Mansoul*, said they. But pray call him not a cowardly General, for whether any from the East to the West has done more service for our Prince *Diabolus*, than has my Lord *Incredulity*, will be a hard question for you to answer. But had they catched him they would for certain have hanged him, and we promise you hanging is but a bad business. Then said the old *Gentleman*, I would that all the ten thousand *Doubters* were now well armed in *Mansoul*, and my self in the head of them, I would see what I could do. Ai, said they, that would be well if we could see that: But wishes alas! what are they! and these words were spoken aloud. Well, said old *Evil questioning*, take heed that you talk not too loud, you must be quat and close, and must take care of your selves while you are here, or I'le assure you, you will be snapt.

Talk betwixt the *Doubters*, and old *Evil-questioning*.

Why? quoth the *Doubters*.

Why! quoth the old *Gentleman*, why, because both the Prince, and Lord *Secretary*, and their Captains and Souldiers are all at present in Town; yea, the Town is as full of them as ever it can hold. And besides, there is one whose name is *Wilbewill*, a most cruel enemy of ours, and him the Prince has made Keeper of the Gates, and has commanded him that with all the diligence he can, he should look for, search out, and destroy all, and all manner of *Diabolonians*.

And if he lighteth upon you, down you go though your heads were made of Gold.

They are overheard.

And now to see how it happened, one of the Lord *Wilbewills* faithful Souldiers, whose name was Mr. *Diligence*, stood all this while listning under old *Evil-questionings Eaves*, and heard all the talk that had been betwixt him and the *Doubters* that he entertained under his roof.

The Souldier was a man that my Lord had much confidence in, and that he loved dearly, and that both because he was a man of courage, and also a man that was unwearied in seeking after *Diabolonians* to apprehend them.

They are discovered.

Now this man, as I told you, heard all the talk that was between old *Evil-questioning*, and these *Diabolonians*; wherefore what does he but goes to his Lord, and tells him what he had heard. And saist thou so, my trusty, quoth my Lord? Ay, quoth *Diligence*, that I do, and if your Lord shall be pleased to go with me, you shall find it as I have said. And are they there, quoth my Lord? I know *Evil-questioning* well, for he and I were great in the time of our Apostasie. But I know not now where he dwells. But I do, said his man, and if your Lordship will go, I will lead you the way to his den. Go! quoth my Lord, that I will. Come my *Diligence*, let's go find them out. So my Lord and his man went together the direct way to his house. Now his man went before to shew him his way, and they went till they came even under old Mr. *Evil-questionings* wall: then said *Diligence*, Hark! my Lord do you know the old Gentlemans tongue when you hear it? Yes, said my Lord, I know it well, but I have not seen him many a day. This I know, he is cunning, I wish he doth not give us the slip. Let me alone for that, said his servant *Diligence*. But how shall we find the door, quoth my Lord? Let me alone for that too, said his man. So he had my Lord *Wilbewill* about, and shewed him the way to the door. Then my Lord without more ado, broke open the door, rushed into the house, and caught them all five together, even as *Diligence* his man had told him. So my Lord apprehended them, and led them away, and committed them to the hand of Mr. *Trueman* the Gaoler, and commanded, and he did put them in Ward. This done, my Lord *Mayor* was acquainted in the morning with what my Lord *Wilbewill* had done over night, and his Lordship rejoiced much at the news, not only because there were *Doubters* apprehended, but because that old *Evil-questioning* was taken; for he had been a very great trouble to *Mansoul*, and much affliction to my Lord *Mayor* himself. He had also been sought for often, but no hand could ever be laid upon him till now.

They are apprehended, and committed to Prison.

The Lord *Mayor* is glad at it.

Well, the next thing was to make preparation to try these five that by my Lord had been apprehended, and that were in the hands of Mr. *Trueman* the Gaoler. So the day was set, and the Court called and come together, and the Prisoners brought to the Bar. My Lord *Wilbewill* had power to have slain them when at first he took them, and that without any more ado, but he thought it at this time more for the honour of the Prince, the comfort of *Mansoul*, and the discouragement of the enemy, to bring them forth to publick judgment.

They are brought to trial.

But I say, Mr. *Trueman* brought them in chains to the Bar, to the Town-Hall, for that was the place of Judgment. So to be short, the Jury was pannelled, the Witnesses sworn, and the Prisoners tried for their lives, the Jury was the same that tried Mr. *No-truth*, *Pitiless*, *Haughty*, and the rest of their companions.

And first old *Questioning* himself was set to the Bar; for he was the receiver, the entertainer and comforter of these *Doubters*, that by Nation were outlandish men; then he was bid to hearken to his Charge, and was told that he had liberty to object, if he had ought to say for himself. So his Indictment was read, the manner and form here follows.

Mr. Questioning, *Thou art here Indicted by the name of* Evil-questioning, *an intruder upon the Town of Mansoul*, *for that thou art a* Diabolonian *by nature, and also a hater of the Prince* Emanuel, *and one that hast studied the ruin of the Town of* Mansoul. *Thou art also here indicted for countenancing the Kings*

His Indictment.

enemies, after wholsome Laws made to the contrary: For, 1. *thou hast* questioned *the truth of her Doctrine and State.* 2. *In wishing that ten thousand* Doubters *were in her.* 3. *In receiving, in entertaining and encouraging of her enemies, that came from their Army unto thee. What saist thou to this Indictment, art thou guilty or not guilty?*

His Plea. My Lord, quoth he, I know not the meaning of this Indictment, forasmuch as I am not the man concerned in it; the man that standeth by this Charge accused before this Bench, is called by the name of *Evil-questioning*, which name I deny to be mine, mine being *Honest-Enquiring*. The one indeed sounds like the other, but I trow, your Lordships know that between these two there is a wide difference; for I hope that a man even in the worst of times, and that too amongst the worst of men, may make an honest enquiry after things, without running the danger of death.

The Lord *Wilbewills* Testimony. *Wilb.* Then spake my Lord *Wilbewill*, for he was one of the Witnesses: *My Lord, and you the Honourable Bench, and Magistrates of the Town of* Mansoul, *you all have heard with your own ears that the prisoner at the Bar has denied his name, and so thinks to shift from the charge of the Indictment. But I know him to be the man concerned, and that his proper name is* Evil-questioning. *I have known him (my Lord) above this thirty years, for he and I (a shame it is for me to speak it) were great acquaintance, when* Diabolus *that Tyrant had the Government of* Mansoul*; and I testifie that he is a* Diabolonian *by nature, an enemy to our Prince, and an hater of the blessed Town of* Mansoul. *He has in times of rebellion been at, and lain in my house, my Lord, not so little as twenty nights together, and we did use to talk then* (for the substance of talk) *as he, and his* Doubters *have talked of late: true, I have not seen him many a day. I suppose that the coming of* Emanuel *to* Mansoul, *has made him to change his lodgings, as this Indictment has driven him to change his name; but this is the man, my Lord.*

The Court. Then said the Court unto him hast thou any more to say?

His Plea. *Evil.* Yes, quoth the old *Gentleman*, that I have; for all that as yet has been said against me, is but by the mouth of one

Witness, and it is not lawful for the famous Town of *Mansoul*, at the mouth of one Witness to put any man to death.

Dilig. Then stood forth Mr. *Diligence*, and said, *My Lord, as I was upon my watch such a night at the head of* Badstreet *in this Town, I chanced to hear a muttering within this Gentlemans house; then thought I, what's to do here? so I went up close, but very softly to the side of the house to listen, thinking, as indeed it fell out, that there I might light upon some* Diabolonian *Conventicle. So, as I said, I drew nearer and nearer, and when I was got up close to the wall, it was but a while before I perceived that there were outlandish men in the house (but I did well understand their speech, for I have been a traveller my self) now hearing such language in such a tottering cottage as this old Gentleman dwelt in, I clapt mine ear to a hole in the window, and there heard them talk as followeth. This old Mr.* Questioning *asked these* Doubters *what they were, whence they came, and what was their business in these parts? and they told him to all these questions, yet he did entertain them. He also asked what numbers there were of them, and they told him ten thousand men. He then asked them why they made no more manly assault upon* Mansoul? *and they told him; so he called their General coward for marching off when he should have fought for his Prince. Further, this old* Evil-questioning *wisht, and I heard him wish, would all the ten thousand* Doubters *were now in* Mansoul, *and himself in the head of them. He bid them also to take heed and lye quat, for if they were taken they must die, although they had heads of gold.* Mr. *Diligence* testimony.

Then said the Court, Mr. *Evil-questioning* here is now another Witness against you, and his Testimony is full: 1. He swears that you did receive these men into your house, and that you did nourish them there, though you knew that they were *Diabolonians*, and the Kings enemies. 2. He swears that you did wish ten thousand of them in *Mansoul*. 3. He swears that you did give them advice to be quat and close lest they were taken by the Kings servants. All which manifesteth that thou art a *Diabolonian*; but hadst thou been a friend to the King, thou wouldest have apprehended them. The Court.

Evil. Then said *Evil-questioning*, *To the first of these I answer, the men that came into mine house were strangers, and I took them in,* His Plea.

and is it now become a crime in Mansoul *for a man to entertain strangers? That I did also nourish them is true, and why should my charity be blamed. As for the reason why I wished ten thousand of them in* Mansoul, *I never told it to the Witnesses, nor to themselves. I might wish them to be taken, and so my wish might mean well to* Mansoul, *for ought that any yet knows. I did also bid them take heed that they fell not into the Captains hands, but that might be bècause I am unwilling that any man should be slain, and not because I would have the Kings enemies as such escape.*

My Lord *Mayor* then replied, That though it was a vertue to entertain strangers, yet it was treason to entertain the Kings enemies. And for what else thou hast said, thou dost by words but labour to evade, and defer the execution of Judgment. But could there be no more proved against thee but that thou art a *Diabolonian*, thou must for that die the death by the Law; but to be a receiver, a nourisher, a countenancer, and a harbourer of others of them, yea, of outlandish *Diabolonians*; yea, of them that came from far on purpose to cut off and destroy our *Mansoul*: this must not be born.

His Conclusion. Then said *Evil-questioning*, *I see how the game will go: I must die for my name, and for my charity.* And so he held his peace.

Then they called the outlandish *Doubters* to the Bar, and the first of them that was arrainged, was the *Election-doubter*; so his Indictment was read, and because he was an outlandish man, the substance of it was told him by an Interpreter: to wit, *That he was there charged with being an enemy of* Emanuel *the Prince, a hater of the Town of* Mansoul, *and an opposer of her most wholsome Doctrine.*

The *Election doubter* tried.

Then the Judg asked him if he would plead? But he said only this, That he confessed that he was an *Election-doubter*, and that that was the Religion that he had ever been brought up in. And said moreover, If I must die for my Religion, I trow, I shall die a Martyr, and so I care the less.

His Plea.

Judg. Then it was replied, To question Election is to overthrow a great Doctrine of the Gospel, to wit, the *Omnisciency*, and *Power*, and *Will* of God, to take away the liberty

The Court.

of God with his Creature, to stumble the faith of the Town of *Mansoul*, and to make Salvation to depend upon works, and not upon Grace. It also belyed the Word, and disquieted the minds of the men of *Mansoul*, therefore by the best of Laws he must die.

Then was the *Vocation-doubter* called, and set to the Bar; and his Indictment for substance was the same with the other only he was particularly charged with denying the calling of *Mansoul*. The *Vocation-doubter* tried.

The Judg asked him also what he had to say for himself?

So he replied, *That he never believed that there was any such thing as a distinct and powerful call of God to* Mansoul; *otherwise than by the general voice of the Word, nor by that neither otherwise than as it exhorted them to forbear evil, and to do that which is good and in so doing a promise of happiness is annexed.*

Then said the Judg, Thou art a *Diabolonian*, and hast denied a great part of one of the most experimental truths of the Prince of the Town of *Mansoul*; for he has called, and she has heard a most distinct and powerful call of her *Emanuel*, by which she has been quickned, awakened, and possessed with Heavenly Grace to desire to have Communion with her Prince, to serve him, and do his will, and to look for her happiness meerly of his good *pleasure*. And for thine abhorrence of this good Doctrine thou must die the death.

Then the *Grace-doubter* was called, and his Indictment was read, and he replied thereto, That though he was of the land of *Doubting*, his father was the off-spring of a *Pharisee*, and lived in good fashion among his neighbours, and that he taught him to believe, and believe it I do, and will, that *Mansoul* shall never be saved freely by Grace. The *Grace-doubters* tried.

Then said the Judg, Why, the Law of the Prince is plain: 1. Negatively, *Not of works*: 2. Positively, *By grace you are saved*. And thy Religion setleth in and upon the works of the flesh; for the works of the Law are the works of the flesh. Besides, in saying (as thou hast done) thou hast robbed God of his glory, and given it to a sinful man; thou hast robbed Christ of the *necessity* of his undertaking, and the *sufficiency* Rom. 3. Eph. 2.

thereof, and hast given both these to the works of the flesh. Thou hast despised the work of the Holy Ghost, and hast magnified the will of the flesh, and of the Legal mind. Thou art a *Diabolonian*, the son of a *Diabolonian*; and for thy *Diabolonian* principles thou must die.

The Court then having proceeded thus far with them, sent out the Jury, who forthwith brought them in guilty of death. Then stood up the *Recorder*, and addressed himself to the Prisoner: You the Prisoners at the Bar, you have been here Indicted, and proved guilty of high crimes against *Emanuel* our Prince, and against the welfare of the famous Town of *Mansoul*: Crimes for which you must be put to death; and die ye accordingly.

Their sentence to die.

So they were sentenced to the death of the Cross: The place assigned them for Execution was that where *Diabolus* drew up his last Army against *Mansoul*; save only that old *Evil-questioning* was hanged at the top of *Badstreet*, just over against his own door.

The places of their death assigned.

When the Town of *Mansoul* had thus far rid themselves of their enemies, and of the troublers of their peace; in the next place a strict commandment was given out that yet my Lord *Wilbewill* should with *Diligence* his man, search for and do his best to apprehend what Town-*Diabolonians* were yet left alive in *Mansoul*. The names of several of them were Mr. *Fooling*, Mr. *Letgoodslip*, Mr. *Slavishfear*, Mr. *Nolove*, Mr. *Mistrust*, Mr. *Flesh*, and Mr. *Sloth*. It was also commanded that he should apprehend Mr. *Evil-questionings* children, that he left behind him, and that they should demolish his house. The children that he left behind him were these, Mr. *Doubt*, and he was his eldest Son; the next to him was *Legal life*, *Unbelief*, *Wrong thoughts of Christ*, *Clip-promise*, *Carnal sense*, *Live by feeling*, *Self-love*. All these he had by one wife, and her name was *Nohope*, she was the kinswoman of old *Incredulity*, for he was her *Uncle*, and when her father old *Dark* was dead, he took her and brought her up, and when she was marriageable he gave her to this old *Evil-questioning* to wife.

A new Warrant granted out against the children of *Evil-questioning*, with others.

25 *Letgoodslip*] *Letgoodship*

Wilbewill puts his Warrant into Execution

Fooling taken.

Now the Lord *Wilbewill* did put into execution his Commission with great *Diligence* his man. He took *Fooling* in the streets, and hanged him up in *Wantwit-alley*, over against his own house. This *Fooling* was he that would have had the Town of *Mansoul* deliver up Captain *Credence* into the hands of *Diabolus*, provided that then he would have withdrawn his force out of the Town. He also took Mr. *Letgoodslip* one day as he was busie in the Market, and executed him according to Law; now there was an honest poor man in *Mansoul*, and his name was Mr. *Meditation*, one of no great account in the days of Apostasie, but now of repute with the best of the Town. This man therefore they were willing to prefer; now Mr *Letgoodslip* had a great deal of wealth heretofore in *Mansoul*, and at *Emanuels* coming it was sequestred to the use of the Prince; this therefore was now given to Mr. *Meditation* to improve for the common good, and after him to his Son Mr. *Thinkwell*; this *Thinkwell* he had by Mrs. *Piety* his wife, and she was the daughter of Mr. *Recorder*.

Letgoodslip taken.

Clip promise taken.

After this my Lord apprehended *Clip-promise*, now because he was a notorious Villain, for by his doings much of the Kings Coyn was abused, therefore he was made a publick example. He was arraigned and judged to be first set in the Pillory, then to be whipt by all the children and servants in *Mansoul*, and then to be hanged till he was dead. Some may wonder at the severity of this mans punishment, but those that are honest Traders in *Mansoul*, are sensible of the great abuse that one Clipper of Promises in little time may do to the Town of *Mansoul*. And truly my judgment is that all those of his name and life should be served even as he.

Carnal-sense taken.

He also apprehended *Carnal-sense*, and put him in Hold, but how it came about I cannot tell, but he brake Prison and made his escape. Yea, and the bold Villain will not yet quit the Town, but lurks in the *Diabolonian* dens a days, and haunts like a Ghost honest mens houses a nights. Wherefore there was a Proclamation set up in the Market-place in *Mansoul*, signifying that whosoever could discover *Carnal sense*, and apprehend him and slay him, should be admitted daily to the

Princes Table, and should be made keeper of the Treasure of *Mansoul*. Many therefore did bend themselves to do this thing, but take him and slay him they could not, though often he was discovered.

Wrong thoughts of Christ taken.

But my Lord took Mr. *Wrong thoughts of Christ*, and put him in Prison, and he died there, though it was long first, for he died of a lingering Consumption.

Self-love taken.

Self-love was also taken and committed to custody, but there were many that were allied to him in *Mansoul*, so his judgment was deferred, but at last Mr. *Self-denial* stood up and said, if such Villains as these may be winked at in *Mansoul*, I will lay down my Commission. He also took him from the croud, and had him among his Souldiers, and there he was brained. But some in *Mansoul* muttered at it, though none durst speak plainly, because *Emanuel* was in Town. But this brave act of Captain *Self-denial* came to the Princes ears, so he sent for him, and made him a Lord in *Mansoul*. My Lord *Wilbewill* also obtained great commendations of *Emanuel* for what he had done for the Town of *Mansoul*.

Captain *Self-denial* made a Lord.

Then my Lord *Self-denial* took courage, and set to the pursuing of the *Diabolonians* with my Lord *Wilbewill*; and they took *Live by feeling*, and they took *Legal life*, and put them in hold till they died. But Mr. *Unbelief* was a nimble *Jack*, him they could never lay hold of, though they attempted to do it often. He therefore, and some few more of the subtilest of the *Diabolonian* tribe, did yet remain in *Mansoul*, to the time that *Mansoul* left off to dwell any longer in the Kingdom of *Universe*. But they kept them to their dens and holes; if one of them did appear or happen to be seen in any of the streets of the Town of *Mansoul*, the whole Town would be up in arms after them, yea the very children in *Mansoul* would cry out after them as after a thief, and would wish that they might stone them to death with stones. And now did *Mansoul* arrive to some good degree of peace and quiet, her Prince also did abide within her borders, her Captains also, and her Souldiers did their duties, and *Mansoul* minded her trade that she had with the Country that was a far off, also she was busie in her *Manufacture*.

Live by feeling taken.

The peace of *Mansoul*, she minds her trade.

Isa. 33. 17.
Phil. 3, 20.
Prov. 31.

When the Town of *Mansoul* had thus far rid themselves of so many of their enemies, and the troublers of their peace; the Prince sent to them, and appointed a day wherein he would at the Market-place meet the whole people, and there give them in charge concerning some further matters, that if observed would tend to their further safety and comfort, and to the condemnation and destruction of their home-bred *Diabolonians*. So the day appointed was come, and the Towns-men met together; *Emanuel* also came down in his Chariot, and all his Captains in their state attending of him on the right hand, and on the left. Then was an *O yes* made for silence, and after some mutual carriages of love, the Prince began, and thus proceeded.

Emanuels Speech to *Mansoul*.

You my Mansoul, *and the beloved of mine heart, many and great are the priviledges that I have bestowed upon you; I have singled you out from others, and have chosen you to my self, not for your worthiness, but for mine own sake. I have also redeemed you, not only from the dread of my Fathers Law, but from the hand of* Diabolus. *This I have done because I loved you, and because I have set my heart upon you to do you good. I have also, that all things that might hinder thy way to the pleasures of Paradise might be taken out of the way, laid down for thee for thy soul, a plenary satisfaction, and have bought thee to my self; A price not of corruptible things as of silver and gold, but a price of blood, mine own blood, which I have freely spilt upon the ground to make thee mine. So I have reconciled thee, O my* Mansoul, *to my Father, and intrusted thee in the mansion-houses that are with my Father in the Royal City, where things are, O my* Mansoul, *that eye hath not seen, nor hath entred into the heart of man to conceive.*

Besides, O my Mansoul, *thou seest what I have done, and how I have taken thee out of the hands of thine enemies; unto whom thou hadst deeply revolted from my Father, and by whom thou wast content to be possessed, and also to be destroyed. I came to thee first by my Law, then by my Gospel to awaken thee, and shew thee my glory. And thou knowest what thou wast, what thou saidest, what thou didst, and how many times thou rebelledst against my Father and me; yet I left thee not, as thou seest this day, but came to thee, have born thy manners, have waited upon thee, and after all accepted of thee, even of my meer grace and favour ; and would not suffer thee to be lost as thou most willingly wouldest have been. I also compassed thee about, and afflicted thee on every side, that I might make thee weary of thy ways, and bring down thy heart with* molestation *to a willingness to close with thy good and happiness. And when I had gotten a compleat conquest over thee, I turned it to thy advantage.*

Thou seest also what a company of my Fathers host I have lodged within thy borders, Captains and Rulers, Souldiers and men of war, Engines and excellent devices to subdue and bring down thy foes; thou knowest my meaning, O Mansoul. *And they are my servants, & thine too,* Mansoul. *Yea, my design of possessing of thee with them, and the natural tendency of each of them is to defend, purge, strengthen, and sweeten thee for my self,* O Mansoul, *and to make thee meet for my Fathers presence, blessing and glory; for thou, my* Mansoul, *art created to be prepared unto these.*

Thou seest moreover, my Mansoul, *how I have passed by thy backslidings, and have healed thee. Indeed I was angry with thee, but I have turned mine anger away from thee, because I loved thee still, and mine anger and mine indignation is ceased in the destruction of thine enemies,* O Mansoul. *Nor did thy goodness fetch me again unto thee, after that I for thy transgressions have hid my face, and withdrawn my presence from thee. The way of back-sliding was thine, but the way and means of thy recovery was* mine. *I invented the means of thy return; it was I that made an hedge and a wall, when thou wast beginning to turn to things in which I delighted not. 'Twas I that made thy sweet, bitter; thy day, night; thy smooth way, thorny, and that also confounded all that sought thy destruction. 'Twas I that set Mr.* Godlyfear *to work in* Mansoul. *'Twas I that stirred up thy* Conscience *and* Understanding, *thy* Will *and thy* Affections, *after thy great and woful decay. 'Twas I that put life into thee,* O Mansoul, *to seek me, that thou mightest find me, and in thy finding find thine own health, happiness and salvation. 'Twas I that fetched the second time the* Diabolonians *out of* Mansoul*; and 'twas I that overcame them, and that destroyed them before thy face.*

And now, my Mansoul, *I am returned to thee in peace, and thy transgressions against me, are as if they had not been. Nor shall it be with thee as in former days, but I will do better for thee than at thy beginning. For yet a little while, O my* Mansoul, *even after a few more times are gone over thy head, I will (but be not thou troubled at what I say) take down this famous Town of* Mansoul, *stick and stone, to the ground. And will carry the stones thereof, and the timber thereof, and the walls thereof, and the dust thereof, and the inhabitants thereof, into mine own Country, even into the Kingdom of my Father; and will there set it up in such strength and glory, as it never did see in the Kingdom where now it is placed. I will even there set it up for my Fathers habitation, for, for that purpose it was at first erected in the Kingdom of* Universe; *and there will I make it a spectacle of wonder, a monument of mercy, and the admirer of its own mercy. There shall the Natives of* Mansoul *see all that of which they have seen nothing here; there shall they be equal to those unto whom they have been inferiour here. And there shalt thou, O my* Mansoul, *have such communion with me, with my Father, and with your Lord* Secretary, *as is not possible here to be enjoyed. Nor ever could be, shouldest thou live in* Universe *the space of a thousand years.* 1 Chr. 29. 30

And there, O my Mansoul, *thou shalt be afraid of murderers, no more; of* Diabolonians, *and their threats, no more. There, there shall be no more Plots, nor contrivances, nor designs against thee, O my* Mansoul. *There thou shalt no more hear the evil tidings, or the noise of the* Diabolonian *Drum. There thou shalt not see the* Diabolonian Standard-bearers, *nor yet behold* Diabolus *his Standard. No* Diabolonian *Mount shall be cast up against thee there, nor shall there the* Diabolonian *Standard be set up to make thee afraid. There thou shalt not need Captains, Engines, Souldiers, and men of war. There thou shalt meet with no sorrow, nor grief, nor shall it be possible that any* Diabolonian *should again (for ever) be able to creep into thy skirts, burrow in thy walls, or be seen again within thy borders all the days of eternity. Life shall there last longer, than here you are able to desire it should, and yet it shall always be sweet and new, nor shall any impediment attend it for ever.*

There, O Mansoul, *thou shalt meet with many of those that have been like thee, and that have been partakers of thy sorrows; even such as I have chosen, and redeemed and set apart as thou for my Fathers Court and City Royal. All they will be glad in thee, and thou when thou seest them, shalt be glad in thine heart.*

There are things, O Mansoul, *even things of thy Fathers providing and mine, that never were seen since the beginning of the world, and they are laid up with my Father, and sealed up among his Treasures for thee, till thou shalt come thither to enjoy them. I told you before that I would remove my* Mansoul, *and set it up else-where, and where I will set it, there are those that love thee, and those that rejoice in thee now, but how much more when they shall see thee exalted to honour. My Father will then send them for you to fetch you; and their bosoms* Psal. 68. 17. *are chariots to put you in. And you, O my* Mansoul, *shall ride upon the wings of the wind. They will come to convey, conduct, and bring you to that, when your eyes see more, that will be your desired haven.*

And thus, O my Mansoul, *I have shewed unto thee what shall be done to thee hereafter, if thou canst hear, if thou canst understand; and now I will tell thee what at present must be thy duty and practice, until I shall come and fetch thee to my self, according as is related in the Scriptures of truth.*

First, *I charge thee that thou dost hereafter keep more white and clean the liveries which I gave thee before my last withdrawing from thee. Do it, I say, for this will be thy wisdom. They are in themselves fine linnen, but thou must keep them white and clean. This will be your wisdom, your honour, and will be greatly for my glory. When your Garments are white, the world will count you mine. Also when your garments are white, then I am delighted in your ways; for then your goings to and fro will be like a flash of lightning, that those that are present must take notice of, also their eyes will be made to dazle thereat. Deck thy self therefore according to my bidding, and make thy self by my Law straight steps for thy feet, so shall thy King greatly desire thy beauty, for he is thy Lord, and worship thou him.*

Now that thou maist keep them as I bid thee, I have, as I before did tell thee, provided for thee an open fountain to wash thy garments in. Look therefore that thou wash often in my fountain, and go not in defiled garments; for as it is to my dishonour, and my disgrace, so it Zach. 3. 1, 2. *will be to thy discomfort, when you shall walk in filthy garments. Let not therefore my garments, your garments, the garments that* Jude *v.* 23. *I gave thee, be defiled or spotted by the flesh. Keep thy garments always white, and let thy head lack no ointment.*

My Mansoul, *I have oft-times delivered thee from the designs, plots, attempts, and conspiracies of* Diabolus, *and for all this I ask thee nothing, but that thou render not to me evil for my good, but that thou bear in mind my love, and the continuation of my kindness to my beloved* Mansoul, *so as to provoke thee to walk, in thy measure, according to the benefit bestowed on thee. Of old the Sacrifices were bound with cords to the horns of the Golden altar. Consider what is said to thee, O my blessed* Mansoul.

O my Mansoul, *I have lived, I have died, I live, and will die no more for thee. I live that thou maist not die. Because I live shalt thou live also. I reconciled thee to my Father by the blood of my Cross, and being reconciled thou shalt live through me. I will pray for thee, I will fight for thee, I will yet do thee good.*

Nothing can hurt *thee but sin; nothing can* grieve *me but sin; nothing can make thee base before thy foes but sin: Take heed of sin, my* Mansoul.

And dost thou know why I at first, and do still suffer Diabolonians *to dwell in thy* walls, *O* Mansoul*? it is to keep thee wakening, to try thy love, to make thee watchful, and to cause thee yet to prize my noble* Captains, *their Souldiers, and my mercy.*

It is also that yet thou maist be made to remember what a deplorable condition thou once wast in. I mean when, not some, but all did dwell, not in thy walls, but in thy Castle, and in thy strong hold, O Mansoul.

O my Mansoul, *should I slay all them within, many there be* without *that would bring thee into bondage; for were all those within cut off, those without would find thee sleeping, and then as in a moment they would swallow up my* Mansoul. *I therefore left them in thee, not to do thee hurt, (the which they yet will, if thou hearken to them, and serve them) but to do thee good, the which they must if thou watch and fight against them. Know therefore that whatever they shall tempt thee to, my design is that they should drive thee, not further off, but nearer to my Father, to learn thee war, to make Petitioning desirable to thee, and to make thee little in thine own eyes. Hearken diligently to this my* Mansoul.

Shew me then thy love my Mansoul, *and let not those that are within thy walls, take thy affections off from him that hath redeemed thy soul. Yea, let the sight of a* Diabolonian *heighten thy love to me. I came once and twice, and thrice to save thee from the poyson of those arrows that would have wrought thy death; stand for me, thy friend, my* Mansoul, *against the* Diabolonians, *and I will stand for thee before my Father, and all his Court. Love me against temptation, and I will love thee notwithstanding thine infirmities.*

O my Mansoul, *remember what my Captains, my Souldiers, and mine Engines have done for thee. They have fought for thee, they have suffered by thee, they have born much at thy hands to do thee good, O* Mansoul. *Hadst thou not had them to help thee,* Diabolus *had certainly made a hand of thee. Nourish them therefore my* Mansoul. *When thou dost* well, *they will be* well, *when thou dost* ill, *they will be* ill, *and sick, and weak. Make not my Captains sick, O* Mansoul, *for if they be sick, thou canst not be well; if they be weak, thou canst not be strong; if they be faint, thou canst not be stout and valiant for thy King, O* Mansoul. *Nor must thou think always to live by sense, thou must live upon my Word. Thou must believe, O my* Mansoul, *when I am from thee, that yet I love thee, and bear thee upon mine heart for ever.*

Remember therefore, O my Mansoul, *that thou art beloved of me; as I have therefore taught thee to watch, to fight, to pray, and to make war against my foes, so now I command thee to believe that my love is constant to thee. O my* Mansoul, *how have I set my heart, my love upon thee, watch.* Behold, I lay none other burden upon thee, than what thou hast already, hold fast till I come.

FINIS

An ADVERTISEMENT *to the* READER

SOme say the *Pilgrims Progress* is not mine,
Insinuating as if I would shine
In name and fame by the worth of another,
Like some made rich by robbing of their Brother.
Or that so fond I am of being Sire,
I'le father Bastards: or if need require,
I'le tell a lye in Print to get applause.
I scorn it; *John* such dirt-heap never was,
Since God converted him. Let this suffice
To shew why I my *Pilgrim* Patronize.
It came from mine own heart, so to my head,
And thence into my fingers trickled;
Then to my Pen, from whence immediately
On Paper I did dribble it daintily.
Manner and matter too was all mine own,
Nor was it unto any mortal known,
'Till I had done it. Nor did any then
By Books, by wits, by tongues, or hand, or pen,
Add five words to it, or wrote half a line
Thereof: the whole, and ev'ry whit is mine.
Also for *This*, thine eye is now upon,
The matter in this manner came from none
But the same heart, and head, fingers and pen,
As did the other. Witness all good men;
For none in all the world without a lye,
Can say that this is mine, excepting I.
I write not this of any ostentation,
Nor 'cause I seek of men their commendation;
I do it to keep them from such surmize,
As tempt them will my name to scandalize.
Witness my name, if Anagram'd to thee,
The Letters make, *Nu hony in a B.*

JOHN BUNYAN.

NOTES

p. 1, l. 5. *historiology*: 'the knowledge and telling of old Histories' (Bullokar, 1616).

p. 1, l. 6. *Mansoul's Wars*. The image of the human soul as a city besieged by the devil and the vices is very old and is commonly found associated with the general theme of the *psychomachia* or war between virtues and vices; the first extended literary treatment is the *Psychomachia* of Prudentius (fourth century), but the tower or city of the soul is found as early as *The Shepherd of Hermas* (before 148 A.D.) and the *Homilies* of St. Macarius the Egyptian (300–90 A.D.). The idea of a castle defended by the virtues was made popular by the Anglo-French *Chasteau d'amour* written about 1230 by Robert Grosseteste, Bishop of Lincoln; there were several English prose adaptations. In the *Ancren Riwle*, also thirteenth century, man is a castle defended by the ditch of humiliation. In a Middle English homily the five senses are the gates of the soul by which sin enters, as in Bunyan (Richard Morris (ed.), *Old English Homilies and Homilectic Treatises . . . of the Twelfth and Thirteenth Centuries*, E.E.T.S. 34 (1868), pp. 150–5). In the early thirteenth century *Sawles Warde*, which is based loosely on Hugo of St. Victor, *De Anima*, iv. 13–15, man is a castle of which Wit is the master and Will his wife (cf. Bunyan's Mr. Understanding and Lord Wilbewill). (R. M. Wilson (ed.), *Sawles Warde. An Early Middle English Homily*, Leeds School of English Texts and Monographs, iii (Leeds, 1938).) In the final apocalyptic episode of *Piers Plowman* (late fourteenth century) Antichrist assembles an army against true Christians who are besieged in the city of unity. The siege of the virtues is also found in *The Myroure of Our Ladye*, probably by Thomas Gascoigne (*c.* 1415–30), and in the dramatically powerful *The Castle of Perseverance* (*c.* 1420), one of the morality plays in the Macro MS. The medieval tradition and its antecedents are fully described in Morton W. Bloomfield, *The Seven Deadly Sins* (East Lansing, 1952), *passim*. The tradition is continued in the allegory of the siege of the House of Alma (the soul) in Spenser, *The Faerie Queene*, Book II, canto ix. We do not know whether there was a siege in the lost play on the Seven Deadly Sins by the comedian Richard Tarlton (d. 1588). Bunyan's allegory, as with his treatment of the pilgrimage of the soul, is more likely to have been influenced by the popular sermon tradition than by written sources. In the Dominican John Bromyard's *Summa Praedicantium*, a manual for preachers (*c.* 1370), a symbolic fortress of the soul is described under the heading *anima*; see G. R. Owst, *Literature and Pulpit in Medieval England* (Cambridge, 1933), pp. 56–109.

p. 1, l. 17. *raise such mountains*: tell exaggerated stories, 'make a mountain out of a molehill'. 'And mole-hill faults to Mountains multiply', Phineas Fletcher, *The Purple Island* (1633), vii. 53.

p. 1, l. 30. *Anatomize*: analyse, digest (with 'Mansoul and her wars' as the object).

p. 2, l. 8. *Diabolus, in his possession.* The Latin name for the devil is in keeping with the higher, epic style of *H.W.*; but cf. Apollyon, *P.P.*, 56–60. '... it was my delight to be taken captive by the Devil *at his will*' (*G.A.*, p. 6). 2 Tim. 2: 26.

p. 2, l. 15. *Emanuel*: 'which being interpreted is, God with us' (Matt. 1: 23).

p. 2, l. 31. *Primum mobile*: the soul.

p. 2, l. 33. *slings*: the books of the New Testament assaulting Ear-gate; see p. 51, l. 2.

p. 3, l. 3. *Rams*: the books of the Old Testament; see p. 51, l. 4.

p. 3, l. 23. *Boanerges*: 'sons of thunder', the name given by Christ to the impetuous James and John, who wished to call down fire from heaven on the Samaritan villages who would not receive their Lord: Mark 3: 17; Luke 9: 51–6.

p. 3, l. 35. *clad all in white*: '... they which ... have washed their robes, and made them white in the blood of the Lamb' (Rev. 7: 13–14).

p. 5, ll. 11–12. *a world they will / Have in each Star.* Bunyan may have heard at second hand through Owen of the speculations of John Wilkins, Cromwell's brother-in-law, Warden of Wadham College, Oxford, Bishop of Chester, and a founder member of the Royal Society; in his work on a plurality of worlds Wilkins even envisages space travel (*The First Book. The Discovery of a New World or, A Discourse tending to prove that 'tis probable there may be another habitable World in the Moon* (1640), p. 206).

p. 5, l. 16. *kept thee from the sunshine with a torch*: allowed you only a glimpse of the truth.

p. 5, l. 26. *with my heifer plow*: Judg. 14: 18.

p. 5, l. 27. *in the window*: in the marginal notes.

p. 8, l. 4. *the two worlds*: heaven and hell.

p. 8, l. 6. *Shaddai*: the Hebrew name for God indicating his omnipotence and transcendence; used especially in Job and Revelation.

p. 8, l. 10. *Gods*: angels.

p. 8, l. 11. *and sang for joy*: 'and all the sons of God shouted for joy' (Job 39: 7).

p. 9, l. 16. *Diabolus*: Matt. 4: 1; Rev. 12: 9.

p. 10, l. 12. *the very nick, and first Tripp*: the moment they took their first step: cf. Tilley N160.

p. 11, l. 1. *roared on it as a Lyon*: 1 Pet. 5: 8.

p. 11, l. 37–p. 12, l. 1. *that fierce Alecto*: one of the classical Furies, and female; see *Aeneid*, vii. 323 f.

p. 12, l. 1. *Apollyon*: the demon in dragon shape beaten off by Christian in *P.P.*, pp. 56–60; also pp. 74, 240; Rev. 9: 11.

p. 12, l. 7. *Beelzebub*: 'prince of devils', Matt. 12: 24; 'One next himself [Satan] in power, and next in crime', *Paradise Lost*, i. 79.

p. 12, l. 37. *Legion*: a confusion of the unclean spirit whose name was Legion (Mark 5: 9).

p. 13, ll. 2–3. *what time of day 'twill be with us*: what our situation will be then (cf. Tilley O10).

p. 13, l. 34. *Tisiphane, a fary of the Lake*: another of the classical Furies.

p. 14, l. 13. *My Lord Wilbewill*: 'I tell you the will is all: that is one of the chief things which turns the wheel either backwards or forwards; and God knoweth that full well, and so likewise doth the devil; and therefore they both endeavour very much to strengthen the will of their servants. God, he is for making of his willing people to serve him; and the devil, he doth what he can to possess the will and affection of those that are his, with love to sin . . .' (*The Heavenly Footman*, Offor, iii. 383).

p. 14, l. 14. *Mr. Recorder*: the conscience.

p. 16, l. 23. *Congee* (later *congy*): a low bow.

p. 16, l. 33. *my Lord Innocency . . . sunk down.* The death of Innocency marks the very moment of the Fall, though Bunyan mingles with his allegory the (unallegorical) story of the forbidden fruit, Gen. 3: 3–6. In terms of the individual as distinct from the historical allegory his death and the previous slaying of Captain Resistance indicate the Christian's gradual moral decline once he has succumbed to temptation:

> And, if you grant its [sin's] first suit, 'twill aspire
> From pence to pounds, and so will mount still higher
> To the whole soul.
>
> (*A Caution to Stir up to Watch against Sin in Poems*, vol. vi, p. 177, l. 7–p. 178, l. 9; Offor, ii. 575.)

p. 17, ll. 10–11. *they looked, they considered, they were taken*: corresponding to the traditional three stages of the Fall: suggestion, pleasure, consent; Augustine, *On the Sermon on the Mount* in *Nicene and Post-Nicene Fathers*, ed. Philip Schaff (New York, 1886–90), vi. 15–16; Milton, *De Doctrina Christiana* in *Works*, eds. F. A. Patterson *et al.*, 18 vols. in 21 (New York: Columbia University Press, 1931–8), xv. 193 ff.

p. 17, l. 31. *this Bramble.* The useless bramble, who cannot give shade or protection, accepts the monarchy of the trees in the fable spoken by Jotham from Mount Gerizim; Judg. 9: 7–21; again used symbolically in *Ebal and Gerizzim; or, The Blessing and the Curse*, published with *One Thing is Needful* (3rd edn., 1683), *Poems*, vol. vi, pp. 122–8; Offor, iii. 737–43.

p. 18, ll. 7–8. *new modelling the Town.* The remodelling of corporations all over England in the last years of Charles II was aimed at the control of the boroughs by the royal party and the undermining of the influence of Whigs, Exclusionists, and Dissenters. See David Ogg, *England in the Reign of Charles II* (Oxford, 1956), ii. 634–9; the procedure was to obtain the surrender of the old charters of corporations and the acceptance of new ones. The new charter of Bedford corporation was allowed to pass all its seals and offices gratis on 1 Jan. 1684, but it had been gradually prepared for in the preceding years, especially by a campaign against the Dissenting burgesses undertaken by the local magnate, the Earl of Ailesbury, and others; see *C.S.P.D. 1682*, 1 June and 9 Dec., p. 226; *1 July 1683–5 February 1685* (3 vols., 1934–8), i. 226, ii. 35, 195, 286, 390.

p. 18, marg. The second edition scripture reference has been preferred to that in the first, which seems to be a slip: 'In whom the god of this world hath blinded the minds of them which believe not, lest the light of the glorious gospel of Christ, who is the image of God, should shine unto them' (2 Cor. 4: 4).

p. 18, ll. 32–3. *Mr. Recorder . . . was a man well read in the Laws of his King.* It was customary for a Recorder to have legal experience, but some of the royal appointments after the Corporation Act of 1661 offended against this principle. For the importance of the office in the period of remodelling see Peter Styles, 'The Corporation of Bewdley under the Later Stuarts', *University of Birmingham Historical Journal*, i (1948–9), 92–133, esp. p. 111.

p. 23, ll. 2–3. *some old, rent, and torn parchments*: Bunyan's allusion to the forthcoming reform of the old charter at Bedford. In the spring of 1681 the town chamberlains were suspended for not having taken the sacrament within twelve months of their election; the Recorder, Robert Audley, successfully resisted the Earl of Ailesbury's request for his dismissal in December by an appeal to the King (cf. p. 22, l. 34: 'he maligned Mr. Recorder to death'); *Minute Book of Bedford Corporation*, quot. Brown, p. 318.

p. 23, marg. Neh. 9: 26: 'Nevertheless they were disobedient, and rebelled against thee, and cast thy law behind their backs, and slew thy prophets which testified against them to turn them to thee, and they wrought great provocations.'

p. 23, marg. See also Rom. 1: 26: 'For this cause God gave them up unto vile affections . . .'

p. 23, ll. 25–6. *like to like quoth the Devil to the Collier*: proverb based on the popular notion of the devil as a black man; Tilley L287; also quoted by Bunyan in *Badman*, ed. Harrison, p. 263.

p. 24, l. 16. *Documents*: teaching precepts.

p. 24, ll. 16–17. *relative severities*: corresponding penalties.

p. 24, ll. 24–5. *and they set up his own vain edicts*. On 22 Feb. 1684 Bedford Corporation prayed for a regrant of the surrendered charter 'with such alterations and additions as his Majesty shall think fit' (*C.S.P.D. 1683–5*, ii. 286).

p. 24, l. 20. *the sensual sow*: see 2 Pet. 2: 22.

p. 25, l. 27. *Grammer and settle*: instruct and stregthen.

p. 25, ll. 31–2. *Diabolus made several Burgesses, and Aldermen*. Cf. 'The *Scrutiny* all over the Kingdom, to find out men of *Arbitrary Principles*, that will *Bow the knee to Baal*, in order to their Promotion to all Publick Commissions and imployments' (Andrew Marvell, *An Account of the Growth of Popery and Arbitrary Government* (1677), p. 154). The names of the new magistrates which follow bear some resemblance to the catalogue of the jury of vices which tries Christian and Faithful in Vanity Fair, though no particular name is reproduced: *P.P.*, pp.96–7.

p. 27, l. 12. *to a very circumstance*: in exact detail.

p. 29, ll. 7–8. *having stricken hands with his Father*: in conformity with Jewish custom; see Job 17: 3, Prov. 6: 1, 17: 18, 22: 26.

p. 29, l. 32. *molestation*: vexation.

p. 31, l. 17. *a new Oath, and horrible covenant*: an allusion to a new municipal charter in Bunyan's England.

p. 31, l. 35. *Mr. Filth*: possibly a covert reference to Sir Roger L'Estrange, Charles II's licenser of the press, who wrote some witty and vigorous pamphlets against Nonconformists, including *An Account of the Growth of Knavery under the Pretended Fears of Arbitrary Government* (2nd edn., 1681), a reply to Marvell's *An Account of the Growth of Popery . . .* (1677).

p. 33, l. 15. *die the death*: an A.V. Hebraism.

p. 34, marg. Rev. 9: 9.: 'And they had breastplates, as it were breastplates of iron' (of the locusts from the bottomless pit).

p. 34, marg. Ps. 64: 3: 'Who whet their tongue like a sword, and bend their bows to shoot their arrows, even bitter words.'

p. 34, marg. Job 15: 26: 'He runneth upon him, even upon his neck, upon the thick bosses of his bucklers.'

p. 35, l. 14. *Armour of proof*. The whole catalogue of Diabolus's armour is a parody with mock heroic overtones of Paul's description of 'the whole armour of God' (Eph. 6).

p. 35, l. 15. *a Maul*: a club; but cf. Giant Maul who 'did use to spoyl young Pilgrims with Sophistry', *P.P.*, pp. 244–5, 276, and who probably stands for the Roman Catholic Church; cf. also *The Jerusalem Sinner Saved*, Offor, i. 96: 'This is Satan's master argument . . . I say this is his maul, his club, his master-piece' (where the subject is Satan's ability to undermine the confidence of the convert).

p. 36, ll. 13–14. *The Army consisted of above forty thousand*: 'O! that one sentence of the Scripture did more afflict and terrify my mind, I mean those sentences that stood against me . . . more, I say, than an Army of forty thousand men that might have come against me' (*G.A.*, § 246, p. 77).

p. 36, ll. 18–21. *their names and their signs . . . Boanerges . . . Conviction . . . Judgment . . . Execution*: 'And James the son of Zebedee, and John the brother of James; and he surnamed them Boanerges, which is, The sons of thunder' (Mark 3: 17). The other names refer to the awakening Christian's conviction of sin and to its consequence, his contemplation of the final judgement and of the execution of the divine condemnation of sin. Richard L. Greaves has argued for another level of allegory by which Shaddai's four captains would represent four outstanding London Nonconformist preachers of the time, John Owen, George Cokayne, George Griffith, and Anthony Palmer (*Baptist Quarterly* (1975), 158–68).

p. 36, l. 27. *fit to break the ice*: 'After he had a while look'd wise, / At last broke silence, and the *Ice*' (Butler, *Hudibras*, III. ii. 493–4).

p. 36, l. 29. *To each . . . a Banner*. The emblematic standards of the captains symbolize the terrors of the old law. In the Parliamentary armies of the Civil War each company of foot or troop of horse had its distinguishing standard, some of them emblematic; see Sir Charles Firth, *Cromwell's Army* (1912), p. 45.

p. 37, l. 9. *a fruitless tree*. The image of the barren fig-tree from the parable in Luke 12: 6–9 was a favourite with Puritan preachers who applied it to the fruitless professor who does not give evidence of saving faith in his actions. Bunyan devoted a treatise to the theme (*The Barren Fig-tree*, 1673).

p. 38, l. 34. *not hurting or abusing any*. The good discipline of Cromwell's Ironsides is described by Baxter, *Reliquiae Baxterianae* (1696), i. 43–4. Note below that 'they lived upon the Kings cost' and not on the country.

p. 39, l. 31. *cap-a-pe*: (accoutrements) from head to foot. Cf. *Hamlet*, I. ii. 199–200.

p. 39, l. 36. *a been*. This unemphatic colloquial form of 'have' is also found in *P.P.*, first edition. Cf. the unemphatic 'a' for 'of' in 'push a pike' below.

p. 40, ll. 6–7. *Iron . . . the nether Milstone*: 'His heart is as firm as a stone; yea, as hard as a piece of the nether millstone' (Job 41: 24).

p. 41, ll. 11–12. *a Council of War*: 'But now, when a Councel is held in *eternity* about the Salvation of sinners in *time* . . .' (*Saved by Grace*, *1692 Folio*, p. 565).

p. 42, l. 4. *lift up the heel*: Ps. 41: 9.

p. 42, ll. 24–5. *you shall see the black Flag . . . upon the mount tomorrow*. The parallel to the black tents of Tamburlaine, indicating, after successive white and red ones, the total destruction of a besieged city, may be coincidental (Marlowe, *1 Tamburlaine*, IV. ii. 111–22).

p. 43, marg. Zach. 7: 11: 'But they refused to hearken, and pulled away the shoulder, and stopped their ears, that they should not hear.'

p. 45, l. 28. *if he touches the Mountains they smoak*: Ps. 104: 32.

p. 45, l. 34. *golden Scepter*: Esther 5: 2.

p. 47, l. 1. *is required thy repentance*: 'If timely repentance prevent not, the end of that soul is damnation' (*The Barren Fig-tree*, Offor, iii. 573).

p. 47, ll. 10–11. *a three years rebellion*: 'Behold, these three years I come seeking fruit on this fig tree' (Luke 13: 7).

p. 47, l. 18. *a cumber ground*: 'A cumber-ground professor is not only a provocation to God, a stumbling-block to the world, and a blemish to religion, but a snare to his own soul also' (*The Barren Fig-tree*, Offor, iii. 561).

p. 50, l. 6. *mattered*: regarded as of no importance.

p. 50, l. 16. *the word*: in seventeenth-century armies a word or phrase serving as a recognition signal or charging-cry on the field of battle; that of Cromwell's army at Dunbar was 'The sword of the Lord and of Gideon'. See M. A. Denham, *Slogans of War and Gathering Cries* (Newcastle, 1851). On the place of the war-cry in the O.T. holy war tradition see Gerhard von Rad, *Der heilige Krieg im Alten Israel* (Zürich, 1951).

p. 51, ll. 24–5. Mr. *Tradition*, Mr. *Human-wisdom*, and Mr. *Mans Invention*. Strictures on the insufficiency of human learning are frequent in Bunyan's doctrinal works and sermons: 'Take notice of this, you that are the despisers of the least of the Lazaruses of our Lord Jesus Christ; it may be now ye are loath to receive these little ones of his, because they are not gentlemen, because they cannot, with Pontius Pilate, speak Hebrew, Greek, and Latin' (*A Few Sighs from Hell*, Offor, iii. 695).

p. 52, l. 31. *Ancient-Bearer*: standard-bearer.

p. 53, l. 2. *Mr. Swearing*: 'But how it came to pass I know not, I did from this time forward so leave my swearing, that it was a great wonder to my self to observe it' (*G.A.*, § 28, p. 12).

p. 54, l. 2. *I doubt he will not receive us*: 'At this I felt my own heart began to shake, as mistrusting my condition to be nought' (*G.A.*, § 39, p. 15).

p. 54, marg. *Conscience speaks*: 'For my conscience now was sore, and would smart at every touch' (*G.A.*, § 82, p. 26).

p. 56, l. 25. 2 Tim. 2: 19: 'Let every one that nameth the name of Christ depart from iniquity.'

p. 57, l. 25. *at their points*: at the sword's point, hence, in fierce debate; 'at the point', *1 Henry IV*, v. iv. 21.

p. 57, ll. 33–4. *rub over this brunt*: clear this hurdle.

p. 62, marg. *revel-rout*: disorderly brawl.

p. 62, l. 21. *closing with our summons*: doing as we have commanded.

p. 62, ll. 32–3. *ye fools delight in your scorning*: Prov. 1: 22.

p. 63, l. 3. *afraid as a Grass-hopper*: Eccles. 12: 5.

p. 63, l. 8. *or stay the bottles of heaven*: Job 38: 37.

p. 64, l. 4. *the thoughts of his holiness, sunk them in despair*: 'Thus, by the strange and unusual assaults of the tempter, was my Soul, like a broken Vessel, driven as with the Winds, and tossed sometimes head-long into dispair' (*G.A.*, § 186 p. 58).

p. 66, ll. 27–8. *I delight to do thy will*: '. . . as a sacrifice / Glad to be offer'd he attends the will / Of his great Father' (*Paradise Lost*, iii. 269–71).

p. 66, ll. 34–5. *he leaped over the mountains for joy*: S. of S. 2: 8.

p. 68, l. 12. *golden shield*: the shield of faith (Eph. 6: 16).

p. 68, ll. 16–17. *three golden anchors*: 'Which hope we have as an anchor of the soul, both sure and stedfast' (Heb. 6: 19); Offor finds another anchor in Joel 3: 16: 'the Lord will be the hope of his people, and the strength of the children of Israel', but is unable to explain the third anchor (Offor, iii. 285). Christiana is given a golden anchor at the House of the Interpreter (*P.P.*, p. 233).

p. 68, ll. 20–1. *three naked Orphans imbraced in the bosom*. This emblem is not explained by the marginal scripture reference as are the colours of the other four captains; charity is often depicted in medieval and Renaissance iconography as a mother-figure surrounded by infants (Forrest, p. 78, and cf. *Macbeth*, I. vii. 21–2: 'Pity, like a naked new-born babe, striding the blast').

p. 68, ll. 25–6. *three Golden Doves*: 'as harmless as doves' (Matt. 10: 16).

p. 68, ll. 29–30. *three Arrows through the Golden Heart*: Ps. 38: 2; 45: 5.

p. 69, l. 4. *the Colours*: as described in the previous list. Bunyan follows traditional colour symbolism which is also often that of ecclesiastical usage: red for faith, blue for hope, green for youth, white for innocence, black for suffering.

p. 69, l. 8. *Reformades*: volunteer officers attached to an army; *O.E.D.*, s.v. *N.Q.* clxvii. 440, clxviii. 52.

p. 69, l. 13. *forty four Battering Rams, and twelve slings*. Something is wrong with the arithmetic since these numbers do not add up to the sixty-six books of the Bible mentioned in the marginal gloss; George Offor remarks 'it would be a task for Aquinus [sic] to discover which are rams and which are slings' (Offor, iii. 286). He proposes a way out of the numerical difficulty by suggesting that the printer mistook 'Mr. Bunyan's figures, 22 for 12', and that the division should be as follows: the forty-four battering rams are the thirty-nine books of the Old Testament with the addition of the Gospels and Acts, and this leaves the Epistles and Revelation for the twenty-two slings. This seems ingenious but not entirely convincing, since no basis for such a separation of the New Testament books can be traced in Bunyan's theology. In the second edition the issue is evaded by the omission of the entire paragraph, while later editions retain the passage and repeat the error. After a mid eighteenth-century edition tacitly alters to 'fifty-four battering-rams', this emendation is apparently followed by all subsequent editors up to Mabel Peacock in her Oxford edition of 1892.

p. 70, ll. 15–36. The parallel between Emanuel's display of the white, red, and black flags and Tamburlaine's tents of the same colours to indicate a mounting threat against a besieged city is a striking one (*1 Tamburlaine*, IV. ii. 111–22; see also n. on p. 77, ll. 28–9). But it should be noted that the display of significant flags follows late medieval military practice; white was the accepted symbol for truce, before battle was to be joined, red the heraldic sign of open war, and black the withholding of quarter. The custom had legal importance 'because deeds done in those circumstances were performed in *actu belli* . . .' (M. H. Keen, *The Laws of War in the Late Middle Ages* (1965), p. 107, and see especially the chapters in that work on 'Signs of War' and 'Sieges').

p. 72, l. 2. *buffed*: blustered. Cf. 'To be expos'd i' the end to suffer / By such a braggadocio *buffer*' (Butler, *Hudibras*, II, iii. 1034–5).

p. 72, l. 12. *and that by a twofold Right*. That Diabolus should appeal to the legality of his conquest is, of course, ironic.

p. 72, ll. 13–14. *And shall the prey . . . delivered?* Isa. 49: 24.

p. 74, l. 27. *The Palace*: the heart, the seat of the soul: see 8, 17–18, 26 etc.

p. 75, l. 8. *by right of purchase*: 'Jesus Christ, by what he hath done, hath paid the full price to God for the souls of sinners' (*Light for Them that Sit in Darkness*, Offor, i. 416). 'Thy Advocate pleads to a price paid, to a propitiation made' (*The Work of Jesus Christ as an Advocate*, Offor, i. 176).

p. 75, l. 20. *became a surety*. On Bunyan's view of the Atonement in terms of a contractual relationship between God and Christ see *Law and Grace*, Oxford Bunyan, ii. 166, 168–92 and Greaves's comment ibid., pp. xxvii–xxviii; cf. *An Exposition of the First Ten Chapters of Genesis, 1692 Folio*, p. 67 (Offor, ii. 491) and *Paradise Lost*, iii. 228–41.

p. 75, ll. 23–4 *life for life*: 'Behold mee then, mee for him, life for life / I offer' (*Paradise Lost*, iii. 236–7).

p. 76, ll. 31–2. *the strong man armed that keeps the house*: Luke 11: 21–2; Isa. 53: 12.

p. 77, ll. 28–9. *to bid Diabolus Battel.* The doctrine of salvation solely by the free grace of Christ involves Bunyan in some difficulty with his fable here. Although Emanuel summons Mansoul to surrender, he must actually take the town by assault so as to establish a suitable image for the supremacy of his imputed righteousness; the call to surrender is thus a mere formality, and yet it does correspond to the formal courtesies of medieval siege-warfare (see Keen, *Laws of War*, pp. 119–20).

p. 78, l. 23. *All that the Father giveth me*, etc.: John 6: 37 and 17: 12.

p. 78, l. 25. *not a hoof, nor a hair*. As 'hair and hoof' the phrase appears in Jean Irvine, *A Collection of Dying Testaments* (1705).

p. 78, l. 31. *as a way-faring man.* The reference is to Nathan's parable of the rich man who steals the poor man's ewe lamb to feed 'the wayfaring man', a parable related in order to denounce David's adultery with Bathsheba (2 Sam. 12: 1–5).

p. 79, ll. 21–2. *some tokens of his love.* The marginal reference to Romans is to the text 'Let not sin therefore reign in your mortal body', addressed to the saved, 'those that are alive from the dead'. The condition Loth-to-stoop refers therefore to the survival of fleshly concupiscence in the justified Christian; and though Emanuel rejects this, the later state of the town is indeed marked by the revival of such concupiscence.

p. 81, marg. *plays the man.* Cf. *P.P.*, p. 117. Cf. Latimer: 'Be of good comfort, Master Ridley, and play the man. We shall this day light such a candle by God's grace in England, as (I trust) shall never be put out.' Foxe, *Actes and Monuments* (1570), p. 1937.

p. 82, ll. 8–9. *at Eyegate . . . they had almost broken it quite open*: 'The serpents that bit the people of old were types of guilt and sin. Now these were fiery serpents, and such as, I think, could fly. Is. xiv. 29. Wherefore, in my judgment, they stung the people about their faces, and so swelled up their eyes, which made it the more difficult for them to look up to the brazen serpent, which was the type of Christ. Jn. iii. 14' (*A Defence of the Doctrine of Justification by Faith*, Offor, i. 320).

p. 82, l. 28. *stickler*: persistent advocate.

p. 83, l. 35. *bend . . . to thy bow*: make obedient to your every whim.

p. 84, ll. 13–14. *a sufficient Ministry, besides Lecturers.* Diabolus is proposing an established church, possibly of a presbyterian kind, like that proposed by the Westminster Assembly. On the duties of the Puritan lecturers in parishes before the Civil War see William Haller, *The Rise of Puritanism* (New York, 1958), p. 53.

p. 85, l. 6. *a curse pronounced against him.* See Gal. 3: 10; also *Law and Grace*, Oxford Bunyan, ii. 57.

p. 85, l. 17. *I am not come to put Mansoul upon works.* Cf. Gal. 2: 16, 3: 11–13.

p. 85, ll. 21–2. *by the Law they cannot obtain mercy*: Rom. 3: 20.

p. 86, l. 33. *the hottest front of the Battel.* There are echoes of 2 Sam. 10: 7–10.

p. 88, l. 24. *a snow-ball loses nothing by rolling*: folk idiom. (Cf. 'News, like a snowball, is more by telling', Tilley N150.)

p. 88, ll. 35–6. *death and destruction now attended Mansoul.* Cf. Bunyan's own terrors of conscience as described in *G.A.*, §§ 84–8, pp. 27–9.

p. 90, l. 8. *they were they that fought with Mauls.* See n. on p. 35, l. 15.

p. 91, ll. 19–20. *as did Josephs Brethren . . . the quite contrary way*: Gen. 44.

p. 91, ll. 27–8. *as an Angel . . . done in the earth*: 2 Sam. 14: 20.

p. 92, ll. 6–7. *as a ball tossed*: Isa. 22: 18. '. . . sometimes one end would be uppermost, and sometimes again the other' (*G.A.*, § 205, p. 65).

p. 92, ll. 13–14. *the Judgment that he had appointed for him*: Jude 6.

p. 92, ll. 15–16. *send him into the deep*: Luke 8: 31.

p. 92, ll. 18–19. *stript him of his armour*: Luke 11: 22.

p. 93, l. 7. *He hath led captivity captive*: Eph. 4: 8; Col. 2: 15.

p. 95, l. 23. *a rope about his head*: 1 Kings 20: 31; 'I thought also of Benhadad's servants, who went with ropes upon their heads to their Enemies for mercy' (*G.A.*, § 251, p. 78).

p. 96, l. 24. *as white as a clout*: like Little-faith, *P.P.*, p. 125.

p. 97, ll. 30–1. *got this story by the end*: an allusion to spinning and to drawing the fibres out from the end of the distaff to spin them into a thread; cf. *P.P.*, p. 2: 'For having now my Method by the end; / Still as I pull'd, it came . . .'

p. 103, ll. 6–7. *death seem'd to sit upon some of their Eyebrows.* The whole episode of the doubts and fears of Mansoul before Emanuel announces his pardon for the town recalls the final stage of Bunyan's spiritual anxieties in *Grace Abounding*; see, for instance, *G.A.*, § 210, p. 66: 'These, as the Elders of the City of Refuge, I saw were to be the Judges both of my Case and me, while I stood with the avenger of blood at my heels, trembling at their Gate for deliverance; also with a thousand fears and mistrusts, that they would shut me out for ever.'

p. 103, ll. 6–7. *they must all drink of the same cup*: Tilley C908; cf. Spenser, *Faerie Queene*, v. i. 15.

p. 106, l. 4. *sealed with seven Seals*: Rev. 5: 1–9.

p. 106, l. 29. *their steps were enlarged*: 'Thou hast enlarged my steps under me; so that my feet did not slip' (2 Sam. 22: 37).

p. 106, ll. 32–3. *this place*: Eze. 3: 12.

p. 107, l. 35. *in White*: Rev. 19: 8.

p. 109, l. 25. *Tabret*: a timbrel or small tabor.

p. 110, l. 34. *They marched, they counter marched*, etc.: another passage which evokes the drill of a seventeenth-century army and which may therefore contain reminiscence of Bunyan's service in the Parliamentary garrison at Newport Pagnell (1644–5).

p. 112, l. 16. *no trust in his Saints*. Cf. Job 4: 18.

p. 112, l. 29. *let light go before, and let love come after*: John 1: 8–9.

p. 113, ll. 12–13. *to gather boughs and flowers*: reminiscent both of the Biblical account of Christ's entry into Jerusalem, Matt. 21: 8, and of the custom of contemporary festivals.

p. 114, l. 5. *to that Captain*: 'purifying their hearts by faith' (Acts 15: 9).

p. 114, marg. Eph. 3: 17: 'That Christ may dwell in your hearts by faith; that ye, being rooted and grounded in love . . .'

p. 115, marg. *Promise after Promise*. The particular promises of God's love in Scripture as additional to the revelation of his general nature and providence: '. . . God hath opened his heart to us in his *word*, and reached out so many sweet *promises* for us to lay hold on, and stooped so low, (by gracious *condescending* mixed with *authority*) as to enter into a covenant with us to perform all things for our good: for *Promises* are (as it were) the stay of the soule in an imperfect condition' (Richard Sibbes, *The Soules Conflict with it selfe, and Victory over it selfe by Faith*, 4th edn. (1651), p. 265).

p. 116, l. 9. *some curious riddles of secrets*. Bunyan's interest in a kind of riddling catechism is demonstrated in the episode at the house of Gaius in the Second Part of *P.P.*, pp. 263–5, when Honest propounds to Gaius a riddle based on the idea that he who gives to the poor increases in riches, and this is followed by others; these riddles bring together his love of similitudes and his concern for growth in spiritual knowledge, and they are closely related to his cultivation of the emblem form, another pursuit of his final decade (*A Book for Boys and Girls: or, Country Rhimes for Children*, 1686).

p. 116, l. 24. *This is the Lamb*, etc.: John 1: 29; Matt. 20: 28; 1 Cor. 10: 4; Heb. 9: 12–14; Num. 19: 2–17; John 10: 9; 14: 6.

p. 117, ll. 1–2. *to new model the Town*: the term usually applied to the reform of corporations in the reign of Charles II, derived from the New Model army commanded by Fairfax and Cromwell in the Civil War. 'The time spent . . . in new modelling their Army' (Clarendon, *The History of the Rebellion and Civil Wars in England* (1707), ii. 630). See n. on p. 18, ll. 7–8.

p. 117, ll. 13–14. *an instrument invented by Emanuel.* From as early as Mason's edition (1782), editors have taken Mouthgate's 'nameless terrible instrument' as 'the prayer of faith', adducing in support Matt. 21: 22, Mark 11: 23, and Heb. 11; but apposite also is Christ's comment on omnipotent prayer in Matt. 18: 18–20, validating the Church's authority to 'bind and loose'. Parallel to Bunyan's description is Bishop Henry Hammond's definition of 'binding and loosing' as 'only an engine of *Christ's* invention to make a battery and an impression on the obdurate sinner' (*Of the Power of the Keyes: or, of Binding and Loosing* (London, 1674), p. 86). Cf. Benjamin Keach: '[Prayer is] like an Engine (as one observes) that makes the Persecutors tremble; and woe to them that are the Buts and Marks that it is levell'd at, when it is fired with the Fire of the Spirit, and discharged in the Strength of Faith' (*Troposchemalogia: Tropes and Figures*, etc. (London, 1682), p. 161). But the paradox involved, that prayer is a weapon divinely appointed to be turned not only against sinners, but also against God Himself, is commonly celebrated among religious writers of the seventeenth century: hence, e.g., Herbert, 'Engine against th' Almightie' ('Prayer (1)', l. 6); and Donne, 'a Canon against God himselfe' (*Sermons*, ed. G. R. Potter and E. M. Simpson, 10 vols. (Berkeley and Los Angeles, 1953–62), iii. 152–3). Cf. also 'Prayers like petards break open heaven gate' (Tilley P557). Bunyan's allegory popularly expresses a sense of this boundless Christian resource that may similarly inform the compacted vision of Milton's 'two-handed engine' (*Lycidas*, ll. 130–1).

p. 118, l. 4. *Mr. Knowledg.* The new recorder is really the instructed conscience; he is evidence of Bunyan's consistent interest in growth in grace and knowledge: '. . . as grace makes men children of God . . . so also it maketh them fathers and ancients in his church; it makes them grave, knowing, solid guides, and unfolders of the mysteries of the kingdom; these are such as are instructed into the kingdom of God, and that can bring out of their treasury things new and old' (*The Holy City*, Offor, iii. 452).

p. 118, l. 17. *his name*: Rev. 3: 12.

p. 119, l. 11. *the time was come, and the Court set.* The working knowledge of court procedure which persecution had imposed upon Bunyan serves him well in the account of the trial of the Diabolonians, as it had done in the description of the trial of Christian and Faithful at Vanity Fair (*P.P.*, pp. 92–7). The prisoners are pinioned and chained as was the practice in treason cases; False-peace denies the indictment by asserting that he is not the person charged: 'not *False-peace* but *Peace*' (p. 125, l. 23). This reflects the importance under seventeenth-century English criminal law of extreme care in the wording of the indictment: a misnomer, or inaccurate naming or entitling of the prisoner, could lead to a defence plea that the whole indictmnet was invalid, so that it would become necessary for a new bill to be drawn up (Blackstone, *Commentaries on the Laws of England* (1766–9), iv. 301, 328; Sir

William Holdsworth, *A History of English Law*, iii (1923), 614–31). But the change of names on the part of the vices belongs to the morality tradition and reappears in Puritan literature; it occurs in Skelton's *Magnyfycence* (1533) and in the Leveller Richard Overton's *The Araignment of Mr. Persecution* where the villain of the title gives his name in court as 'Present Reformation'. An allegorical trial scene which in some ways anticipates that in *The Holy War* is found in Richard Bernard, *The Isle of Man, or the Legall Proceedings in Manshire against Sin* (1627). See Roger Sharrock, 'The Trial of Vices in Puritan Fiction', *Baptist Quarterly*, xiv (1951), 3–12, and Sharrock, pp. 131–2.

p. 120, l. 5. *pestilent fellow*: Acts 24: 5. Bunyan was called 'a pestilent fellow' in court by Justice Chester (*A Relation of my Imprisonment*, in *G.A.*, p. 127).

p. 121, l. 23. *snub'd*: reprimanded.

p. 124, l. 3. *Forget-good, Forget-good.* Repetition of the name of the accused seems to have been a habit of Jeffreys when addressing prisoners from the bench; e.g. to Richard Baxter: 'Richard, Richard, dost thou think we will let thee poison the court?' (*Reliquiae Baxterianae* (1696), p. 257.).

p. 125, l. 32. *Gossips*: Godparents. (Middle English *gossib*: related in God.)

p. 126, ll. 28–9. *the prisoner at the Bar hath denied his name.* See note on p. 119, l. 11. It is to be noted that at the beginning of Bunyan's first imprisonment Sir Matthew Hale advised Elizabeth Bunyan to apply for a writ of error (i.e. a plea of error in the indictment which would make the prosecution's case invalid).

p. 127, l. 4. *Hold, give him his Oath.* The interruption of an over-zealous witness so that he may be sworn also occurs at the trial of Christian and Faithful before Lord Hate-good in Vanity Fair (*P.P.*, p. 93).

p. 129, l. 18. *the horned image*: the traditional image of Astarte, the Assyrian Istar, a moon goddess. Milton, *Paradise Lost*, i. 439. See also John Selden, *De Dis Syris* (1629), p. 246, Milton, *Ode on the Morning of Christ's Nativity*, 200, and Jer. 7: 18. But there is probably no need to look further than the folk characteristics of the Devil for Diabolus's horns.

p. 130, l. 1. *bowels of compassion.* This use of the Old Testament form 'bowels' to express mercy or tenderness (see Isa. 63: 15, Jer. 31: 20, 1 Kgs. 3: 26, etc.) is a favourite with Bunyan. Cf. 'Bowels becometh Pilgrims' in *P.P.*, p. 186. It was, however, common Puritan usage, as is illustrated in the title of Richard Sibbes's book, *Bowels Opened.*

p. 130, l. 2. *condole*: the transitive use is common in Bunyan, e.g. *P.P.*, pp. 9, 114.

p. 131, l. 2. *hang down the head like a bulrush.* Cf. the phrase 'weak as a bulrush'.

p. 131, l. 3. *veil*: doff, lower.

p. 131, l. 33. . . . *the Foreman, began.* The omission from the statements that follow of any by Mr. Upright is probably a slip. The technique of having a short statement in character for each allegorical member of the jury parallels a similar passage in the trial at Vanity Fair, *P.P.*, pp. 96–7.

p. 133, l. 4. *Incredulity by name.* The escape of Incredulity, which is the key to the rest of the story, signifies that it is the lack of an entire faith in God, and therefore in the sureness of its own election, that is the cause of the later troubles of Mansoul.

p. 134, l. 25. *the Cross*: the instrument of crucifixion, rather than the market-cross, the traditional site of public executions. '. . . if ye through the Spirit do mortify the deeds of the body, ye shall live' (Rom. 8: 13).

p. 135, ll. 9–10. *put his hands upon the hands of the men of Mansoul*: as when Elisha placed his hands upon those of Joash to shoot the arrow of deliverance (2 Kgs. 13: 14–19).

p. 136, l. 31. *the dead Lion, and dead Bear*: 'The Lord that delivered me out of the paw of the lion, and out of the paw of the bear, he will deliver me out of the hand of this Philistine' (1 Sam. 17: 37).

p. 137, l. 6. *renew their Charter*. Cf. pp. 25 ff. The formal charter is an admirable vehicle to express the rationalistic and legalistic implications of seventeenth-century covenant theology: 'I am willing to enter into Covenant with thee, that is, I will binde my selfe, I will ingage my selfe, I will enter into bond, as it were, I will not bee at liberty any more, but I am willing even to make a Covenant, a compact and agreement with thee' (John Preston quoted in Perry Miller, 'The Marrow of Puritan Divinity', *Transactions of the Colonial Society of Massachusetts* (1933–7), p. 263).

p. 139, l. 15. *the Lord chief Secretary*: the Holy Ghost.

p. 139, ll. 34–5. *your other Teacher*. The role of Mr. Conscience as subordinate teacher has not yet been defined.

p. 140, l. 27. *terrene*: '. . . That blessed souls have no respect at all to things terrene and created' (Samuel Shaw, *The Voice of One Crying in the Wilderness* (1667), p. 201).

p. 144, marg. *Mark* 7: 21: 'For from within, out of the heart of men, proceed evil thoughts, adulteries, fornications, murders.' 'Lasciviousness' and 'an evil eye' are listed in the catalogue that follows.

p. 144, ll. 36–7. *the Lord Evil-eye*: more likely to stand for a mean and covetous person than one with the power of cursing: 'He that hasteth to be rich hath an evil eye' Prov. 28: 22).

p. 145, ll. 23–4. *my four first Captains*. The ministry given to Emanuel's chief officers recalls the preaching captains of the Parliamentary army during the Civil War.

p. 146, ll. 22–3. *white and glistering robes*: one of the many millenarian references, as the marginal Scripture indicates; cf. the dressing of Christian by the three Shining Ones in *P.P.*, pp. 158–9.

p. 147, ll. 1–2. *terrible as an Army with banners*: S. of S. 6: 10.

p. 149, l. 20. *milk and hony out of the rock*: Exod. 17: 6; Deut. 26: 9.

p. 151, ll. 19–20. *some little smattering . . . by the end*: metaphor from spinning; cf. p. 97, ll. 30–1.

p. 152, l. 18. *their peace have been as a river*: Isa. 48: 18.

p. 152, l. 24. *Oh that my people had hearkened unto me*: Ps. 81: 13–16.

p. 152, ll. 28–9. *acknowledg their offence*: Hos. 5: 15.

p. 153, l. 23. *the methods of his withdrawing*. Carnal Security's influence in Mansoul makes God resistant to the prayers of its citizens. Thus in Bunyan's analysis of his own case in *G.A.* a temporary release from spiritual doubts brings on complacency and puts him in a state of unpreparedness for further temptations: 'for though, as I can say in truth, my Soul was much in prayer before this tryal seized me, yet then I prayed onely, or at the most principally, for the removal of present troubles, and for fresh discoveries of love in Christ: which I saw afterwards was not enough to do; I should also have prayed that the great God would keep me from the evil that was to come' (*G.A.*, § 237, p. 74).

p. 154, l. 34. *bonny and blith*: carefree and happy.

p. 155, l. 12. *obnoxious*: exposed, open to harm: 'who aspires must down as low / As high he soar'd, obnoxious first or last / To basest things' (*Paradise Lost*, ix. 170).

p. 155, l. 30. *sparrow-blasted*: struck down by a sudden and mysterious power; Bunyan could find support in the Apocrypha for the popular belief that a sparrow might harm human beings (Tobit 2: 10).

p. 156, ll. 12–13. *the man that had lost his locks*: Samson (Judg. 16).

p. 158, l. 31. *called for a day of fasting*: as often proclaimed by the authorities during the Civil War and Commonwealth period, though Parliament had prescribed general fasts from 1624 onwards; fast sermons, often having political importance, were preached before Parliament on the last Wednesday of every month from 1642 to 1649 (see H. R. Trevor-Roper, 'The Fast Sermons of the Long Parliament', in *Religion, Reformation and Social Change* (2nd edn., 1972), pp. 294–344). After the Restoration, fasts were appointed for unseasonable weather, for the commemoration of the death of Charles I, and on account of the Dutch war, as well as for the Plague and the Great Fire (Pepys, *Diary*, ed. William Matthews, vi (1972), p. 155: 'July 12th 1665 It being a monthly fast day for the plague growing upon us').

p. 158, l. 36. *a very smart Sermon.* The text is that of Bunyan's *The Barren Fig-tree, Or, the Doom and Downfal of the Fruitless Professor*, which was first published in 1673 and went into a second edition in 1688; it was a parable taken much to heart by zealous Puritans concerned about the evidence of grace in the outward life; the description that follows of the Subordinate Preacher's sermon is a classic summary of the Puritan sermon: the preacher opens the text, states the doctrine therein, then gives reasons or proofs of the doctrine, and finally offers uses or applications to the moral and spiritual life of his congregation (cf. W. Fraser Mitchell, *English Pulpit Oratory from Andrewes to Tillotson* (1932), ch. 4).

p. 162, ll. 1–2. *destroy any, or all that they could lay hands of.* The Diabolonians who survive in their dens, all moral vices, stand for the continuing struggle of concupiscence, even in the justified soul. The Scriptural text Bunyan had in mind in this passage may be Num. 33: 55: 'But if ye will not drive out the inhabitants of the land from before you; then it shall come to pass, that those which ye let remain of them shall be pricks in your eyes, and thorns in your sides, and shall vex you in the land wherein ye dwell.'

p. 162, l. 34. *wise as foxes.* Cf. Tilley F629.

p. 164, l. 6. *Cerberus*: the three-headed dog, keeper of the gates of hell in the classical underworld.

p. 165, l. 24. *the Law of that Prince*: 'When the unclean spirit is gone out of a man, he walketh through dry places, seeking rest, and finding none. Then he saith, I will return into my house from whence I came out; and when he is come, he findeth it empty, swept, and garnished. Then goeth he, and taketh with himself seven other spirits more wicked than himself, and they enter in and dwell there: and the last state of this man is worse than the first. Even so shall it be also unto this wicked generation' (Matt. 12: 43–5).

p. 167, l. 10. *into desperation*: despair of salvation, the principal temptation of *G.A.*

p. 167, l. 25. *change their names*: as in the previous trial scene; cf. note on p. 119, l. 11.

p. 168, l. 9. *sheepsrusset*: a coarse, home-spun woollen cloth.

p. 170, l. 1. *an army of Doubters*: '. . . Satan, who is the great cause and incentive to sin, will not cease after our truest repentance, to vex, and sad, (if he could, to) despaire our hearts with the fresh memory of former and forsaken sins, so that we seldome or never lay hand on a blessed promise, or gaine ourselves into the comfortable savour of God, or delight ourselves in the sweet peace of conscience, but he falls in, and checks, and troubles us with the representations of former sins, and perchance makes us let go our gracious hold' (Obadiah Sedgwick, *The Doubting Beleever* (1641), pp. 319–20).

p. 170, l. 14. *took pepper in the nose*: became offended; as French idiom, 'La moutande monte au nez.'

p. 171, l. 11. *The sickness also . . .*: the physical sickness of Mansoul may be suggested by the language of the penitential psalms, dwelling as it does on the physical symptoms of distress: e.g. Ps. 6, 22, 31, 69, 88.

p. 171, l. 21. *as great as beggers*: variant of 'as thick as thieves'.

p. 171, l. 24. *By St. Mary.* As in the reference to Lord Wilbewill's receiving of the disguised Lord Lasciviousness at the end of Lent, this is a thrust at Popish practices (p. 168, l. 19).

p. 171, l. 33. *a foot in their dish*: a foot in their camp.

p. 172, l. 14. *a Coranto*: a lively dance in 3/4 time: *Twelfth Night*, I. iii. 120; Pepys, *Diary*, ed. William Matthews iii. 300.

p. 172, ll. 26–7. *they consulted . . .* This second infernal council is in some ways a more considered and successful piece of writing than the first, held before the original attack on Mansoul (pp. 11–13), since there is more impression of debate and conflicting points of view; the manner in which the counsels of the leaders are thrust aside by Diabolus through sheer force of personality cannot fail to remind the reader of Satan's oratorical triumph in *Paradise Lost*, ii. 1–466. Whether or not Milton's account had been brought to Bunyan's attention, it is likely that he knew the work of a fellow Baptist, Benjamin Keach, who had described the debate of the fallen angels in *The Glorious Lover* (1679), pp. 190 ff. and where Beelzebub and Lucifer are for open war; Keach's verses are manifestly inferior to both Bunyan's attempts at the subject.

p. 172, ll. 32–3. *this is Probatum est.* Of a Latin phrase he uses elsewhere, Bunyan wrote, 'The Lattine I borrow' (*P.P.*, p. 229).

p. 172, l. 33. *Balaam.* This allusion and the marginal gloss 'Lucifer' give a somewhat one-sided view of the Biblical character. In Num. 22–4 he is represented as an almost heroic figure who blesses Israel in response to God's will, and does not curse her as the King of Moab desires; he is compelled to bow to the superior insight of God's grace, an irresistible power, as his clear-sighted ass recognizes. Balaam's poor reputation in the New Testament may be explained by the interweaving of different traditions; and in Rev. 2: 14, to which Bunyan refers, it has been suggested that St. John was attracted by the possibility of a play on his name ('master of the people') suitable for a denunciation of false prophets (Austin Farrer, *The Revelation of St. John the Divine* (Oxford, 1964), p. 74).

p. 177, l. 21. *endure the Drum.* Cf. 'It is for want of hope, . . . that so many brisk professors, that have so boasted and made brags of their faith, have not been able to endure the drum in the day of alarm and affliction' (*Israel's Hope Encouraged*, Offor, i. 580).

p. 178, l. 4. *fall as the fig into the mouth of the eater*: 'All thy strong holds shall be like fig trees with the first ripe figs: if they be shaken, they shall even fall into the mouth of the eater' (Nahum 3: 12).

p. 179, l. 1. *Does he!*: a common idiom in Bunyan's colloquial writing: e.g. Christian's 'Know him!' in response to Faithful's query about his knowing Talkative; or Mr. Sagacity's 'Hear of him!' answering what he hears of Christian (*P.P.*, pp. 77, 175).

p. 180, ll. 16–17. *a rouling thing before the whirlwind*: Isa. 17: 13.

p. 180, l. 24. *go to handigripes*: close in hand-to-hand combat.

p. 180, ll. 31–2. *more than eleven thousand*: Ps. 91: 7.

p. 181, l. 29. *an horrible plot*. Mr. Prywell's report of the secret meeting at Vile-hill is strongly reminiscent of the early statements of Protestant informers during the Popish Plot even to the threat of invasion by a large foreign army.

p. 183, l. 18. *a publick fast, and a day of humiliation*. Cf. note on p. 158, l. 31.

p. 184, l. 1. *Scoutmaster-general*: an appointment peculiar to the Parliamentary army and held in 1645 by William Rowe (*The Writings and Speeches of Oliver Cromwell*, ed. W. C. Abbott, iii. (Cambridge, Mass., 1945), p. 295). As with other details of military practice Bunyan seems to have been ineradicably impressed by what he learned either at first or second hand as a young recruit in a Parliamentary levy towards the end of the first Civil War.

p. 185, ll. 21–2. *a very deep Consumption*: the jail fever which caused the death of so many prisoners in the seventeenth and eighteenth centuries.

p. 185, l. 27. *the manner of penance*. The open confession of faults of the offenders seems to be modelled on the penances prescribed by the Bedford church in this period when Bunyan was pastor; see *The Church Book of Bedford Meeting*, ed. H. G. Tibbutt (*Bedfordshire Historical Records*, lv, 1977), pp. 74, 76, 77.

p. 186, ll. 15–16. *Their highest Captains shall be named*. The catalogue resembles that of the captains, their colours, and ancients, in the earlier wars between Diabolus and Mansoul. All the captains' names represent variations on the theme of spiritual despair and destruction and their ancients and their colours are likewise related verbally to particular scriptural texts; the iconography of the 'yawning jaws' of Satan ('seeking whom he may devour'), so common in late medieval religious art (Bosch, Breughel, etc.) is present in Bunyan's broad-sheet *A Mapp Shewing the Order and Causes of Salvation & Damnation* (*c.* 1664) in the monster with open jaws and exposed teeth at the right-hand foot of the sheet.

p. 187, l. 21. *they were in number seven*. The number agrees with the numerology of Revelation (the seven last plagues: Rev. 15: 1).

p. 187, l. 23. *Python*: the serpent hatched from the mud in Deucalion's deluge which devastated the region about Delphi until slain by Apollo (Ovid,

Metamorphoses, i. 432–51). Though it is impossible to decide what could have been Bunyan's source for his classical mythology it is not open to doubt that there were Nonconformists in Bedford who could have supplied him with information suitable to the epic side of his work.

p. 187, l. 24. *Belial*: used as a proper name in A.V. (following the Vulgate) to denote the wicked: Deut. 13: 13; Judg. 19: 22; 1 Sam. 1: 16; in 2 Cor. 6: 15 the name has become a synonym for the Devil: 'And what concord hath Christ with Belial?'

p. 188, ll. 9–10. *the roaring of their DRUM*. The terror aroused by Diabolus's drum recalls the effect on Christian of the noises heard in the Valley of the Shadow of Death: 'also he heard doleful voices, and rushings too and fro, . . . these dreadful voices were heard by him for several miles together' (*P.P.*, p. 63); these in turn seem to be modelled on the voices of temptation in the form of reiterated texts which are recorded in Bunyan's spiritual autobiography (*G.A.*, §§ 93–4, p. 30).

p. 188, ll. 30–1. *Mount Alecto, Mount Megaera, and Mount Tisiphone*. The addition of Megaera completes the trinity of the classical Furies, the other two having already been introduced at the first council in hell, Tisiphone as 'a fury of the lake' (p. 13, l. 34).

p. 189, ll. 1–2. *the North-side of the Town*. The tradition that the north was the quarter in which hell lay goes back to the Old English *Genesis* and originates from Isa. 14: 13 where Lucifer plans to exalt himself 'upon the mount of the congregation, in the sides of the north'.

p. 189, l. 35. *when all came to all*: when all was done.

p. 191, ll. 20–1. *fell like a milstone upon them*: 'for this sentence stood like a Mill-post at my back' (*G.A.*, § 189, p. 60).

p. 191, marg. *Lam.* 1: 3: 'Judah is gone into captivity because of affliction, and because of great servitude: she dwelleth among the heathen, she findeth no rest: all her persecutors overtook her between the straits.'

p. 191, ll. 30–2. *this unavoidably follows upon the saying of my Lord, That we must yet suffer for our sins*. Cf. *G.A.*, §§ 237–8, p. 74.

p. 191, l. 35. *more critical*: an interesting usage.

p. 192, ll. 2–3. *pry into them*: examine them closely.

p. 192, l. 22. *the sling-stones*: as the marginal gloss points out, these are passages of Scripture directed against the doubts of election Diabolus has caused: in fact, the promises.

p. 193, l. 2. *all to be sugared*: completely sweetened. Cf. Judg. 9: 53: 'all to brake'.

p. 194, l. 10. *Og of Bashan*: Deut. 3: 1–13; Josh. 9: 10; Ps. 135: 11; 136: 20.

p. 194, l. 34. *Feelgate*. The fact that Feelgate is attacked first suggests that

Bunyan wishes to recapitulate the tactile symptoms of the worst phase of his spiritual sickness: 'I felt also such a clogging and heat at my stomach by reason of this my terrour . . . as if my breast-bone would have split in sunder' (*G.A.*, § 164, p. 50).

p. 195, ll. 18–19. *to land up*: silt or block.

p. 196, l. 4. *ticking and toying*: fondling and flirting.

p. 196, l. 5. *jealoused*: suspected.

p. 197, l. 12. *quat and close*: hidden and secluded.

p. 197, l. 25. *a troop shall overcome him, but he shall overcome at the last*. The verse is from Jacob's testament to his sons, prophesying the future of the twelve tribes of Israel (Gen. 49: 19).

p. 197, l. 37. *horrible rage and blasphemy*: 'one of the wicked ones got behind him, and stept up softly to him, and whisperingly suggested many grievous blasphemies to him . . .' (*P.P.*, p. 63).

p. 198, l. 2. *objections*: assaults.

p. 198, l. 14. *the leaves of a tree*. After his combat with Apollyon Christian is revived with 'some of the leaves of the Tree of Life' (*P.P.*, p. 60); the text in Revelation has 'the leaves of the tree were for the healing of the nations'; cf. *The Faerie Queene*, I. xi, stanzas 41–3.

p. 198, l. 22. *about the Stomach*: the seat of the heart in the old physiology and therefore the source of the passions: 'the seat and fountain of life . . . the seat and organ of all passions and affections' (Burton, *Anatomy of Melancholy*, I. ii; II. iv).

p. 199, l. 31. *documents*: teachings, admonitions.

p. 200, l. 7. *the Forlorn hope*: a body of men chosen to begin the attack (Dutch, *verloren hoop*, the lost troop). 'Besides . . . that seeing God of his mercy should chuse me to go upon the forlorn hope in this country' (*A Relation of the Imprisonment*, p. 106).

p. 201, l. 14. *as safe and good a retreat as they could*. The sudden reversal of fortune, turning what seemed a victory into a rout, is matched by events in many of the cavalry battles of the first Civil War, especially Naseby (June 1645) which was fought during the time when Bunyan was mustered in the garrison of Newport Pagnell.

p. 201, ll. 33–4. *as the bird . . . fell into the hands of the fowler*: the subject of the twenty-third emblem in *A Book for Boys and Girls* (1686), *Poems*, p. 226:

> This Fowler is an Emblem of the Devil,
> His Nets and Whistle, Figures of all evil.
> His Glass an Emblem is of sinful Pleasure,
> And his Decoy, of who counts sin a Treasure.
> This simple Lark's a shadow of a Saint,
> Under allurings, ready now to faint.

Cf. Ps. 124: 7.

p. 202, l. 30. *hurricaning*: making a great commotion.

p. 203, ll. 10–11. *all their force against Feelgate*. Cf. pp. 9, 194.

p. 204, l. 25. *They made great havock*. The occupation by the Doubters, which is moralized in the marginal comment, has all the circumstances of the seventeenth-century sack of a town.

p. 205, ll. 21–2. *Red-coats, and Black-coats*: soldiers and clergy: another instance of tilting at the contemporary establishment in a period of repression of Nonconformists and Whigs following the Rye House Plot (David Ogg, *England in the Reign of Charles II* (Oxford, 1956), ii. 652–6).

p. 205, l. 35. *make stroy*: destroy.

p. 206, l. 18. *about two years and an half*: the length of the period of the author's great temptation of fearing that he had betrayed Christ: 'well-nigh two years and a half' (*G.A.*, § 198, p. 62).

p. 207, ll. 16–17. *implore him to lend you his aid*: 'The Spirit helpeth our infirmities, for we know not what we should pray for as we ought' (Rom. 8: 26); 'He will give the Holy Spirit to men that ask him' (Luke 11: 13).

p. 208, l. 5. *the ink and paper must be yours*: an interesting detail of the allegory to illustrate the degree of Mansoul's responsibility and co-operation with the work of the Spirit.

p. 209, l. 1. *our enemies are lively, and they are strong*, etc.: 'Now hell rageth, the devil roareth, and all the world resolved to do the best they can, to bring the soul again into bondage, and ruine. Also the soul shall not want enemies, even in its own hearts lust, as covetousnesse, adultery, blasphemy, unbelief, hardness of heart, coldness, half-heartednesse, ignorance, with an innumerable company of attendants, hanging like so many blocks at its heels, ready to sink it into the fire of hell every moment . . .' (*Law and Grace*, Oxford Bunyan, ii. 150–1).

p. 209, ll. 17–18. *had it presently by the end*: learned of it at once.

p. 210, l. 22. *be kept out of the dungeon*. Cf. the Doubting Castle episode in *P.P.*, pp. 114–18.

p. 211, ll. 3–4. *And him that cometh to me I will in no wise cast out*: John 6: 37.

p. 211, ll. 4–5. *all manner of sin and blasphemy shall be forgiven . . .*: Matt. 12: 31.

p. 211, l. 15. *the water stood in his eyes*. Cf. *P.P.*, p. 201.

p. 213, l. 35. *a to side*: aside.

p. 215, l. 34. *refell'd*: refuted.

p. 216, l. 23. *witty*: ingenious, crafty. (Cf. Prov. 8: 12.)

p. 216, ll. 26–7. *Get ith'-hundred-and lose-ith'-shire*: small gains wiped out by greater losses, the 'hundred' being a territorial division of a county with its own court. The allusion expresses a foolishness similar to that of losing a pound to gain a penny.

p. 216, l. 33. *Laodicea*: Rev. 3: 14–18.

p. 217, l. 28. *Mansoul with a fulness of this world*. Diabolus's new strategy is to abandon spiritual assaults and wait for Mansoul to succumb to Worldliness.

p. 217, l. 32. *the third day*: obviously invoking the day of the Resurrection. Cf. Red Cross Knight's three-day battle with the dragon: *Faerie Queene*, I. xi.

p. 218, l. 32. *Boot and saddle, nor horse and away, nor a Charge*: the usual trumpet-calls; the first is a corruption of French *boute-selle*, place saddle: an order for cavalry to mount.

p. 219, ll. 1–2. *this melodious charm of the Trumpets*: a recurring feature of Bunyan's fictions; cf. *P.P.*, p. 160: 'These Trumpeters saluted *Christian* and his Fellow.'

p. 219, l. 11. *terrene and terrible manner*: an example of the occasional high epic style of *H.W.*

p. 219, l. 29. *like oyl to a flaming fire*. Cf. the 'Man with a Vessel of Oyl' in the House of the Interpreter who stands for Christ's grace maintaining the work already begun in the heart (*P.P.*, p. 32).

p. 220, l. 7. *Crutches*: the promises. The same allegorical detail is employed in the Second Part of *P.P.*, where Bunyan emphasizes it by a pun: Ready-to-halt 'could not Dance without one Crutch in his Hand, but I promise you, he footed it well' (p. 283).

p. 223, ll. 8–9. *Lift up your heads*, etc.: Ps. 24: 7–10.

p. 223, l. 21. *They have seen thy goings O God*, etc.: Ps. 68: 24–5.

p. 223, l. 35. *of purple*: the imperial colour to signify that Emanuel is come in glory.

p. 224, ll. 30–1. *Weep not, but go your way*, etc.: Neh. 8: 9–10.

p. 225, l. 9. *they made their garments white*: Rev. 7: 14–15: 'These are they which came out of great tribulation, and have washed their robes, and made them white in the blood of the Lamb': at the millenarian level of the allegory this signifies the rejoicing of the saints at the second coming of Christ.

p. 226, l. 15. *set up a mark thereby, and a sign*: Ezek. 39: 14–15.

p. 227, l. 22. *a short-for-ever*: an eternity.

p. 227, ll. 33–4. *the Valley of the shadow of death*. Cf. *P.P.*, pp. 61–5, 241–6.

p. 228, l. 4. *Blood-men*. The Bloodmen stand for the civil persecution of the saints under Charles II; the penal laws against Dissenters were strenuously applied in the period 1681–2. But at another level of meaning the Bloodmen stand for the forces of Antichrist in the struggles of the last days (Rev. 17: 14; 20: 17–21). Cf. *Of Antichrist and His Ruin*, Offor, ii. 65–8.

p. 228, l. 7. *under the Dog-star*: Sirius in *Canis Major*, supposed to exercise a malignant influence.

p. 231, l. 26. *shrewd brush*: short, sharp encounter.

p. 232, l. 32. *by fives, nines, and seventeens*. The numerals correspond to the five fallen angels who are the leaders of Diabolus's army, the nine companies of Doubters and (added to the latter) the eight companies of Bloodmen. See Offor, iii. 364.

p. 235, l. 3. *down boys*. Editions subsequent to the first (apparently until 1720) reject this reading in favour of *town boys*, which may seem reasonable enough, given the setting of Evil-questioning's query about the Doubters' being 'all of a town'. But there is surely no need to emend. The phrase *down boys* not only suits the context, but is also significant in itself, as 'down' was formerly used as an intensive with the force of 'downright' (see *O.E.D.*, a. 4). Thus the 'old *Gentleman*' here gleefully recognizes his ruffian visitors as 'downright good fellows' after his own rascally heart.

p. 235, l. 4. *have the very length of my foot*: fully understand me.

p. 234, l. 8. *conventicle*: the word used by their opponents for the unlawful religious meetings of Nonconformists; there is therefore a certain irony.

p. 241, ll. 12–13. *otherwise than by the general voice of the Word*: the Vocation-doubter believes in a doctrine of general rather than particular salvation (as did John Preston and the General Baptists).

p. 243, l. 19. *Clip-promise*. The name suggests deliberate impairment of the promises, just as current coin of the realm might be defaced by paring or 'clipping' the edges, a fraud not uncommon in Bunyan's day.

p. 245, l. 27. *that eye hath not seen*, etc.: 1 Cor. 2: 9.

p. 246, l. 24. *an hedge and a wall*: Job 1: 10; Jer. 1: 18–19; 15: 20–1.

p. 247, l. 7. *in such strength and glory*: a forecast of the last things and the reign of the saints: 2 Cor. 5: 1; Rev. 21: 2–3.

p. 247, l. 18. *to make thee afraid*. Cf. Isa. 35: 4–10.

p. 248, l. 20. *fine linnen . . . white and clean*: Rev. 19: 8; 16: 15.

p. 248, l. 23. *a flash of lightning*: Ezek. 1: 14.

p. 248, l. 28. *he is thy Lord*: Ps. 45: 11.

p. 248, ll. 34–5. *Let not therefore my garments . . . be defiled*. There are multiple references to Zech. 3: 3–4, John 13: 10, Rev. 21: 2–3.

p. 248, ll. 35–6. *Keep thy garments always white*: Eccles. 9: 8.

p. 245, ll. 5–6. *the Sacrifices were bound with cords to the horns of the Golden altar*: Ps. 118: 27.

p. 249, l. 10. *I reconciled thee*: Col. 1: 20.

p. 249, ll. 29–31. *Know therefore that whatever they should tempt thee to, my design is that they should drive thee, not further off,* etc. The continual testing of the devout soul by evil in order that it can gain virtue is the continual theme of Bunyan as it is of Milton; cf. 'That which purifies us is triall, and triall is by what is contrary' (*Areopagitica*, in Oxford Bunyan, iv. 311).

p. 250, l. 9. *made a hand of thee*: destroyed thee.

p. 250, l. 23. *hold fast till I come*: Rev. 2: 25. The ending in which nothing is concluded and the struggle continues closely resembles that of *Piers Plowman* (*Piers Plowman, an edition of the C-text*, ed. Derek Pearsall (York Medieval Texts, 1978), p. 376).

INDEX